100 Reasons to Celebrate

We invite you to join us in celebrating Mills & Boon's centenary. Gerald Mills and Charles Boon founded Mills & Boon Limited in 1908 and opened offices in London's Covent Garden. Since then, Mills & Boon has become a hallmark for romantic fiction, recognised around the world.

We're proud of our 100 years of publishing excellence, which wouldn't have been achieved without the loyalty and enthusiasm of our authors and readers.

Thank you!

Each month throughout the year there will be something new and exciting to mark the centenary, so watch for your favourite authors, captivating new stories, special limited edition collections...and more!

DAX

Welcome to Penhally Bay!

Nestled on the rugged Cornish coast is the picturesque town of Penhally. With sandy beaches, breathtaking landscapes and a warm, bustling community—it is the lucky tourist who stumbles upon this little haven.

But now Mills & Boon® Medical™ Romance is giving readers the unique opportunity to visit this fictional coastal town through our brand-new twelve-book continuity… You are welcomed to a town where the fishing boats bob up and down in the bay, surfers wait expectantly for the waves, friendly faces line the cobbled streets and romance flutters on the Cornish sea breeze…

We introduce you to Penhally Bay Surgery, where you can meet the team led by caring and commanding Dr Nick Tremayne. Each book will bring you an emotional, tempting romance—from Mediterranean heroes to a sheikh with a guarded heart. There's royal scandal that leads to marriage for a baby's sake, and handsome playboys are tamed by their blushing brides! Top-notch city surgeons win adoring smiles from the community, and little miracle babies will warm your hearts. But that's not all…

With Penhally Bay you get double the reading pleasure… as each book also follows the life of damaged hero Dr Nick Tremayne. His story will pierce your heart—a tale of lost love and the torment of forbidden romance. Dr Nick's unquestionable, unrelenting skill would leave any patient happy in the knowledge that she's in safe hands, and is a testament to the ability and dedication of all the staff at Penhally Bay Surgery. Come in and meet them for yourself…

THEIR MIRACLE BABY

AND

MAKING MEMORIES

Caroline Anderson

First published in Great Britain 2008
Harlequin Mills & Boon Limited,
Eton House, 18-24 Paradise Road, Richmond, Surrey TW9 1SR

ISBN: 978 0 263 86338 3

Set in Times Roman 10½ on 13 pt.
03-0808-98544

Printed and bound in Spain
by Litografia Rosés S.A., Barcelona

CONTENTS

THEIR MIRACLE BABY 9

MAKING MEMORIES 195

BRIDES OF PENHALLY BAY

*Bachelor doctors become husbands and fathers—
in a place where hearts are made whole.*

**At Christmas pregnant Lucy Tremayne
was reunited with the man she loved**
Christmas Eve Baby by Caroline Anderson

**We snuggled up in January
with gorgeous Italian, Dr Avanti**
The Italian's New-Year Marriage Wish by Sarah Morgan

Romance blossomed for Adam and Maggie in February
The Doctor's Bride by Sunrise by Josie Metcalfe

Single dad Jack Tremayne found his perfect bride in March
The Surgeon's Fatherhood Surprise by Jennifer Taylor

In April a princess arrived in Penhally!
The Doctor's Royal Love-Child by Kate Hardy

In May Edward Tremayne found the woman of his dreams
Nurse Bride, Bayside Wedding by Gill Sanderson

**We attended gorgeous Chief Inspector
Lachlan D'Ancey's wedding in June**
Single Dad Seeks a Wife by Melanie Milburne

**The temperature really hotted up in July—
Dr Oliver Fawkner arrived in the Bay…**
Virgin Midwife, Playboy Doctor by Margaret McDonagh

**This month Francesca and Mike try one last time
for the baby they've longed for**
Their Miracle Baby by Caroline Anderson

**September brings sexy Sheikh Zayed
to the beaches of Penhally**
Sheikh Surgeon Claims His Bride by Josie Metcalfe

Snuggle up with dishy Dr Tom Cornish in October
A Baby for Eve by Maggie Kingsley

**And don't miss French doctor Gabriel,
who sweeps into the Bay this November**
Dr Devereux's Proposal by Margaret McDonagh

A collection to treasure for ever!

THEIR MIRACLE BABY

CHAPTER ONE

'DADDY!'

'Hello, pickle!' Mike scooped Sophie up into his arms and whirled her round, their laughter ringing round the yard and echoing off the old stone walls of the barn, bringing a lump to her throat.

These two adored each other, and now both their faces were lit up with a joy so infectious Fran couldn't help but smile.

'How's my favourite girl today?' he asked, hugging her tight and looking down into her beaming face.

'I'm fine— Daddy, where's Fran? I've got something really special to show her— Fran! Look!' she yelled, catching sight of her and waving madly.

She wriggled out of his arms, running across and throwing herself at Fran. She caught her little stepdaughter, hugging her close and laughing, kissing her bright, rosy cheek and holding out her hand for the little box Sophie was thrusting at her eagerly.

'It's a model—I made it at school!' she confided in a stage whisper. 'It's Daddy milking a cow—see, here's Amber, and this is Daddy, and this is the cluster…'

She pointed underneath the misshapen reddish blob that could just conceivably have been a cow, and there was a thing like a mangled grey spider stuck on her underside. She supposed if the blob could be Amber, then the spider could be a milking machine cluster. Why not? And as for Mike…!

'I'm going to give it to him for his birthday,' she went on, still whispering loud enough to wake the dead. 'We've got to wrap it. Have you got paper?'

Fran smiled and put the lid back on the box. 'I'm sure we've got paper,' she whispered back. 'It's lovely. Well done, darling. I'm sure he'll be really pleased.'

A flicker of doubt passed over Sophie's earnest little face. 'Do you think so? Amber was really hard to make.'

'I'm sure, but you've done it beautifully. He'll be so pleased. He loves everything you make for him. It makes him feel *really* special.'

Sophie brightened, her confidence restored, and whirling round she ran back to her beloved father and grabbed his hand. 'I want to go and see the cows— Oh, Brodie!' she said, breaking away again and dropping to her knees to cuddle the delighted collie who was lying on her back, grinning hideously and wagging her tail fit to break it. 'Hello, Brodie,' she crooned, bending right down and letting the dog wash her face with meticulous attention.

'Sophie, you mustn't let her do that!' Kirsten protested, but Sophie ignored her mother, laughing and hugging the dog while Brodie licked and licked and licked for England.

'Yeah, not your face, it's not a good idea,' Mike chipped in, backing Kirsten up simply because he just did. It was one of the many things Fran loved about him, the way he defended Sophie's mother's decisions to their daughter even if he didn't agree, and then discussed it with her rationally when Sophie wasn't around.

The fact that Brodie washed his face whenever it was in reach was neither here nor there! Now he held out his hand to Sophie and pulled her to her feet—and out of range of Brodie's tongue—with a grin.

'Come on, scamp, say goodbye to your mum and then let's go and see the cows. I'm sure they've missed you.'

Missed the treats, no doubt, because the six-year-old always seemed to have her little pockets bulging with pellets of feed, and she'd happily give it to them despite the cows' slippery noses and rough, rasping tongues. Nothing fazed her, and she was deliriously happy trailing round after her father and 'helping' him.

'Fran?' Sophie said, holding out her hand expectantly after they'd waved Kirsten off, but she shook her head. This was their time, precious and special to both of them, and she wouldn't intrude.

'I've got to make supper,' she said with a smile. 'You go with your father and say goodnight to the cows. I'll see you both soon.' And with a little wave she watched them head off towards the field where the cows were grazing, Mike shortening his stride to accommodate his little sprite, Sophie skipping and dancing beside him, chattering nineteen to the dozen while her pale blonde bunches bobbed and curled and flicked around her head.

They went round the corner out of sight, Brodie at their heels, and with a soft sigh Fran went back inside, the little cardboard box containing Mike's present in her hand. She opened the lid and stared down at the little lumps of modelling clay so carefully and lovingly squashed into shape, and her eyes filled. He was so lucky to have her. So very, very lucky.

If only it could happen to them.

They'd come so close—twice now.

It often happened, she'd been told. Miscarriages were common, and her first, three years ago—well, that had just been one of those things, they'd said. It probably wouldn't happen again.

And it hadn't, of course, because she hadn't conceived again, and so they'd undergone endless intrusive and humiliating tests, all of which had proved nothing except that there wasn't any obvious reason why they hadn't had a baby yet.

So they'd gone through the difficult and challenging process of a cycle of IVF, and she'd become pregnant, and then, just like before, she'd lost it.

Not unusual, they were told again, especially with IVF, possibly because the embryos weren't always as perfect as they might be with a normally conceived embryo, and this, it seemed, was probably what had happened to theirs.

All very logical, but she didn't feel logical about it, because there was nothing wrong with either of them, they just hadn't managed to make a healthy baby yet, and it was tearing her apart.

Looking on the bright side, they hadn't made an unhealthy one either, so if that was why the embryos had both failed, maybe it was for the best.

Small consolation.

Whatever the reason, she'd lost the embryos, and she wasn't sure she had the strength to go through it again. If she had another miscarriage…

And, anyway, they still had Sophie coming to visit them

and bringing so much sunshine into their lives. OK, it wasn't like having her own child, but Sophie was gorgeous, and she loved her to bits. Was it greedy to want more?

To want a child of their own who would come home from school bubbling with excitement and giving them some little blob of modelling clay to treasure?

She dragged in a breath, pressing her fist against the little knot of pain in her chest. Not now. She couldn't think about it now. Blinking hard, she put the little box in a safe place, opened the fridge and started pulling things out.

Supper. Practicalities. Forget the rest.

Just like the funny, amazing little present, she had to put her feelings in a box and put the lid on and put them all away.

It was the only way to survive.

They were sitting at the kitchen table.

Mike had finished milking on Saturday morning and he was hurrying back to join them for breakfast. Glancing through the window, expecting to see them cooking, he was surprised to see them seated side by side, Sophie's untamed blonde curls close to Fran's sleek, dark hair, and he could hear them laughing.

They were busy wrapping something that could well have been the little box Sophie had been brandishing yesterday so, instead of kicking off his boots and going in, Mike opened the door a crack to give them warning and said, 'Just going over to the shop to make sure everything's OK. Anything you need?'

'Daddy, go away, you can't see!' Sophie shrieked, plastering herself over the table.

'I'm not looking, I've got my eyes shut,' he said,

squashing a grin and screwing his eyes up tight. 'Want anything, Frankie?'

'Bacon?' she said, a smile in her voice. 'I thought we could have a nice cooked breakfast if you've finished milking.'

'OK. I'll be five minutes.' That should give them long enough to wrap whatever it was, he thought with the smile still tugging at his mouth.

'Fine.'

He went out, leaving Brodie behind to fuss over Sophie, and had a quick chat to his sister-in-law, Sarah, in the farm shop. She was just about to open up, and she threw him a smile as he went in.

'Hiya. How are you? Looking forward to tomorrow?'

'What—getting older, you mean? I can't wait.' He chuckled and picked out a packet of local dry-cured bacon. 'I've been sent to fetch breakfast,' he told her. 'You OK here? Need anything?'

'More blue cheese from the store, when you've got time. It's gone really well this week and we've only got half a wheel left.'

'I'll drop it in later,' he promised.

'Oh, and eggs? We've had a run on them—must be all those desperate women in Penhally making you a birthday cake in the hope of tempting you away from Fran!'

He chuckled again. 'Hardly. But I'll get Sophie on it right after breakfast. She likes collecting the eggs. We'll do it in the next hour or so, OK?'

'Fine. See you later.'

He sauntered back, whistling cheerfully so they could hear him coming and get the present out of the way, and when he opened the door a crack and called through it,

Sophie dashed over and opened it, her eyes twinkling mischievously.

'We're all finished. You can come in now,' she said primly, and he tweaked one of her curls and hugged her against his side.

'I'm glad to hear it. Give this to Fran, could you, sweetheart?'

She skipped across the kitchen with the bacon in her hand. Fran turned and met his eyes over her head, and they shared a smile.

'Here,' Sophie announced, handing it over, then sat down on the floor next to Brodie and sang, 'Bacon, bacon, bacon, we're having bacon! Do you want some?'

'Of course she does but she's not allowed,' Mike reminded her.

'Not even just a teeny, tiny, weeny little bit?'

'Not even a sniff.'

'Oh. Never mind, Brodie,' she said comfortingly, and cuddled the dog, who promptly rolled over and sprawled right in front of Fran.

'Come on, guys, out of the way,' she said patiently, and they decamped to the far end, Sophie propped up against the wall, Brodie propped up against her, both watching the bacon intently.

'Time to wash your hands,' Mike reminded her, washing his own and laying the table while Fran finished the cooking. He made a pot of coffee, poured some juice for Sophie and they settled down to eat.

Well, he and Fran did. Sophie couldn't even eat quietly, humming and jiggling while she ate, making appreciative noises and pretending that she wasn't sneaking bits of food down to Brodie, clamped firmly to her side.

'Brodie, go and lie down,' he said, and the dog, crest-fallen, went and flopped apparently casually in a pool of sunshine and watched Sophie's every move.

Poor old thing. She adored Sophie, loving every moment of her visits, and she'd wander around like a lost soul after she'd gone, looking for her.

She wasn't allowed in the bedrooms but somehow, when Sophie was here, she seemed to find her way out of the kitchen door and up the stairs to the foot of her bed, and there she slept, one eye on the door and grinning manically every time they went in to tuck Sophie up, rolling onto her back and wiggling her tail, her melting amber eyes beseeching.

And getting away with it, because Sophie adored her and he couldn't see any harm in it, so they turned a blind eye, even to the point where they'd bathe Brodie before Sophie's visits. She'd been in there last night, and Mike had no doubt she'd be in there tonight, but he didn't care. Kirsten didn't approve, but she'd made her choice and she'd chosen to leave, and he'd moved on.

He'd met Fran four years ago when she'd come back to the village; they'd fallen in love on sight and were blissfully happy.

Or they had been.

If only they could crack this baby thing…

He put their plates in the dishwasher, bent and kissed Fran on the forehead and ushered Sophie towards the door. 'We've got to pick up eggs and take some cheese to the shop. Want to join us?'

Fran shook her head and smiled. 'I've got things to do. You go and have fun,' she told him, but the smile didn't go all the way to her eyes, and in their depths was something he couldn't bear.

He loved his present.

Sophie came creeping into their bedroom with the first rays of the sun, Brodie on her heels, and they ended up with her in the bed between them, with Brodie lying on Mike's legs and Sophie snuggled under his arm, watching in a dreadful mixture of excitement and trepidation as he slowly, carefully peeled the wrapping paper off and opened the box.

A frown creased his brow, and then a smile, and then a great big laugh as he hugged Sophie hard against his side and kissed her. 'It's me and Amber, isn't it?' he said, and Sophie turned to Fran with a huge grin before bouncing up and taking the models from Mike's hands and showing him the intricacies of her design.

'Look—see the cluster.' She showed him, turning Amber over. 'And you've got your hat on. It was meant to be red but I'd used up all the red making Amber and there wasn't enough, so you had to have pink.'

'Close enough,' he said, but Fran could see his mouth twitching and she had to bite her lip to keep the bubble of laughter inside.

'Do you like it?' Sophie asked, bouncing on the spot, and he reached out and hugged her again, his eyes suspiciously bright.

'I love it. Thank you, darling. It's really nice.'

'I was going to make Brodie too but Mrs Pearce said I

couldn't have any more clay, so you'll have to have her for Christmas.'

His lips twitched again. 'I'm sure she won't mind waiting.'

Sophie sat back on her heels. 'So can I help you milk the cows today?'

'I'm not doing it. My brother's doing it so I can have a lie-in,' he said, and Fran, glancing at the clock, stifled a sigh.

It was only five-thirty. So much for his lie-in! And Sophie was looking crestfallen. 'Does that mean I have to go back to bed?' she asked. 'Because I'm *wide* awake now.'

Mike wasn't. He looked exhausted, and without his usual alarm he might well have slept another couple of hours.

'I tell you what,' Fran said quickly. 'Why don't you and I go downstairs for a little while and see if we can find something to do while your daddy has a birthday lie-in, and then, when he's up, maybe we can go to the beach?'

'Brilliant! We can make sandcastles!' Sophie shrieked, leaping up and down on the bed until his present nearly fell off the edge. He made a grab for it, and Fran threw back the bedclothes and got up, holding out her hand to Sophie.

'Come on, you, I've got something I want us to do together.'

Sophie slid over the bed, bouncing on her bottom until her skinny little legs hung off the side. 'What?' she asked.

Fran bent over and whispered in her ear, 'We've got to make his birthday cake.'

Sophie's eyes sparkled. 'Can I help?'

'Of course. I'll need your help—lots of it.'

She spun round, kissed Mike and pulled the bedclothes back up round his chin. 'You go back to sleep, Daddy, for a nice long time,' she ordered. 'And don't come in the kitchen without knocking. We're going to be busy making a secret.'

He winked at her, and Fran ushered her away, throwing him a smile over her head as she closed the door.

'Dog!' he yelled, and she opened the door again, called Brodie and they went down to the kitchen and left him in peace.

'How many eggs?' Sophie asked, kneeling up on a chair at the table to help.

'Three.'

'Can I break them into the bowl?'

'No—break them into this cup, and we can check they're all right before we add them to the mixture, just in case.'

'Just in case what?'

Just in case she mashed the shell, Fran thought, but couldn't dent her pride. 'In case one's a bit funny,' she flannelled.

'Funny?' Sophie said, wrinkling her nose.

'Sometimes they smell a bit fishy or they have bits in.'

'And we don't want a fishy, bitty cake,' she said sagely, and Fran suppressed her smile.

'We certainly don't.'

'Can I measure the flour and the sugar and the butter?'

'Sure.'

It took longer—much longer—and they didn't use the mixer but a wooden spoon in a bowl, the way Fran's grandmother had always done it, because that way Sophie could be more involved and Mike got a longer lie-in. They grated the rind of an orange, and squeezed in some juice, and then, when it was all mixed together they spooned it into the tin, put it in the top oven of the Aga and set the timer.

'An hour? Really? That's *ages*! Can we make Daddy breakfast in bed?'

'We can make him breakfast in bed if you like, but not yet. He's tired, Sophie. He works very hard.'

Too hard, for too long, and the strain was beginning to tell. And no matter how badly she wanted to crawl back into bed beside him and go back to sleep herself, for now she had to entertain his daughter and keep her out of his way so he could rest.

'Want to help me make some things for the project I'm doing with my class?' she suggested, and Sophie, bless her, responded with her usual boundless enthusiasm.

If only Fran could say the same for herself…

'Bye-bye, sweetheart. Love you.'

'Don't forget I'm coming next Sunday for tea 'cos I'm going on holiday the next week!'

'I haven't forgotten. You take care.'

Fran watched as Mike kissed his little sprite of a daughter goodbye and closed the car door, lifting his hand to wave farewell. Sophie waved back, her hand just visible through the water streaming down the car window, and Fran waved too, her feelings mixed.

She adored Sophie; she was a lovely girl, sweet and bright, just like her mother to look at, and for that Fran was profoundly grateful. If she'd been the image of her father, the knife would be twisted every time she looked at her. As it was, it was easy enough most of the time to pretend she was just another little girl, just like the many little girls Fran taught all day.

But delightful though Sophie was, the very fact of her existence only served to underscore Fran's own failure to successfully carry a baby to full term.

Having Sophie to stay every other weekend, for a couple of weeks every holiday and at half-term once or twice a year was like a two-edged sword. When she was there, she brought sunshine and laughter into their lives, and after she'd gone, the house—a beautiful old house that should have been filled with the sound of children—rang with silence.

It might be better if she didn't come, Fran thought, and then shook her head. No. That was ridiculous. They both loved her to bits, and without her their lives would be immeasurably poorer. They'd had a lovely weekend, and even the rain today hadn't spoilt things, because by the time it had started they'd finished at the beach and were home, making sandwiches to go with Mike's birthday cake for tea.

And Sophie had been an absolute delight.

The car moved off across the streaming concrete yard, and Fran turned away from the cover of the doorway, steeling herself for the silence. Not that she had time to sit still and listen to it. She had a lot to do. Mike's parents and Joe and Sarah had joined them for tea, and the sitting room was smothered in plates and cups. Brodie went with her, tongue lashing, and cleared up the dropped birthday cake crumbs from the floor while she dealt with everything else.

She saw Mike's feet come into range as she was fishing for a fallen knife beside the sofa. There was a hole in the toe of his left sock, she noticed absently. Another failure in her wifely duties. She gave a muffled snort, and Mike dropped down onto his haunches beside her, his hand warm on her shoulder.

'You OK?'

Her fingers coaxed the knife closer. 'Of course. Why shouldn't I be?'

'I just— I thought you looked—'

'I'm fine, Mike,' she said firmly. 'I just have a lot to do and I'm a bit tired. *I* didn't get a lie-in.'

He sighed and stood up, and she could hear him scrubbing his hands through his damp hair in frustration. 'I'm sorry. I'll go and get the cows in, then. I'm late starting the milking.'

She straightened, the errant knife in hand at last, and threw him a tight smile. 'Good idea. I'll do supper for seven.'

'Don't bother to do much, I'm really not hungry after all the cake. Come, Brodie.'

And that was it. No offer of help. No thanks for his birthday tea, or having Sophie for the weekend.

No hug, no cuddle, no 'Don't worry, darling, it'll be all right.'

Not that she'd believe him, anyway. How could it be all right? They'd run out of time on the NHS, and she was wondering if she could psych herself up for another IVF cycle and failing miserably. Not that they could afford it, although the way things were going, she wasn't even sure Mike wanted a child with her. It was so much hassle and, despite his assurances, he seemed more than happy with just Sophie.

And why wouldn't he be? She was gorgeous.

Gorgeous, and his, and if she was honest Fran had to admit that she was simply jealous of his relationship with her. They'd spent hours together over the weekend, and every time she'd looked up they'd been there, giggling about something, Mike chasing her, catching her and throwing her up in the air, turning her upside down, leading her by the hand and showing her the chicks, showing her how to feed a calf—just being the doting, devoted father that he was, with Sophie right there being the doting, devoted daughter.

And every laugh, every hug, every smile had turned the knife a little more. Sure, Sophie spent time with her, and they'd had fun, but it wasn't the same as Sophie's relationship with Mike. That relationship was special, different, and Fran yearned for one like it.

Yearned and ached and wept for it.

She picked up a plate, catching it on the edge of the table, and it flew out of her fingers, clipped the edge of the hearth and shattered. She stared at it, at the wreckage of the plate, splintered into a thousand pieces, just like her dreams, and a sob rose in her throat.

She crushed it down, threw the bits back onto the tray and carried it through to the kitchen. She didn't have time to be sentimental and stupid. She had a pile of project work to mark before school tomorrow, and the house hadn't seen the vacuum cleaner in nearly a fortnight. Not that they'd been in it much. Mike was busy on the farm, she was busy with the end of the summer term coming up and lots of curriculum work to get through in the next week. And just as if that wasn't enough, they'd extended the farm shop in time for the summer influx of tourists and were run off their feet.

Which was just as well with the amount of money they'd sunk into that and the new cheese-making equipment, not to mention last year's investment in the ice-cream venture that her sister-in-law, Sarah, was running, but the result was that there weren't enough hours in the day.

So she needed to clean the kitchen, which was pointless since it was raining and Brodie coming in and out didn't help in the least, even if Mike wiped the dog's feet on an old towel, and she needed to clean the bathroom and their bedroom and change Sophie's sheets. That pretty much was it, because they hadn't had time to make the rest dirty.

Except for the sitting-room floor, of course, which now had crumbs, dog hair and bits of broken plate all over it.

She got the vacuum out and started in there.

'Hello, my lovely,' Mike murmured, wiping down Marigold's teats with a paper towel before attaching the cups to them. He rested his head against her flank for a moment, feeling the warmth of her side and the gentle movement of her breathing. She smelt safe and familiar. Nothing unexpected there, no emotional minefield, just a cow doing her job, as he was doing his.

He pulled the cluster down and slipped the cups over her teats, one at a time, the suction tugging them rhythmically, and watched in satisfaction as the milk started to flow in a steady, creamy stream.

Beautiful. He loved his Guernseys. Their milk was fantastic, the cheese and ice cream and clotted cream they made from it a lifesaver in the current dairy-farming climate. 'Clever girl,' he murmured, running his hand over her rump and patting it before moving on. Clever, uncomplicated, undemanding, a lovely old girl who still, after six calvings, delivered the goods better than any other cow. If only his own life were as straightforward.

Her daughter Mirabelle was next to her, her head in the trough, and he ran his hand over her udder and frowned. There was heat in the right front quarter, and when he tugged the teat down gently, she raised her head and lowed in protest.

She had mastitis. Damn. As if he didn't have enough to do.

'Sorry, sweetheart,' he murmured, and he wiped her other teats, attached the cluster to the three which were OK and then, taking advantage of the let-down reflex which the routine of the milking parlour always stimulated, with gentle, rhythmic movements he stripped out the infected quarter, discarding the milk. After dodging her disgruntled kick, he carefully inserted the nozzle of an intermammary tube of antibiotic ointment into the teat canal, squirted it into the udder and left her to finish.

The others were waiting patiently, the sound of their gentle mooing and soft, warm breath endlessly relaxing.

Funny. Most people who came to watch him milk, and it could be hundreds over the course of the summer, were fascinated from a distance, but thought it was smelly and dirty and couldn't understand why anybody in their right mind would want to get up at four-thirty in the morning and work right through till seven at night.

Including his ex-wife.

Kirsten had thought he was insane, but he loved it, and couldn't imagine doing anything else in the world. He could have been a vet, and he'd thought about it long and hard. He was clever enough, his school exam grades more than adequate for the entry requirements, but he'd gone instead to agricultural college because the farm was in his blood.

OK, it was hard work, but he was young and fit and it didn't hurt him. You had to do something with your waking hours, and the warmth of the animals and the relationship he had with them was all the reward he needed.

It was servicing the investment in the ice cream, clotted cream and cheese-making equipment and expanding the farm shop that made him tired and brought him stress, but that was only the other side of the coin, and he could deal with it.

Or he would be able to, if only Fran wasn't so stressed out herself.

He let the first batch of cows out and let the next ten in. It never ceased to amaze him the way they came in, all bar the odd one or two, in the same order, to the same places every time. It made his job that much easier.

Too easy, really. So easy that he had far too much time to think, and all he could think about was the look in Fran's eyes every time she saw him with Sophie. Which, when she was with them, was always. Sophie was his shadow, trailing him, helping with the calves and the chickens and the milking, asking endless questions, nagging him about having a pony, tasting the ice cream and chattering about the cheese, wanting to stir it and cut it and sieve it.

She was too small to reach right across the vat so he had to lift her and hold her, and she'd been known to drop the spoon into the vat. Not that it mattered if the paddles weren't turning, but if they were still at the mixing stage, he had to strip off to the waist, scrub his arm and plunge it nearly to the armpit in warm milk to fetch the spoon out so it didn't foul on the paddles.

Yes, she was a hazard, but he missed her now she was gone, and he knew Fran missed her too, although her presence just rubbed salt into the wound.

He sighed and let the last ten cows in. They were nearly all pregnant now. The last three had calved in the past six weeks, and it would soon be time to artificially inseminate them.

He was trying to build the herd on really strong genetic lines, and he'd got a young bull growing on his brother's farm which had excellent breeding and was showing promise. When he was mature, they'd see about using him, but until then they did it the clinical way, in the crush, with a syringe of frozen semen.

He gave a hollow laugh.

Not quite the same, not for the bull or the cows. He could empathise. He'd done his share of producing semen for his and Fran's fertility investigations and treatment, and it was the pits.

It was all the pits, the whole damn process. So many questions, so much personal intervention that in the end they'd felt like lab rats. He couldn't remember the last time he and Frankie had made love for the hell of it.

Not had sex, not timed it to coincide with her ovulation, or gone at it hammer and tongs for a fortnight in an attempt at quantity rather than quality, or done it out of duty and guilt because it had been months since they had, which was the current state of affairs, but made love in the real sense of the words, slowly, tenderly, just for the sheer joy of touching each other.

Or, come to that, clawed each other's clothes off in desperate haste to get at each other! There hadn't been any of that for ages.

Years. Two years? Three? Damn, so long he couldn't even remember what it had felt like. Certainly he hadn't touched her at all since the miscarriage in April.

He propped his head against Amber's flank and rubbed her side absently. The calf shifted under his hand, and he swallowed the sadness that welled in his throat. Would he ever feel his own baby like that, moving inside Fran, stretching and kicking and getting comfortable?

'You're getting a bit close, aren't you, girl? Last milking tonight, and tomorrow you can go and munch your head off in the meadow till you have your baby.'

She mooed, a soft, low sound of agreement, and he laughed and let them out.

He still wasn't finished. He'd milked them, but he had to flush the lines through and hose down the yard before he could go in for supper.

Not that he minded. The longer the better, really, because Fran would be in a foul mood and they'd eat their supper in an awkward, tense silence.

It was always the same after Sophie had been to stay.

'Mirabelle's got mastitis.'

'Oh. Badly?'

'No, just one quarter. I've given her a tube of antibiotic. It might be enough. I'll watch her.'

'Mmm.' Fran poked the cake crumbs around on the plate and pushed it away.

'Don't you want that?' he asked, and she shook her head.

'No. I've had too much cake.' Which was a lie. She'd hardly had any, but he wouldn't know that. She pushed the plate towards him. 'Here, finish it off. I know you're always starving.'

He picked up the almost untouched slice of cake and bit into it in silence while she cleared her plate away and put it in the dishwasher, then she heard the scrape of his chair against the tiles as he stood. 'That was lovely. Thanks.'

She took the plate from him. 'Don't lie,' she said with a pang of guilt for giving him such a scratch supper on his birthday. 'It was just a slice of cake, not a romantic candlelit dinner.'

The sort of dinner most wives would give their husbands on their birthdays. Shortly before they went to bed and made love…

A puzzled frown flickered across his face and was gone, leaving his eyes troubled. 'Fran, what's wrong?'

'Nothing,' she said, shutting down her runaway thoughts in case he could read them.

'That's not true. You didn't eat your cake just now, you hardly had anything this afternoon— And don't argue,' he added, as she opened her mouth. 'I saw you give that sandwich to the dog. And except for the time this morning when I was having my lie-in, you spent the whole weekend sending me off with Sophie and keeping out of the way. What the hell is it, love? Talk to me.'

She looked away, her conscience pricking. Had it been so obvious? She didn't want to hurt Sophie, but having her there…

'Frankie?'

She couldn't. It was a real Pandora's box and there was

no way she was opening it now. 'I'm fine. Just preoccupied. I've got a lot to do before tomorrow morning. You know what the end of the summer term is like—so many things to finish off.'

He just looked at her for a long moment, then turned away with a sigh. She watched him out of the corner of her eye, her peripheral vision picking up the moment he gave up. Damn her, then, she could almost hear him thinking. Damn her, if she wants to be like that.

'I'll be in the farm office,' he said. 'Don't wait up.'

And he went out, the dog at his heels, the door banging shut behind them. She felt the tears threaten, but swallowed them down, straightened her shoulders and got her class's project work out, spreading it out on the dining-room table and forcing herself to concentrate. The last thing she could afford to do was neglect her job and end up losing it. At the moment, with the farm overstretched because of the expansion, her income was the only thing keeping them afloat.

She gave a ragged little laugh. Perhaps it was just as well she wasn't pregnant.

CHAPTER TWO

IT WAS obviously going to be one of those weeks.

Mirabelle's mastitis had cleared up overnight, but Betsy had gone down with milk fever and needed IV calcium. Guernseys were prone to milk fever, and Betsy had had it before. And Mike should have been on the alert for it as she'd just calved, but his mind had been elsewhere.

Still, he'd caught her in time and given her the injection, so she'd made a rapid recovery. And he'd turned Amber out that morning to await the arrival of her calf. Her milk had dwindled to a halt, and it was time for her to rest and gather her strength. He'd have to take a walk up there later and check on them. They were near Ben and Lucy Carter's, grazing on the field by Tregorran House, the one with the barn where Lucy had had her baby at Christmas.

He could go with Fran when she got back from school—or perhaps not. It was a gorgeous day today, unlike yesterday, and no doubt Lucy would be out in the garden with the baby and would want to say hello.

He didn't think either of them needed that at the moment.

Fran had been moody for the past week, short with him

for no particular reason. And every time he tried to talk to her, she changed the subject. Whatever it was.

He went into the farm office and put a mug under the spout of the coffee-machine. It was one of those new pod ones, which meant he could have real coffee without fiddling around too much, and when reps from the wholesalers and farm shop outlets came to visit, he could give them decent coffee quickly that hadn't been stewing for hours. It also meant they didn't have to go into the house.

And recently, for some reason, he just didn't want to go into the house if Fran was around. She was always busy making something for school, and it was simpler to keep out of her way.

Not that that was going to sort anything out, but if he left her alone, she'd get over it. She always did, but usually quicker than this.

He was just taking the milk jug out of the little fridge when there was a tap on the door. Since it wasn't closed, knocking was a bit of a formality, but nevertheless he was surprised to see Nick Tremayne there.

'Hello, Nick,' he said, summoning up a smile. 'Come on in. Coffee?'

'Oh—yes, why not. Thanks.' He propped his hips against the battered old desk and Mike could feel the searching stare of those dark brown eyes burning into his back. They'd seen enough of their GP in the previous three years to know that Nick Tremayne never did anything without a reason, and Mike had no idea what it could be. Not unless Nick knew something that he didn't.

'So—what can I do for you?' he asked, turning round with the coffee in his hand and holding it out to Nick.

'Oh, nothing. I've just finished my visits and I was just passing, thought I'd have a look in the farm shop, pick something up for Ben and Lucy. You've got some interesting things now.'

'We try. The ice cream's going well, and the blue cheese is a runaway success. We can't keep up with the demand—but I'm damn sure you aren't here to talk about that.'

Nick's smile was wry. 'Am I so transparent?'

Mike just grunted, and Nick smiled again. 'OK. Point taken—but I really was just passing!' He hefted the farm-shop paper carrier in evidence. 'Ben's got a few days off and my daughter's invited me for lunch, and I didn't want to go empty-handed. And as I was here, I thought I'd just see if you were around. We haven't seen you recently—I wondered if you were both OK.'

Mike snorted softly and stared down into his coffee-cup, swirling the dark brew while he tried to work out how to reply. Honestly, he decided, and put the cup down.

'Not really. We haven't been since the miscarriage. Fran's preoccupied, her temper's short, she's lost all her sparkle—I don't know, she doesn't have anything to say to me any more, and I think it's pretty mutual. Frankly, Nick, I'm beginning to wonder if the strain of all this isn't going to be too much for our marriage.'

'Do you still love her?'

He hesitated, his eyes locked with Nick's, and then he looked away, scrubbing his hand through his hair and letting his breath out on a harsh sigh. 'Yes. Yes, I still love her. I just don't know if she still loves me.'

He swallowed hard, emotion suddenly choking him,

and Nick tutted softly and put his cup down as well. 'Time for a stroll?'

'Yeah. You going to Tregorran now?' Mike asked.

'I am.'

'I'll come with you. If you give me a lift there, I've got some stock to check and I'll walk back. It only takes five minutes across the fields.'

They pulled up on the drive at Tregorran House, and while Mike stood waiting by the car, Nick handed over the bag of shopping to Ben. 'There's some strawberry ice cream in there that needs to go in the freezer,' he said. 'Back in a minute. Mike's just going to show me something.'

A likely story, Mike thought with a mental snort, but he raised his hand and dredged up a smile for Ben. He liked his neighbours, and he was delighted they'd bought Nick's old family home, but it would have been easier if Ben hadn't come to the door with baby Annabel gurgling on his hip and rubbing salt into the wound.

'Mike, I'm glad I've seen you,' Ben said now, coming out onto the drive. 'I've been meaning to talk to you about something. Any chance we could have a chat some time?'

He nodded. 'Sure. Give me a call when you're not busy, or drop round. I'm usually about.' Mike gave him his mobile number and Ben keyed it into his own phone, then slipped it back into his pocket and smiled.

'Cheers. I'll call you.'

Ben waved, lifting the baby's chubby little hand as Mike himself had done with Sophie so many times, and Mike waved back to them both, his breath jamming in his throat as Annabel's face split into a cherubic smile, and he turned away.

Nick fell in beside him, and they went down the track at the side of the house and to the field at the side. It wasn't right on the cliff top, because that field had a footpath through it, part of the Cornish Coastal Path, and he didn't want his dry cows disturbed in their last few weeks of pregnancy by all the walkers.

'Here we are—my ladies-in-waiting,' he said to Nick, his eyes scanning the field to check that the six cows in there were all looking well. Amber came over to him, her gorgeous coat, fox-red splashed with white, gleaming with health in the summer sun, and he rubbed her poll and spoke softly to her for a moment.

'You love your farm, don't you?' Nick murmured, and Mike nodded.

'Can't imagine doing anything else, but it's a constant reminder of our own failure. With a dairy herd, all you do all the time is monitor their pregnancies and deliver their calves and manage their lactation. And it's impossible not to draw parallels.' He smiled, but he could feel it was off kilter. 'If we were livestock, Fran and I would be shot. It seems we're useless together. Giant pandas have more success.'

'That's not true. Fran's been pregnant before, and you achieved a pregnancy on your first cycle of IVF.'

'Yeah—which we also lost. We can't afford another cycle at the moment, and we've run out of NHS funding, so where do we go from here? It wouldn't be so damned frustrating if they could find anything *wrong* with us! But they can't, Nick. We're both well, there are no physical problems, we just can't seem to get it right. And right now I'm not sure I even want to, the way we are. Well, the way Fran is, anyway. I just can't get through to her at all.'

'But that's probably just a reaction to the miscarriage. Perhaps she needs to talk it through. Will she come to see me?'

Mike snorted again and shook his head. 'Not a chance. She might talk to Kate—woman to woman and all that.'

Nick's mouth tightened, and then he nodded. 'That could work. She knows Kate. It's an idea.'

One that was growing on Mike by the second. Kate was working as a midwife again now, and Fran had known her for years because of her son, Jem, who was at the school. Maybe she'd be able to get through to her. 'She could catch her at school,' he suggested, but Nick shook his head.

'Not really the place. But she could call in—maybe one day after school? On her way to see Ben and Lucy? Kate does drop by from time to time to cuddle the baby. I could make sure she doesn't have Jeremiah with her, and maybe you could make yourself unavailable?'

He laughed shortly. 'That won't be hard. I don't have a lot of time to hang around. By the time Fran's home, I'm usually milking so Kate should be able to talk to her undisturbed between four-thirty and six, and if I know she's going to be here, I can always drag it out.'

'Sure. Give me your mobile number. I'll let you know what she's planning so you're forewarned.'

He pulled out his phone and they swapped numbers, and then Mike turned his back on the cattle and stared out over the sea, which was flat and smooth and sparkling, the lazy swell scarcely visible. The surfers wouldn't be happy today, but the families with little children would be having a great time, just as they themselves had had with Sophie last weekend—just as they might one day be doing with another child of their own. His chest tightened with longing and he hauled in a breath and turned back to the GP.

'Thanks, Nick,' he said gruffly. 'I don't know if it'll do any good, but thanks for trying.'

'You're welcome. And you can call me whenever you want a chat, you know. Any time.'

Mike nodded, and they strolled back to the house in thoughtful silence. Nick went in, lifting his hand in farewell, and Mike nodded and set off back across the fields to the farm.

Fran would kill him for interfering, but he couldn't watch her falling apart any longer. He just hoped that Kate was able to reach her, because frankly he was at a loss, and if something didn't happen soon, the remains of their marriage would be unsalvageable.

He tried a little salvage that night.

They'd had supper, and for once they were sitting down together in front of the television. There was nothing on that either of them really seemed to want to watch, though, so he turned it off, found an easy-listening CD, soft and lazy and romantic, and instead of going back to his chair he went over to the sofa and sat down beside her, giving her shoulder an affectionate little rub.

'You OK, my love?'

She nodded, but she didn't meet his eyes and there wasn't a trace of a smile. 'Just tired. I'll be glad when the holidays come.'

'So will I. You can give me a hand—we'll try that new fresh curd cheese you've been talking about.'

Beneath his hand her shoulder drooped a little, then she

straightened up. 'Yes, we can do that. I might give Sarah a hand with the ice cream as well. See if we can get the raspberry one smoother. It's a bit too juicy and it tends to get ice crystals.'

'It's gorgeous. Maybe it just needs stirring for longer as it cools, and agitating more often. You've got it cracked with the strawberry, doing that. Maybe it just needs more of the same.'

'Maybe. We'll try a few things, see how we do.'

She stood up, moving away from him, and went out, coming back a moment later with a book. So much for cuddling up together on the sofa. He peered at the cover.

'Anything interesting?' he asked, and she lifted the book so he could see it.

'CBT—cognitive behaviour therapy. One of my pupils is having it, so I thought I'd read up a bit.'

And she curled up in the corner of the sofa again, opened the book and shut him out as effectively as if she'd left the room.

So *he* did.

He went upstairs, had a shower for the second time that day and came back down in a clean pair of jeans. He hadn't bothered with a T-shirt. It was still hot and, anyway, she'd never been able to keep her hands off him when he took his shirt off. All that rippling muscle, she'd say with a smoky laugh, and grab him.

But she didn't even look up.

The CD had finished, so he put the television back on and settled down to watch a repeat of something he hadn't enjoyed a lot the first time round.

Anything rather than be ignored.

* * *

What was happening to them?

She raised her eyes slightly from the book and let them dwell on his body. Long, lean and rangy, his muscles sleek and strong, not the muscles of a weightlifter but of a man who worked hard with his body, and it showed.

Lord, it showed, and there'd been a time not so very long ago when she would have got up and gone over to him and run her hand over that bare, deep chest with its scattering of dark hair, teasing the flat copper coins of his nipples until they were tight and pebbled under her fingertips. Then she'd run her hands down his ribcage, feeling the bones, the muscles, the heat of his body radiating out, warming her to her heart.

He would have pulled her onto his lap, his eyes laughing, and then the laughter would fade, and he'd kiss her, his hands exploring her body, searching out its secret places, driving her crazy with his sure, gentle touch.

What was that song about a lover with a slow hand? That was Mike—or it had been. Just lately he didn't seem to be interested, and if he had been, she wouldn't have. Just the thought of him touching her so intimately made her shrink away. She didn't think she could cope with the intimacy, baring her soul to him as well as her body. Not when her soul was hurting so much and her body had become public property with all the investigations. Even the idea of being touched there…

And he'd give her a lecture on getting too thin, which probably wasn't unjustified but wouldn't make her feel sexy. Right now, she didn't think anything would make her feel sexy.

Not that he'd tried recently. He'd been too busy, and

every night he was buried in the farm office until late. It was almost as if he was avoiding her. Hard to say, when she was so busy avoiding him, holding herself back because if she did that, if they didn't try, then it didn't hurt so much.

If you didn't try, you couldn't fail, could you?

The book—interesting under other circumstances—couldn't hold her attention, so she shut it and unfolded herself from the corner of the sofa and winced as the circulation returned to her foot. 'I'm going to have a bath,' she told him, limping for the door. 'Don't bother to wait up for me. I feel like a wallow.'

He flicked her an enigmatic look, nodded and turned his eyes back to the television, and swallowing down her disappointment she headed up the stairs.

'Kate, have you got a minute?'

She paused and glanced at Nick, then at the clock. 'Literally. I've got a meeting with Chloe—'

'It won't take long,' he said, holding open the door of his consulting room, and after a tiny hesitation she braced herself and went in, wondering what was coming as he shut the door behind them.

'I saw Mike Trevellyan yesterday.'

'Oh.' She felt the tension drain out of her shoulders and turned to face him. 'How are they?'

'Not sure. He's worried about Fran. They don't seem to be talking.'

She gave a soft snort. 'There must be something in the water.'

Nick's mouth tightened and he looked away, but not before his eyes flicked over her in contempt. 'You've had nearly ten years to talk to me about that, so don't get stroppy if I don't seem to be in a hurry to talk to you about it now.'

'That? It? We're talking about your son, Nick.'

'We don't know that.'

'We do.'

'It was just the once.'

She sighed and rolled her eyes. 'How many times have I heard that from a pregnant woman? And you only have to look at him. His eyes…'

A muscle worked in his jaw, and she gave up. For now. A gentle sigh eased out of her and she squared her shoulders. 'So—about Fran. What do you want me to do? She had a follow-up appointment with me after her miscarriage and she cancelled it. I don't know if I can get her into the surgery.'

'No, we thought of that. I've got Mike's mobile number. I thought if you could drop by there after school one day, when Fran's around and Mike's milking, maybe you could engineer the conversation.'

She stared at him in silence for a long moment, and eventually he turned and looked at her.

'Well? What do you think of it?'

'I think it's a conversation I should have without Jem—*your son*—since I'll have him with me after school.'

'Well, perhaps you could find someone to leave him with for an hour.'

'Mmm. His *father* springs to mind.'

His eyes widened with horror. 'I can't.'

'Well, then, neither can I,' she retorted. 'Not at short notice.'

'He must have school friends,' Nick said, looking a little desperate, but she wasn't going to back down.

'I'm sure he does—but I need to save them for emergencies, and my childminder's not feeling great at the moment so I can't ask her. Besides, Jem needs me. It's our time together—so if you want me to do this, and I agree it seems like a very good idea, then I think it would be an excellent opportunity for you to get to know him a little bit better. As his other parent.'

She watched him struggle, knew the moment he gave in. His jaw tightened, his eyes became shuttered and he gave a curt nod. 'Just don't let it become a habit.'

She laughed. 'What—dropping in on Fran?' she said, deliberately misunderstanding him. 'Hardly. She'll smell a rat before I get up the garden path! What am I supposed to tell her, Nick?'

'Tell her you're visiting Ben and Lucy. Tell her you're going to the farm shop and wondered how she was.'

'I'll tell her I was worried about her, because I am. I've been watching her at school, and a couple of times when she's been outside when I've picked Jem up, she's looked very tired. Don't worry, Nick,' she said soothingly, with only a trace of patronage. 'I'm sure I can manage to manoeuvre the conversation in the right direction.'

He shot her a blistering look and opened his mouth, then clearly thought better of it as a fleeting, rueful smile cracked his face just for a second. 'Thank you. When were you thinking of doing it?'

'Tonight? I can't tomorrow,' she said, thinking ahead. 'I've got a clinic, and on Thursday there's the school sports day, and Friday's the end of term.'

Nick nodded, a muscle working in his jaw. 'OK. I'll get Hazel to shift my patients to Dragan or Oliver. You can drop Jeremiah round to me on your way there, and I'll give him supper.'

'I'll do that. Now, if that's all…?'

'That's all,' he agreed, opening the door for her with something that could have been relief. Poor Nick, she thought as she walked away. He really, really didn't like this. The truth was obviously much too much to take, but that was tough.

He was going to have to get used to it, no matter how unpalatable—get used to the fact that ten years ago this summer, on the very night of the storm that had torn a hole in their community, while his father and brother had lain cooling in the mortuary and her husband's body was being sucked out to sea and shattered on the rocks, their frenzied, desperate coupling had given rise to a child.

And that child was their son.

She looked out of the window, across the bay to the headland where Nick had found her staring out to sea, her body drenched and buffeted by the wild storm, her eyes straining into the darkness. Not that there had been any hope. Even the coastguard had given up, at least for the night, but she hadn't been able to tear herself away.

So Nick had taken control—taken her back to her house, stripped off her sodden clothes, dried her—and then somehow, suddenly, everything had changed. It could have been put down to that old affirmation-of-life cliché, she thought, but it had been more than that. She'd loved him since she'd been fifteen, had wanted him for ever, and it had seemed entirely natural to turn to him for comfort.

And it seemed he had felt the same, because, laid bare by their emotions, when the world had been falling apart all around them and it had seemed as if they were the only people in the world left alive, they'd finally done what they'd come so close to before he'd gone to university and met Annabel. The timing had been awful, but maybe it had been because it was so awful that they'd been able to break through those barriers and reach for each other. And in that moment, when they'd both been too racked with grief and guilt to know what they were doing, they'd started another life.

Like it or not—and he clearly didn't—Nick Tremayne would have to acknowledge the result of their actions that night, and learn to live with it every day of his life, just like she had for the past ten years. After all, it had given her a son, a child she'd never thought she'd have, and he'd brought her so much joy.

So she'd learned to live with herself, with the shame she felt at having given in and taken comfort from Nick at that dreadful time, and she'd slowly, painfully, learned to forgive herself.

Now it was Nick's turn. He'd have to learn to live with himself, too, and maybe, with time, forgive himself.

And perhaps, in the end, he could even learn to love his son.

'Fran!'

She heard the knock, heard the voice calling and went to the window, leaning out and seeing Kate there, to her surprise. 'Kate, hi! Come in, the door's open. I'm just changing Sophie's sheets— Come on up, I'm nearly done.'

And then she wondered why on earth she'd said that,

because the house wasn't looking fantastic and Kate wasn't a close friend, not the sort of person who you just invited in—although maybe she was exactly the sort of person, she amended as Kate arrived in the bedroom with a smile, got hold of the other side of the quilt cover and helped her put it on.

'Thanks.'

'Pleasure. It's always easier with two.'

Fran plumped up the pillow and straightened up. 'I only did it yesterday, that's the frustrating thing, in time for Sophie's next visit, but the dog sneaked up here last night with filthy feet, and I didn't realise till this morning. So—what brings you here on a Tuesday afternoon?' she asked, finally voicing the question that had been in the forefront of her mind ever since she'd heard Kate calling her.

'Oh, I was just passing. I've been to see Ben and Lucy and I popped in at the farm shop. I thought I'd say hello and see how you are. It's always so busy at school and I haven't seen you for ages, not to chat to.'

Not since before the miscarriage but, then, you didn't really need antenatal care when there wasn't going to be any natal to worry about, Fran thought with a sharp stab of grief.

'I'm fine.'

She scooped up the washing and carried it downstairs, leaving Kate to follow. She ought to offer her a cup of tea, but that would open the door to all sorts of things she didn't want. A cosy chat. A more penetrating 'How are you'. A 'How are you really, now your dream's been snatched away' sort of 'How are you'.

But the teapot was there on the side of the Aga, and the kettle was next to it, and without being offered, Kate went over to it, lifted it and raised an eyebrow at Fran. 'Got time to give me a cup of tea?' she asked, and put like that, it would have been too rude to refuse.

She gave in.

'Of course. I'll make it.'

'No, you deal with the washing. I can make a cup of tea. I spend my life making tea and drinking it. That's what midwives do—didn't you know that?'

'Really? I thought they interfered.'

Kate met her eyes and smiled. So the gloves were off, their cards were on the table and they could both start being honest.

Kate lifted the hotplate cover and put the kettle on the hob. 'Fran, I haven't seen you for ages—not since the miscarriage. I'm worried about you,' she said gently.

Fran looked up from the washing machine, slammed the door on it and stood up. 'Don't be.'

'I am. You've got a lot of pressures on you. Sometimes talking them through can help.'

'Kate, I don't need counselling,' she said firmly and a little desperately.

'I never said you did. But a friend who understands the pressures you might be under and the choices open to you might be a help—a sounding board, someone to rant at that isn't your husband?'

Had Mike been talking?

'I don't rant at him.'

'But maybe you want to. Maybe you need to—not because he's done anything wrong but just because you need to rant, to let out your anger. It's all part of the grieving process, Fran. And you have to grieve for your baby.'

Fran swallowed. 'It was just a failed embryo—just like my other miscarriage. There was no baby.'

'But there was—there were two, and you loved them,' Kate said gently, and that was it. The dam burst, and Kate took the washing powder out of her hands, wrapped her arms firmly around her and held her tight. At first Fran could hardly breathe for the wave of pain, but then it got easier, just slightly, so she could actually drag in the air with which to sob.

And sob she did, cradled against Kate's comforting bosom, her hand smoothing rhythmically up and down her back, telling her without words that it would be all right.

'That's it, let it go,' Kate murmured, and when the tears had slowed to a trickle, when the pain had eased to a dull ache instead of the slice of a sword, Kate let her go, and she sat down at the table and groped for a tissue.

'Sorry—heavens, I must look a wreck,' Fran said, sniffing and patting her pockets until Kate handed her a clump of kitchen roll. She mopped her face, blew her nose, sniffed again and tried to smile. It was a wobbly effort, but it was rewarded by an answering smile and a mug of tea put in her hand.

When had Kate made it? In the few seconds she'd been mopping up? Must have. God, she was losing it.

'Thanks,' she said, wrapping her nerveless hands around the mug and hugging it close.

'Better now?'

She nodded, and Kate smiled sympathetically.

'Good. It always helps to get all that backed-up emotion out of the way. Helps you see things more clearly. Was that the first time?'

'Since April? Yes. Properly, like that, yes. I've always tried to stop it before, because it didn't help with the first miscarriage, and I cried so much then. Silly. I might have known it would come out in the end.'

'And Mike's too close to allow him to see it. Because he's hurting, too, and you don't want him to feel bad for you.'

'When did you become so clever?'

A fleeting shadow passed over Kate's face, and Fran was so preoccupied she nearly missed it. Not quite, though, but she had no idea what had prompted it, and Kate was smiling now.

'Oh, I'm not clever, Fran,' she said softly. 'Just human. Maybe I just try and put myself in someone else's shoes, and I know the difference Jem's made in my life, so it's not hard to imagine how I would feel if I'd been unable to have him.'

Fran didn't know what to say. She hadn't been in Penhally when Kate's husband had died, but she'd heard about it from her parents, and how sad it was that he couldn't have known that Kate had been pregnant after several years of marriage. But she didn't feel she could say anything about that now. It had been years ago, intensely private and nothing to do with her.

So she sipped her tea, and sniffed a bit more, and blew her nose again, and all the time Kate just sat there in a companionable silence and let her sift through her thoughts.

'Have you noticed,' Fran said finally, as the sifting came to a sort of conclusion, 'how just about everybody seems to be pregnant at the moment? I don't know if it's just because I'm hypersensitive, but there seems to be a plague of it right now, especially among the school mums. Every time I look up, there's another one.'

Kate nodded. 'And it hurts.'

'Oh, yes,' Fran said very softly. 'It really hurts. You have no idea how much I want a baby, Kate. It's like a biological ache, a real *pain* low down in my abdomen— No, not a pain, it's not that sharp, but a sort of dull awareness, an emptiness, a sort of *waiting*—does that sound crazy?'

'No,' Kate murmured. 'It doesn't sound crazy at all. I've heard it before, so many times.'

'The frantic ticking of my biological clock—except it's not ticking, is it? The spring's broken, or it needs oiling or something, but nobody can find out what exactly, and sort it out. And in the meantime we've run out of time on the NHS, we don't have any money to pay for another cycle of IVF privately, and even if we did, Mike's been so odd recently I don't even know if he *wants* a baby with me!'

Kate studied her tea thoughtfully. 'Do you want a baby with him?' she asked gently. 'Or do you just want a baby?'

That stopped her. She stared at Kate, opened her mouth to say, 'Of course I want a baby with him!' and then shut it again without saying a word, because suddenly she wasn't sure, and she felt her eyes fill again.

'I don't know,' she replied instead, looking down and twisting the tissue into knots. 'I really, really don't know.'

'Do you still love him?'

Again she opened her mouth, then shut it, then said softly, her confidence wavering, 'Yes. Yes, I do, but I don't know if I can live with him like this. And I don't know if he loves me any more.'

'Then you need to talk. You need to spend time together, find out if you've still got what it takes, because there's no point killing yourselves to have a baby together if you don't in the end want to be together. If being with Mike, with or without a child, is the first and most important thing in your life, then go ahead and keep trying for a baby. But if it's not, if the baby's more important than being together, then you need to think very carefully before you go ahead. And so does he.

'Think about it,' she went on. 'Talk to Mike. Take some time together. And play, Fran. Take time out. The weather's gorgeous now. As soon as you break up at the end of the week, try and find some time away from the farm and all its distractions. Is there any chance you can get away?'

She laughed, but with very little humour. 'Not exactly. There's the milking, and the cheese making, and then we share the weekends with Joe, so they each get one weekend off in four. Well, Saturday afternoon and Sunday.'

'And when's your next one?'

'This weekend,' she said slowly. 'But Mike won't stop. He'll just use the time to catch up on paperwork.'

'So stop him. Find a little hotel or a guest house or something, and go away for the night.'

'I doubt if he'll wear that. Anyway, we've got Sophie coming for tea on Sunday because she's away the next weekend.'

'You can be back by teatime.' Kate stood up and put a hand on Fran's shoulder. 'Try it. You've got nothing to lose. And you might have everything to gain. And in the meantime, I've heard some very interesting things about miscarriage and diet and the relationship to damaged and defective sperm.'

Fran frowned. 'Are Mike's sperm defective? I don't think they said anything about it at the fertility clinic—well, not to me, anyway.'

Kate shook her head. 'Not particularly, according to the report from the clinic, but although there were a good number, a slightly higher proportion than one might hope for were defective or sluggish. That in itself might have been enough to cause your miscarriage, if it was a damaged sperm that fertilised the ovum. And this diet is supposed to reduce the numbers of defective sperm quite significantly, according to the study I've heard about. If you're going to try again, maybe you need to take a while to make friends again, and while you do that, you could try the diet to boost Mike's sperm production. It might as well be as good as it can be, and even if you decide not to go ahead and try again, it won't do either of you any harm.'

It sounded a good idea, but she wasn't sure she'd get it past Mike. 'Is it freaky?' she asked. 'I don't want to start giving him weird stuff. He'll ask questions or refuse to eat it. You know what men are like. And he's always starving.'

Kate laughed softly. 'Typical man, then—and, no, it's not freaky. It's more a supplement to his normal diet rather than any radical alteration. I can let you have all the details, if you like—why don't you come and see me tomorrow after school? I've got time, and we can go through it then properly.'

Fran nodded slowly. 'OK. Thanks. I will.'

And in the meantime, she'd try and talk him into going away. Just a few days, right away from the pressures of the farm.

She felt a shiver of something that could have been fear and could have been excitement. Maybe both. Probably.

She'd ask him tonight.

CHAPTER THREE

'THIS is ridiculous.'

Fran stared out across the yard. She couldn't see the farm office on the other side, but she could see the spill of light from the window, and she knew exactly what he'd be doing.

Avoiding her.

Night after night, week after week for months now.

It was becoming a pattern. He'd get up at the end of their evening meal, kiss her absently on the cheek and thank her, then go out, Brodie at his heels, to the farm office.

And he'd stay there, wrestling with the accounts and the endless paperwork, until nearly midnight. Sometimes she'd hear him come to bed, sometimes she wouldn't. And in the morning, when the alarm went at five, he'd get up and go into the bathroom and dress, then go out and do the milking.

On a good day, or at the weekend, she'd see him for breakfast before she went to work herself. On a bad day, and there were increasingly more of them, she wouldn't see him at all.

Tonight was no exception. He'd kissed her vaguely on her cheek, said, 'Don't wait up for me, I want to get those quota forms filled in,' and he had gone.

Well, she was sick of it.

Sick of not having a relationship, sick of not having anyone—not even the dog, for heaven's sake!—to talk to in the evenings, sick of going to bed alone. Even on his birthday.

No wonder Kirsten had left him.

She sighed and turned away from the window, sick, too, of staring out and willing him to come back in. It hadn't always been like this. At first, when they'd started going out together, he'd been able to find time for her, and after they'd married he'd been lovely. OK, he'd worked late and started early, but when he'd come to bed he would wake her, snuggling up, either for a cuddle or to make love to her, slowly, tenderly, languorously—or wildly, as if he couldn't get enough of her.

When had it changed? she asked herself, but she knew.

The miscarriage—the most recent one, three months ago.

That was when it had changed—when he'd withdrawn from her so completely. When she'd lost the baby she'd thought they'd been so thrilled about.

Except maybe she'd been wrong. Maybe he hadn't been thrilled at all. Maybe this last miscarriage had been a lucky escape, a narrow squeak in the midst of all the happy, fluffy stuff—choosing the colour of the paint for the nursery, discussing names, telling both sets of parents. Thank God they hadn't told Sophie, but they'd been waiting till after the three-month watershed, till it was safe.

Except it hadn't been.

She scrubbed away the sudden, unexpected tears and swallowed hard.

No. She wouldn't cry again. Not after all this time. She'd cried all over Kate today, embarrassingly, but she wasn't doing it again. It didn't help. She'd cried an ocean after the first miscarriage, and it hadn't done any good.

And neither had anything else they'd tried, because she still hadn't conceived again until they'd gone down the IVF route.

Of course, the opportunity wouldn't have gone amiss and, looking back on it, she realised that ever since the first miscarriage things had been different. She'd put it down to too much work and the pressure of the farm, but really he'd been avoiding her for years, she thought with shock, and she'd been more than happy to let him, because it meant she didn't have to confront her fears and feelings.

Well, not any more.

She stared out of the window again, and decided it was time to act. If she was going to save her marriage, she was going to have to fight for it—she just wished she knew what it was she was fighting…

'We can't go away!'

'Why not?'

Mike stared at her, puzzled by her sudden insistence, but maybe more puzzled by his own curious reluctance.

The truth was, with Joe already fixed to cover him for the coming weekend there was no reason at all why they couldn't go away. Sophie was coming on Sunday afternoon, but otherwise they were free—the animals were taken care of, and Brodie would be perfectly content down at Joe and Sarah's house with their two dogs. They spent a lot of time together anyway.

So there was no reason, no reasonable excuse he could give, and he wasn't sure why he wanted to get out of it, but he did.

'I've got a lot of paperwork.'

'You always have a lot of paperwork.'

'Yes, and it won't just go away because we have!'

'No, it won't,' she agreed. 'It'll still be there when we come back. Mike, nobody's going to die if you don't do the paperwork this weekend. We can do it together.'

'No. Fran, I can't go.'

'Or won't.'

He met her eyes, wondered what the hell was happening to them, and, abandoning his coffee, he walked out of the farm office and headed for the machinery store. 'I haven't got time to talk about this now,' he said shortly. 'I've got to get on. Brodie!'

And he walked away, haunted by the look of hurt in her eyes and kicking himself, but he couldn't imagine what the hell they'd do for the whole weekend.

He laughed bitterly. His own wife, the woman he loved, and he couldn't work out what they'd do alone together for a night? 'Hell, man, you're losing it,' he muttered, and Brodie nudged his hand, her face anxious.

'It's all right,' he said reassuringly, giving her a pat, but it wasn't. It was far from all right, and he didn't quite know how they'd ended up there.

He threw the chainsaw into the back of the pickup, loaded in the other tools he'd need for his day's work, opened the cab door for Brodie and followed her in, starting up the engine and getting out of the farmyard before Fran came up with any other excuses for—what? Finding time with him?

Was that really such a bad thing?

Yet just the other night, when he'd sat with her and tried to get through to her, she'd stonewalled him and got a book out. Well, let her run after him. Maybe she'd find she wanted him after all…

'So how did it go with Fran?'

Kate gave a 'so-so' shrug. 'Not sure, really. I think I gave her something to think about. She's coming in to see me at the end of the afternoon, before my clinic. I'm going to give her the details of that fertility-boosting diet I was telling you about, so that if they decide to go down the IVF route they're starting from the best possible position.'

'Do you think they will? IVF's not cheap and they've invested a lot in the farm recently. I don't know if they can afford it.'

'I don't know if they even want it,' Kate admitted quietly.

Nick sighed. 'It seems such a damn shame that they got pregnant and then she lost it.'

'But at least we know she can get pregnant, which is a good starting point.'

Nick nodded and pushed a hand through his hair, the fingers parting it, leaving it rumpled. It was greying now, pepper and salt, but still thick, and her fingers itched to feel it, to thread through it as his had, to see if it still felt as soft and heavy as before…

She was going crazy. She had no business thinking things like that. She had to get on.

'Just seems so tough, when the rest of the world seems to have babies at the drop of a hat.'

'Well, you would know,' she said, a touch bitterly, reminding herself of all the reasons why Nick was so very bad for her. 'And at least if and when *they* have a child, it'll know it was wanted.'

'My children are wanted!' he retorted.

'All of them?'

He coloured and turned away, staring out of the window and stabbing his hand through his hair again. 'We still don't know—'

'Yes, we do,' she said with quiet emphasis. 'James was sub-fertile. He'd had a test.'

Nick turned slowly and stared at her, his eyes carefully expressionless. 'So—he really is mine?'

She felt her heart kick. 'Yes, Nick. He really is. There's no doubt at all. Jem is your son.'

The colour seemed to drain from his face, and for a moment he just stood there, rooted to the spot. Then he swallowed, dragged in a breath, straightened his shoulders. 'Right. Um—got to get on.'

'That's it—run away.'

He stopped, paused, then started walking again, then paused once more with his hand on the doorhandle. 'I'm not running, Kate,' he said, defeat in his voice. 'There's no point. There's nowhere to go.'

And, opening the door, he strode out into the waiting room and left her there.

'Brodie, get out of the way! Come on. Stupid dog—what the hell are you doing?'

Brodie was tugging Mike's trousers, trying to get him to play, but he wasn't interested. He'd been clearing up fallen and dead timber all day, and he'd just found an old willow which had snapped halfway up the trunk but stayed attached, the top swinging down to make a ragged arch, but it was still hanging by a thick rope of twisted wood and bark, propped on a lower branch that had dug into the ground and broken its fall.

Under normal circumstances he'd get up the tree and cut it off at the trunk, but it was straddling the river, one end high in the air, the other, in a tangle of broken branches and twigs, sprawled across the ground on this side. There was no way to get to it without crossing the river, and he didn't have time to keep driving backwards and forwards over the nearest bridge.

And Joe had the forklift with the long reach for bringing in the hay and silage bales, otherwise he could have used that. No, he'd just have to tackle it from this side.

But it was big.

He'd tried levering it off the supporting branch with a smaller branch wedged under it and over another log, but he wasn't heavy enough to shift it. He couldn't leave it there, though, because it was unstable and if the wind got up again, it could fall—and the cattle had been grazing down here around it. So he had to shift it now, before the end of the day, so he could let the cows back into the field in safety.

He tried Joe again, but he wasn't answering his mobile. Probably couldn't hear it. Damn. And the dog was still begging for a game.

'Brodie, give it up,' he said crossly, and, picking up the chainsaw, he cut away a few more branches so he could roll the tree when it fell. But the dog was in the way, and he'd get her with the saw in a minute, so he put her in the cab and told her to stay, then went back to it.

'Right, you stubborn bloody thing,' he said, glaring at the tree, and touched the underside with the saw. It creaked, sagged a fraction.

Better.

He touched it again, but the tree was weaker than he'd thought, and the creaking was more ominous.

Too ominous.

He looked up, to where the fallen part of the tree was joined to the trunk on the other side of the river, and watched in horror as, almost in slow motion, the wood started to split away and flip up, freeing the hugely heavy upper section of the tree. It was going to fall, and he was right in its way.

He didn't have time to think. He didn't have time to do anything but turn and run, throwing the saw aside, and as he turned, he heard a loud crack and a sound like thunder, then a branch whipped round and felled him at the same time as the trunk rolled down and came to rest across his legs.

The pain was blinding, but the adrenalin was kicking in, his heart racing, and gradually the pain receded to a dull scream.

He lay motionless, waiting, listening, but apart from Brodie's frantic barking, there was silence. The tree had settled, and he could still feel his feet. And his legs. Hell, he could definitely feel his legs, especially the right one.

Well, the ankle really. The left one was OK, and he could even move it a little. It was in a bit of a hollow, but the right—there was no way he could move that, and no way he was going to try. Just lying there was agony.

So now what?

He was lying there, contemplating his very limited options and trying not to retch with the pain, when he felt the vibration of his phone against his hip. Great. It might be Joe. He'd be able to get him out of this mess. He wriggled around a little, gasping at the pain in his ankle and his ribs, and the tree creaked again and shifted in a little gust of wind, sending pain stabbing through him.

Hell! He'd thought it had settled! He tried again for the phone, and finally managed to get it out of his pocket. 'One missed call,' he read, and tapped the keys with a shaking thumb to bring up the number. Not Joe.

Ben Carter.

Well, it was a start. If that tree kept shifting, an emergency consultant might not be a bad man to have around. He called him back. 'Ben? It's Mike.'

'Mike, hi. I was just calling to have that chat—is this a good time?'

Mike gave a strangled laugh, his breath constricted by the branch over his back. 'Um…I've had better. Bit…um… stuck at the moment.'

'Oh, I'll call you later—'

'No! I mean—really stuck. I'm lying under a tree.'

There was a pause. 'As in lying under a tree on the grass, contemplating the meaning of life, or—?'

'Lying under a fallen tree that I was cutting up,' Mike finished for him. 'Sort of literally stuck. And I think my leg might be broken, and the tree's not stable.'

Just to underline that fact, the tree groaned again, and he felt sweat break out all over him. 'I'm down by the river—only a short way from you over the fields, but you'll need help. I'm trying to get hold of Joe, but maybe we need the fire brigade—they've got a few strong lads who could help shift this thing.'

'Tell me where to come, and I'll get them on their way, too,' Ben said, his voice all calm business, and Mike felt his confidence like a soothing hand.

'Out of your drive, turn left, down the hill to the river, then there's a track to the right. Follow it—shut the gates behind you—and you'll find me there. You'll see the pickup and hear the dog barking.'

'Right. Are you bleeding?'

He considered that for a second. 'I don't think so.'

'OK. Stay still, don't move and I'll be with you.'

'Like I can move,' he said, but the line was dead, and he tried Joe again, getting him this time. Joe's language was colourful, and he could hear the fear in his brother's voice, but he'd know what to do and how to get him out, and he could use the chainsaw.

They arrived simultaneously, Joe on the tractor, Ben in his BMW, grounding on the track, and Mike felt a stupid, stupid urge to cry with relief.

'Nice one, guys,' he said, cracking a grin, and Joe swore and knelt down beside him, reaching through the twigs covering him to squeeze his shoulder hard.

'Stupid bastard. This tree's huge, far too big to tackle alone—why didn't you call me?'

'I did. Several times. You weren't answering.'

Joe swore again. 'Sorry, I was clearing the auger. Right, let's have a look at this tree. If I could only get the tractor in here I could lift it off you with the forks, but there isn't enough room. The other trees are too close.'

'So what's plan B?'

Joe looked around. 'I'm going to get this branch off you first, so you can breathe better. Then we can get a closer look.'

'Great.' Mike grunted. 'Just make sure it's not holding up the tree.'

'It's not. There's a good-sized branch wedging it.'

'Good. Cut this one off, then, because I really can't breathe. The chainsaw's about somewhere.'

He got up, and Ben took his place, hands running confidently over Mike's body. 'Tell me what hurts.'

'My leg? My pride?'

'Idiot. Not your back? Only your legs?'

'No, my back's fine—well, in comparison to my legs. The right one, anyway—and, believe me, it's enough,' he said, fighting down bile and wondering how the hell Joe was going to get him out. The scream of the saw sounded, and the pressure on his back and ribs eased, but it didn't take away the other pain.

'What kind of pain is it?' Ben was asking. 'Sharp? Sickening? Dull? Raw? Tender?'

'No. More—excruciatingly sharp. And sickening, yeah.'

'Right. Sounds like a fracture.'

'Feels like it, but I'm not an expert.'

'Can you feel your foot?'

He gave a choked laugh. 'All too well.'

'That's good.'

Good? Mike snorted and turned his face down, resting his head on the back of his hand and closing his eyes. He felt sick—sick and scared. If he'd died, what would have happened to Fran? Or the farm? Joe couldn't cope alone, and his father was too old to want to start all over again. He'd just retired, handed over the reins to his sons and put his feet up.

That damn tree had better not fall any further, he thought, and, craning his neck, he saw Joe shifting logs, making a pile under the trunk so it couldn't roll any further and couldn't sag any more.

Or that was the theory, but it was so heavy it could probably shift the logs quite easily.

Then he heard a fire engine lumbering down the track, felt the ground tremble under the weight of it, and the tree shifted again. Just a fraction, but enough to make him swear and eye the pile of logs nervously. Would they hold?

'We need to clear these branches to get the airbags under it,' someone said, and he could hear people running, and then the sound of the saw, then the weight shifted again and he groaned as pain shafted up his leg.

'Stop! It's moving on him. He needs pain relief—where are the paramedics?' That was Ben.

'There's been a big pile-up. All the ambulances are out. They're having to send one from Plymouth. It'll be another twenty minutes, and I don't think we're going to be able to use the airbags. There isn't enough room to get them underneath without cutting off the branches, and they're supporting it. We need to get heavy-lifting gear and it'll take a while—it's at the pile-up too.'

Great. Sweat dribbled down his face and into a graze, stinging it. He turned his cheek against his sleeve to wipe it away and caught Ben's troubled eyes. He smiled reassuringly but for some reason it didn't work. Nothing to do with the tons of timber hovering over his body just waiting to crash the rest of the way down and kill him…

'Right. I'll get Nick.'

Mike heard Ben key in a number, then heard rapid instructions, and a hand came back on his shoulder. 'Nick's going to bring some drugs.'

'Excellent,' he mumbled. 'I love drugs. Drugs are good.' The tree creaked again, and he bit down on his hand and gave a grunt of pain as the fire crew started to shift whatever they could to prop the broken trunk.

'Fran, come on in, have a seat,' Kate said, her smile welcoming, and Fran sat down at the desk, her fingers knotted tightly together in her lap.

'Are you OK?'

She consciously relaxed her hands and smiled back. 'Fine. So—tell me about this diet.'

'I've got the details here for you.' Kate straightened up and reached for a sheet of paper, sliding it across the desk towards her. 'It's very simple—suggestions, really, for how to include certain things, trace elements and so on which, although probably present in your diet, might not be there in sufficient quantity.'

'Things?'

'Zinc, selenium, folic acid, vitamin C. You need Brazil nuts and shitake mushrooms and oysters—not together, obviously,' she said with a chuckle, and Fran smiled with relief.

'I wondered how I was going to work them in!' she said.

'Well, oysters are out of season at the moment, you'll have to wait until the end of October if you want local ones, but the mushrooms and Brazil nuts you can get any time. And fruit smoothies. Fruit and veg smoothies—do you eat a lot of fruit and veg?'

'I do. Mike's usually crunching an apple and he eats what I give him but he's not over-fond of salads so he tends to eat cooked veg. He drinks apple juice sometimes—does that count?'

'Not really, but it makes an excellent base for the smoothies, so make him smoothies with apple juice instead of giving him coffee—it's hot now, so you've got the perfect excuse. And you should both be avoiding having a high caffeine intake as well. It's been related to delayed conception, so avoid coffee if you can, and also colas, dark chocolate and black tea—that's not tea without milk, by the way, but any tea that isn't green, white, fruit or herbal. Oh, and cut out alcohol. It can reduce a man's sperm count by half.'

'Good grief. I don't mind that but I think he'll kill me if he can't have tea or coffee! Apart from the odd glass of wine and the occasional apple juice, that's all he drinks!'

'He'll love the smoothies. You can use the veg ones as chilled soups—lovely in the summer. And they'll do you good as well—boost your vitamin levels. If they help sperm production, they might have a beneficial effect on your ovaries, too. Just try, Fran. If it does nothing else, it'll improve your general health and make you feel much better. In fact, it'll do you a power of good to eat something nutritious. You've lost too much weight recently, and being underweight can harm your chances of conception—did you know that?'

She shook her head, wondering why they were having this conversation when Mike clearly didn't even want to spend one night—one miserable, solitary little night!—alone with her, without the dog or his daughter or the endless bloody paperwork to hide behind.

'Encourage him to take cool showers and not hot baths—does he have baths?' Kate went on.

'Sometimes—if he's been doing something very strenuous and he's aching. Usually he showers.'

'What about underpants? Does he wear loose boxers or

tight briefs? Because if they're too tight, the testicles can overheat and that can affect the sperm count as well. The whole design of the scrotum is to allow the testicles to be at a slightly lower temperature, but because we wear clothes and bundle them up nice and tight, they cook a bit. Of course, going commando is the best answer, but I can imagine he might object if you steal all his underwear.'

Fran chuckled. 'I'll just steal the tight stuff and tell him it was worn out. To be honest, as long as there's something in the drawer I don't think he'd care what it was. I can tell him I had a crisis with the washing machine or the dog ate it or something.'

Or she could just tell him the truth, but the whole thing was irrelevant at the moment. She was hardly going to get pregnant if they didn't—

'You need to eat lots of dairy, too,' Kate was saying, 'but be careful with the soft cheese and unpasteurised milk products if there's the slightest possibility you might be pregnant.'

A humourless little huff of laughter escaped from Fran's mouth. 'Chance'd be a fine thing.'

Kate clicked her tongue sympathetically. 'Did you broach the subject of going away?' she asked gently.

Fran laughed again, but it was just as bad as the last one and utterly unconvincing. She swallowed hard. 'He's— He hasn't got time.'

'Is that true?'

'Probably, but if he wanted to, he'd make time—wouldn't he?'

Kate smiled. 'Don't ask me. Men are a mystery.'

'Tell me about it,' Fran murmured.

'So do something romantic at home. Cook a nice meal, put something pretty on…'

'He'll think I've run up a credit card,' she said dryly, and then felt saddened that they'd come so far down the line that they'd come to this, her talking about her marriage to a woman she hardly knew, trying to gain insight into her husband's behaviour. Not to mention her own…

'Kate, sorry— Ah. Fran. I'm glad you're here,' Nick said, his face troubled. 'Um, I've had a call from Ben. Mike's got a bit of a problem. He was apparently cutting down a tree—'

'What?' The word came out soundlessly from lips suddenly numb. She felt the colour drain from her face, her limbs curiously heavy and her heart lumping with dread. She lifted a hand to her mouth. 'Not the chainsaw…'

'No—no, a branch rolled onto him and it's pinning his leg down. Ben's with him—thinks he's got a fracture but the ambulances are all out on a big RTA and it'll take them ages to get to him, so I'm going to pop over there with a bit of pain relief while the fire crew get the branch off him. I'm taking morphine, but I just wondered if we'd got Entonox, Kate.'

'Yes—I'll get it. And we'll come. Come on, Fran, I'll drive you.'

The props weren't working. The weight of the upper trunk was too great, and they couldn't shift enough wood to secure it. The fire crew was gathered round Mike, having a muttered conference that didn't inspire confidence. He just wanted to get the hell out, and he needed those drugs.

'I'm going to dig it out,' Joe said. 'If I undermine it,

under that leg and foot, we can ease him out. The other one's free.'

'Sounds like a plan,' he mumbled, but the fire officer in charge had other ideas.

'Sorry, I can't let you get that close,' he said.

Joe's reply was pithy and not in the least bit polite, and it made Mike smile. Seconds later he felt him digging, felt Joe's hands under his leg while Ben supported it, stripping away the shale that was digging into his shin, and then his foot moved a fraction and he let out a whimper as he felt his leg sliding down gradually, away from the weight of the trunk.

He bit down on his lip, knowing it was necessary to dig around his foot so he could wriggle free but not sure he could take it.

Not without pain relief, but Nick was there, bringing him Entonox. He knew about that—Kirsten had had it when she'd been in labour with Sophie, and he sucked greedily on the mouthpiece while Joe tunnelled away like a mole, shifting the stony soil away from his leg and foot while he tried not to yell. Nick was putting something in his hand—some kind of IV set—and then injecting something that made him feel woozy and light-headed.

'Whazat?' he mumbled.

'Morphine, and metaclopromide, to stop you feeling sick from the morphine.'

''S lovely,' he replied. It was. The pain was going, fading a bit, less global.

'Right, that's as good as it gets,' Joe said.

'OK.' That was Ben. 'Mike, can you get your legs out yourself? Just slowly and carefully.'

He took a deep breath of the Entonox, wriggled his left leg free, took another suck of the gas and tried to move.

Pain lanced through him despite the drugs, and he swore viciously, suddenly wide awake. 'I need a hand, guys,' he said, sweat beading on his brow. 'Just pull me out, nice and carefully. I can't do this myself.'

'It is free,' Ben said, feeling round his leg gently. 'We should be able to do it. It's a very unstable fracture, though, and I don't want to drag you. And you need a spinal board.'

'To hell with that. What I need is to get out of here now,' he muttered as the tree groaned again. He felt it shift against his calf, and yelled, 'Just get me—Joe and Nick maybe?—and he could feel Ben's hands on his leg, steadying it. On the count of three they pulled, he gasped and swore and bit hard on his lip, and then he was free, and they were dragging and lifting him away from the tree while everything went black for a second and he fought the urge to scream with the pain.

As they put him down and shifted him to his back, Fran's white, terrified face swam into view. He thought she was going to yell at him, but she just smiled a little shakily and said, 'I didn't know you knew half of those words.' And then with a last tortured groan the tree slipped and fell the last few feet with a thundering crash, and she burst into tears.

'What the *hell* were you doing down there on your own with the chainsaw?'

He gave a rueful smile, and Fran felt a terrible urge

to smack him. She'd hung on as long as she could, but the 'what the hell' question just wouldn't stay locked up any longer, and she sat by his bed in the hospital and clamped her hands together. So she didn't strangle him, or so they didn't shake?

She didn't know. She didn't care. All she cared about was that Mike was alive—damaged, but alive—and only because Ben, Joe and Nick had got him out when they had.

She and Kate had got there just as he had been yelling at them to pull him out, and she'd watched in horror as his face had blanched and he'd let fly a string of words she'd never heard him use before.

And then the trunk had dropped, right where he'd been lying, and one of the firemen had been lucky to duck out of the way of the flying branches.

It could have been so, so much worse.

Infinitely worse. Unimaginably worse—

'I've done the milking for you, you idle skiver—and can you stick to Monopoly and not pick-up-sticks in future?' Joe said, walking up behind her and saving him from the strangling he so surely deserved.

'Hi, Joe,' she said with a smile of welcome. 'Give your brother a hard time for me, could you? I'm just going to ring your mother again and let her know they've moved him.'

'She's here. She and Dad have just pulled into the car park. I told them where to come.'

Ensconced in his hospital bed, Mike groaned. 'Did you have to? They'll make such a fuss.'

'A fuss? *A fuss!*' Fran all but shrieked. 'I'll give you *fuss*,

Michael Trevellyan! If that tree had fallen a minute earlier—ten seconds, for heaven's sake—'

'Michael! Oh, my goodness, are you all right? We came as soon as we heard but we were on our way back from Plymouth and there was a huge tailback because of this accident—'

'I'm fine, Mum,' he said, grimacing as he caught sight of his father's stern face.

'How many times have I told you—?' Fran's father-in-law started, and Fran just smiled, stepped back and left them to it. She didn't need to strangle him. His parents would do it for her. In the meantime, she might go and get herself a cup of coffee.

'So how's the invalid?' Ben asked as she bumped into him at the ward entrance.

'Getting an earful from everyone,' Fran told Ben with a wry smile.

Ben smiled back, but his eyes were gentle with concern, and she felt hers fill again. 'You OK?' he asked, and she nodded, then shook her head, then shrugged a little helplessly and laughed, her traitorous eyes welling.

'I don't know. Yes. Maybe. At least he's alive.'

'He'll be fine. He'll be going to Theatre shortly to have it plated, and he'll be in for a couple of days, then they'll send him home in a cast to rest.'

'He'll be horrible. He'll be so bored,' Fran said with a sigh, and Ben raised an eyebrow.

'So entertain him,' he said with a smile. 'He'll be laid up and fizzing over with all that pent-up energy. I'm sure you'll be able to find something to do together to alleviate the boredom!'

She felt herself colour slightly, and found a smile. If only, she thought. 'I'll buy him a Sudoku book,' she said, and Ben chuckled.

'Yeah, right. Like that'll do it!' He tipped his head on one side. 'You going anywhere important?'

'Yes—to get a coffee,' she said, wondering if it mattered if she started Kate's diet a day later and deciding that today justified it. She could have lost Mike—so easily. And today had proved to her beyond any doubt that she wasn't ready to lose him. Not in any way. There was nothing like staring that dreadful possibility in the face to bring it home to her, so, yes, today justified a delay in the start of the diet, because at the moment whether or not they had a child was way down the list of her priorities.

And Mike—her beloved, darling, infuriating, broken Mike—was right at the top.

'Mind if I join you?' Ben was saying. 'I was just about to make a drink when I called him, and I still haven't had one yet. I'll even treat you to a chocolate muffin.'

She laughed. 'You truly know the way to a woman's heart,' she replied, and wondered when she and Mike had last laughed like that, about nothing in particular, just for the sake of laughing. Ages. A lifetime.

But they would again. She'd make sure of it…

CHAPTER FOUR

THEY were sending him home on Friday, and he couldn't get out of hospital quickly enough.

Not that he'd really known that much about it for the first twenty-four hours, because he'd been in so much pain he'd been drugged up to the eyeballs.

It was the bottom of his fibula where it joined the tibia on the outside of his ankle—the lateral maleolus, or some such bone—that had sheared off, and his fibula was fractured again just above the ankle joint. Such a skinny little bone to cause so much pain, although the ligaments between the two bones hadn't ripped. This, apparently, was a good thing, or it would have been ages before he could bear weight.

Even so, he'd have to be in a cast for weeks.

Fabulous. In the summer, when he relied on the longer hours of daylight to do all those endless jobs about the farm that he couldn't simply do in the dark. Hedging, fencing, repairing the fabric of the buildings—cutting up fallen trees?

But on the bright side, luckily the skin hadn't broken. It seemed a very slight thing to worry about, considering they'd had to cut it open anyway, but apparently it made a great difference to the sort of repair they could do, and it meant it could be plated and screwed, and he didn't have to have an external fixator.

Thank God, because there was no way he could work on the farm with a metal frame on the outside of his leg and pins going through into the bone, carrying filth and infection right into the heart of the injury. And, anyway, even the sight of them made him feel sick. There were several people in the orthopaedic ward with them on, and others in traction, even one screwed into a special revolving frame, bolts into his head and shoulders and hips and legs…

Hideous. God only knows what it must feel like to be in there, he thought, but the man didn't seem to be aware of too much. That had to be a good thing—probably the only good thing, if the drawn faces of his relatives were anything to go by.

He glanced across at the man. On second thoughts, maybe it wasn't a good thing. He discovered he was extremely grateful he wasn't in so bad a way that he wasn't aware of his surroundings, never mind his ankle.

Although he felt all too aware of it most of the time, and he was desperate for a good night's sleep in his own bed, with soft cotton sheets, their lovely down duvet and his own pillow.

And Fran.

God, he missed her. She'd been in to visit him each evening, but it wasn't enough, and he couldn't believe he'd been so reluctant to go away with her this coming weekend for the night. He'd give his eye teeth for the chance to do it now, he thought, lying there waiting for someone to come and discharge him.

And then Ben strolled in, hitched his hip onto the edge of the bed and grinned. 'Want to cut loose?'

'Oh, do I ever!' he said fervently. 'Got the power to spring me?'

'Absolutely. Well, not really, but I've just seen your consultant and he's happy to lose you. They're just filling in the paperwork, and I thought, as I've got the afternoon off, I'd give you a lift—unless you're organised?'

He shook his head. 'No, not at all. I was going to ring my father or my brother, but I haven't done that yet. I'm supposed to be getting a lesson on my crutches.'

'Yeah, the physio's on her way. I'll get them to give me a call when you're done, and I'll get you out of here.'

'You're a star. Cheers.'

'My pleasure.'

It took another hour, but finally he was ready to go, and Ben came up, put him into a wheelchair and trundled him out into the fresh air. He dragged in a great lungful of it, closed his eyes and sighed hugely. 'Oh, that feels so good. You can't imagine what it's like when you're used to being outside all the time, to be cooped up in there without feeling the wind in your hair and the sun on your face. I just kept telling myself I was lucky not to be six feet under.'

'Shouldn't think you needed to,' Ben said dryly, pushing him through the car park to his BMW. 'I would have thought you'd got Fran doing that for you, on the minute every minute. She was beside herself, you know, when she realised how dangerous it might have been.'

Mike gave a rusty chuckle. 'She wasn't alone. When I heard that tree go—well, let's just say I won't be taking chances like that again.'

'Good. I'm glad to hear it, and I'm sure she will be. Right, shift across and I'll get rid of the wheels while you settle yourself.'

Easier said than done, he realised. God, how could anything so simple be so profoundly awkward? It took him ages, while Ben stood holding the wheelchair and telling him to take his time.

But so much? Finally there, he slumped back in the seat, his skin breaking out in a cold sweat, and concentrated on getting his breath back. Not easy with his ribs screaming in protest.

He was shocked at how hard he'd found it, how even such a comparatively minor injury could have taken such a toll on him. And once he was at home, he'd have to go up and down stairs. How the hell was he going to manage that? And bathing, for crying out loud. He'd have to shower with his leg in a bin bag.

He gave the cast a jaundiced look and wondered for the umpteenth time how he could have been so stupid. It was going to be weeks before he was fixed—months, even. Certainly a couple of weeks before he could do anything even remotely useful on the farm. Even the dreaded paper-work would be too much for him at the moment.

He swore under his breath, hauled his broken leg into the car, swung the comparatively uninjured one in beside it and eyed the bruises with disgust.

Pity he couldn't have worn trousers to hide them a bit, but he didn't have any that would go over the cast, so he was wearing shorts and a T-shirt and his Technicolor injuries were all on display.

Well, not quite all of them. His body under the clothes

was also black and blue all over, a million points of pain and mutilation. He'd caught a glimpse of the bruises over his cracked ribs in the bathroom mirror this morning and had nearly had a fit. Fran would take one look at him in the nude and run, if she had any sense. Probably just as well, because he didn't have the strength to argue with her about how stupid he'd been and just now she wasn't wasting a single opportunity to lecture him.

He closed his eyes and dropped his head back against the seat. He just wanted her to come home and hug him. He'd missed her so much, and his family had all been in telling him off, so their visiting times had hardly been cosy, intimate occasions.

'Come on, Ben,' he muttered. 'Take me home.'

As if he'd heard him, Ben opened the driver's door, slid behind the wheel and shot him a smile. 'Sorry about that. Somebody wanted the chair and then couldn't manage to get her husband into it. As he was having a heart attack, I didn't feel I could leave them.'

'Of course not,' Mike said, trying for a smile and probably producing a grimace.

'Right, let's get you home.'

He hadn't heard anything so good in ages.

'Mike?'

Fran ran lightly up the stairs, crept down the landing and pushed open the bedroom door, tiptoeing round the bed so she could see his face.

He was fast asleep, his lashes dark crescents against his cheeks. He looked pale under his tan, drained of warmth, and she bit her lip and blinked back tears. He looked awful. Washed out and exhausted, and it made her want to cry.

She'd been fighting the urge since it had happened, moaning at him about being stupid when all she'd really wanted to do was curl up in his arms and howl her eyes out.

She backed away, meaning to leave him alone, but her foot hit the creaky board and his lids fluttered open, those gorgeous brown eyes fixed on hers.

'Hi.'

'Hi,' she replied softly, perching carefully on the edge of the bed and giving him a shaky smile. 'Welcome home.'

His answering smile was tired but contented. 'Thanks. It's good to be back.'

'How long have you been home?'

He glanced at his watch. 'Two hours? Ben gave me a lift.'

'Ben?' she echoed, surprised. 'That was kind of him. I thought Joe or your father would do it.'

Mike shrugged. 'He was there, he offered, and they were busy.'

'Can I get you anything—a drink?'

He shook his head, his eyes intense. 'Not yet. The first thing I want is a hug from my wife without an audience.'

'Oh, Mike…'

She kicked off her shoes, lifted the quilt and slid carefully under it, turning towards him as his arms reached for her and he gathered her up against his chest with a sigh. She breathed deeply, drawing in the scent of him, a strange mixture of hospital and warm, earthy man, and she squeezed her eyes shut and slid her arms carefully round him and hugged him.

He grunted, and she froze, lifting her arms away. 'Mike?'

'It's OK. I've got a few bruised ribs.'

She lifted the quilt back and propped herself up, staring down at the vicious bruises over his side and back, a huge spreading stain of vivid, deepest purple where the branch had fallen on him, the bruises so many they'd all run together in a great blotchy sheet. She hadn't seen them before, because he'd been in a T-shirt and boxers in the hospital, but now, with his T-shirt removed and just the boxers on, she could see them, and they brought tears to her eyes.

'Bruised?' she questioned sceptically, a give-away shake in her voice. 'Is that what you call it? Just...bruised?'

His smile was a little crooked. 'Well, the odd rib might be cracked.'

She shut her eyes again and lay down, keeping her arms well away from his ribs, one hand lightly resting on his shoulder, her face cradled against his chest. It rose and fell slowly, then stopped, and she looked up and saw his lips pressed hard together.

'What is it? Are you OK? Where do you hurt?' she asked, panicking, and he turned his head and stared at her, his eyes raw with emotion.

'It's just so good to be home—to hold you,' he said, and she was stunned to hear a catch in his voice. 'I've missed you.'

'Oh, Mike...' She broke off, the words dammed up behind the tears, and she lifted a hand to his cheek, letting it linger as she feathered a kiss over his lips. 'I've missed you, too,' she said, knowing that they weren't just talking about this last two nights but the months and months before, the aching void since things had been good between them, natural and relaxed and just plain happy.

A sob broke free, and his arms tightened around her,

easing her closer. 'Don't cry,' he murmured gruffly. 'I can't bear it when you cry. It tears me apart.'

'You could have died,' she whispered, her chest shuddering, and his arms squeezed tighter.

'But I didn't, and I'm home now. Stay with me, just for a while. Dad's here, doing the milking, and Joe and Sarah have still got Brodie—it's just us, Fran, and we don't have to do anything or be anywhere. So stay with me. Let me hold you—just for a little while.'

It had been so long since he'd held her that she'd have been happy to stay there for ever. He didn't need to talk her into it. She tilted her head and kissed him again. 'Just for a while,' she agreed, and, closing her eyes, let herself relax against him.

She was asleep.

It felt so good to hold her after all this time, but he needed the bathroom, and he didn't think he could get up without help. He couldn't bear to disturb her, though.

Not that they could stay there for long, because he could hear his mother moving around in the kitchen, and his father would have finished milking now. With a sigh he bent his head and brushed his lips against her cheek.

'Wake up, darling,' he murmured.

'Mmm,' she said, snuggling closer and ignoring him.

'Fran, I need a pee and I can't get up when you're holding me.' He probably couldn't get up at all, but they'd cross that bridge when they got to it.

She eased away, lifting herself up on one arm and turning back the quilt, her eyes widening as he sat up with his back towards her and she saw the full extent of his bruises. Her lips pressed together but she didn't say a word, just slid out of bed and came round to his side, moving the quilt the rest of the way off him and helping him shuffle forwards to the edge of the bed.

'Stay there for a moment, give yourself time,' she said, and handed him a clean T-shirt. 'Here, put this on. You don't want to frighten your mother to death.' When he'd carefully eased his way into it, trying not to wince, she gave him his crutches. 'OK?'

He nodded, shifted his weight to his left foot and the crutches and stood up carefully. Hell. He was still wobbly, and she was so tiny that if he started to go he'd crush her.

He gave it another second, then tried a step. Fran reached up, steadying him by the shoulders as he adjusted his weight and swung slowly forwards on the crutches. OK. So far, so good. He took another step, then another, and he was at the bathroom door in a few more steps without incident.

'Can you manage?' she asked, and only his pride made him say yes.

'I'll be fine,' he assured her with more confidence than he felt.

'OK. I'll go and put the kettle on.'

'Great. I could kill a decent cup of tea,' he said. Shutting the bathroom door, he leant on it quickly before he fell over. Damn.

Triple damn with a cherry on top.

He eyed the loo in disgust. Who on earth had decided to put it right on the other side of the bathroom?

'How is he?'

Fran shook her head, sat down at the kitchen table and

smiled unsteadily at his mother, still ridiculously close to tears after watching him struggle to the bathroom. 'OK, I suppose, but he's very sore. I didn't realise— I thought it was just his legs, but it's everywhere. He says he might have a cracked rib.'

Joy nodded. 'Joseph said there was a big branch across his back. He was lucky—'

She broke off, biting her lip, and Fran realised she wasn't the only one who'd been through hell. And it was so stupid!

But she wasn't going to fight with him any more about it, or tell him off. He was well aware of how close he'd come—he had to be, he wasn't an idiot. Although how anyone as clever as him could be so frustratingly dense was incredible.

His father, Russell, came in, followed by Sarah and Brodie, and then Joe, shucking off his overalls and grinning at her.

'You look a bit rumpled,' he said, and she ran a hand through her hair and smiled self-consciously, colour warming her cheeks.

'I just lay down next to him for a minute and fell asleep,' she said, oddly embarrassed to have been caught napping with her own husband, but Sarah hugged her as if she understood.

'Are you OK?'

'I am now he's home. He's in the loo—I must go and help him back to bed.'

But he was there, in the doorway, as white as a sheet and fending off Brodie with one hand while he leant heavily against the doorframe.

'So where's that tea, then?' he said, cracking a smile. 'I don't know, five of you in the kitchen and the kettle isn't even on.'

'We were just debating on the slowest and most painful way to kill you,' Joe said mildly, scrubbing his hands in the sink. 'I've cleared the slurry pit.'

'I can tell—I can smell it on you,' Mike said, wrinkling his nose.

'The lengths some people will go to to get out of the worst jobs,' Joe quipped, and, shaking his hands, he wiped them on his jeans and gave his brother a crooked smile. 'Take a pew, for God's sake, before you fall down.'

He pulled a chair out, steered his brother towards it and propped his broken leg on another chair while Joy put the kettle on. Fran moved to his side, laying her hand gently on his shoulder, afraid to hurt him until her mental map of his bruises was more accurate, but he just tilted his head and smiled at her, covered her hand with his and squeezed her fingers.

In the busy, crowded kitchen you would have thought such a tiny gesture would go unnoticed, but suddenly you could have heard a pin drop. Everyone stopped talking and stared at them, then looked away, finding things to do, a burst of conversation ending the brief, deafening silence.

Was it really so strange that she should go to him, that he should touch her, that his entire family had stopped in their tracks and stared?

Evidently it was.

Mike, looking up at her, hadn't even noticed, but she had, and it made her wish they'd all go away. Their marriage felt so fragile at the moment; they needed to work on it, to find out if they had anything left, to piece together, slowly and painstakingly, the fragments of their love, and she wasn't sure she could do that under the penetrating gaze of their relations.

Because what if, like Humpty Dumpty, they couldn't put it together again? If, at the end, they found there simply weren't enough pieces left to make it work…?

They had to make it work. Anything else was unthinkable. And so, burying her natural reticence, she bent her head and kissed him. It was the merest touch of her lips to his, but it was a sign, and a promise, and his eyes met hers and held them for a long moment. Then he squeezed her hand again where it rested on his shoulder, and the world started to breathe once more…

CHAPTER FIVE

'SHALL I sleep in the spare room?'

Mike looked up, frowning, but Fran's eyes were unreadable. 'You don't have to do that.'

'I didn't want to crowd you. With your foot—if I hit it in the night, I might hurt you.'

'You won't hurt me. It's all pinned and plated, Fran—it's not going anywhere. You're more likely to stub your toe on the cast.'

'But what about your ribs? If I shift around…'

'You won't. You never disturb me. Anyway,' he added, sure that there was more to it than just concern about hurting him but not knowing what, or how to deal with it, just that he had to keep her with him come hell or high water, 'what if I need to get up in the night? I might need help.'

For the longest moment she hesitated, then with a tiny, almost imperceptible sigh her shoulders sagged in defeat and she nodded.

'You're right. I'll try and keep out of your way.'

'You're not in my way,' he said, feeling a wave of relief at her submission. He'd really thought she was going to sleep in another room, and it had scared the living daylights out of him.

It was the thin end of the wedge, the beginning of the end, and for all they were hovering on the brink, he couldn't let it go that far. Not yet. Not now. Hopefully not ever.

He was curiously reluctant to let her out of reach, even though he'd actively avoided her for months. But he'd better not scare her off. Shucking off his dressing-gown and letting the new, loose boxers she'd got him that fitted over his cast fall down around his ankles, he kicked them carefully away and lay down, wondering if he could find a position that didn't hurt his leg and then deciding that it was his leg and not the position that hurt, and it wouldn't frankly matter if he hung the damn thing out of the window…

'You haven't had your painkillers, have you?' she said, and he wondered if she was a mind-reader.

'I didn't think I needed them,' he lied. He knew perfectly well he needed them, but they made everything blurred at the edges and he was worried he'd say or do something—

What? Something affectionate? Romantic?

Desperate?

Damn. Perhaps he should have kept the boxers on.

She handed him the pills and a glass of water, and he swallowed them down. What the hell. He'd just lie with his back to her and keep his hands to himself and his mouth shut, and hopefully he'd be asleep soon…

He was restless.

Fran lay awake beside him, keeping a careful distance and wondering how much pain he was in.

A lot. He must be. She'd seen the X-rays, seen the metal

framework holding his leg together, seen the screws that went right into the bones…

It made her feel sick just to think about it, sick and scared and as if she wanted to gather him up against her and hold him close, to ease it, to take away the pain in any way she could.

Except she couldn't take it away, of course, and, besides, he'd lain down with his back firmly towards her, discouraging any repeat of their earlier cuddle. But then he mumbled something in his sleep, and she reached out a hand and laid it gently on his side, and he sighed softly and went quiet.

Comforted by her presence? She felt a tear leak out of the corner of one eye. She'd missed him so much. He'd only been gone two nights, but they'd been lonely and endless. Crazy when, apart from their earlier hug, they'd hardly even touched each other by accident in bed recently, never mind deliberately, but nevertheless she'd missed his presence there.

He murmured again, and she moved closer, curling her body behind his and snuggling up, her hand resting lightly on his hip, afraid to wake him. But the painkillers must be keeping him under because he didn't stir, just sighed and relaxed against her, the tension she hadn't even been aware of seeping out of him, and she felt her own tension dissipate into the night.

Her eyes drifting shut, she laid her cheek against his shoulder and fell asleep…

He woke to find her curled around him.

It was his leg that had woken him—that and the ribs he

was lying on—and he really needed to turn over, but she was in the way and he couldn't bear to wake her.

She'd move away—he knew that, knew she must have ended up lying against him by accident, because, God knows, apart from their cuddle when she'd got home from work and the briefest of brief kisses in the kitchen, if there'd been a way to avoid it she hadn't touched him in ages. There could have been chainlink fencing down the middle of the bed since April for all the difference it would have made, they'd kept so strictly to their own sides of the bed.

He straightened his leg a fraction and, as if she'd read his mind again, she shifted away, giving him room.

'You OK?'

'Mmm. Just need to move my leg.'

'Sorry.' She scooted across to the far side of the bed, and he rolled carefully over towards her.

'Better?'

'Mmm,' he said again. Better, but too far from her. He lifted a hand, almost reached for her, then, letting his breath out on a silent sigh, he lowered his hand back to the mattress. No. Too dangerous. He didn't trust himself, and the last thing he wanted to do was drive her away.

He shifted a fraction, trying to get comfortable, and listened to the sound of her breathing. It took her ages to fall asleep again, and he wondered if she was listening to him breathe as well, so he deliberately slowed his respiration rate down and after a few more minutes he heard a subtle change in hers as she slid into sleep.

But it wasn't a happy sleep. She was restless, murmuring, and he reached out a hand. Should he?

Yes.

This time, he let himself touch her, let his fingers curl over the slender, fragile curve of her shoulder, and with a contented little sigh she wriggled backwards until she was touching him, the soft roundness of her bottom brushing his thighs, her back against his chest, and she relaxed again.

Lucky her. He didn't. He couldn't.

It had been so long since he'd touched her. She was wearing a nightshirt, not much more than a long T-shirt, and it had ridden up so that the soft, bare skin of her bottom was against his legs, silky smooth and unbelievably arousing; he ached to rest his hand on her thigh, to slide it up and round her slender, tiny waist, up over her ribs, curling his fingers round to cup one of her small, firm breasts in his palm—

His body reacted instantly, and he felt his erection brush against her, sending shockwaves racing through him. Dear God, he wanted her. Wanted to hold her, touch her, bury himself in her, but he couldn't. Couldn't risk it. Couldn't put her in that position again.

He shifted his hips, pulling back away from her, but she followed him, her bottom bumping against his penis, and then he heard a soft gasp as she came suddenly, instantly awake.

Fran froze.

What the hell was she doing? Snuggling against him, her back against his chest, her bottom spooned—oh, lord. She couldn't move away. If she moved, he might know she was awake, and if she didn't…

If she didn't, and he reached out for her again, wanted to make love to her—could she do that? Let him? After so long, she really wasn't sure, wasn't sure at all that she could let him touch her, kiss her…

She felt the brush of his erection again, felt the stillness in his body and knew he was awake. Awake, and aroused, and waiting for her to make the next move.

Oh, dear God. She couldn't deal with this. Her emotions were too close to the surface, and if he touched her, all hell might break loose. So she faked a mumble, shifted away, rolling onto her front with her head turned away from him, and after an endless moment she heard him sigh.

Had she fooled him? She closed her eyes, squeezing them shut against the threatening tears, and after a few more minutes she heard the rustle of the quilt, felt the mattress shift and heard him grunt with pain as he sat up.

What was she to do? Pretend he'd disturbed her and get up and help him? Stay put with her eyes closed and listen out for him until he'd got down the corridor to the bathroom?

He was naked. If he was still aroused…

She stayed put, her ears straining as he picked up the crutches, took a step, swore softly and moved again. The bedroom door was open and as he went unsteadily down the corridor, she turned her head and watched him until he was in the bathroom.

The door closed softly, and she dropped her face into the pillow and sighed. What now? Pretend she'd been asleep? If she was a decent wife she'd get up and make him a drink, but that would mean talking to him, and she felt awkward—gauche and nervous and oddly apprehensive. What if he said something about it?

What if he knew she'd been awake?

Oh, why on earth had she wriggled up against him? Because she had, of course. She'd been right on her side of the bed after he'd rolled towards her, and when she'd woken, she'd been slap in the middle, her bottom rammed firmly up against him—as in, Sit on my lap and we'll talk about the first thing that comes up, she thought, and groaned with embarrassment.

No wonder he'd had an erection. He'd have to be dead not to react to that, whether he'd wanted her or not. He was a relatively young man after all, fit and healthy and in the prime of his life. And it had been literally months since they'd made love. After such a long time, he'd surely react to anything female.

He came back to bed, and she heard the crackle of the pill packet, heard the swallow as he took his painkillers, felt the mattress dip slightly as he lay down with a muffled groan.

She cracked an eye open. He was lying on his back, staring at the ceiling with one arm flung up over his head.

'Fran?'

His voice was soft, little more than a breath, but she ignored it, afraid to answer, afraid to open that Pandora's box.

After an age, he sighed quietly, the arm settling over his eyes, and eventually a soft snore heralded his slide into sleep.

She wasn't so lucky. Every cell of her body was aware of him, every breath he took, every slight shift, every grunt. She daren't relax, daren't go to sleep in case she ended up curling into his side. So she lay awake, staring at the ceiling and listening to him breathe, until the sky lightened and she could creep away…

Mike woke alone.

Odd, that. He was always the first to wake, the first to get up, the last to come to bed. He was *never* alone in bed.

He hated it.

He had no idea where Fran was, what she was doing, and how she'd greet him when he finally caught up with her.

He thought back to the night, to the way she'd recoiled from him, pretending to be asleep and rolling away from him—because she *had* pretended, she *had* been awake, and in the end he'd had to get up and move around or he'd have screamed with frustration.

So he'd gone to the bathroom, and the pain in his leg had dealt with his untimely arousal, and he'd gone back to bed and stared at the ceiling for ages while Fran had lain rigid beside him and feigned sleep. Again.

He swore, softly and comprehensively. Where on earth did they go from here?

The kitchen would be a good start. He could hear voices, and he got up, slowly and carefully, and struggled into his boxers. He didn't bother with his dressing-gown. It was hot today, and he needed a shower. Maybe Joe was about.

He made his way slowly and carefully downstairs, shuffling down on his bottom because he'd been warned in no uncertain terms not to put any weight through his leg yet—not that he needed warning. Even resting it on the floor made it ache like hell.

The kitchen, when he eventually got there, was rammed again. It had obviously become Party Central since his accident, he decided, and discovered that he was relieved, because otherwise he'd have to deal with Fran without anyone to run interference.

Except she wasn't there.

'Morning.'

They looked up, Joe and his father from breakfast, his mother from the sink, Sarah from sorting a pile of vegetables by the fridge. 'Hi,' she said. 'Fran's gone over to the shop to get some fruit. Joe, shove up, let him sit down. Want a cup of tea, Mike?'

'Um—thanks,' he said, sinking gratefully into the chair Joe had vacated and stretching his leg out cautiously. Brodie propped herself against the other one and gazed soulfully up at him as if she couldn't understand why he'd deserted her. He rubbed her behind her ears, and she washed his hand, her eyes still on him anxiously. Sarah brought his tea over, set it down and stared at him open-mouthed.

'Wow,' she said, and his brother grunted.

'That's my brother you're eyeing up,' he reminded her, and she laughed.

'Really? I thought he was a refugee from a film set. The last time I saw bruises like that was a post-mortem in a forensic science drama. Impressive. You ought to take photos.'

'Don't overdo the sympathy,' Mike said, but he was smiling, knowing that in her way Sarah was telling him how sorry she was that he was hurt. 'Any more of that bacon, Mum?'

She dragged her eyes from his side and tried for a smile. 'Coming up. Want it in a sandwich?'

'Lovely. With an egg in it. You're a star.'

And then Fran was back, with a box full of fruit, and he stared at it in surprise. 'Is that all close to its sell-by date?' he asked. They often got a surplus of one kind of fruit or another, but not normally so much at once unless it had been over-ordered, and they tried not to do that. It dented profits.

But to his surprise she coloured a little and put the box down on the side. 'There was a lot and I just thought it looked nice,' she said, avoiding his eyes. 'Fruit's good for you, and I've got some cheese and yoghurt as well. You need all those vitamins and minerals to help you mend and build your strength up.'

What for? he thought. What have you got in mind for me? Because it's clearly not sex…

He felt his body reacting at the thought, and regretted leaving his dressing-gown upstairs, but his mother put the sandwich down in front of him and he leant forwards, giving himself a bit of privacy until he got his crazed libido under control. Hell, he must be nuts, but all he could think about was her bottom, soft and warm and snuggled up to him…

She bent over, putting the fruit in the fridge, and he was treated to the curve in question, her jeans, loose now since she'd lost weight, pulling taut as she bent and giving him a tempting view of the very part of her that was giving him so much trouble.

He yanked his eyes off her and concentrated on not dribbling the softly fried egg down his chest.

'You around for a while?' he asked Joe around a mouthful of sandwich.

'Why?'

'I need a shower.'

Joe arched a brow. 'Long time since we shared a shower,' he said dryly, and Mike felt himself colour.

'I don't want to share it with you, you jackass. I need someone to grab me when I fall over, and Fran's too little. I'd squash her.'

Joe looked disbelieving, but he shrugged and nodded. 'I can give you a hand. Be more fun with Fran, though.'

He felt himself colour again, his neck reddening, and his

hands itched to strangle Joe. Not that his brother realised he was being tactless. How could he? Only they knew their marriage was in tatters.

'Don't tease him, Joe,' their mother said gently, and Mike heard something else in her tone. A warning? A warning to tread softly?

So maybe their problems weren't as private as he'd thought.

Damn.

He pushed the plate away. 'That was lovely, Mum. Thanks. Right, Joe, are you ready? I don't want to hold you up, I know you've got loads to do.'

'Tell me about it,' Joe said, dropping his mug into the sink and handing his brother the crutches. 'Come on, then, Hopalong, let's get you scrubbed. Pity we haven't still got the sheep-dip.'

'Ha-ha. I need a bin bag and some elastic bands,' he said, and while Joe found those, he headed upstairs the same way he'd come down.

He turned the shower on, got the temperature right and then Joe trussed his leg up like a turkey and he swung round into the bath, getting awkwardly to his feet and pulling the shower curtain closed. 'So how are we going to manage this, Joe?' he asked.

'Hell, you want me to wash you?' Joe asked in disbelief.

'Not the shower—the farm,' Mike retorted, struggling with the soap and wondering if a little help *wouldn't* go amiss.

There was a heavy sigh from Joe, and the curtain twitched back a little. 'We'll cope, bro. You get yourself right. Don't worry about the farm. Dad's quite enjoying having a bit to do with it again, and at least the weather's nice.'

'Yeah—and Mum was probably planning all sorts of work on their house in the next few weeks and it won't get done.'

'It doesn't matter. There's always another day. Want a hand with your hair?'

'No, I'm fine,' he lied, struggling to scrub it with one elbow propped against the tiles so he didn't lose his balance. He rinsed it quickly, swilled the water over his body one last time and turned off the taps. 'Might need a hand getting out,' he confessed, and Joe steadied him while he sat on the edge and swivelled round, grunting with the pain in his side.

'Your ribs OK?' Joe asked, giving him a searching look.

'Not really, but what are you going to do about it? What I could really do with is a good night's sleep. I couldn't get comfortable last night.'

Except when I was snuggled up to Fran, he thought, but didn't voice it. Too much information, and he didn't want to think about it when he was stark naked. His body was all too keen to betray him at the moment.

Joe towelled off his back and leg, took the bin bag off his cast and washed his toes carefully with a flannel, then looked round. 'Got any clean boxers?'

'In the bedroom. It doesn't matter, I'll go like this.'

'What, and shock Mum rigid? You've grown up a bit since she changed your last nappy.'

'Well, then, hopefully she won't be foolish enough to be in my bedroom.'

She wasn't. Fran was, bending over the laundry basket, and he grabbed another pair of new boxers out of the drawer, struggled into them and then lay back under cover of the quilt to get his breath.

'You OK now?'

He nodded. 'Thanks, Joe. You go and get on. I'm sorry to hold you up—and I'm sorry about all this...' He waved in the general direction of his leg, and Joe shot him a wry grin.

'Could have been a whole lot worse, big bro,' he said softly, and left them.

Alone.

Fran stood up, washing in her arms, and eyed him warily. 'Are you OK? You have to go to the fracture clinic in a bit.'

He nodded. 'Can you take me?'

'Of course I can,' she said, frowning slightly. 'I need to put the washing on. Can you manage to dress yourself?'

He nodded again, not wanting to make her do anything intimate for him—not if it was so repugnant to her—and her recoil in the night couldn't have been clearer. 'I'll be fine. I'll come down in a little while,' he said.

'Take your painkillers first,' she advised, and left the room as if it was on fire.

The fracture clinic seemed happy with him.

He told them he was having trouble getting comfortable, and they gave him some advice for propping up his leg in the night—advice which Fran was relieved to know would make it impossible for her to end up snuggled on his lap, thank goodness, because he'd have to lie on his back. At least it didn't seem to be swelling, so long as he kept it propped up, and that seemed to be what worried them most.

She drove him home, and when they were almost

there, he asked her to drive down to the river. 'I want to see it,' he said.

'What, the tree?' she asked, a cold shiver of dread running over her. 'Whatever for?'

'To know how big an idiot I was?'

She gave a strangled little laugh. 'Oh, I can tell you that.'

'I thought you had,' he pointed out. 'But I want to see for myself.'

So she detoured, turning left instead of right and running down past Tregorran House to the gate at the bottom of the hill, opening it and driving along the river until they reached the fallen tree.

'Here you go,' she said. 'The crime scene.'

He opened the door, got out with difficulty and swung himself over to the tree on his crutches, standing there and staring down at it for an age.

He could see the depression where Joe had dug away the ground under his leg. It was about five feet from where the tree had ended up—which would put it right across the back of his shoulders, maybe even his head. Whatever, he wouldn't have survived it.

He felt goose-bumps coming up all over him, and he gave a sudden shiver.

Fran took his arm. 'Come on, Mike. You've seen enough,' she said softly, and he looked at her and realised she was as white as a sheet.

Poor Fran. He wanted to hug her. Was it wise?

'Ah, hell,' he muttered, and turned back to the Land Rover. He couldn't hug her, could he, with the crutches hanging on his arms? And anyway, she probably wouldn't want it. He got back in, swung his legs in—he was getting good at it now, although his ribs still hurt like hell to do it—and Fran shut the door.

She walked round the bonnet, giving the tree one last wary look, and slid behind the wheel, starting the engine and heading back towards the road.

'I'm sorry.'

She shot him a startled look. 'What for?'

'Being so bloody stupid. Scaring the living daylights out of you. Making you come back here when you obviously didn't want to. Take your pick.'

She sighed softly and gave him a hesitant little smile. 'Idiot. Put your seat belt on. I don't want you flying through the windscreen if we meet a lunatic tourist. We've all got enough to worry about at the moment.'

He fastened his seat belt obediently, tried to find a comfortable position against the backrest as they jolted down the track and then sighed with relief when they hit the flat, even surface of the road again. They were home in moments, and he slid down out of the Land Rover and swung himself towards the back door.

'Gosh, it's hot,' Fran said, following him in. 'Fancy a drink?'

'Coffee would be good.'

There was a second's hesitation, then she said, 'Oh. I was thinking more of something cold—a fruit smoothie? Use up some of that lovely fruit I sorted out this morning.'

He would rather have had a coffee, but she was right, the fruit needed to be used up and with all the painkillers he was on, if he didn't have fruit his system would grind to a halt. 'Sounds good,' he lied, and eased himself into a chair. Brodie wasn't around—gone off with Joe and Sarah, probably, so it was just him and Fran and a rather awkward tension between them which he'd never felt before.

She peeled and chopped the fruit—strawberries, a chunk of melon, two bananas and a handful of blueberries—threw in a good glug of locally sourced apple juice and turned on the liquidiser.

At least it drowned out the silence, he thought, and then she handed him a glass of purplish mush, clinked hers against it and said, 'Welcome home, Mike.'

What could he do? He picked up the glass, took a breath and sipped, then frowned at it. 'This is really nice,' he said, surprised, and she smiled—in relief?

'Good. Drink up, and you can go and have a lie-down. You look tired.'

He was, and, curiously, what he wanted more than anything was to ask her to join him, but he didn't think he could. Not easily. Not after last night.

So he drank up, took some more painkillers and went to bed.

Alone.

CHAPTER SIX

HE SLEPT most of that day, and the night was made easier by the stack of pillows under and around his leg, propping it up and protecting his toes from the pressure of the quilt. Not that he needed it, because it was hot, and in the end they abandoned it in favour of a sheet.

But then it grew cooler, the wind picking up a little, and because their bedroom was on a corner and there was a cross-draught from the windows, Fran found herself snuggling closer to him for warmth.

Only her head and shoulders, her body carefully kept out of reach, but he slid his arm round her and held her, and together they slept the rest of the night till the fingers of light crept over the horizon and woke them.

Well, woke her. And when she looked up, Mike was watching her, his eyes curiously intent, and her heart thumped.

'Want a drink?' she asked him, easing away and stretching out the kinks in her neck.

'Mmm. Tea would be nice.'

She hesitated. 'How about juice? It's quicker and it won't keep you awake.'

He gave a short laugh. 'Fran, I've slept for nearly eighteen hours straight, apart from waking up for supper. I don't think sleep's an issue.'

'OK.'

She slipped out of bed and went down to the kitchen, foraging in the back of the cupboard for the decaf tea bags she'd bought for them. 'Oh, Brodie, it would be so much easier if I could tell him what I was doing and why, but I don't know if I can. What do you think he'll say?'

And that was the trouble, of course. Mike was avoiding her, she was avoiding him, and they just weren't talking. Not that they ever had, really. Maybe that was the trouble, but once the lid was off that box…

'I can't talk to him, Brodie. Not about getting pregnant again. Not until I know how he feels about me.' And, of course, without talking to him, she never would.

'So—what are we going to do today?'

Mike dragged his eyes from the window and looked at her. They were in the sitting room overlooking the garden and the sea in the distance, the church and lighthouse just visible on the horizon.

'I don't know. You tell me,' he said, wondering if he sounded like a spoilt brat. He felt like one. If it wasn't for the physical impossibility, he would have stamped his foot, but because he couldn't he just ground his teeth and crossed his arms over his chest, drumming his fingers on the other arm.

God, he *hated* the inactivity! Hated sitting still, being unable to do anything, just—sitting, for heaven's sake! He *never* sat! Well, not unless he was in front of the computer, filling in endless farm returns and tweaking the farm-shop website. Maybe he should do that.

'How about going for a drive?'

He thought about it, but his ribs probably weren't up to being jostled and he'd quickly discovered that if he didn't have his foot up, the cast got uncomfortably tight. Although comfort wasn't really a word he could have used truthfully and it was all a matter of degree.

'We could play Scrabble.'

Fran stared at him. 'You hate Scrabble.'

'Not as much as I hate lying here doing nothing. Got any better ideas?'

She looked away, and he was stunned to see a warm sweep of colour brush over her cheeks. Fran, blushing? She got up hastily and crouched down, rummaging in the cupboard where the games were kept, and by the time she straightened up her colour had returned to normal.

She still didn't look at him, though, and he was fascinated. Fascinated, and very curious, and strangely a little edgy.

'If I move the coffee-table over by you, can you manage on that?' she asked.

'I'll give it a try.'

It worked. Sort of. It was a little low, but that was fine, because every time she leant over to put her letters down on the board, he got a view straight down the V of her T-shirt, and it was worth every second of the discomfort he felt when he put his own letters down.

Especially when she realised it was hurting him and started taking the letters from him and putting them down for him. So he got twice as many opportunities to see the soft, warm shadow between her breasts.

The effect was predictable, and he shifted a little on the sofa, pretending it was to do with his ribs but actually trying to ease the tension in his boxers.

'Grackle? You can't have that!' she said. 'It doesn't exist.'

'Want a bet?'

'What is it, then?'

'It's a type of mynah bird.'

She sat back and stared at him. 'Really?'

'Look it up.'

'And lose my go? No way. I know you and animals.' She added the score, and he leant over and shifted one of the letters to expose the coloured square.

'Don't forget it's on a double word score,' he pointed out, and she scribbled out the score and wrote the correct one in.

'I'm not going to let you win,' she said fiercely, scowling at her letters and checking the board. 'You always win—even though you hate it, you always win.' She put down 'lathe', and he added an 'r' to it and got another double word score.

'Don't sulk,' he teased, and she glared at him, then laughed and threw a letter at him.

'Don't gloat, then! I was going to do that when I got an "r".'

'You should have hung on.'

'No doubt.' She shuffled her letters, grinned and hung 'runcible' on the 'r' of 'lather', getting a triple word score and a bonus for using all her letters.

'Runcible? You can't have that, it's not a proper word!' he protested.

'Yes, it is.'

'Rubbish. It's Edward Lear—he has a runcible spoon in "The Owl and the Pussycat"—"They dined on mince and slices of quince which they ate with a runcible spoon." It's just nonsense.'

'*And* a runcible cat in "The Pobble Who Has No Toes",' she said, and quoted back at him, '"He has gone to fish, for his Aunt Jobiska's runcible cat with crimson whiskers." I rest my case,' she said smugly.

He tried not to laugh. 'It's not in the dictionary.'

'Oh, yes, it is.'

'I bet it isn't.'

'What do you bet?'

He took a slow breath, his eyes locked with hers. 'A kiss.'

She coloured, and then looked away and laughed a little oddly. 'You're on.' And she handed him the dictionary.

Except he didn't take it. He caught her wrist, gave it a gentle tug and toppled her towards him. She gave a little shriek and grabbed the back of the sofa with her free hand so she didn't fall on him, but his nose ended up in her cleavage, and he turned his head and brushed his lips against the soft, shadowed skin.

She caught her breath and straightened, sinking down onto the edge of the sofa, and their eyes locked. Slowly, carefully, he leant forwards, stifling the groan as his ribs pinched, and touched his mouth to hers.

For an endless, aching second she was still, then she moved away. 'Uh-uh,' she said, her voice over-bright and her smile pinned in place. 'You have to win a kiss, and you haven't looked it up yet.' And she stood up and moved back to the other side of the coffee-table and safety.

He found it—of course. She was never so definite if she wasn't sure about something, and he'd bet she'd looked it up recently when they'd been doing Lear at school.

'See? It's a three-pronged fork with a curved edge on one side.'

'Shame,' he said softly, closing the dictionary, and her eyes flew up and met his, then slid away again, but he'd had his kiss. Sort of. And it had left him aching for more.

He wanted to drag her off to bed, kiss her senseless and drive out this reluctance of hers, but he had a feeling it wouldn't and, anyway, it was as much as he could do to drag himself there, never mind an unwilling woman.

Besides, he didn't want to. Not if it meant her going through hell again with another failed pregnancy somewhere down the line because of him.

He reached out, letters in hand, but she tutted and put another word down before him. 'My turn,' she pointed out. 'You forfeited your turn when you looked in the dictionary.'

He gave up trying and let her win, as much as anything because he couldn't sit there any longer and look down her cleavage at something he wasn't able to touch…

Sophie came later, running into the sitting room with her eyes wide with worry and fascination. 'Wow, you've got a proper cast!' she said in awe. 'Can I draw a picture on it?'

'Sure—when I've had a hug.'

'Mind his ribs, darling,' Fran warned her. 'He's a bit sore.'

Her eyes widened. 'Will I hurt you if I hug you?' she asked, nibbling her lip, and he shook his head and pulled her up onto his lap, snuggling her close on his right side, the side that didn't have the bruises. Well, not so many, anyway, and he needed a cuddle from his little girl.

She wriggled down tighter, burrowing under his arm, and then lay almost motionless, even breathing carefully in case she hurt him. It made him want to laugh and cry at the same time, and he hugged her gently.

'So—are you all ready for your holiday?' he said, and she shuffled round so she could see him, gently kneeing him in the groin as she did so. He grabbed her leg and held it still, and over her shoulder he could see Fran biting her lip and trying not to laugh.

'Yup. I've packed my things already. I want to see Nessie again. Last time we went to Scotland we saw Nessie,' she said. 'Didn't we, Mummy?'

Kirsten smiled. 'Well, there were some ripples on Loch Ness that might have been caused by an animal, but they could have been the wind.'

'It was Nessie, I know it was,' Sophie said adamantly. 'And we had haggis. I'm not eating *that* again!' She pulled a face, and Mike chuckled.

'Didn't you like it?'

'It was dis*gust*ing!' she said. 'All greasy and smelly and made of a sheep's *stomach*! It was horrid. But we had lots of shortbread and I like that. Mummy says we can go back to the shop we bought it from and get some more. Oh, and we're going up Ben Nevis again! We walked halfway up last time, to the little lake, and Andrew had to carry me down 'cos I had bendy legs, but I'm bigger now. Maybe we'll even get to the top!'

He smothered the laugh and hugged her again. 'Poor old Andrew! Let's hope you make it both ways this time. Coming down's always the hardest bit.' He knew—he'd carried Sophie down his fair share of hills over the years, and it got your knees like nothing else. 'Hey, how about some cake? I know Fran's brought some over from the shop and I'm getting really hungry.'

'Good idea,' Fran said with a smile. 'Come on, guys, let's go and make tea for Mike.' She held out her hand to Sophie, who slithered over his chest, grabbed her hand and cuddled up to her side.

'Can I make him banana sandwiches?'

'I expect so.' Fran chuckled, and Mike listened to them making their way towards the kitchen and smiled at Kirsten.

'Sounds like you'll have a busy holiday.'

'Well, we will if she has anything to do with it, but we all love Scotland and Andrew's parents spoil her to death. So—are you OK to have her for the week when we get back?'

'Fine. Make it Sunday afternoon, can you? I should be able to help out in the shop over the weekend by then, and I feel I ought to be pulling my weight.'

'Sunday's fine. It'll give me time to unpack and wash her stuff.' She stared at his leg. 'I'm sorry about your accident.'

He shrugged. 'I was being stupid.'

'So I gather. And I always thought you were clever. Maybe we should get Sophie screened for the reckless gene.'

He snorted. 'So rude.'

'You asked for it.' She stopped smiling and perched on the edge of the sofa. 'Actually, I've got something to tell you.'

He looked up into her face, and his heart sank. He knew, before she opened her mouth, what she was going to say.

'When's it due?' he asked.

She frowned, then said sadly, 'Is it so obvious?'

He nodded. 'I've seen that look in your eyes before, don't forget. So when is it? February? March?'

'February—the very end. We haven't told Sophie yet, but I wanted to warn you, because of Fran and—well, you know.'

Yes, he knew. What he didn't know was how on earth he was going to tell Fran. He dredged up a smile. 'Congratulations, Kirsten,' he said softly, and, drawing her down, he hugged her gently and brushed a kiss against her cheek. 'I hope it all goes well for you. Sophie's dying for a little brother or sister and we don't seem to be getting any closer to achieving that for her, so I'm really pleased for you.'

She blinked hard and smiled. 'Thank you. I know it isn't easy for you.'

'Mummy—Mummy! It's a chocolate fudge cake! Absolutely my favourite! And I've made some banana sandwiches, and Fran's made a huge pot of tea—she's bringing it on a tray.'

'How lovely—I'll help her,' Kirsten said, standing up and giving him another slightly worried smile. 'Mike, are you sure you're OK about it?'

'About what?' Sophie asked, bouncing around the room with the dog on her heels.

'Having you for the week once you're back,' he said quickly. 'I think if Fran's OK with it, we could have you from the weekend after next? I should get a walking cast so I might be a bit more mobile by then. And we're pushed on the farm at the moment, because one of the shop ladies is off on holiday, so we'll have you from Sunday afternoon, perhaps? Then we'll have plenty of time to hear about your holiday.'

Kirsten shot him a grateful look for his hasty intervention. 'That would be fine. I'll bring her over—we'll go and talk to Fran now and sort out the times,' she said, and went out to help with the tea things.

Sophie went too, dithering and skipping and chatting to Brodie as she went, and Mike laid his head back against the sofa and closed his eyes.

Pregnant.

Hell. It was going to kill Fran—and he was going to have to strike the fatal blow…

Mike seemed much more comfortable with the new cast.

Maybe it was because his leg was starting to recover from the insult of the fracture and the repair, or maybe he was giving in and taking the painkillers regularly and not trying to be heroic.

Whatever, he was sleeping better, and that meant Fran was too.

Just as well, she thought, because with him out of action, now she was on holiday from school she was doing as much as she could on the farm to help out. She didn't do the milking—Russell seemed more than happy to do that, and she didn't like to stop him. She sensed that he missed the farm, and also that he needed to be needed, something that Mike wasn't very good at understanding.

He was so busy trying to take the pressure off his father that sometimes she wondered if they'd taken too much too soon, but it was certainly back on now, and Russell seemed to be thriving on it.

And Joy was helping in the farm shop, as usual, and so Fran ended up making the cheese.

She didn't mind. It was quite therapeutic, really, and because of the tight timings—adding the starter culture once the milk was the right temperature, then stirring it, then leaving it, then adding the rennet, and the mould if it was to be a blue cheese, then cutting it, then scooping out the curds into the strainers, and all the time checking the temperature of the various processes, washing out the vats, scrubbing down the tables, sterilising everything, endlessly hosing the floor and brushing it clean—there was no time to think and yet the steady rhythm of the work was curiously restful.

There was all the work in the cheese stores as well, turning and salting and testing, and then packaging the cheeses for sale, either in wheels or cut into wedges and shrink-wrapped.

It all took time, and as they were so busy with the summer tourist influx it kept her well out of Mike's way, but it was quite hard physical work, and she was feeling drained this week. Just because it was another thing, another turn of the screw at a time when things were already tough enough, she'd started her period on Sunday evening, and although she *knew* she couldn't be pregnant—well, after all, how could she without any contact with Mike?—nevertheless it still made her feel down.

She'd just finished a long session of salting and turning in the blue cheese store on Thursday and was cooking their supper when she saw Ben heading towards the house with a book in his hand. She went to the door and opened it with a smile. 'Hi, Ben!' she said, and he smiled back.

'Hello, Fran. Is Mike in? I've got something for him.'

'Yes—go on through. He's in the sitting room. He's bored to death. He'll be delighted to see you. Want a cup of tea?'

He shook his head. 'No, I won't hold you up, I can see you're cooking. I'll just go and have a chat for a few minutes.'

'If you're sure?'

'I'm sure. You carry on, I won't be long.'

* * *

'Is the invalid up for a visit?'

Ben was standing in the doorway, and Mike chuckled and shifted up the sofa, propping himself up against the backrest and moving his leg into a more comfortable position.

'Absolutely. Come on in, make yourself at home.'

'So how are you?'

'Oh, you know—bored, sore, frustrated with the ceaseless inactivity…'

'Peachy, then.'

'Oh, utterly.'

Ben grinned and dropped into the armchair opposite. 'Thought so. I've brought you a book—it's an autobiography I've just finished reading. The guy was unfortunate enough to become one of my patients and he gave it to me. Nice man. I thought you might enjoy it. It's quite funny and very touching—he used to be a farmer.'

He slid it over the coffee-table and Mike picked it up, flicked through the pictures and put it down. 'Thanks. I've heard about it—if I'd thought I'd have the time, I would have bought a copy, so I'll enjoy reading it. God knows, there's not much else to do at the moment.'

Ben chuckled. 'I can imagine. So when did they change your cast?'

'Tuesday. It doesn't seem to be swelling too much, so they were happy to do it. I have to say it looked pretty grim.'

Ben nodded. 'I expect it's black.'

'Mmm—like this,' he said, lifting up his T-shirt and making Ben wince.

'That's a goody. You were lucky your chest didn't cave

in. You could have had a flail segment there and it would have made it much more exciting.'

Mike groaned. 'No, thanks. It was quite exciting enough. In fact, I'm not sure I've thanked you for coming to my rescue.' He tipped his head on one side. 'Actually, I seem to remember you rang me at a rather opportune moment for that chat, and you never did say what it was about.'

'Oh, that. It's nothing to worry about—it'll keep.'

'Well, if it's nothing to worry about, bring it on, frankly, because all I've had to do for the last week is sit here and worry about all the things I should be doing and can't, and how much work this has put on everybody else, and how far behind we'll be if I can't get all the summer jobs done—so, please, if it's something to think about that isn't a worry, tell me!'

Ben laughed and sat back, studying him for a moment. 'OK. It's about the field in front of the house. Well, all round it, really, but especially the bit between the house and the road. It's not huge, but when we had the christening you let us use it for parking, and it was hugely helpful. The drive's really not big enough if we have more than one visitor, and if we had that field, we could extend the parking at the front and make a bit more of a garden on that side of the house. And if you got really carried away and wanted to sell the bit between us and the clifftop, and maybe a little strip round each side too…?'

Mike thought about it for a moment, then nodded slowly. 'It would make a lot of sense for you, but we tend to move the cattle through from one side of you to the other along that field, and if you've got the whole section from the cliff to the road, we'd have to move them on the lane, and we try to avoid that. And it wouldn't help you with access to the beach—I take it you've found out how steep it is there? You can't walk down.'

'No, I know. It was just an idea. It's the other bit, really, that's the most significant, and Lucy's decided she loves gardening—takes after her grandmother, I think, and she really wants to expand it. She says I only want it so I can have a little red tractor mower and drive around on it, pretending to be a farmer—'

Mike laughed out loud at that. 'Any time you want to play at being a farmer, give us a shout and you can get up at five and do the milking.'

Ben grinned. 'I'll stick with the mower,' he replied. 'So—think about it, ask Joe what he thinks. There's no rush, and we certainly don't want to put any pressure on you, but if the land's going begging, we'd be more than happy to pay you amenity rates. We'd have to get it valued to make it fair.'

Amenity rates? They doubled the price of agricultural land, sometimes more than doubled it. And the land Ben was talking about wasn't in any way fundamental to the running of the farm. They had plenty of grazing, and certainly the area between the house and the road was only ever grazed just to keep it down. It wasn't good enough for hay, it wasn't big enough for crops and the most sensible thing would be to sell it to the Carters.

And, God knows, cash at the moment was tight.

'Have you got a plan of the plot?'

'Not here,' Ben said. 'I have at home. Want me to draw it up so you can see?'

'Or I can walk over it with you.'

Ben arched a brow ironically, and Mike sighed. 'Well, drive, then. I can get Joe to bring me up. We could all talk it over on site. I'll speak to him and Dad first.'

'Do that. And now I'm going to leave you in peace. Fran was cooking something that smelled really gorgeous, and I don't want to be responsible for ruining your supper. Enjoy the book—and drop in when you're next in the hospital. The fracture clinic's right next to A and E, and if I've got time, I'll stop for a coffee with you.'

'I'll do that,' Mike promised.

Ben went out, and he could hear his voice in the kitchen, talking to Fran for a moment before the back door shut.

So Ben wanted to buy the land.

And if he did, Joe and Sarah would get enough money to refit their kitchen, which was absolutely falling apart, and he and Fran—they'd have enough money, he thought, the realisation slowly dawning, to pay for another cycle of IVF.

He swallowed. If Fran felt brave enough to go for it. And if she did, he'd have to find the strength from somewhere to support her when it all went wrong.

Assuming she even wanted a baby with him any more. Right now, he wasn't sure she did. He didn't know what was going on in her head, and that made life with her an absolute minefield.

And to make matters worse, Sophie was coming back on Sunday week and he still hadn't worked out how to tell Fran that Kirsten was pregnant.

Oh, damn.

CHAPTER SEVEN

THERE was only one way to do this, Mike decided, and that was to tell Fran straight.

So he did—eventually.

She'd prepared a lovely meal—chilled watercress and tomato soup with basil and garlic croutons, a really tasty chicken dish in a creamy blue cheese sauce with shiitake mushrooms on a bed of wild rice served with the freshest, crunchiest runner beans out of their own garden, and then a fabulous fruit salad rammed with fresh summer fruits topped with a dollop of clotted cream. It was streets away from the usual food they ate, when she was up to her eyes in schoolwork and he was milking until six-thirty and then fighting with the paperwork. He didn't care if it was geared to helping his leg mend, it was gorgeous, and he scraped the last dribble of cream off the edge of the bowl and pushed it away with a sigh of regret.

'That was delicious, darling, thank you,' he said with a smile, and she smiled back and took his plate.

'You're welcome,' she said.

It would have been easier if he hadn't felt so guilty because he was about to wreck it all by telling her about

Kirsten. In fact, he was so preoccupied with working out how to do it he was surprised she hadn't picked up on it.

But apparently she hadn't, because she cleared the table, loaded the dishwasher and topped up his glass of apple juice without commenting on his silence.

He wished he didn't have to do this. Telling her about the baby was going to spoil their evening, and good times between them were so few and far between. She'd made a real effort tonight—did he *really* have to say anything to spoil it?

Yes, because otherwise Sophie would come next weekend and if she knew she was bound to say something, and he owed Fran a few days to get used to the idea without having to pretend enthusiasm to a delighted little girl who was finally having her dream realised.

But not now. Later, perhaps. When they'd gone to bed. When he could lie there and hold her, and hug her when she cried—because she would, of course. She was bound to, and if she was already in his arms, maybe she wouldn't run away and cry in private.

Although he hated it when she cried, he hated even more the idea that she'd run away and do it in a corner somewhere, like a wounded animal. That he really, *really* couldn't bear.

'Coffee?' he suggested.

She hesitated, then smiled. 'OK. Just a little one. I don't want to keep you awake.'

He'd love her to keep him awake, but that wasn't what she was talking about, and, anyway, there was still this whole pregnancy minefield.

Oh, hell. Life was so incredibly complicated.

'What's wrong, Mike? You've been frowning all evening.'

He turned towards her in the darkness. With the bedroom

curtains open, as they always were, he could just about make out her features, but he couldn't read her expression. That was a definite disadvantage of doing this in the dark, but it was more intimate, easier to say the things that would hurt her so badly.

'Nothing's wrong, exactly,' he said, not knowing where to start. He reached out and found her hand, curling his fingers round it and squeezing gently. 'It's just—Kirsten's…'

He let it hang, and after a few seconds she sucked in her breath and he knew she'd worked it out.

'When?' she said, her voice almost inaudible.

He ached to gather her into his arms. 'February,' he told her, although he couldn't see that it made any difference, but it had been his first question, too, and he supposed it was only natural, part of the process of establishing just when the changes would start to show. Soon, he thought, remembering Kirsten's first pregnancy.

Fran's fingers tightened on his, and he squeezed back and didn't let go.

'Does Sophie know?' she asked eventually, her voice hollow.

'I don't know. She didn't when Kirsten told me.'

'When did she tell you?'

'On Sunday.'

'Sunday?' she exclaimed, pulling her fingers away. 'But—it's Thursday!'

'I know,' he said heavily. 'I didn't know how to tell you.'

'Oh, Mike, that's silly,' she said, her voice more normal now—or was it? 'It's lovely for them. And Sophie will be delighted.'

'Are you going to be OK with it?' he asked, wishing to God he could read her face. If only he'd done this in daylight…

'I'll live. It was always going to happen, Mike.' But this time there was a little wobble in her voice, and without thinking about it, because if he did he'd talk himself out of it, he reached out and gathered her against his chest.

For a moment she resisted, then he felt her chest hitch, and her arms slid round him and she squeezed him tight. Right over his cracked ribs, but he stifled the groan and held her, running his hands gently up and down over her back to comfort her.

'I'm so sorry,' he murmured, and she sniffed and her chest jerked again, but she wouldn't let the tears fall, wouldn't give way to them.

Damn, she was so ridiculously *brave*! If only she'd cry—let it out, let him hold her while she worked through all her feelings, but she wouldn't, and he could understand that. He wouldn't lie and cry in her arms either. It was just all too revealing.

'I knew it would happen,' she said finally. 'I mean, why not? Everyone else in the world seems to be pregnant.'

Everyone but her. He knew that, knew without a shadow of a doubt that she wasn't pregnant because she'd had a period this week. Not that it made any difference without the means to conceive, but it must just rub it in when something like this happened.

And she'd been in a foul mood earlier in the week, distant and unapproachable, and he didn't know if she was still angry with him about the accident or unhappy because she wasn't pregnant again or if it was just PMT.

In the good old days, if she'd been grumpy like this he

would have made a wisecrack about her hormones. Not now. He knew better now, because PMT was an indicator of just how monumentally unsuccessful they were being in the baby department, and frankly it just wasn't funny.

He pressed a kiss to her hair, and she snuggled closer, letting him hold her. He wasn't really comfortable. He should have had his leg up on a pillow, but it wasn't as bad as it had been and for now it wasn't his priority.

Fran was, and he wasn't going to do anything that might make her leave his arms. He wished he knew what to say, how to comfort her, but he didn't, so he just held her, and after an age she fell asleep.

It was hot—too hot to lie so close—and he shifted slightly, easing away from her and stretching his leg out, wishing he'd propped it up on the pillows first before they'd started this conversation.

She'd rolled to her side away from him, and he shifted to face her, hunting for a better position. It wasn't, but his good leg brushed hers, and she wriggled back towards him, seeking him out in her sleep the way she always did if things were tough.

The way she always *had*, he corrected himself, and let his arm circle her waist, drawing her back more firmly against his chest. To hell with the heat. She needed him, and it was little enough to do for her.

Even if the feel of her soft, warm body in his arms was killing him…

Fran woke to Mike's arm around her, his fingers curled gently around her breast, the insistent nudge of his erection against her bottom.

Heat speared through her, flooding her with a fierce, desperate need, a hollow ache that only he could fill. It was so long since she'd felt it, felt anything at all except empty and cold. And she wanted him—wanted the old Mike, the man who laughed and chased her around until she let him catch her, who made love to her, tormenting her until she was sobbing with need, then taking her with a wild and uncontrolled passion that left her spent and boneless in his arms.

Where was that man? Gone for ever? Or was he still here? If she only had the courage to reach out…

'Mike?' she whispered.

For a moment he said nothing, so she almost wondered if he was asleep, but he was too still, too silent, and then he spoke, his voice gruff and low.

'I'm sorry. It's just— I'll move.'

'No!'

The word was out before she could stop it, and he froze again. 'Fran, please. I can't do this. Can't lie here night after night, wanting you like this, and—'

'Wanting me?' she breathed, stunned. Turning, she stared at him in the moonlight. 'Do you want me? I thought you didn't.'

'Of course I want you,' he whispered roughly. 'I'll always want you.'

'But—you've been avoiding me. Going over to the farm office, telling me not to wait up, getting out of bed in the morning without waking me.'

'I've always done that. I never wake you that early.'

'Not like this, Mike. Not like this, so I thought you didn't love me any more.'

'Oh, Frankie, of course I love you.' He sighed. 'I just…'

'Just can't bring yourself to touch me?' she said, her voice hollow to her ears—hollow and empty, like her heart.

'No! How could you think that?'

'Then why are you avoiding me?' she wailed softly, ridiculously, all but inviting him to make love to her when she couldn't even contemplate his intimate touch.

He sighed again, his hand coming up, the knuckles grazing her cheek with infinite tenderness. 'It's not that I can't bring myself to touch you, Fran. It's—oh, hell, much more complicated than that.'

'Then tell me! Talk to me, Mike!'

He didn't answer, but she could hear the cogs turning, feel the tension radiating out of him.

'Mike?'

'Frankie, I'm no good with words. I'm a farmer, for God's sake. I don't talk about my feelings.'

'Why?' she asked. 'Why not? Dammit, I'm not enjoying this either, but we *have* to talk. Our marriage is in tatters, we're falling apart and I'm trying here, really trying to get through to you, to sort it out, to find out if we've still got anything, and I can't do that on my own! I can't lay myself bare, wide open to you—not on my own! You have to do it too, Mike. You *have* to tell me how you feel. You *have* to share. Please…'

Her voice cracked, and with a ragged sigh he reached out and found her hands in the darkness, gripping them so tight she nearly cried out, but she wasn't letting go, not now, when they were so close…

'It's not that I can't bring myself to touch you,' he said gruffly. 'Far from it. It's more that—I daren't.'

'Daren't?' she breathed. 'Why ever not?'

He hesitated an age, then said, so softly she could hardly hear him, 'In case you get pregnant.'

She froze with shock. So she was right, she thought numbly, her eyes searching his but unable to read them in the shadows. Her voice cracking, she said desperately, 'I knew you didn't want a child with me—'

'Oh, Frankie, no!' He reached out, wrapped her in his arms, dragged her against his chest with a groan of protest. 'Of course I want a child with you. But every time you're pregnant, every time you lose it—I just can't bear to watch you go through that, sweetheart—not again. I can't bear watching you fall apart, seeing what I've done to you destroying you—'

'What you've done?' She pushed away, tilting her head so she could look into his eyes, her hand cradling his face. 'Mike, don't be silly! You've done nothing to me.'

'Except get you pregnant with dodgy sperm.'

'We don't know that. It could be my eggs. Maybe they're dodgy. What makes you think it's you? There's nothing dodgy about Sophie.'

'Maybe she was a one-off. My lucky break. And anyway, you've been avoiding me, too,' he added softly. 'Sometimes, when I've reached the end of my tether and I really, really needed you, you've turned away, reading a book or going to have a bath or—I don't know, almost anything rather than be alone with me. I've even wondered…'

'Wondered what?' she asked, when the silence stretched on.

'If there was someone else.'

'Mike! You know I wouldn't!'

'I know. I do know. Or I know you wouldn't have an

affair, at least, but—you can't stop yourself falling in love, Frankie. And if there's someone else—someone you'd rather be with— I know you don't want me to touch you. I've felt you recoil...'

'When?'

'The other night?'

'Oh, Mike.' She felt tears fill her eyes, felt the anguish in his voice cut through her like a knife. 'It wasn't that.'

'What, then? What is it that makes you flinch away from me as if I'm somehow...repugnant to you?'

'Oh, darling, you're not. Not at all. It's just—I feel like a medical investigation. As if so many people have looked at me there, touched me, talked about me—as if the part of me that had belonged to us is suddenly public property. And I don't know if I could bear for you to touch me, or if it'll just bring it all back—' She broke off, biting her lip, then went on unsteadily, 'Mike, I don't know if I can respond to you any more. I don't know if it hasn't just killed it for me, and I'm scared to find out.'

His breath sighed against her face, warm and reassuring. 'Oh, Frankie. Oh, my love—what's happened to us?' he whispered, folding her against his chest again and rocking her. She could still feel the brush of his erection, but softer now, less urgent, and as he cradled her so her confidence grew, her need to hold him, to touch him building until finally she found the courage to reach out.

'Mike?' Her voice was soft, gently questioning, and her hand stroked against his shadowed jaw, the rasp of stubble unbearably erotic against her palm. Leaning in to him, she brushed her lips lightly against his, tentatively, not sure of her reception or how she'd react if he took it further than this, but he wasn't going to let her find out.

He drew back, taking her hand and turning his face into it, pressing a kiss against her palm. 'No,' he said softly. 'Not tonight. Not when you're still unsure—still not ready.'

'I am,' she lied, but he knew her better than that. So much better. And he was right, of course. She wasn't ready, and maybe he wasn't either. They still had a long way to go, a lot to unravel, much to talk through.

And for a man who didn't talk and a woman usually too shy to reveal her inner self, it was going to be uphill all the way.

They slept in each other's arms, only waking to the sound of his family in the kitchen at seven.

She groaned, and he chuckled and hugged her closer to his chest. 'Maybe they'll cook us breakfast,' he suggested.

'And maybe I should be up and helping them, not lying here with you and—' She broke off, and he let her go.

Lying here with him and—what? Wanting him, the way he wanted her? God, he hoped so, because a few more nights of persistent arousal was going to give him a serious medical problem.

But what if she didn't? What if she never wanted him, couldn't ever bear his touch? What if all the investigations had turned her off so thoroughly that they never made love again?

The thought took his breath away.

'Coming down?' she asked, and he shook his head.

'I'll have a shower first.'

'Need a hand?'

'No,' he said firmly. Not to have a cold shower. And it

would need a bucket of ice to settle him down after last night. He watched her as she walked down to the bathroom, the nightshirt hitched up slightly by the clothes she'd scooped up to take with her, revealing an incredibly tempting glimpse of the crease below her left buttock as she walked.

The softly shadowed fold did nothing to help his state of arousal, and with a groan he shut his eyes and dragged his mind to something dull. Anything. The paperwork? Farm records?

Funny how his mind had emptied, how he couldn't think of a single thing except that soft shadow and the warm, silky feel of her skin…

She was busy all day, out on the farm, and he was driven crazy. He started to read the book Ben had given him, but it couldn't hold his attention. Not against such fierce competition.

And he was getting so unfit it was driving him mad.

He went into the kitchen, poked about in the larder and found an unopened bag of rice. That might do the trick. He sat down on one of the chairs, draped the rice bag over his cast and did some lower-leg lifts until his thigh and abdominal muscles were burning. Then he shifted onto his right hip and lifted the leg up and in towards the centre, over and over, then stood up and held on to the sink and lifted his leg out sideways until the muscles round his hip were screaming in protest.

He looked at the clock and sighed. Ten minutes. Barely that, and he was cream-crackered. Still, it was a start.

He put the kettle on, then went to the freezer and hunted around for the packet of coffee. Funny, he had been sure there'd been one in here, but he couldn't find it. Oh, well. He picked up his crutches and went slowly over to the farm office. Joe was in there with his father, and he stuck a coffee-pod in the machine and put a mug under the spout.

'So how are things?' Mike asked while he waited for the coffee.

'OK. How about you?'

'Bored to death. Doing exercises so my leg doesn't wither and drop off. Why?'

'I'm going to cut up that tree,' his brother said. 'Want to come and keep an eye on me?'

'I can't do anything.'

'You can dial 999 when I cut my leg off,' Joe pointed out dryly, and Russell snorted.

'I hate to point this out to you two but I can't run the entire farm alone without either of my suicidally reckless sons.'

'Don't worry, Dad, I'll look after him,' Mike assured him. 'And tell Fran not to worry about lunch, we'll grab something from the shop.'

He drained his coffee—the first decent one for days, he realised—and climbed into the cab of the pickup with Joe. Maybe if he was careful he could stack some of the logs…

'Cheers. You've been a real help—hope you haven't overdone it.'

'I'm fine. It was good to get some fresh air,' Mike told Joe, and slapped his shoulder. 'Right, I'm going in. No doubt I'll get a lecture. I'll see you later.'

He went into the kitchen and sniffed appreciatively.

'Wow, that smells good.'

'It's more than you deserve,' Fran growled, but when she

turned she was smiling and he hobbled over to her, stashed his crutches in the corner of the worktop and hugged her.

'I was sensible. I was just going crazy, stuck in the house, sweetheart.'

'I know.' Her arms were round him, holding him close, and she felt so good he could have stayed there for ever, but she pushed him away and told him to wash.

'You've got ten minutes before supper,' she said. 'And I want you clean and presentable. We're eating in the dining room.'

He peered through the door on the way past and did a mild double-take. Candles?

He yelled back, 'Give me fifteen minutes. I'm having a shower.'

A nice hot one, followed by a shave and a slosh of the citrusy cologne she'd given him for Christmas two years ago. He contemplated the cast with disfavour, pulled on a fresh pair of the baggy boxers, then his favourite aqua-blue soft cotton shirt and his decent shorts—his dress shorts? he thought with a chuckle—and went downstairs.

Wow.

She'd said clean and presentable, but she hadn't expected him to go to so much trouble. He was even wearing aftershave!

She was wearing a sundress—she'd changed into it after she'd finished turning the cheeses and had a shower, and she'd been out in the garden picking fresh herbs and dead-heading the roses. She could feel the warmth in her shoulders, even though she'd been out of the sun at midday, but it had obviously been enough.

Now, though, looking at him in his shorts and that lovely shirt, which did incredible things to his fabulous chocolate-brown eyes, she wished she'd made more effort—put on a touch of make-up, her best underwear—

She cut herself off. This was supper for her husband. Nothing more. Nothing huge. They were going to eat, and they were going to talk and make friends again. And if tonight went like last night, he wouldn't let it go any further.

'Anything I can do?'

'Yes—sit down in the dining room and light the candles. I know it's not dark yet, but it's gloomy in there.'

'You're an old romantic, do you know that?' he murmured softly, right behind her. Feathering a kiss over her bare shoulder, he stumped out, the clatter of his crutches almost drowned out by the beating of her heart.

Brodie was looking hopeful, but she was banned. 'Sorry, sweetheart, two's company and all that,' she said, and shut the dog out.

They had oysters to start with. Not Falmouth oysters, because they were out of season, but imported oysters that she'd found on the supermarket fish counter. Normally she wouldn't have dreamed of buying anything so unlocal, out of season and environmentally unsound, but they were on the list, they were reputedly an aphrodisiac and, besides, Mike loved them and he deserved a treat.

'I can't believe we're having oysters,' he said, raising his eyebrows.

'They were on special offer,' she lied, and wondered how many more lies she'd have to tell him before the end of the meal.

He squeezed lemon juice over them and sucked one off the shell. 'Mmm,' he said. 'Not bad. The Fal ones are fresher.'

'Well, they would be. They've only come fifty miles.'

He chuckled. 'Fair point. These are still good, though. Thanks.'

'Pleasure.'

'So—are they part of this diet you've got me on?' he asked casually. 'Because, if so, I think I like it. And I should certainly heal fast.' He looked up, laughing, and was arrested by the guilty look on her face. 'Fran?' he said, slowly lowering the next shell to the plate untouched. What the hell was going on?

She swallowed and knotted her fingers together. She always did that when she was nervous—but why?

'Talk to me,' he said, and she looked up and met his eyes, her own filled with remorse, and he *knew*—he just knew—that she was hiding something. 'It's nothing to do with my leg healing, is it?' he said slowly. 'So what's it all about?'

She got up and went out, coming back seconds later with a folded sheet of paper. She handed it to him, and he opened it and scanned it.

'Fertility-boosting diet?' he said, noticing all the things that were on it that should have rung alarm bells. The lack of tea and coffee, the extra fruit, the smoothies, the raw veg soups, the lack of alcohol—not that they drank much, but if she was going to this much trouble they'd usually share a bottle of wine, but there was fruit juice by their plates, and a jug of water on the table.

He lifted his head and met her wary and slightly defiant eyes. 'Fran?'

'I saw Kate—about the baby thing. She discussed our diet with me.'

She looked guilty, and he had a feeling they'd talked about a lot more than diet. Good, because he'd wanted her to have someone to talk to, but he'd never dreamt she wouldn't discuss things like this with him.

'Why didn't you say anything?' he said, hurt and puzzled that she'd felt the need to lie—*lie, for heaven's sake!*—about something so uncontroversial and trivial. Or was it? Was it that she hadn't been sure if he wanted a child with her? She'd said that last night—did she really believe he didn't? If so, maybe that was why she'd been reluctant to get it out in the open.

'She said it wouldn't hurt to try it, to improve our diet, to get fitter—and then, if we decided we wanted to go ahead and try again for a baby, we'd be in the best possible position.'

He felt a flicker of fear for her, dread that yet again she'd be faced with crippling disappointment or a gut-shredding loss that would leave her devastated.

'If?' he said softly.

Her eyes flicked back to his. 'I wasn't sure if you wanted one—if you didn't feel it was just a lot of angst and hassle, if Sophie wasn't enough for you.'

'This isn't about me, Fran, it's about you, and if you want a baby.'

'I do—but I want yours. And I need you to want it, too. And right now I'm not sure you do.'

He sighed. 'It's not so urgent for me,' he pointed out. 'I've got Sophie, and my clock's not ticking the way yours is. And anyway…' he scanned the paper again, noted the section about boosting sperm production and reducing

DNA damage '...if you want a baby, maybe you'd be better off with someone else.'

'What?'

Her soft, shocked exclamation tore at him, but he went on regardless. 'Maybe, if you want a healthy baby, you'd be safer trying with someone who hasn't already got you pregnant twice with an embryo that was probably flawed.'

'We don't know that that was you!'

'We know that some of the sperm were damaged—that the motility was down a little, that they weren't all perfect.'

'But—everyone's are like that, Mike! It's perfectly normal to have a proportion of sperm that aren't a hundred per cent. It could just as easily have been something to do with the IVF process.'

'Not the first time.'

'Mike, miscarriage is really common,' she said, repeating to him all the things he'd told her again and again, trying to encourage her, to give her confidence to try again, but it sounded as hollow now as it had when he'd said it, and he felt the burden of guilt settle firmly on his shoulders.

'But if it is me,' he said quietly. 'If it is my fault, then I may not be able to give you a baby, Fran. And how many times are you prepared to try? How many miscarriages are you going to go through before you give up? And what if—just consider, for a moment—what if we have a baby that you *should* have miscarried but didn't? A baby nature would normally have rejected as unviable? What if we have a baby with problems—physical or mental disabilities, developmental problems—what then, Fran? Will you be able to forgive yourself for not choosing a better partner? Will you be able to forgive *me*? Because I'm not sure I could.'

She stared at him for an age. 'That could happen to anyone at any time. Are you telling me if we had a disabled baby you couldn't love it?'

'Of course not!' He didn't even have to stop and think about that one. In fact, for a while now he'd been on the point of suggesting to Fran that they adopt a child with special needs, but he'd held back, not ready to concede defeat in the fight for their own child until she was. But she didn't know that, didn't realise that he'd considered it, and now she thought he just couldn't hack it if they had a child with problems.

'Of course not,' he said again. 'But I don't know if I could forgive myself for bringing a child into the world if I had a fair idea that that child would be damaged in some way because of my contribution to its existence. And if that was the case, maybe it would be better to adopt. That's all I meant. Nothing more sinister. And if it *is* me—'

'But I don't want anybody else's baby,' she said with a certainty that brought a lump to his throat. 'I want yours, Mike—and if I can't have yours, then I don't want one at all. We've got Sophie. That's enough. We should be grateful and concentrate on loving her.'

Her voice cracked, and he was up and round the table in a second, his crutches abandoned, hauling her into his arms and cradling her against his chest, unable to bear the desolate look in her eyes. 'Don't give up,' he said gruffly, his eyes prickling. 'We'll take our time, try the diet, have some more tests. And then—if you want to, if you think you can cope with it—we'll try the IVF again.'

'But we can't afford it, Mike, so it's pointless,' she said, her voice clogged with tears.

'Maybe we can,' he told her. 'Ben and Lucy want to buy some of our land around their house. Joe and I are going to have a look at it at the weekend. Ben's talking about paying amenity rates—that's about double what it's worth, at least. I don't want to fleece them, but it'll add significantly to the value of their property, and Joe and Sarah want to do their kitchen—and it would mean we could afford to try again. If you want to.'

She looked up at him, her eyes uncertain, and as he watched, a flicker of hope came to life. 'Really?'

'Really.'

She smiled slightly. 'You'd better sit down and finish your oysters, then,' she said with a return of her old spirit, 'because we've got baked sea bass and new potatoes and mangetout, followed by hazelnut meringue ice cream with mango coulis and chocolate Brazil nuts with decaf coffee to finish up.'

'And then?'

She smiled again, and he could see a pulse beating in her throat.

'Then we go to bed.'

CHAPTER EIGHT

IT WAS the longest meal of his life.

He didn't want it. Every mouthful, delicious though it undoubtedly was, was just another step on the path to the bedroom, and the anticipation was killing him.

Not just the anticipation, though. There was also the fear of failure, of letting down.

What if he rushed her—if, while she was still uneasy about her body, he was too fast for her, in too much of a hurry for his own satisfaction that he left her behind?

No. He couldn't. Not tonight, when it was clearly so significant in the salvation of a marriage he'd realised he wanted more than anything else in the world.

So he ate his meal slowly, mouthful by mouthful, and he talked to her about what he and Joe had done that day down by the river, and they laughed about him taking the saw from Joe and cutting up the part that had trapped him into tiny little bits.

'It's just matchsticks now,' he said, and she laughed again.

'That'll teach it,' she said, and then her laughter faded. 'I was so scared,' she confessed. 'When I saw you trapped under it, when they were just about to pull you out and I saw it shift—I knew it was going, and I thought I was going to lose you.'

'But you didn't.'

'No—but it came too close, Mike. It scared me. It was bad enough that you were injured, without having to watch you die—' She broke off, her eyes filling, and he felt a lump in his throat.

'Well, it didn't happen, and I'm fine.'

'Only because they got you out in the nick of time. Just because you're big and tough, you think nothing can hurt you.'

'You think I'm tough?' he asked, flexing his muscles and flirting with her for the first time in years, and she laughed again, softly.

'You look pretty tough to me.'

Her eyes strayed over him, and he felt the heat building until he thought he'd scream with frustration. But he didn't scream, and he didn't leap to his feet and drag her upstairs. Not that he could, unless he sat down and dragged her up backwards!

Instead they stayed in the dining room for their coffee, but he didn't eat any of the chocolate Brazils. He was full enough—and with the workout he had in mind, he didn't want to be over-full. Even by one mouthful.

And then, at last, it was finished.

The sun was setting, the last fingers of the day pulling back and leaving them alone in the candlelight.

He met her eyes—they were wary, a little nervous, but unflinching, her lips parted, the breath easing in and out of the top of her chest, rapid and unsteady.

It was time.

He pushed back his chair and stood, holding out a hand to her. 'Come to bed with me,' he said softly, and she got to her feet, taking his hand, her eyes locked with his.

'I ought to clear the table,' she said, giving it a guilty glance, but he cupped her chin and turned her back towards him, his fingers gentle.

'Later,' he murmured. 'It'll keep.'

Still she hesitated, killing him, and then she gave a tiny nod, as if she'd made the decision, and, letting go of his hand, she passed him his crutches and headed for the door.

'You go on up. I'll let the dog out,' she said.

He paused. 'Don't be long.'

'I won't.'

He wanted to stay with her, didn't trust her not to change her mind and run away, but by the time he was finished in the bathroom, he could hear her calling the dog in, locking the door, running up the stairs.

Running?

He opened the bathroom door and she was standing there, backlit by the landing light, looking just like the girl he'd fallen in love with, and he smiled.

'Five minutes,' he said, and she smiled back.

'Five minutes,' she agreed.

Lord, she was so nervous!

She'd never felt like this with him, not even the first time, but that had been then and this was now, and so much had happened.

She cleaned her teeth, washed her face and stared at herself in the mirror, wishing she had a gorgeous silk night-dress she could put on, or some really fabulous underwear—something to bolster her confidence and take his eyes off the fact that she was so thin.

But she didn't. Because she hadn't expected things to go so far tonight, she was wearing a pretty but still fairly ordinary bra and a pair of lacy knickers, not very new and not overly glamorous even at the beginning, and a sundress which with the best will in the world was very simple.

But at least it covered her.

Oh, help.

She was so scared that her whole body was shaking. What if she froze at the crucial moment? What if she just couldn't *let* him?

She looked herself in the eye, took a steadying breath and straightened her shoulders.

'You can do it, Fran,' she told herself firmly. 'You can do it.'

He was standing by the window, watching the sun go down.

The room was tinted pink from its last rays, and he held out his hand to her.

'Come here,' he ordered softly, and she went to his side, standing in front of him with his arms around her and his head close to hers. She could feel his heartbeat against her back, feel the steady, solid pounding of it as the sun slipped down into the distant sea, melting away in a flare of crimson and gold.

Then he turned her in his arms, staring down at her, his eyes serious.

'I love you, Francesca,' he said quietly. 'You mean everything to me. You're the reason I get up in the morning, and the reason I come to bed at night. You make the sun shine for me, put colour into everything I do. But if this—my love, our marriage, being here with me—isn't what you want, then I'll let you go. All I'm asking for is one last night, one last chance to put things right between us. Can you give me that? Give me this chance?'

She couldn't believe it. This man, who never showed his feelings, certainly never spoke about them, was baring his soul to her in words that brought tears to her eyes.

And nothing—*nothing*—could have convinced her more that their marriage was worth saving.

She couldn't speak, couldn't find any words to match his, so instead, swallowing the tears and stepping back, she held out her hand to him.

He took it, squeezed it, then swung himself over to the bed, less awkward now on his crutches, and propped them up against the wall, then took her hand again and drew her close.

'I love you,' he breathed, bending his head and touching his lips lightly to hers. She parted her lips but he eased away, cradling her close, pressing soft, breathy kisses to her hair, her temple, her cheek, his lips grazing her skin like the wings of an angel.

She let her head fall over to one side, giving him access to the incredibly sensitive skin of her throat, and she felt the hot trail of his breath as his lips traced slowly down to the hollow at the bottom, the rasp of stubble unbearably erotic.

She could feel her heart beating there, his lips pressed softly to the pulse point. A little cry rose in her throat, and he must have felt it vibrate under his lips because he moved then, lifting his head, staring down into her eyes as if he was trying to read her soul.

He ought to be able to. It was there for him to read, everything she was, everything she felt for him laid out there for him to see.

And maybe he did, because he smiled then, a tiny flicker of encouragement, before his mouth lowered again and he captured her lips with his. She opened to him on a sigh, and this time he settled his mouth against hers, his arms tightening, supporting her as his kiss grew bolder, deepening until she thought her knees would go out from under her.

But he had her, held close against his heart, and finally he lifted his head and stared down at her again.

'I want you, Fran,' he said unsteadily. 'I need you. Not just tonight, but every night, for the rest of our lives. I need you more than I need to breathe.'

'Oh, Mike,' she whispered, the tears that had threatened earlier finally spilling over. 'I need you, too. I love you—so very, very much. I just don't know if I can be the woman you want.'

'You are the woman I want,' he said, his voice vibrating with sincerity, 'and if you can't do this—if you really don't want to, then you're still the woman I want. I still love you. Whatever happens, I'll always love you.'

'I can do this,' she said, her doubts dissolving like mist in the sunshine, leaving her certain. 'Make love to me, Mike. I've missed you so, so much.'

He gave a ragged, broken groan, and his mouth came down on hers hard, seeking, demanding her response, and she rose up on tiptoe, threaded her fingers through his hair and kissed him right back, her tongue tangling with his, stroking, suckling, pleading until he dragged his mouth away and reached for the hem of her dress, pulling it over her head and throwing it aside, his eyes settling on her hungrily.

The bra was gone in a second, then he pushed her back onto the mattress, one hand capturing hers and holding them over her head, the other cupping her heat, his fingers curling hot against her, slipping under the edge of the lace and tracing the soft, aching flesh that wept for his touch.

'Mike, please…' she gasped, and he straightened and stripped them away, leaving her there exposed to his eyes. The bedroom light was off, but the landing light was on and she knew he could see her clearly. Knew by the way his eyes darkened, the way his lips parted and the air hissed out of them.

He grasped her thighs, kneeling, awkward in the cast, and laying hot, open-mouthed kisses from her knee slowly, slowly up her thigh, so near and yet so far…

'Mike, please!'

He looked up, his eyes black. 'Not yet,' he said tightly. Turning his attention to the other leg, his tongue teased the trembling, quivering flesh behind her knee, the soft graze of his stubble torture as he worked his way slowly up her thigh until at last, finally, he was there, his mouth closing over her…

'Mike!'

She felt the tremors start, felt the sensation build as his tongue flicked against her, and then she felt his fingers there, thrusting into her in time with his tongue, and her body arched, a scream leaving her throat as wave after wave of sensation crashed through her, leaving her shaking and stunned in its wake.

'Mike?'

'I'm here,' he growled, his voice rough with need, and she felt a button ping off his shirt and flick against her skin.

He struggled out of the shorts, swearing as they caught on the cast, and then he was beside her, dragging her up the bed and taking her in his arms. With a shuddering sigh he drew her tighter against him, taking her mouth in a wild, desperate kiss that she thought would never end.

It did, finally, but only because he'd moved on, his breath hot against her throat, his lips parted, nipping, nibbling, his tongue like fire licking over her, leaving her shaking and wild with a need every bit as desperate as his own.

Her hands clung to him, plunging into his hair, holding him against her as his chin grazed her chest, her breasts, tormenting her, his breath sighing over her skin until finally, when she thought she would have to scream if he left it another second, his mouth closed hotly over a nipple and she did scream, a sobbing scream of need and frustration satisfied at last.

Except not, because it just made it all much worse, and the need was building again, another need, much greater, and she bucked against him, feeling the hard, urgent thrust of his erection against her thigh. And tonight she was ready for it.

More than ready.

'Mike, please,' she sobbed, her hands dragging at him, and with a fractured groan he shifted over her, settling against the intense, liquid heat, the fire he'd lit in her burning recklessly out of control as he stared down into her eyes and drove deeply into her.

'Oh, God, Fran, I love you,' he said brokenly, and then he started to move, the long, slow thrusts driving her higher, higher, until with a sobbing cry she felt her body tighten around him and sensation flooded her again. He drove into her one last time, then stiffened against her, a great groan torn from his chest as his body convulsed with the devastating power of his release, and then with a ragged sob he rolled to the side, taking her with him, cradling her against his heart as if he'd never let her go…

He held her all night.

She woke towards dawn, and he made love to her again, slowly, tenderly, afraid he'd hurt or frighten her, but she clung to him, her breathy sighs sweet music to his ears, and as she curled against him to sleep again, there was a smile on her face.

He didn't smile. He was too close to tears, too moved to speak. He just held her, thankful for the chance, hoping that the future wouldn't prove too much for them but a little more confident now that they would make it.

They had to, because without her he would be nothing.

Fran woke again later, the sun well up, and found Mike gone.

She could hear his voice in the kitchen, and she slipped out of bed, hot colour scorching her cheeks as she saw the trail of underwear strewn across the floor. She scooped it up, showered and dressed quickly and went downstairs.

'Hi, Fran,' Joe said, and then did a mild double-take before turning away, just a fraction too slowly to hide his smile.

She felt the heat climb her cheeks again and went over to the kettle. 'Any tea in the pot?' she asked brightly.

'I should make some fresh,' Joy said. 'It's been there a while. I would have brought you up a cup but Mike said to let you sleep.'

'Mmm,' she said, filling the kettle and avoiding Mike's eye. They hadn't exchanged a word since last night, and she felt ludicrously self-conscious and aware, her body still humming from his touch. If she looked at him…

'How about a fruit smoothie?'

Oh, lord. He was right behind her, his body big and powerful and radiating heat. He rested his hand on her hip, and she leant against him, wondering what his family would make of their closeness and deciding it was none of their business. 'OK,' she said, surprised by his suggestion as well as his closeness. 'Want one?'

'Please.'

She met his eyes, saw the unspoken message and smiled. So he was engaging with this diet, taking it seriously, even though she knew he was afraid for her in case it all went wrong again. She went up on tiptoe, brushed a kiss over his lips and then pulled a selection of fruit out of the fridge.

'Two smoothies coming up,' she said lightly. Chopping the fruit, she wondered how long his family were going to hang around before they left them in peace so they could go back to bed and carry on where they'd left off…

It was a glorious few days.

Fran absconded from the farm, taking Mike to get his cast changed again and his stitches removed. The skin had healed well, and the swelling had subsided a lot, so they put on a lightweight walking cast and told him to start bearing weight.

Which meant they could do more, and so they did. They drove down to Penhally and had lunch in the Smugglers, then sat on the harbour wall in the sunshine and watched the children crabbing off the jetty, and then they went home and went back to bed and made love until the racket in the kitchen told them that milking was over and Joe was returning Brodie to them.

She pulled on her clothes and went down, Mike following her a few moments later when he'd dressed himself more slowly, and if the family was studiously avoiding looking at them, she didn't care, because she'd got her husband back, the man she'd loved for years and thought she'd lost, and she wasn't going to be ashamed of spending time with him in their own home.

Even if it was the afternoon!

'Can you guys manage without us for a day or so?' Mike asked, coming up behind her and wrapping his arms round her, the declaration so blatant they couldn't fail to understand it.

In unison they chorused, 'Of course!'

'Going anywhere nice?' Sarah asked.

Joe started to say something and got her elbow in the ribs for his pains, and Joy and Russell just looked at each other and smiled.

'We might take a run down to Falmouth if the weather stays fair,' Mike said. 'Don't really know. We haven't made any plans, but as I can't really do anything and Fran hasn't had a holiday for ages, we thought we might just take off for a night or so. Could you hang on to Brodie till Sunday?'

'Sure.' Joe nodded. 'Got a hotel in mind?'

Fran felt Mike shrug. 'No plans. We'll see where the road takes us.'

In the end they found a fabulous hotel right on the clifftop with spectacular views of the rugged Cornish coast, and booked in for two nights, taking advantage of a late cancellation, and spent most of the day in bed, making love slowly and lazily, getting to know each other again—and talking.

Talking like they'd never talked before, talking about anything and everything.

Everything except the whole baby thing. That was taboo, a sort of tacit avoidance, because at the end of the day all that really mattered was that they loved each other. Anything else was just the icing on the cake.

And then, relaxed and comfortable with each other, closer than they'd ever been, they went home because Sophie was coming, and Mike broke the taboo.

'Will you be OK?' he asked, and she smiled, realising with surprise that she would.

'I'll be fine,' she told him. 'And I'm looking forward to seeing her again.'

Sophie was fizzing with excitement, of course, because Kirsten and Andrew had told her about the baby and she was utterly obsessed with the prospect. She talked about it non-stop, her holiday hardly getting a mention, and Fran thought it was just as well she was OK with it, because if this had happened before she and Mike had spent the last few days together in their glorious idyll, it would have been intolerable.

But then Sophie snuggled up to her that evening, her restless little body finally still, and said, 'I wish you could have a baby too, 'cos then I could have a baby in *both* my homes!'

It was the 'homes' that did it for Fran. The fact that Sophie still considered this to be her home, even though she and her mother had moved out of it years ago and she now had another home, nearly moved Fran to tears. She hugged the little girl tighter, looking up and meeting Mike's eyes and giving him a supporting smile, because his mouth had pressed together and his eyes were over-bright.

'That would be nice, wouldn't it, Mike?' she said. 'We'll have to think about it.'

'Maybe one day, sweetheart,' he said softly, looking at Sophie, but Fran felt his words were for her. 'And, anyway, you might like coming here and having a bit of peace at night without the baby crying,' he added, this time definitely to his daughter, and her nose wrinkled.

'Babies do cry a lot, don't they? And they smell. Suzie's mum's got a baby and she had to change his nappy the other day when I was there and it was *really* smelly!'

Fran chuckled and hugged her again, then stood up. 'Come on, young lady, it's time for bed.'

'Oh, do I have to? I haven't seen you for *ages*!'

'It's only two days longer than usual, so don't give us that rubbish,' Mike said with a laugh, standing up and scooping his daughter off the sofa and throwing her over his shoulder. He winced as his ribs twinged, but Fran handed him the crutch he was using as a stick and he hobbled out of the room, Sophie draped over his shoulder and giggling.

'Mike, are you sure you're OK to put her to bed, or do you want me to do it?' Fran asked as he limped away.

'I can do it. I'm fine,' he assured her. Sliding Sophie down to the floor at the bottom of the stairs, he clapped his hands behind her and chased her up. She won easily, because he still found the stairs hard, but she heard him stumping along the landing, a great roar and a little shriek echoing back down the stairs, and Fran hoped he wasn't doing too much for his ankle.

Whatever, she thought. He was a grown man, he knew if it hurt or not and she wasn't his mother. He had one of those already, making more than enough fuss over him, so she really didn't need to join in.

She went into the kitchen and made them some fennel tea, letting it brew while she loaded the dishwasher, and by the time she'd finished he was down. 'All tucked up?'

'Mmm.' He came up behind her, put his arms round her and sniffed. 'Smells interesting.'

'Fennel tea,' she said, turning her head to look at him, and his eyes narrowed suspiciously.

'Really?'

'Really. Try it, it's really refreshing.'

He looked doubtful, but then his eyes twinkled mischievously. 'One condition.'

'What's that?'

'I get a reward for drinking it.'

'Such as?'

He smiled lazily. 'Oh—I'm sure you can work it out.' He bent his head and brushed a feather-soft kiss over her shoulder, trailing his lips up the side of her neck and nibbling her ear with his lips.

'Michael Trevellyan, behave,' she said, giggling and swatting him away, but her knees were like jelly and her heart was pounding and she could feel her body responding to his instantly.

'I don't want to,' he said, suddenly serious. 'I've missed this, Fran. It's been too long. Come here.'

And he turned her into his arms, stepped forwards so he

trapped her between the cupboards and his long, hard body and, wedging his thigh between hers, he took her mouth in a kiss that surely would have set the kitchen on fire if the phone hadn't rung to interrupt them.

'Rats,' he said mildly, easing away from her, his eyes blazing with promise. 'Remember where we got to.' And he picked up the phone. 'Trevellyan.'

He winked at her, then said, 'Sure. That'll be fine. I'll have Sophie with me, but she's no trouble.' His eyes flicked to Fran's, his gaze assessing, the mischief gone, and he said, 'That would be lovely. Thanks. I'll check with Fran and get back to you if there's a problem. See you tomorrow—two? Fine.'

He put the phone down. 'That was Ben Carter,' he said, and she thought his voice sounded a little wary. 'He's got a couple of days off, and they've invited us for a barbeque tomorrow. He wants to look over the land with me, show me where he's talking about so I can discuss it with Joe later.'

And, of course, the baby would be there. 'That's nice,' she said, summoning a smile, and it was, of course. It would be lovely. Annabel was gorgeous, and she couldn't isolate herself from everyone just in case she ever encountered a baby. She taught the reception class of a primary school, for heaven's sake! She was surrounded by babies and toddlers and pregnant women at every turn.

And just because, for now at least, she wasn't able to join them, it didn't mean she wanted to avoid them.

'You really OK with it?'

She smiled again, a bit more convincingly. 'Yes, Mike. I'm OK with it. It'll be lovely. Stop worrying. I can cope—I have to. And Sophie will be in her element. She'll be able to tell Lucy all about the new baby that's coming and practise on Annabel. Why don't you ring them back and say yes? I'll make a salad and we can take some steaks and burgers from the farm shop. It'll be fun.'

And if she told herself that enough times, maybe she'd believe it…

CHAPTER NINE

IT WAS an absolutely gorgeous day, and Sophie was up with the larks, bursting into their bedroom and clambering onto the bed, effectively putting an end to their early-morning cuddle.

Especially as the dog came too, trampling all over them and lashing Mike with her tongue.

Fran ducked under the bedclothes with a little shriek, Mike yelled at Brodie and told her to get down, then he must have grabbed Sophie because she started to giggle hysterically.

'No, no, stop!' she screamed, then there was a yelp from Mike, and Fran emerged from the bedclothes to find him sitting up and holding his ribs, his mouth open as he gasped with pain.

'I only tickled him back,' Sophie said, her eyes flooding with tears, and Mike reached out and tucked her under his right arm, well away from the damaged ribs, and kissed the top of her head as she burrowed into him, sobbing heartbrokenly.

'It's OK, sweetheart, don't cry, I'm fine,' he said softly. 'It wasn't you, it was because I jumped. You didn't hurt me.'

Her head came out from his side and she stared up at him soulfully. 'Are you sure?'

'I'm sure. Come here.'

So she snuggled back into his side and, reaching out her hand, caught hold of Fran and tugged her over, pulling her into the cuddle, too.

'That's better,' she said, and for a few minutes they all lay there quietly until Sophie's natural ebullience returned. 'So—what are we going to do today? Can we go to the beach?'

'Not while your dad's got his cast on,' Fran said, saving him from having to tell her. 'Anyway, we're doing something much more exciting. We're going to see Ben and Lucy Carter, just down the road at Tregorran House, and they've got a little baby girl called Annabel. I expect you'll be able to play with her.'

Sophie wriggled round and looked up at Fran, eyes sparkling. 'Is she very new?'

'Not very. She was born on Christmas Eve, but she's still pretty tiny. She can't do a lot, but you can play peep-bo with her and teach her how to play with her toys, I expect.'

'Can I hold her?'

'I don't know. Maybe.'

'That means no,' Sophie said with an exaggerated sigh.

'No, it means maybe,' Fran reiterated, 'and it depends on Lucy.'

'That's not till this afternoon, though,' Mike put in, 'so what do you want to do this morning?'

'Go riding,' Sophie said promptly. 'Can I? Please? Mummy said you might let me.'

Mike met Fran's eyes. 'Got any other plans?'

She shook her head. 'No. I've got things to do here, like

picking up the eggs and mucking out the chickens, and they might need a hand in the farm shop, but if I get up early and get on with it—since I already seem to be awake,' she added, wriggling her fingers into Sophie's ribs and making her giggle, 'I might as well get on. Why don't you two have a bit of a rest and make some breakfast for me? And by the time you've done that, I'll have finished with the chickens. And I'll take Brodie with me, she could do with a bit of a run. It might be late enough then to ring the stables and see if they can fit you in.'

They could, and they set off at a quarter to eleven, Sophie fizzing with excitement. They turned into the stableyard and pulled up, and she was out of the door and hopping from foot to foot with impatience while Mike sorted out his crutches.

'Come on, you, hold my hand and let's go and find Georgina,' Fran said to her, and Sophie slipped her hand into Fran's and all but dragged her over to where a few fat little ponies were tied up to a rail by the stables. Children were milling around them, brushing and fussing over them, and the ponies stood patiently and tolerated it with what Fran felt was very good grace.

'Hi, Sophie, haven't seen you for a while,' Georgina Somers said, coming over and smiling at them. 'You're looking well, unlike your dad—he's been in the wars, hasn't he?'

'He broke his leg,' Sophie said, a little unnecessarily as Mike hobbled towards them in his cast, leaning heavily on one crutch and grinning.

'Really?' Georgina teased, then flashed a smile at Mike which might have made Fran jealous if she hadn't been loved so very thoroughly by him the night before. 'The wounded soldier. I heard about your accident. Good to see you up and about.'

'Good to be up and about. They gave me a walking cast the other day—it's so much better, but I must say I'm a bit scared about my toes. I'm used to steel toecaps, and I feel a bit vulnerable.'

'Mmm. I did when I broke my leg. Right, Sophie, let's get you a hat sorted out and then pop you up on your pony. You're riding Bracken today.'

'Oh, goody, I love Bracken! He's really nice.'

'She says that about every one of them,' Mike murmured as Georgina took Sophie to get her hat. 'She'd love us to buy her one—that's the trouble with bringing her here, we'll have nothing else for the rest of the week, and there's no way she's having a pony part time, it just isn't fair. Apart from anything else, I've got more than enough to do without pooh-picking and grooming and changing rugs and so forth, and that's never the end, is it? There's always another one, and then another one, because the first is too small and then the next one will be lonely and then you can't get rid of the old one and it just goes on. I know so many farmers who're overrun with their children's first ponies and they just can't get rid of them.'

Fran chuckled. 'Sounds to me like a done job,' she teased, but he shook his head.

'No way, Fran. To tell you the truth, I don't really like her riding. It's dangerous, and the odd ride from time to time is OK, but all the time? She's only six—it's too risky. So I'm just going to keep saying no to her own pony and letting her come here instead. She's too precious to us.'

She was. Fran watched her skipping out of the tack room in a body protector and a hat with a shocking pink silk cover on it, looking utterly delectable, and she felt her eyes fill.

'I have to keep her safe, Fran,' Mike said, and she heard the little catch in his voice.

'Don't worry. I'll back you up.'

His hand found hers and squeezed. 'Thanks.'

The lesson passed without incident. Well, more or less. One little girl ended up on her bottom in the sand school, but she was all right and got up laughing, and another ended up in tears because her pony ran off with her and wouldn't stop, and a boy wanted to change ponies because his wouldn't go, and Georgina refused and told him that when he gave the pony the correct cues, it would understand. And of course, eventually, when he got it right, the pony trotted forwards nicely and Fran suppressed a smile.

'Know him?'

'Oh, yes. I know most of them. He's a bit of a bully. It's nice to see something big enough and stubborn enough to beat him. Take him down a peg or two. It'll do him good.'

'OK, everybody, that's it now. Give your ponies a nice big pat and take them back out and tie them up. Well done, all of you.'

Georgina opened the gate, and the ponies filed out.

'That was so cool! Daddy, can I have a pony? I really, *really* want one!' Sophie said, the pleading starting before she'd even dismounted, and Mike rolled his eyes at Fran and gave a hollow laugh.

'Kids,' he said under his breath. 'Do we really need another one?'

Fran stopped in her tracks, and after another step Mike came to a halt and turned back to her, his face stricken.

'Oh, hell, Fran, I didn't mean that! Darling, I'm sorry.'

'It's OK,' she said, struggling to find a smile. 'I know it was a joke.'

'No, it was a stupid, thoughtless remark—I'm so, so sorry, Fran. I don't know what I was thinking about.'

She shook her head. 'Not here, Mike. Not now. I'm fine—really. Just let it go.'

But it put a dampener on the drive back and, while Sophie chattered happily about the pony and how she wanted one of her own and what she was going to call it, Mike stared straight ahead, and Fran tried to concentrate on driving and wondered just how much of a joke it really had been, and how much he'd meant it.

Many a true word is spoken in jest, she thought. Maybe he really doesn't want another child after all and he's just playing along with me out of pity? It would explain the way he'd kept his distance all these last months, and although he'd said it was because he was afraid of getting her pregnant again, that he couldn't bear the possibility of her having another miscarriage, maybe that was just an excuse, something legitimate he could use to hide his real feelings behind.

They got back to the farm, and Joy was just coming out of the farm shop as they pulled up.

'Grannie!' Sophie yelled. Sliding out of the car, she ran over to her grandmother and started telling her about her riding lesson.

Mike opened the car door and swung round, eased himself out and hobbled over to his mother. 'Are you busy?'

'No, not at all. Why?'

'Just wondered if you'd like to spend a little time with Sophie—who, incidentally, knows she's not having a pony of her own, so don't let her try and talk you round—while I have a bit of a rest? And Fran's got some things to do, so if you don't mind?'

Fran watched them, heard his words, saw his mother nod agreement and look up, meeting her eyes with concern.

'Is everything OK?' she was asking, but Fran couldn't take any more. She turned away and, locking the car, went into the house, leaving Mike to follow her.

He couldn't believe he'd said that.

Of all the crass, stupid remarks!

He limped into the house, calling her name, and found her eventually in their bedroom, stripping the bed with fierce concentration, her movements almost savage. He went over to her, took her hands in his, held them against his heart.

'Frankie, talk to me.'

'No, you talk to *me*,' she cried, wrenching her hands away and stripping off the pillow case with enough force to tear it. 'You tell *me* what you really feel, what you really want. Because I thought I knew, and then I suddenly realised that maybe I didn't know at all, maybe you don't really want a baby with me despite all the stuff you've said over the last few days, and I have to *know*, Mike,' she said, throwing down the pillow with a ragged sob. *'I have to know!'*

Her eyes were filled with tears, and with a rough sigh he hauled her up against his chest and hugged her tight. 'I want a baby,' he said emphatically. 'I want your baby. Our baby. And what I said was just a knee-jerk reaction to kids in general, and nothing to do with us. I know it was stupid, but I thought—Frankie, I thought we'd sorted this out? Thought you knew how I felt. Of course I want a baby. You know I do.'

'No, I don't, Mike,' she said, her body still and unresponsive in his arms. 'I really don't, not any more.'

'Oh, God.' He sighed, and let her go, frustration at his stupidity making him want to scream. He paced away, then turned back to her, scrubbing his hands through his hair. 'How can I prove it?' he asked desperately.

'Let me try again,' she said. 'I know you said you couldn't bear the thought of me having a miscarriage, but it isn't you that has to bear it. It's me. So let me. Or, at least, let's think about it, because for the last few days we haven't talked about it at all, and I want to, in the context of our relationship now. Not what it's been, but what it is now. I know you love me. I know you want me. But I need the truth from you about this, Mike. I need to know that you really, really want a child with me, not that you're just going along with me, humouring me. Indulging me.'

'I'm not,' he said instantly. 'Never. I want a baby with you, Fran. I've said it over and over again. I know what it means to you, how it's tearing you apart, but it means a lot to me, too. It's not just for you. I want a child as well—a child who'll live here with us, a child to share every moment of our lives, not just the odd weekend. I adore Sophie, and I wish she could be here with us more, but if I'd stayed with Kirsten I would have wanted more children. Sophie shouldn't be alone, and this house needs kids, Fran. Either ours or somebody else's. And if we can't have a baby of our own, then I'd like to adopt one—or more. Maybe disabled in some way, a child nobody wants. Not necessarily a pretty little baby but a real person with needs that maybe, with enough love, we could meet. The farm's a wonderful place to be a child, and nature has a way of healing all sorts of hurts. This would be a good place to let that happen.

'So, yes, I do want a child. With you. And I'll do whatever it takes, for as long as you want to try. And failing that, I'd like to adopt, because I want to be a full-time father. I love being a father. It's part of who I am, and I want to share it with you. Does that answer your questions?'

She stared at him, then gave a scratchy little laugh. 'Pity I wrecked the bed,' she said, 'because I could just do with lying down in it with you and having a really big cuddle.'

'Oh, you idiot,' he said, his voice cracking. Limping quickly back to her, he grabbed the pillows off the floor, shoved the quilt out of the way and lay down, pulling her down after him. 'Come here,' he said gruffly. Wrapping his arms round her, he sighed deeply and pressed a kiss to her forehead. 'I'm sorry,' he murmured. 'Forgive me?'

She tilted her head back and smiled. 'I forgive you. Actually, I more than forgive you. Maybe I need to push you more often, because you get really honest then, and tell me all the things you've been keeping to yourself. Like this adoption business. How long have you been thinking about that?'

He shrugged. 'I don't know. Ages. Years, probably. Since I married Kirsten.'

'Then let's do it. If I have a baby, great. If I don't—well, we'll do as you said. Maybe do it anyway.'

He looked down at her, saw new determination in her

eyes and kissed her. 'One thing at a time,' he cautioned, and she smiled.

'It's all right, Mike,' she said. 'You won't wake up one morning and find we're running a children's home, but it's something to think about. Something for the future.'

She settled her head down on his chest. 'Now go to sleep. We've only got a short time before we have to get ready to go to the Carters'.'

'Seems a shame to waste it,' he murmured, and she lifted her head again and looked up at him.

'Are we making up for lost time?' she asked.

He chuckled. 'Is that a problem?'

'No problem,' she said, and kissed him.

The baby was gorgeous.

Sophie was captivated, and when the men wandered off to look at the fields, Fran asked Lucy if there was anything she could do to help and ended up with Annabel in her arms.

'Oh, that's better. She can pull your hair instead of mine,' Lucy said with a laugh, kissing the baby's nose and making her giggle deliciously. She clapped her chubby hands in delight, and Fran caught one of them and blew a raspberry on it, making her giggle even harder.

'I want to blow a raspberry,' Sophie said, and Fran crouched down so Sophie could reach, and the baby giggled again and grabbed Sophie's curls.

'Ouch!' Sophie said with a laugh, gently pulling her hair out of Annabel's fingers. She danced over to Lucy and said, eyes sparkling, 'I'm going to have a baby too!'

'Oh!' Lucy spun round, her eyes also sparkling, and

said, 'Oh, Fran, that's so lovely, because so am I! When's yours due?'

Oh, lord. 'Um…it's not me, it's Kirsten—Sophie's mother,' she explained, wondering if everything today was going to be destined to floor her, 'but congratulations! That's really lovely for you.'

'Oh, well—it's a bit quick. Fran, I'm really sorry,' she added, her eyes conveying her regret.

'It's a shame it's not you and Daddy,' Sophie chipped in, looking up at her with wistful eyes. 'That would have been so nice.'

Wouldn't it just? Fran thought, and banished it. She was going to enjoy herself this afternoon. One thing at a time, Mike had said, and she was starting now, having a lovely cuddle with little Annabel to fill her achingly empty arms.

'But perhaps you could have one too,' Sophie went on, as relentless as ever. 'Daddy said maybe one day, so maybe it could be a *soon* maybe instead of a never maybe. He usually means never, though. Like the pony. He said maybe once, when I was four, but now he just says no.'

Lucy laughed a little awkwardly. 'I think a baby's a bit different, Sophie. I'm sure Fran and your father will have a baby when it's right for them.'

'What if it's never right?'

'Then you'll have your mother's new baby anyway,' Fran pointed out. 'And, like your father said, it might be nice to come to us and have a bit of peace.'

Lucy rolled her eyes. 'Amen to that,' she said fervently. 'This one still doesn't always go through the night and by the time she does, I expect I'll have the other one.'

A shadow fell across the room, and Mike and Ben walked into the kitchen.

'All right, girls?' Mike asked, scanning their faces and picking up on the atmosphere.

'Fine,' Fran said.

But then Sophie opened her mouth and said, 'Guess what, Daddy? Lucy's having another baby!'

'So—what do you think about the fields, Mike?' Lucy asked.

They'd finished eating, Annabel had been put down for a nap and Sophie was standing on the other side of the track, talking to Amber through the fence. The adults were all sitting round in the shade, sipping a nicely chilled rosé.

'Oh, I think we should be able to do something,' he said, very conscious of the need for money so they could afford another IVF cycle, and yet wondering how they could possibly charge the Carters the going rate for a bit of land that was little more than useless to the farm.

'You're having a fit of conscience,' Ben said astutely, narrowing his eyes. 'Don't. We want it, you've got it—it's called supply and demand, Mike.'

'I think we need an independent valuation,' he said, wondering if he was shooting himself in the foot and if they'd end up without the land and with not enough money to do anything. Not that losing the land mattered, because the bit the Carters were most interested in was essentially worthless to the farm. And that was the problem, of course. Oh, damn.

'I'll get the auctioneer who sold us the house to have a look, shall I?' Ben said. 'Unless you've got a better suggestion?'

'No, he's fine. He's the man, I would have said.'

'Well, we'll do that, then,' Ben said, picking up the wine bottle. 'Top-up?'

Mike shook his head. 'No. I'm still on painkillers. I shouldn't, really,' he lied, although he had taken one the night before after chasing Sophie up the stairs, so it wasn't really a total lie.

'Fran?'

She shook her head. 'No, I'm fine, Ben, thank you. It was lovely.' She looked at Mike. 'We ought to go, darling. I promised Sarah I'd give her a hand to restock the shelves in the shop, and Sophie could do with a bath. She's covered in cow slobber.'

'Right. Ben, I'll have a chat to Joe—I might see him tonight. He's doing the milking. I'll talk to you when we've got the valuation.'

They took their leave, Sophie reluctant to drag herself away from Amber and wanting to stay until Annabel woke up. But Mike bribed her with the promise of hot chocolate in the bath, and Fran drove them home and went over to the farm shop, leaving Mike to deal with Sophie.

He was clearing up the bathroom while Sophie was getting into her pyjamas when Joe called up the stairs.

'Sophie, come down when you're ready,' he said, sticking his head round the door, and he hobbled downstairs to the kitchen.

'Hi. I'm glad you popped in. We've been with Ben and Lucy, and he's walked me over the fields and shown me what he wants. I've got the plans.'

'OK.'

He looked at his brother's face, wondering what was wrong. Something, that was for sure, because Joe was looking troubled. 'What is it? Don't tell me we've got foot and mouth or something, because I don't want to know.'

'No!' Joe laughed awkwardly. 'No, it's nothing like that. It's just—oh, hell, bro, I don't know how to tell you, so I'm just going to say it. Sarah's pregnant.'

Oh, God, not another one. Mike stood motionless for a second, then forced his face into a smile. 'That's really great news,' he said, but his voice sounded hollow and Joe couldn't fail to notice.

He didn't. He said something very rude, and then added, 'You don't have to lie. I know what this news means to you, and I'm so sorry. It wasn't really planned, but actually we're thrilled to bits—or we would be, if it wasn't for you guys.'

'You *be* thrilled to bits,' Mike said gruffly, grabbing his brother and hugging him hard. 'It's fantastic news, and I really, really am pleased for you. Just because we're having trouble, it doesn't mean nobody else in the county can have a baby.'

'But it's not just us, is it?' Joe said quietly. 'Sarah told me Kirsten's pregnant.'

'And Lucy,' Mike said flatly. 'But, hey, that's life. We're all the right age, it's bound to happen. Anyway, we're talking about maybe trying the IVF again. That's why I want to talk to you about this land. We're getting the agent who sold the house to have a look and value it, but I don't know what we should ask.'

'How about splitting the difference between agricultural rates and what it would add to the value of their house?' Joe suggested. 'That would seem fair. And if it isn't enough, we don't have to refit the kitchen. It all works—

and with the baby coming, I don't know if we'll want that much upheaval. You could have it all.'

'That's not fair.'

'Life isn't. Sometimes it sucks. And if you need help, you just have to ask. This is more important than the kitchen, and the clock's ticking, Mike. We don't want Fran to run out of time because we want some fancy new cupboards and a bigger fridge.' He glanced at his watch. 'Got to go, I've still got to feed the calves again before I can stop. Let me know if there's any news on the valuation.'

'Will do. And tell Sarah congratulations for me.'

Joe nodded and went out, leaving Mike alone with his thoughts. Not a happy place to be. He couldn't believe it was happening again.

It was going to kill Fran. And once again he was going to have to be the one to tell her.

'Everything all right, Fran?'

His eyes held hers for a second then slid away, something that could have been guilt lurking in their depths, and Fran stared at him, her heart breaking. He knew. He actually knew, and he hadn't said anything! He'd been upstairs putting Sophie to bed when she'd come back from helping Sarah, and just when she'd needed him, he hadn't been there.

And now she discovered that he'd already known, and he hadn't told her. Just when she'd thought there were no secrets. Why hadn't he told her?

'Oh, just peachy,' she said flatly.

'Fran, I'm sorry,' he began, but she cut him off.

'How long have you known?'

He sighed. 'About half an hour,' he said heavily, taking the wind out of her sails. 'Joe told me while Sophie was getting her pyjamas on. I'm really sorry, darling.'

And he was, she could see that. His throat was working, his eyes were sad and he held out his arms to her. She walked into them, laid her head on his chest and sighed, the fight going out of her and leaving only sadness.

'I'm sorry, too,' she said. 'Sorry I jumped down your throat. I thought you'd been keeping it from me for a while.'

'No. So I take it Sarah told you?'

She gave a strangled little laugh. 'Not exactly. I found some coffee that was past its sell-by date and handed it to her, commenting on the lovely smell, and she dropped it and ran. Bit of a give-away, really.'

He rubbed her shoulders with his hand, the other hand lying lightly in the small of her back and holding her against him comfortingly.

'I'm sorry. If I'd known, I would have told you, given you some warning.'

She sighed and eased out of his arms. 'Don't be silly. You can't protect me from every pregnant woman in Cornwall, Mike.' Although there did seem to be an extraordinary number of them. It just seemed so hard, when they wanted a baby so much, and they hadn't done anything wrong. Surely they *deserved* a baby of their own as much as anyone else?

She looked up and met Mike's worried eyes and smiled, but the honeymoon was over, and the yearning was back in spades.

Mike saw the change in her eyes, saw the fragile happiness of the past few days recede and the longing take its place, and he felt a flicker of dread return.

Damn. He'd hoped for longer to build on their relationship, more time to celebrate the joy they'd found in each other, to cement the foundations of their marriage before they'd had to face this.

And now it had all caught up with them again.

It came to a head later, after they'd made love and were lying in each other's arms. He was stroking her, his hand running lightly up and down her spine, and he could feel the tension in her, the determination in every line of her body, and he knew it was coming.

Her voice was just a murmur. 'Mike?'

'Mmm?'

'I want to try again,' she said softly.

He didn't pretend not to understand. 'Maybe we should persevere with this diet for another few months,' he suggested, stalling because he couldn't bear to lose this newfound closeness, and he was afraid that when they started the awful business of the injections and whatever all over again, that was exactly what would happen. 'Really give it time to work.'

'Maybe. I'll talk to Kate,' she said, but although she was lying still against him, he could sense the restlessness in her, the urge to do something *now*, and he knew she wouldn't be stalled, that this was it.

'Fran?' he prompted. 'Talk to me.'

She shifted slightly, sighed. 'Oh, Mike, I want a baby—I *need* a baby—and I can't afford to waste time. I'm thirty-four—my clock's ticking. I'm getting old for this, and if we can get the money from Ben and Lucy—I think we have to try.'

He sighed softly and drew her closer. She was right. She was getting on, in reproductive terms, and if her system was starting to shut down, they didn't have the luxury of waiting. But it wasn't easy.

'Are you sure, my love?' he said quietly. 'It's so hard on you—the hormones made you so sick before, the headaches…'

'I don't mind,' she said, her voice soft but firm. 'I can do this, Mike. I'm not looking forward to it, and I won't pretend I'm not scared that it'll all go wrong again, but I'll do it, and if it ends in a baby, I'd go through it ten times. Fifty.'

Oh, lord. So much courage. He'd seen what it had done to her, the side-effects of the treatment, the indignity and invasion of personal space—it had nearly cost them their marriage, and then when she'd lost it…

'Mike?'

Her voice was tentative now, seeking reassurance, and he pressed his lips to her hair and held her close. 'I'm here,' he promised. 'I'll always be here. There's not much else I can do to help you, but I can do that. I can be here for you, and support you, and we'll do whatever you feel you can bear.'

He just hoped Ben's surveyor came up with the goods.

CHAPTER TEN

'I'VE got Fran and Mike Trevellyan coming in to see me on Monday.'

Nick cocked his head on one side and raised a brow slightly. 'Any idea why?'

'They didn't say, but I suspect they want to talk about trying another cycle of IVF,' Kate said. 'You know I gave Fran the fertility-boosting diet sheet and lots of other advice and information?'

'Mmm—that was the day of his accident, wasn't it? They'll need longer that that. It was only a few weeks ago—three, wasn't it?'

'Something like that. It's certainly not long enough to have made a great deal of difference, and if they want to go ahead I'll encourage them to wait a bit longer, but I don't know if that's what they want.'

'Well, we know she's not pregnant,' Nick told her, lounging back in his chair and fiddling with his pen. 'Lucy told me she made a bit of a faux pas the other day—Sophie said she was going to have a baby brother or sister and Lucy assumed it was Mike and Fran having the baby and congratulated Fran, but it turned out it's Sophie's mother, Kirsten. Lucy felt dreadful.'

'I can imagine. Poor Fran.' Kate sighed softly. 'She said to me last time how it was funny that everyone seemed to be pregnant. And now Lucy and Kirsten are pregnant as well. Oh, dear.'

'And Joe and Sarah, although I don't know if Mike and Fran know that yet.'

Kate sat down, deeply troubled. 'I hope this isn't going to push them into a hasty decision.'

'Hardly hasty. They've been trying for years.'

'But they weren't ready, Nick. Only weeks ago when she came to see me their marriage was in ruins.'

'Well, not now. Not according to Lucy. They were there on Monday for a barbeque, and she said the air between them was sizzling.'

'Interesting.' Kate frowned. 'So maybe they just want to chat through the next stage in the process.'

'What time are they coming? I could drop in if I'm free.'

She gave a dry chuckle. 'I think I can manage to counsel a couple trying for a baby rather better than you,' she pointed out.

'Why do you say that?' he protested, bristling, and she gave him a wry look.

'Because I spent six years trying to have a baby and so I know where they're coming from?' she said softly. 'Because—correct me if I'm wrong—not one of your four children was planned or anticipated in any way, and infertility just doesn't even cross your mind? And neither, apparently, does your fertility, so if it's all the same with you, I'll handle the Trevellyans my way. And if you're very good, I'll tell you what it's all about.'

She got up and walked out, his growl of frustration clearly audible, then his barked 'Shut the door, then!' followed her down the corridor.

'Pretty please,' she said, sticking her head back round it, and got a sour look for her pains.

'I can't believe you think I'd be so bad at this,' he muttered, scowling. Oh, dear, poor Nick. He obviously felt insulted, but she didn't care. Her feelings were all with Mike and Fran, and Nick was big enough and ugly enough to take care of himself.

'Get over it,' she advised, and shut the door.

It was the longest week of Fran's life.

Well, no, it wasn't. Waiting to hear that she was pregnant after their IVF at the beginning of the year had been dreadful. This, waiting for their appointment with Kate to find out when they could start the process again, was different, but she felt so impatient to be getting on with it that every day dragged.

Mike was doing a bit more on the farm now, serving in the farm shop and doing the dreaded paperwork, but he didn't start at stupid o'clock in the morning and he wasn't coming to bed late, so they had plenty of time together to reinforce their new-found closeness.

With his gentleness and passion he'd repossessed her body from the grip of the medical profession, and their relationship was stronger and better than it had ever been. And it would have been wonderful if it wasn't for the suspense.

A few things broke it up. Amber had her calf, and

Sophie was there and saw it born, something Mike had no problem with and Kirsten was annoyed about.

'It's nature—she needs to know,' he said when Sophie was out of earshot.

'And I'm pregnant, and I don't want all sorts of embarrassing questions!' Kirsten protested. 'I can hear them all now— Oh, God, I could kill you sometimes, Mike.'

'Feel free to try,' he said blandly. 'She's my daughter, too, and I grew up knowing where babies come from. It didn't do me any harm. It was just one of those things. Better to know from the start than to be totally grossed out by the idea when you're twelve or so.'

'But to *see* it!'

'It was lovely,' Fran chipped in in his defence. 'She was captivated. Believe me, Kirsten, I teach in a rural area, and the kids that see animals reproduce have a much greater acceptance of sexual matters and their parents' subsequent pregnancies than those who don't. They just accept it as normal and natural and part of everyday life.'

'And what about my pregnancy? Did she say anything? Anything about my baby and where it's going to come from?'

'Actually, yes,' Mike confessed, looking a little uncomfortable. 'She asked if you'd stood up too when you had her, or if you were lying down, and what you'd do with the new baby.'

Kirsten closed her eyes and made a tiny screaming sound. 'And?'

'And I said people were all different, and it depended on how you felt at the time. I told her you walked round and round till the end then lay down to have her, but you might not feel like doing that with this baby.'

She groaned. 'Too much information, Mike. She doesn't need it at her age.'

Mike opened his mouth, then shut it, and Fran wondered if he'd thought better of telling Kirsten how fascinated Sophie had been with the afterbirth and the fact that Amber had eaten it. But then Sophie came back into the room with Brodie in tow and the subject was swiftly dropped.

'All ready to go?' Kirsten said, and Sophie nodded reluctantly.

'I want to stay and see Amber's calf some more. She's really cute—she's called Ama—something.'

'Amaryllis,' Mike supplied. 'And she'll still be cute when you come next time. Maybe cuter, because Amber will let you get closer. Right, come on, into the car. Your mother's in a hurry and we've got to go out.'

'Where are you going?' Sophie asked.

'The memorial service at the church in Penhally,' Mike told her. 'You remember, I told you about it. Lots of people died in a storm, and it was ten years ago today, so we're all gathering together to remember them.'

'That was four years before I was born,' Sophie said, counting on her fingers. 'That's *ages* ago.'

Not for the people who were still grieving, Fran thought, and wondered how Kate Althorp and the Tremayne family would be feeling. Had they moved on?

'We'd better go,' she said to Mike as soon as Kirsten and Sophie had gone.

There was standing room only, and Kate would rather have been outside with the majority of the villagers than trapped inside the pretty little church. At least outside she could look out to sea and communicate with James somehow, instead of being trapped inside this box with thoughts and feelings that were too painful to contemplate in public.

So she shut them down, sat quietly and still, and remembered him for the good man and loyal husband he'd been. She didn't let herself think about Nick, sitting with the rest of his family in the pew to her right, there to remember his father and brother. And she certainly didn't let herself think about that night ten years ago.

Reverend Kenner was leading the service, and when he read out the names of those lost, Jem leant closer to her, his hand in hers. For comfort, or to comfort her? She wasn't sure any more. He was growing up, turning into a fine young man, and James would have been proud of him.

Except, of course, the boy who was here to mourn his father wasn't that man's son at all.

Dear lord, it was so complicated. So sad and veiled in secrecy. She squeezed his hand, and he squeezed back.

Did he have the right to know who his real father was? She had no idea. No idea at all if it was better to mourn a man who had been a hero than to know that the man who really was your father was refusing to acknowledge your existence in his life.

The service moved outside and down to the beach, and as she and Jem stood on the rocks and threw their wreaths into the water and watched them carried away, as James had been, she blinked away threatening tears and straightened her shoulders.

They didn't need Nick in their lives. They could manage without him.

And if sometimes, at night, she still cried herself to

sleep for the love of a man she had no business loving, that was between her and her maker.

'Hello! Come on in and sit down. How are you, Mike?'

He gave a dry chuckle. 'Better than the last time you saw me,' he said, and Kate laughed.

'Yes, I think I'd probably agree. And Fran. How are you?'

Fran smiled, not knowing quite where to start and what to say. 'Um—good,' she said in the end, because it was true. She felt good—a bit sick with nerves, because now they'd decided to go for this, she was having to face all her demons all over again, but she could do it.

She reached out, and Mike took her hand, folding it in his and holding it tight. 'Um…we wanted to talk to you about the IVF. Trying again. We've spent a lot of time talking…' Her voice faltered, but she could feel Mike's fingers tightening on hers, and out of the corner of her eye she could see his reassuring smile.

'Anyway,' she said, firming her voice, 'we've been talking and thinking and we've been sticking to the diet and all the other things you said—the boxers and the showers and so on—and—'

'Boxers?' Mike said, frowning in puzzlement, then the light dawned. 'I thought they were because of the cast,' he murmured, but she could see a smile lurking in his eyes, and she smiled back.

'Sorry. And the coffee and alcohol and so on have all been strictly rationed.'

'And are you feeling better?' Kate asked, looking at them both.

'Probably, yes,' Mike said, looking thoughtful. 'I'm

sleeping better, but that could be all sorts of things. Less pressure, we're talking again—all sorts. And I feel energetic and optimistic, but again that could be because I'm not killing myself on the farm.'

'Looks like your broken leg's been quite useful, then,' Kate said with a smile, and turned to Fran. 'How do you feel?'

'Scared. Sick. Dreading the injections and all the intrusive stuff, but…' She shrugged and tried for a smile. 'Generally better. Like Mike. Sleeping better, more energy, happier—but there are lots of reasons for that.'

Kate smiled again. 'I'm so glad you're both happier,' she said quietly. 'An unhappy relationship is never a good start to this journey, and I must say from my point of view you both look light years better.'

'We feel it, and we were wondering if you could check us over,' Mike said. 'You know, run a ruler over us and make sure everything's up to scratch before we start again.'

'Of course. You probably haven't given the diet and the other changes long enough yet, but if you really feel you can't wait, we can start getting ready for the process of referral. You'll have to go to a different centre for private treatment, but we can run a lot of the preliminary checks from here, to rule out anything that's going to make them send you away. I'll need blood from both of you, so can you roll your sleeves up? That's great.'

She put a strap round Fran's arm, slid a needle into the vein and took several vials of blood from it, then, giving Fran the swab to press down on the vein, she repeated the process with Mike. 'You aren't still on painkillers or anything, are you?' she asked him, and he shook his head.

'I'm not on anything at the moment. Neither of us are.'

'Not even caffeine,' Fran said, giving him a rueful smile. 'I think that's probably been the hardest for him.'

'It's nothing,' he said, pressing down on the swab. 'Not compared to what's at stake.'

'Indeed. Right, let's weigh you both.'

She noted down their weights, commenting on the fact that Fran had put on three much-needed kilos, and took their blood pressure.

'OK. That's that. And I'll need a urine sample from each of you to make sure you haven't got diabetes or any sub-clinical infections, and you know what we're going to want from you,' she said, sliding a little pot across the desk to Mike with a smile.

He gave a wry laugh. 'Oh, yes. Do I ever. My favourite bit.' He pushed the ominous little pot around, picked it up and tossed it in the air, then said, with a tension in his voice that probably only Fran would have noticed, 'Will they be able to check for damaged sperm? Because if there's any likelihood that it was my sperm quality that caused Fran to miscarry, I want to do something about it before we try again.'

Kate's smile was reassuring. 'Of course. If there's a significant number of non-swimmers or sluggish ones, they'll have a closer look. It might be that you have to persevere with the diet for longer, or there might be something more significant wrong, although I doubt it. That would have been spotted before, I'm sure, and if you remember they never did find anything significantly wrong with either of you last time. But let's get the first tests out of the way and see what they come up with before we worry about what's next.'

'And then if everything comes back all right?' Fran asked, feeling the tension ratchet up a notch.

'Then we refer you to the clinic in Exeter, and they take over from us.' She finished labelling all the bottles of blood, slipped them into the plastic sleeves, filled in the various request forms and looked up. 'The semen sample needs to be as fresh as possible, so I would do it at the hospital, Mike, preferably near the beginning of the working day,' she said. 'Would you have time to do it this morning?'

He nodded, and Fran's heart hitched.

'Then I'll give you all this stuff to take to the lab as well,' she said, handing over all the blood samples and request envelopes, together with the urine sample bottles. 'The sooner they get them, the better the results. And I'll see you next week when they're all back—I'll give you a call when they're in.'

She smiled and pushed back her chair, stood up and shook their hands and opened the door. 'Good luck. I'll see you next week.'

'I can't believe I've got to go into that ghastly room again,' Mike muttered as they walked down the corridor towards the path lab. 'It's just awful, Fran—even thinking about it's enough to put me off. The girly magazines and the smutty videos—it's just horrible.' He suppressed a shudder, and then without warning she got hold of his arm and yanked him through a doorway.

'What the hell are you doing?' he asked as she shut the door and turned on the light. 'Fran? Why are we in the loo?'

She pushed him against the wall, took the pot out of her

handbag and put in on the basin, then reached for his zip. He grabbed it and held her away from him, unable to stop the splutter of laughter that rose in his chest.

'Fran, stop it! We can't do this here!' he hissed.

'Why not? Why ever not?'

'Because it's a public toilet!'

'Don't be silly, it's a single cubicle off the corridor and it's a lot more private than that dreadful room. Now, stop fighting.'

She pinned his hands out of the way, grabbed his zip and slid it down, reaching inside and curling her fingers round him.

Dear God. He was already hard, the thought of her touching him enough to bring him to the edge even though they were both still laughing. But then she moved her hand, the firm, rhythmic strokes enough to bring him to his knees, and he dropped his head forwards on his chest and stared down at her, her hand curled round him, her lip caught between her teeth, her pupils darkening as she looked up and met his eyes.

'God, you are so sexy, Trevellyan,' she muttered, flicking her nail across the tip of his penis, and he fisted his hands in her T-shirt and closed his eyes.

'I'm going to come any second if you do that,' he said through gritted teeth, and she gave a sexy little chuckle.

'I thought that was the general idea,' she said, and reached for the pot…

'Kate? It's Jan, at the fertility clinic. We've got a lot of results here from some patients of yours, Francesca and Michael Trevellyan. I think they were probably for you and

I'll send them through to you straight away, but I thought you'd want to know the results anyway.'

'Of course,' Kate said, surprised to feel a little kick of apprehension. 'I was going to chase them up, it's been over a week now. OK, fire away. I've got a pen.' She listened, frowned, raised her eyebrows and jotted down all the information. 'Really? Thanks, Jan. I'll pass all that on,' she said. Cutting the connection, she dialled the Trevellyans' number.

'Fran? It's Kate. Are you both in? I've got your results, and I was just about to leave the surgery. I thought I might drop by on my way to collect Jem from my mother and have a chat about what happens next.'

'Oh. Um…yes, sure,' Fran said, sounding instantly worried. 'We'll be here. Mike's in the office. I'll get him.'

'I'll be with you in ten minutes,' Kate said, and replaced the phone in its cradle.

'Mike?'

He glanced up at Fran and got straight to his feet, one look enough to know something was going on. 'What is it?' he asked, his chest tight with dread.

'I don't know. Kate's coming to see us. She's got our results.'

He felt his heart lurch and went over to her, gathering her in his arms and hugging her tight.

'We can handle this, Frankie,' he said softly. 'Whatever it is. Come on, let's go into the house and wait for her. I take it she's coming here now?'

'Yes. She said she'd be ten minutes. Mike, I feel sick.'

'Me, too,' he said. 'Come on.'

* * *

She would have fallen down without his support. They left the door open, standing there in the kitchen facing it, him behind her, his hands on her shoulders, steadying her, and so when Kate came in they couldn't see her face because the light was behind her.

'Well, I'll get straight to the point,' Kate said. 'It wasn't the news I was expecting to give you, but we aren't going to be referring you for the IVF programme.'

'No!' Fran wailed, her knees threatening to buckle, and she felt Mike's arms tighten round her.

'Fran, no,' Kate said hurriedly, and Fran couldn't work out why on earth she was smiling. 'It's not bad news! You can't have the IVF because you don't need it. You're pregnant, Fran,' she said, and her smile widened. 'Congratulations, both of you. You're going to have a baby.'

Fran stared at her for an age, numb with shock, and then with a fractured little sob she turned and fell into Mike's waiting arms…

They talked for hours.

Once Fran had stopped crying, of course, and they realised that Kate had left.

She was sitting on Mike's lap, one arm round his neck and his hand resting lightly over their baby, and she said softly, 'It's going to be OK this time, Mike. I feel so different. Much sicker. I thought it was just fright, but of course it isn't. My period is two days overdue, and I feel really different. And tired, but I thought that was just you keeping me awake half the night.'

He chuckled and tilted his head back, smiling up at her tenderly. 'You're to take care of yourself,' he said. 'Nothing silly. No unpasteurised milk or soft cheese or any of the other things—and no cheesemaking either. I can do that with a bin bag on my foot. And I'm sure Kate will give you a huge list of dos and don'ts.'

'I'm sure she will.' His hair had flopped forwards, and she lifted it back with her fingers and smoothed it out of the way so she could see his eyes. 'I don't want to tell Sophie yet, though,' she said, not wanting to acknowledge the possibility of failure but all too aware that it might lurk round the corner for them. After all it had before, twice.

'It'll be fine. Third time lucky, Fran,' he murmured. 'But I agree, we won't tell her yet. We won't tell anyone. Not till you're past the three-month mark.'

'I lost both the others at eight weeks,' she reminded him sadly.

His arm tightened. 'I know.'

'Three weeks and five days to go.'

'We'll make it,' he assured her, his voice quietly confident. 'And even if we don't, we've still got each other. As far as I'm concerned, that makes me the luckiest man alive. The rest is just the icing on the cake.'

She rested her head against his and sighed. 'I'm so lucky to have you,' she said softly. 'Have I told you recently how much I love you?'

He chuckled. 'Only about ten times today, but feel free to do it again.'

The phone rang, and she hung on to his neck and reached over, grabbing it from the charger without leaving Mike's lap. 'Hello? Oh, hi, Ben. Yes, he's here. I'll hand you over.'

She gave Mike the phone, and after a brief conversation he hung up and smiled at her. 'The valuer's been.'

'And?'

'If we'd ended up having to go the IVF route, we'd have had more than enough, but Joe and Sarah can do their kitchen, and Mum and Dad can change the car. And we can put the money on one side and spend it on something later. We're going to make it this time, Fran,' he said with conviction. 'I know we will.'

'We can spend it on the nursery,' she said, allowing a little bloom of hope. 'The house could do with a bit of decorating, and the heating's not great.'

He laughed. 'Don't get too carried away,' he said, and then kissed her. 'Time for bed?'

'Sounds good,' she said.

He lay watching her sleep, a little knot of fear in his chest. They had to make it. If she lost this baby…

Then he'd cope, he told himself firmly. If Fran had the courage to do this, then he had to find the courage to support her if it all went wrong. And they'd have the money put on one side for the IVF, should they need it. Please, God, it wouldn't be necessary…

Fran thought The Day would never come.

That was how she'd started thinking about it—with capital letters, because it seemed so huge, so important, so very far away that somehow nothing else would do.

Her pregnancy was a nightmare. Not because anything went wrong, because it didn't. She got through it, day by day, hour by hour, focusing on the end, planning for the magical day when she could bring her baby home, but somehow not daring to believe that it would ever happen.

The eight-week deadline passed.

Safely.

She gave a shaky sigh of relief when she reached nine weeks and realised she was probably over that hurdle. The next danger point was twelve weeks, and she got through that, too.

Then she had a scan—an image of her baby, just a tiny curl of a thing, but with an unwavering heartbeat.

'Oh, Mike,' she said, clinging to him and staring mesmerised at the screen, not knowing whether to laugh or cry. So she did both, and so did Mike, and they were given a photo to keep.

Their first, in the album she started with a trembling hope.

Then at twenty weeks she had her second scan, and another photo for the album.

'Do you want to know what sex it is?'

She looked at Mike for guidance, and he shrugged, passing the ball back to her.

'I don't care, so long as everything's all right,' he said, and she smiled.

'No, then,' she said. 'We'll wait and see.'

And then she kicked herself, because they started decorating the nursery, the little room off their bedroom that had always been the nursery, where Mike and Joe had slept for the first year of their lives, where their father, Russell, had slept, and so on back for generations. And because they didn't know the sex of the baby, they didn't know what colour to paint it.

'Yellow?' Mike offered. 'That's sunny and sort of neutral.'

'It makes them look jaundiced,' Fran said doubtfully, and he chuckled.

'Not daffodil yellow. Something softer. A pale creamy primrose?'

So that was how it ended up, a lovely soft colour, and when she was thirty-six weeks, they bought a cot. They didn't assemble it, though. It was as if, by tacit agreement, they didn't want to push their luck. So it stayed in the room, propped up behind the door, and for the next three weeks they didn't look at it.

It was as if they were holding their breath, but every night Mike would hold her in his arms, cuddled together like spoons in a drawer, with his big, strong hand splayed tenderly over the baby, soothing it with gentle strokes when it kicked and squirmed.

It had hiccups, too, which made them chuckle once they realised it was nothing to worry about.

And then Fran woke one morning tired and grumpy, and the house was a tip. So she cleaned it, furiously, from end to end, which frankly would have been stupidly ambitious when she hadn't been pregnant, she thought in a rare pause when she'd changed their sheets and vacuumed the bedroom floor, but she just had to do it, because the baby was coming soon and it couldn't be brought back to a place hanging with cobwebs.

Well, one cobweb, and it wasn't exactly hanging, but it was soon banished with a flick of the feather duster, and after another half-hour the dining table was gleaming, the old mahogany nourished within an inch of its life.

And she ached. Lord, how she ached! She straightened

up, the beeswax in her hand, and arched her back. She'd done too much, she thought. Much too much.

Time to sit down for a while.

Except she couldn't sit down, because it was so horrendously uncomfortable suddenly, and then she had one of those lightbulb moments and couldn't believe she'd been so stupid. She'd watched Brodie do just the same thing only two weeks ago, dragging her bedding round and round to get it comfortable, before finally settling down and giving birth to three puppies.

And she hadn't even realised she was doing the same thing!

She phoned Mike on his mobile. 'Um, can you come?'

'Sure—is supper ready?'

'Not exactly.'

He must have picked up on the tone of her voice, because he swore softly and she could hear him running. 'I'm on my way,' he said, and five minutes later he burst into the kitchen and found her standing leaning over the sink, a pool at her feet, panting.

'Fran?'

'Mind the floor,' she warned, worried he'd slip.

'What have you spilt?'

'I haven't. My waters have broken.'

'Oh, God.' He went pale, then lifted her out of the way and scrubbed his hands. 'I'd better take you to hospital now. Are you having contractions?'

'Um, sort of— Ah-h-h!'

It poleaxed her. It was the first time she'd felt anything other than a horrendous ache, but this was different. This was strong, and powerful, much bigger than her, and it took her over completely.

'Fran?'

'Bed,' she said through gritted teeth. 'Now.'

And Mike peered down at her, stopped flapping and turned into the father, stockman and one-time-maybe vet that he was, scooped her up and carried her up the stairs.

He dumped her on the edge of the bed, grabbed the plastic sheet they'd had for Sophie out of the airing cupboard, spread it over the mattress, covered it in thick, soft towels and lifted her into the middle of it.

She couldn't move, couldn't do anything to help him, but she didn't need to. He was doing fine, his smile reassuring, his hands slow and steady and confident as he stripped off her wet underwear.

'In a bit of a hurry, I think,' he said, rubbing her back gently and smiling at her.

She suddenly realised why the livestock trusted him so much, why his cows were so content and relaxed around him.

'I've called an ambulance,' he told her, but they both knew she wasn't going anywhere till she'd had the baby, and she felt a great peace steal over her. Generations of his family had been born here, in this room, and their baby would be the next in line.

'Help me out of my clothes,' she said, struggling to get out of them. She didn't know why, she just wanted to get rid of them, get rid of anything that wasn't natural, anything tight, anything constricting that would come between her and nature, because nature was taking her over and she was following her instincts blindly.

Mike eased the dress over her head, pulled off her

T-shirt, unclipped her bra and took it off, then drew her naked body into his arms and held her, rubbing her back through another contraction.

'I need to push,' she said a minute later, shoving him out of the way and struggling to her knees. 'Now!'

She couldn't have done it without him. She locked her hands around the back of his neck and hung on him, whimpering, and he knelt there in front of her and cradled her, then turned her so she was lying over the pillows, hanging on to the headboard for dear life while he concentrated at the business end, and as the baby let out a lusty howl, she turned and sagged back onto the bed, her empty arms outstretched.

Mike lifted their son, slippery and shuddering with rage, and put him into her waiting arms. 'It's a boy,' he said, his voice unsteady, and his hand came out, trembling, and he brushed the back of his knuckles gently over the soft, soft skin. 'We've got a boy, Fran. A son.' And his tears welled over and splashed onto her hand.

She stared down at them, the tears he'd shed, and the child they'd made together, the child they'd feared they'd never have, and she looked up at him, her own eyes flooded with tears.

'Come here,' she said, and he covered them both with the quilt, lay down beside them and drew them into his arms. The baby was nuzzling now, and she looked up at Mike helplessly. 'I don't know how to do this,' she confessed.

'Yes, you do. Remember the classes?'

And wrapping his big hand round his son's tiny head, he steered him in the right direction, brushed his cheek against her nipple, and as his mouth opened instinctively, Mike pressed him firmly against her and she felt the baby start to suckle.

'Oh! It's so strong!' she whispered, and stared down at him in wonder. 'Oh, Mike. He's beautiful.'

'He is. Incredible. Amazing. Our little miracle.'

His tiny fingers were splayed over Fran's breast, the transparent nails so small she could barely see them, but he was strong, a real fighter. He was suckling hard, his tiny rosebud mouth making little sucking noises, and she looked up at Mike and laughed softly.

'He's got his father's appetite,' she said, and Mike chuckled and hugged her closer.

'We haven't talked about names,' she said, remembering their reluctance to take that much for granted.

'Sophie has,' he confessed with a groan. 'She's been nagging me. She's had hundreds of ideas, but her favourite seems to be Thomas.'

'Thomas. I like that. Thomas Trevellyan. Sounds good.'

'I think so.'

She stroked his tiny cheek. 'I think we ought to let your sister name you, little man, don't you? She'll be so excited. You have to tell her, Mike.'

'Not until we've got you sorted out,' he said, easing away from her. 'The ambulance is here. I'll talk to her later.'

'Daddy!'

'Hello, pickle!' Mike scooped Sophie up into his arms and hugged her. 'How's my favourite girl?'

'I'm fine—Daddy, where's Fran? I've got something really special to show her. Fran! Look!' she yelled, catching sight of her. Fran hugged her close and took the little box Sophie was thrusting at her eagerly.

'It's a model—I made it at school!' she said. 'Look, it's Brodie and her puppies!'

'So it is,' Fran said, smiling down at the little model nestling in its bed of cotton wool. 'It's lovely. Give it to your daddy, then.'

'It's not for him, it's for the baby. Can I see him? I'm dying to see him. I can't believe Mummy made me wait *two whole days*!'

She was beside herself with excitement and, taking her by the hand, Fran looked up at Kirsten, still in the car. 'Coming in?'

She shook her head and smiled. 'I'll see him when I pick her up on Sunday,' she said, and drove away, leaving them with Sophie.

Fran led her through the kitchen, past Brodie and her three little puppies all snuggled up together in her basket, into the sitting room to where Sophie's brand-new little brother was lying sleeping in his crib.

'Oh, he's tiny!' she said in a stage whisper. 'Much smaller than Millie. Daddy, he's just like you! All that black hair—and he's got your nose!'

'Poor kid,' Mike said with a proud grin, wrapping his arms round Fran and hugging her close.

'There's nothing wrong with your nose,' Fran told him, turning and kissing the tip of it with a smile. 'Nothing at all. And there won't be anything wrong with Thomas's either. It's just a bit squashed, but I'm sure he'll grow into it.'

'I'm sure he will,' Mike said, staring down at his

with an expression of wonder and love so profound it brought tears to Fran's eyes.

'Can I hold him?'

'Of course. Sit down.'

Sophie sat on the sofa, with Fran next to her just in case, and Mike slipped his big hands gently under his son's small body and lifted him, resting him carefully on Sophie's lap.

'Hello, Thomas,' she whispered, and kissed her little brother gently on his forehead. His eyes fluttered open and he stared at her, and they were both transfixed.

It was magical, Fran thought as Mike sat down beyond Sophie and put his arm around them all. Perfect.

Then Sophie looked up, her eyes shining and her smile as bright as the sun, and said, 'We're a proper family now.'

And Brodie, wandering in to see what was going on, rested her head on Sophie's knee and thumped her tail in agreement…

MAKING MEMORIES

CHAPTER ONE

THE little shop was busy. It was good, Max thought, to see such support for a tiny rural supermarket. It implied a thriving community—not that he would be part of it for long. He wasn't part of anything for long these days.

Stifling a pang of regret, he went in, grabbed a basket and threw in a few basic essentials. Bread, butter, milk, cheese, tomatoes, a local paper, marmalade for breakfast, and biscuits for late-night snacking. Chocolate biscuits, for a change, a housewarming present to himself.

He gave a wry snort, went round the corner of the aisle and tripped over something small and soft and indignant.

His basket went flying, he crashed into the magazine stand and scattered the contents wildly. Muttering a quiet oath, he bent and scooped up an armful of machine knitting patterns and gardening periodicals, then lifted his eyes to see what he'd fallen over and met the worried gaze of a small boy.

Good grief, he was so like his nephew! All eyes, lurking with mischief and now distinctly worried—because he had been playing with a toy car in the middle of the aisle when Max had fallen over him.

He smiled, and the child gave him a tentative smile in return. 'Oops,' Max said in a conspiratorial stage whisper, and the boy giggled. Had they got away with it?

'Are you all right?' he asked, and the boy nodded.

'I banged my hand.'

'I'm sorry. I wasn't looking.'

He stood up, dusting off his grubby little knees. "S OK. Doesn't hurt.'

Max put the magazines back, grabbed his basket and looked up, just as a young woman came round the corner.

'Harry? Are you all right?'

She bent down, her hair falling over her face, and Max's heart jolted.

Don't be a fool, he told himself in disgust. You think every woman between twenty and fifty looks like her.

And then she stood up, and he felt the colour drain from his cheeks. He straightened, the basket dangling forgotten at his side, his eyes locked with hers.

'Annie?' he said hoarsely, and then he looked again at the boy, so like his nephew it was uncanny, and knew with a shock that took his breath away that this beautiful, healthy, mischievous child was his son.

Annie wanted to run. She wanted to grab Harry and leg it, out of the shop, into the car, miles away where he couldn't find them. Anything rather than stand there and explain, in front of Mrs Bootle and the rest of her cronies, just what this man meant to her.

And so she did the only thing left open to her. She met his eyes, dragged in a deep breath and said, 'Hello, Max.'

He looked hardly any different, she thought absently.

Older, of course, but weren't they all? Harry had been a mere embryo the last time he'd been in the vicinity of his father. Scarcely that. In fact, Max's contribution to his son had probably still been swimming at the time.

Anna dragged Harry to his feet.

'Excuse us. We have a lot to do.' She turned, heading for the door, and Mrs Bootle's voice followed her.

'Don't forget your shopping, Anna!'

Muttering words Harry didn't know about under her breath, she turned back to the checkout, snatched up her carrier bag and made for the door again, her son trailing behind her.

A shadow fell across her path, and her way was suddenly blocked.

'I think we have some catching up to do,' he said in a soft voice that still sent shivers down her spine.

Did he know? Had he realised about Harry, or was he talking about them? It didn't matter. Either way, she wasn't talking—not after what he'd done to her.

She forced herself to meet his eyes—startling eyes, denim blue eyes that matched the jeans he was wearing and found an echo in her son's own eyes. She thought they were the most beautiful eyes she'd ever seen—and she'd hoped never to see them again.

'I don't think so,' she replied frostily. 'I can't think of a single thing I want to say to you that wouldn't consign me straight to hell. Please, move out of my way.'

He hesitated, his eyes so like Harry's searching hers, and deep within them she thought she saw a flicker of something that could have been pain.

Then he moved, stepping aside to let her pass, and she

felt his eyes on her back all the way across the square, until she rounded the corner out of sight.

She let out her breath in a ragged sigh, and suddenly became aware of Harry, tugging her hand.

'You're hurting me,' he said petulantly, and she realised she had his wrist in a death-like grip.

She released it, crouching down and smoothing back his dark blond hair, another legacy from his father. 'Sorry, darling. I forgot what I was doing.' She hesitated, looking up her front path just feet away. She had an idea. 'Shall we go and see if Grannie's in?'

Harry started to whinge, a sure sign that he was tired after a busy day at nursery school, and Anna realised with resignation that she was going to have to go home and couldn't escape.

However, she felt strangely reluctant. It was almost as if she could still feel Max's eyes on her, watching her, following her.

She turned, scanning the edge of the square, but there was no one to be seen. At least, no one like him, tall, broad, dressed in denim jeans and a cool chambray shirt, with sun-tipped hair and eyes that could caress at one minute and cut holes in steel in the next.

She slipped her key into the lock, went through the door and closed it softly behind them. The cat ran to greet them, trotting down the stairs with a staccato 'Mreouw!'. Harry scooped him up.

'Want some juice and a biscuit?' she offered her son's departing back, and Harry nodded as he sauntered towards the sitting room.

'Two,' he said.

'One.'

'Two.'

Seconds later the television was on, and she trailed into the kitchen with her shopping, put the kettle on and sank down at the table, her head in her hands.

Max Carter was in town—and she was in big trouble, unless he decided to go quietly away and leave them in peace.

Somehow she doubted it, and the very thought sent shivers up her spine. Almost five years, she thought numbly. Five years without a word, without a murmur, and then he turns up out of the blue, on the other side of the country.

She tried to remember if she'd told him where her parents lived, but she didn't think so. They hadn't talked much. Their relationship had been wild and wicked and based on instinct and had lasted a grand total of three weeks. She'd given her heart to him, and he'd absconded with it, leaving her pregnant and alone. There had been little time for niceties of social exchange.

So what on earth was he doing here, in Wenham Market?

Causing trouble, that was a sure bet. It was one thing Max Carter did as easily as breathing.

And Anna's life would never be the same again.

It got worse. She hadn't imagined it could, of course, but, then, she'd reckoned without the tinkering and mischievous hand of fate.

He was working at the practice, as a locum.

Terrific. She'd be thrust into his company umpteen times a day, forced to work with him whether she liked it or not, and her only consolation was that it was a distinctly temporary post until Suzanna had had her baby and came back to work.

He was in a meeting with the other doctors, fortunately, and so she grabbed a cup of coffee, picked up a handful of notes and went into her treatment room. She could hide, at least, until later.

Her first patient—fate muscling in on the act, again—was one of Suzanna's, a man with a history of slight chest pain. Just her luck, the trace was abnormal, and so she had to take it in to Max immediately.

She debated seeing one of the other doctors, but that wasn't fair to them. With a resigned sigh she knocked on his door and popped her head round.

'Excuse me, Dr Carter—could I have a word?'

He gave her an unreadable look, stood up and stepped outside the door, pulling it to.

'On Friday you wouldn't talk to me,' he reminded her, his voice deadly quiet and edged with reproach.

'Today I have to,' she said acidly, thrusting the notes and the trace at him. 'Mr Jenks—history of mild intermittent chest pain. I thought you ought to see his ECG.'

He scanned it and frowned. 'I'd better see him—can you ask him to get himself fitted in?'

'Sure.' She turned on her heel and walked away, conscious of the holes seeming to burn in the back of her shoulders as he watched her. She went round the corner of the corridor, sagged against the wall and drew a deep breath.

Her knees felt like jelly, her heart was pounding and she'd lay odds her ECG trace would be highly abnormal as well. Darn the man! How *dare* he turn up and throw her life into confusion?

She shrugged away from the wall, opened the door of her treatment room and went in.

'Hello, Mr Jenks,' she said with a smile. 'I've spoken to Dr Carter, who's taken over from Dr Korrel while she's on maternity leave, and he'll see you shortly. If you ask at Reception, they'll give you a number and fit you in, so you can chat over the result with him—all right?'

He nodded and stood up, looking thoughtful. 'Bad, is it?' he asked.

'I'm not a doctor,' she told him honestly, avoiding answering the question directly. 'He'll go through the trace with you and explain it and set your mind at rest, I'm sure.'

'All right, thank you, Sister,' Mr Jenks said, and went out to arrange his appointment.

Absently Anna unrolled clean paper onto the couch, tore off the used section and put it in the bin, and tidied up the ECG machine. Should she have told him more? Probably not. She didn't know how Max would handle it, or if he'd refer him to a cardiologist. It wasn't her place to discuss the result with patients, just to do the test and pass it all on.

Nevertheless, he'd been right—it was bad. Worse than his symptoms indicated.

She sighed, picked up the notes of the next patient and pressed the call button that buzzed and flashed a light by her name in the waiting room. Max could deal with Mr Jenks. That was why he was there, and he may as well earn his keep.

The morning went. That was all she could say about it. It didn't drag, but it didn't fly, and the whole time she was conscious of the presence, just round the corner, of the man who single-handedly had altered the entire course of her life.

Her last patient dealt with, and nothing left to do in her

room, no further reason she could find to hide, she went back out to the office and bumped straight into him.

Blast. She'd hoped he would still be doing a surgery, but no such luck. She glared at him, just as he lifted his head and met her eyes, and then he smiled at her, a twisted, wry smile, and her whole world tipped upside down.

How could she still feel like this about him? After the way he'd walked out, how could she possibly still fall for that lazy, sexy, wicked mouth and those stunning baby blues?

She just wanted to flee, but it wasn't going to be that easy. David Fellows, the senior partner, put his arm round her shoulders and cut off her escape. 'Ah, Anna,' he boomed in his patronising and slightly irritating manner. 'Come and meet our locum, Max Carter. Max, this is Anna Young, one of our highly valuable and skilled team of practice nurses.'

'We've met,' they said in unison. Max's voice was quiet, matter-of-fact. Hers was—oh, Lord, bitter. He was turning her into a shrew, and she wasn't like that.

Tears stung her eyes and she turned away, heading for the sanctuary of her room again, but she couldn't stay in there all day and she knew it. She went home for lunch, ignoring the deep, slightly gruff voice that called her name, and headed across the square and round the corner with her head down.

He followed her, of course, arriving at her front door almost as she did, so she had no opportunity to slip inside and shut it in his face.

Instead, she turned on him. 'What do you want with me?' she asked, a touch of frenzy in her voice. She steadied herself with a huge effort. 'Why are you here? What do you want?'

'You know why I'm here—covering for Suzanna Korrel.

As to what I want…' He reached out and lifted a tendril of hair which had escaped from her braid, and twirled it idly around his finger. His eyes locked with hers, the message clear, sending shivers of dreadful anticipation through her traitorous body. 'I'd like to know about my son.'

His son? Anna closed her eyes, an icy chill washing over her. So he did know. And very likely, then, had tracked her down.

'What makes you think he's your son?' she asked, clutching at straws.

'The fact that he has my eyes? My father's eyes? My brother's eyes? My nephew's eyes? He's the right sort of age, he looks like me—I would think that's pretty conclusive.'

She turned, opened the door and went in. 'You lost all rights to know him when you walked out on me,' she told him bluntly. 'As far as I'm concerned, he's *my* son, and he doesn't have a father.'

She pushed the door to, but it wouldn't close. A large well-polished masculine shoe was stuck in the crack. She debated slamming the door hard against it to crush it, but thought it more likely that the door would break.

She dropped her forehead against the wood and sighed. 'Please, Max, leave me alone,' she pleaded wearily. 'You can't just waltz back into my life after five years and expect to be welcomed with open arms. Now get your foot out of the door and go!'

Her voice cracked on the last word, and after a second the shoe disappeared. 'I'm sorry, Annie,' he said softly, and then the door closed quietly and she heard the slow, measured stride of his retreat.

Tears scalded her eyes and spilt down on the floor, her head in her hands, the cat rubbing self-indulgently against her shin. He'd just sounded so—what? Forlorn? Penitent? Hopeless?

She sighed thoughtfully. That didn't gel with her reasons for his arrival in her life. Was it possible she was wrong? Was he here just by coincidence?

Or was he just apologising because he wasn't going to let it rest? Because he had no intention of leaving her alone, and wanted his son?

Panic washed over her. What if he wanted to take Harry? What if he decided to go for custody? Or, worse still, kidnap him?

Terror gripped her, and she struggled to her feet and picked up the phone with trembling hands. She rang the nursery school, and was told Harry had gone home with his grandmother, as usual.

She sighed with relief, and told them that under no circumstances was Harry to leave the school with anyone except her or her mother, even with written permission.

'His father has turned up in our lives,' she explained to Carol, the young woman in charge of the school. She hated doing this but was so worried for Harry's safety that she felt she had no choice.

'What does he look like? What's his name?' Carol asked, and Anna hesitated. He was going to be part of the community for some months. Was it fair to him—or her—to discuss this painful secret?

'Max Carter,' she said eventually. 'He's…' How could she describe him? 'He's just like Harry,' she told her. 'Fair hair, blond streaks, bright blue eyes…' Sexy mouth, sinful black lashes, crooked grin calculated to decimate the defences of the most hardened man-hater.

Stick to the facts, she thought. 'About six foot, lean build—perhaps a little on the thin side,' she said, and realised with a jolt of surprise that he'd lost weight. 'Carol, don't say anything,' she added hastily. 'I don't want it getting out, and Harry doesn't know anything about him.'

'OK. Look, are you all right?'

She nodded, then remembered Carol couldn't see her. 'Yes, I'm fine,' she lied. 'I must go, I have to ring my mother.'

She pressed the cut-off button on the phone, dialled her mother and waited. It rang twice, then there was a clatter, and a little, high-pitched voice came over the phone. 'H'llo?'

She couldn't help the smile of relief. 'Hello, Harry, it's Mummy. Is Grannie there, darling?'

'Yup—Grannie!'

She held the phone away from her ear, rubbed it ruefully and switched sides. 'Mum?'

'Hello, darling. Everything all right?'

She suppressed the urge to laugh hysterically. 'Not really. I don't have time to explain, but watch Harry, OK? Don't let him out of your sight, and don't let anybody take him anywhere, no matter how plausible.'

There was a long silence, then her mother sighed softly. 'I take it he's turned up?'

Bless her. She never had to explain anything to her mother. 'Yes. I'll talk later. I have to grab some lunch and go back to work. Love you.'

Lunch was a piece of burnt toast which had got jammed in the toaster, a mouthful of cheese and a raspberry and blackberry yoghurt—always the last to go because she hated the seeds getting stuck in her teeth and Harry, predictably, had had the last strawberry one.

She had a glass of water because there wasn't time to make tea, and headed back across the square to the practice.

Max was sitting outside on the bench in the sun, eating chips out of the wrapper and chatting to an elderly man, one of her less savoury regulars.

'Hello, Sister. You keepin' well?' Fred asked with his singsong, wheezy crackle.

'Fine, thank you, Fred. Yourself?'

'Oi'll do. Oi was just tellin' young Dr Car'er 'ere about my gout. Tha's got so much worse recently—'

'And it's nothing to do with all the booze, of course, is it?' she teased.

He looked shocked and pained. 'Oi ha'n't had a drop in weeks!' he protested, but Anna wasn't fooled.

'Pull the other, Fred. Mrs Bootle told me on Friday that you'd just been in for another bottle of cooking sherry.'

He scowled at her. 'Interferin' old trout,' he grumbled. 'I was going to make a trifle. She ain't got no business spreadin' malicious rumours 'bout me, shrivelled old bag.'

Anna laughed. 'I'm sure she loves you, too, Fred.' She went into the surgery, proud with herself for not once meeting Max's eye during that whole exchange, and made her preparations for the antenatal clinic.

Then a hideous thought struck her.

Suzanna always did the antenatal clinic on Mondays.

And Max was Suzanna's locum…

There was something strangely ordinary about working with Max. Both professionals in their own field, they just got on with the job and worked alongside each other without a hiccup.

How odd, when inside she was seething with doubts and fears and insecurities. Still, as long as he was in his consulting room with a patient he wasn't trying to abscond with Harry, which gave her a small element of comfort in the midst of her confusion.

Not that she thought he really would, but she'd only known him for such a short time, and now he was back in her life without warning, and wanted to talk. About custody?

She realised she wouldn't know what he was doing unless she talked to him—and that thought filled her with so many emotions she didn't know what way to turn.

Max wondered how he was going to be able to concentrate on his antenatal patients with Anna moving quietly around nearby, checking weights and testing urine and taking blood pressure, while he checked the lie of the baby and chatted to the mothers about their problems.

He'd wondered if any of them would object to having a man taking the clinic when they'd been used to Suzanna, but there didn't seem to be any adverse reaction. In fact, it was probably going to turn into the most enjoyable part of the week, he thought wryly. At least the women were there because they were well, and not because they were sick.

That made a refreshing change to the usual run of surgery time.

He caught sight of Anna through the open door as his patient left, and his gut clenched. Her hair was back in order, severely subdued by the French plait, with lighter strands at the front where the sun had caught it, setting off the smooth, clear skin and bright eyes.

She was lovely. Not fat, not thin, with curves in all the right places and a supple grace that he remembered well…

He groaned softly and pressed the buzzer for his next patient. He couldn't allow himself to think about her like that. Not now. Not with little Harry in the wings.

Maybe never.

'Annie?'

'It's Anna.'

He sighed quietly and leant against the wall by the back door of the practice. She'd come outside with her tea, and he'd followed her. Typical. Now she'd have to scald herself drinking it and go back inside.

'Don't run away. I only want to talk.'

'Well, I don't,' she said flatly, throwing her hot tea over a rose bush with a twinge of guilt. She pushed past him, irritated by the shiver of awareness that skimmed through her at the slight contact.

'Later, then.'

'Try when hell freezes,' she muttered under her breath, and went back to her room. She had a few patients in for routine checks, and then she could collect Harry and go home. It was none too soon.

'What does he want?'

Anna shrugged, and trailed a spoon over the top of her tea, bursting the little bubbles. 'He wants to know about Harry,' she said quietly, but her voice was vibrating with emotion. 'He thinks he can just breeze back into my life, persecute me at work and hound me at home.'

'What makes you think he even knows about Harry?' her mother asked.

'Because they've met—he fell over him, in the shop! He could hardly fail to notice him, and then I picked Harry up, and he looked at us—of course he's made the connection, and, anyway, he's told me he wants to know about his son. Trust me, Mum, he knows. Even if he didn't know before he arrived in Wenham Market, he knows now—and he wants to know more.'

Her mother shrugged philosophically. 'Why don't you talk to him, then? Get it over with—show him the photos, the videos of the birthday parties, the little clay things he's made. Bore him to death with the Mother's Day cards and the drawings and the pasta pictures—'

'I don't want to!' she said vehemently. 'It's nothing to do with him! None of it's anything to do with him!'

'Except that Harry is his son.'

She glared at her mother. 'Harry is the biological fruit of his loins, mother. He is *not* his son!'

One eloquent eyebrow arched expressively. 'Strikes me it's one and the same thing. You lost touch. Now he's back—'

'And what if he wants custody? What if he tries to take him from me?' she asked, desperation clawing at her.

Sarah Young tutted reproachfully. 'There isn't a judge in the land who would give him custody—don't be absurd. Is he married?'

'Married?' she echoed incredulously. How odd. She hadn't even given it a thought! 'I don't know,' she murmured. 'He didn't say.'

Her mother took the teaspoon away from her and patted her hand. 'Stop playing with your tea and drink it. Max isn't going to do anything. All he wants to do is talk.'

Anna sighed. 'I wish I could believe you, but I don't know him. I know hardly anything about him. He was a moment of foolishness, Mum, and I have no idea what kind of man he is or what he wants. All I know is that he walked out on me without any kind of explanation, and now he's back and I can't trust him. He could do anything—anything at all.'

She met her mother's eyes. 'Are you busy tonight? Could we stay for supper?'

'Because he knows where you live?'

She looked away. 'You think I'm being silly, don't you?' she said in a soft voice.

'I think you aren't giving him time to explain what he wants. I think that's a little unfair—'

'Unfair? *Unfair!* After what he did to me?' She pushed her tea away and stood up. 'I give up. You clearly don't want to see it from my viewpoint. You can't see how scared I am that I'll lose Harry—'

'You won't lose Harry—'

'I will if he kidnaps him,' she said flatly, and turned away, staring out of the window, her arms wrapped round her waist, hugging herself.

The words hung in the air.

Max sat on the front door step for ages. She'd left the surgery before him, and wasn't home. At least, if she was home, she wasn't answering her bell. Still, it was a pleasant summer evening. He'd gone home and changed into something more relaxed, because he'd thought he'd go for a walk, get to know the neighbourhood.

And he'd ended up here, waiting. Ridiculous. He'd start attracting attention, and then she'd get mad with him. That wouldn't help at all.

He stood up, just as the next-door neighbour came out of her house. 'She's not back yet—I expect she's at her parents'. Can I take a message?'

He smiled and leant over the honeysuckle hedge, his hand extended. 'Hello. I'm Dr Carter—I work with her. I've taken over from Dr Korrel while she's on maternity leave. I just wanted a quick word.'

The neighbour shook his hand and moved closer, relaxing her guard. 'Jill Fraser. Dr Korrel's my doctor—I expect I'll be seeing you with one of my brood in the not-too-distant future, if our track record holds.'

She looked down the road. 'Why don't you go over to her mother's? They often stay late. I'm sure she won't mind, if it's important. It's the big Georgian house on the left, after all the other houses. There's a field, and then it's set back. Painted white—you can't miss it.'

He thanked her, and set off down the road, enjoying the feel of the sun on his face and the scented air. People were pottering in their gardens, watering hanging baskets and pots and tubs, tweaking weeds, picking roses. It was peaceful and domesticated and he envied them.

They smiled at him, said 'Lovely evening!' and things like that, and one or two recognised him and stopped him for a chat.

Then the houses petered out, and the lane narrowed, and

then on the left, after a field full of fluffy, grazing sheep, was the house he was looking for.

It was a pretty house, not huge, but fairly substantial, the proportions elegant, the front garden deep with a gravelled turning circle in front of the house. He crunched over the gravel, rang the doorbell and waited.

A dog barked and was shushed, and then he heard the scrape of a key in the lock and the door swung inwards, revealing a softer, more mature version of Anna—the sort of woman his Anna would turn into given another twenty years. It was a pleasing thought.

'Mrs Young?'

She looked at him, searching his eyes. He obviously passed some sort of test, because she extended her hand. 'Sarah—and you must be Max,' she said calmly. 'Come on in. Anna's in the kitchen. We were just about to sit down to supper—why don't you join us?'

CHAPTER TWO

ANNA couldn't believe her ears. She'd eavesdropped blatantly at the kitchen door, worried that it might be Max, that he might have followed her here, and her mother was letting him in! *For supper!*

Sarah, indeed. She slammed the cutlery down on the table and turned to face the door, uncaring that hostility blazed from her usually gentle grey eyes. 'What the hell do you think you're doing here?' she snarled furiously. 'How *dare* you—?'

'Anna! Max is my guest, and you will treat him with respect—'

'What, like he treated me with respect? He walked out on me when I was pregnant—or have you conveniently forgotten that?'

Max intervened, a pained look on his face. 'At the time I had no idea—'

'And you didn't hang around long enough to find out, did you? Tell me—how many other times have you done this, Max? How many other little bastards are there wandering the streets, with your blue eyes and sexy smile?'

'Was that a compliment?' he asked wryly.

Sarah chipped in. 'Could we, please, discuss this rationally?' she pleaded.

'There's nothing to discuss. I'm leaving. Where's Harry?'

'Out checking sheep with your father. Anna, darling, sit down. Let Max have his say—ah, there they are now. George, come in. We've got a visitor—Max Carter.'

The name meant nothing to her father, but his face stopped George Young in his tracks. Years of diplomacy, however, prevented him reacting with anything but dignity. He nodded his head. 'Max. With you in a minute—Harry and I need to clean up a little bit. Come on, son, let's wash these hands.'

He hoisted the child up to the sink, propped him against the edge with his body and leant over him, soaping and rinsing until all four hands were clean. Then they dried them, and Harry turned and looked up at Max.

'You fell over me,' he said, recognising him for the first time. 'I got a bruise.'

'So've I,' Max said wryly, watching him with a painful intensity.

Anna glared at him. 'Don't you dare say *anything*,' she muttered under her breath for Max's ears alone.

He turned to her, his eyes curiously gentle. 'Don't worry, Anna,' he said softly. 'I'm not here to make trouble.'

It seemed he wasn't. He was charm itself, smiling and laughing at Harry's stories, engaging him in conversation and hanging on his every word.

And Harry adored him.

At least, he enjoyed the attention, and Anna kept trying to catch Max's eye to get him to cool it, but he assiduously avoided her attempts. It infuriated her, but she was helpless to say anything without triggering Harry's abundant curiosity, and so she sat there, and watched father and son together, and a great wave of regret and sadness washed over her for all the might-have-beens that Max had thrown away when he'd left her.

Then finally the meal was over, and Harry dragged Max into the sitting room to meet the dogs while Sarah made coffee. Anna followed with her father, unwilling to leave them alone together for as much as a second.

'Harry, go and ask Grannie if she can find that box of chocolates, would you, son?' George suggested, and Harry took off like a rocket. Her father dropped into his favourite chair with a slight groan, and stretched his legs.

'So, Max, what have you been doing for the past five years?' he asked cordially, settling back in his chair.

Anna held her breath. Was he married? Divorced? Widowed, even?

'Nothing terribly exciting,' Max said in a strangely calm voice. He was fondling the ears of one of the dogs, who was propped against his leg like a faithless hussy, grinning. 'I've done locum work in several practices—done some training courses in surgery and obstetrics, that sort of thing.'

'Never thought of settling down?'

Something flickered in his eyes, but then he leant back in the corner of the settee and gave a lazy smile. 'Maybe one day,' he said easily. 'For now I'm quite happy with variety.'

'And no responsibility,' Anna said under her breath.

'I have responsibilities,' Max corrected. 'Every patient that I see is my responsibility. What I don't have is ties.'

'And where does Harry fit into the great scheme of

things?' she asked rashly, watching the door in case Harry came back in.

Max hesitated, something like regret flickering over his face. 'I don't know. I'd like to see him, obviously, but I don't think it's necessary for him to know exactly who I am. I would like to contribute towards his upbringing, though.'

'Conscience money?' Anna said bitterly.

Her father stood up and left the room, closing the door quietly behind him, and Max sighed and ran his hand through his hair.

'Annie, I don't want to fight with you. I didn't know I had a son until last Friday. I'm still feeling stunned. I'd like to know about him—about his birth, his early years, his first steps…' His voice was suddenly gruff, and he looked down at the dog, still patiently waiting for more attention. He tickled her ears again.

'I don't want you to feel threatened,' he went on after a moment. 'I can't take any real part in his life, for all sorts of reasons, but I would like to help you out with money, and I'd like to keep in touch and know how he's doing and what he's up to—that sort of thing.'

'So you want all the cream and none of the hard work, is that it?' she said, perversely furious that he didn't want to be involved in Harry's life.

'The cream?' he said with a trace of sadness. 'Is that what you call it? Knowing I have a son who doesn't know me, who will never know me as his father? Never know the joy of sharing his successes and the pain of standing back and letting him fail, if that's what's needed? Never sharing those special times, those late-night cuddles and quiet chats? You call that the cream?' He gave a humourless laugh. 'I would call that the crumbs from the table, Annie, but I know it's all I can have.'

'It's more than you deserve.'

He regarded her steadily. 'That's as may be. Whatever, will you allow me that? Will you tell me about him, share those early days and years with me, keep me in touch?'

'And in return you'll pay me to look after him. Is that it?'

He sighed shortly and stabbed his hands through his hair. 'I would contribute to his expenses whether you kept me in touch or not. It would just be nice to know how he's getting on.'

She let out her breath on a shaky sigh and stood up. 'I don't know. I'll show you pictures, tell you about him, but as for keeping in touch over the years—I don't know if I can do that. You hurt me, Max. I gave you everything I had to give, and you walked away. I don't know if I can face having you in my life again.'

He bowed his head. 'I'm sorry. You will never know how sorry I am.'

She snorted and walked to the door. 'I think it's time you went. I have to take Harry home and get him to bed. He can't have too many late nights during the week, he gets crabby and disgusting.'

'Like his mother,' Max said softly. 'You never were a morning person, were you, sweetheart?'

She stiffened at the endearment. 'Don't call me sweetheart. You lost all rights to call me that when you walked out. I'll tell you about your son, I'll share what I can of him with you while you're here, but that's all. No starting up where we left off, no thinking that you can use me and leave again. I won't have it. Do you understand?'

He stood up, crossing to stand behind her at the doorway. 'I understand, Annie. Probably more than you realise. And I'm sorry.'

He moved past her and went down the hall to the front door. 'Thank your mother for supper for me, please. It was very kind of her.'

And he let himself out of the door, leaving her standing in the hall, her mind in a turmoil. Could she cope with him? With being so near him, talking to him, sharing Harry's early moments?

Remembering the things she'd had to do alone, when he should have been there to share them with her?

The thought filled her with dread, but underneath it was a strand of hope, a useless, optimistic thread of anticipation and excitement.

No, she told herself sternly. You don't want anything to do with him.

Even if he is the only man you've ever loved…

It was typical of fate's little tricks that she was scheduled the following day for minor surgery with Max. Just what I need, she thought, being stuck in the same room as him working alongside him for hours!

Still, it could have been worse. There were only three patients, and the first was a relatively simple incision of a cyst. Despite her best attempt at detachment, she was nevertheless interested to see how well and how carefully he worked. He really did have skill, she realised, and wondered again why he was still working as a locum instead of settling down somewhere in a permanent post.

Except, of course, that would give him ties, she thought

bitterly. It still rankled that he didn't want to be part of Harry's life, and she conveniently forgot that just a short while before she'd been paranoid about him going for custody.

She forced herself to concentrate on their patient, and after Max had finished and stitched the little wound, she dressed it, cleaned up the little theatre and prepared it for the next patient.

'This one might be interesting,' Max said. 'A discharging sinus on a farmer's finger. He has a little shard of metal in it from an accident with machinery. It apparently healed and has now started swelling and discharging years later.'

'Is that Mr Bryant?' she asked, something prickling at the back of her mind.

'That's right. Why? Know him?'

'He's a friend of my father's. They farm next to us. I remember him doing it—a flywheel shattered and took off one of his fingers. This must be one of the ones that's left. Right, we're ready for him. Shall I go and get him?'

Max nodded, studying the notes. 'Please.'

She came back with Mr Bryant moments later, and Max shook his hand and introduced himself. 'Right, could we have a look at the offending digit?' he said with a smile.

'Sure. Here it is—I wouldn't have bothered, but every now and then it gets sore and infected, and, to be honest, Doc, it's a darned nuisance.'

He held out his hand, and Anna could see the great lump on the side of the tip of his finger. Half of the nail was missing, presumably lost in the original injury, and in the centre of the swelling was a nasty little black pit. Max pressed it gently, and it oozed.

'Right. Well, that looks straightforward enough. I've

had a look at the X-ray, and it seems to be just one piece of metal—here, can you see?' He pointed the tiny fragment out on the X-ray, up on the light-box on the wall. 'All we have to do is find it.'

Mr Bryant laughed. 'Hope you've got good eyesight, Doc.'

'Twenty-twenty,' he assured him, then said softly under his breath, 'especially my hindsight.'

'What was that?' Mr Bryant said, looking puzzled.

'I said I have special eyesight,' Max lied blithely, and injected the finger to numb it, before scrubbing and gowning in preparation for the operation.

Anna laid out the trolley, taking care with aseptic technique so as not to contaminate any of the sterile packs, and by the time the finger was numb they were all ready.

The little shard of metal proved surprisingly elusive, but after a few moments Max found it and produced it with a florish, like a conjurer with a rabbit.

'Right. That's the little blighter. Now all we need to do is clean up, and it should heal nicely all by itself. I'm not going to stitch it—this sort of thing needs to heal from the inside out. I'll ask Sister Young to dress it for you, and you'll need to come in and have the dressing changed every day for a week. By then it should be just about sorted. OK?'

'Excellent. Thank you, Doc. Lovely job.'

Anna attended to the wound, all the time chattering to him about farming and how her father was and the price of lambs at the market and the state of the industry, and by the time he left Max was staring at her in amazement.

'What?' she said crossly. 'Don't you dare tell me I gossip.'

He laughed. 'I was just stunned by your social skills. You tell old Fred that he's still drinking and Mrs Bootle in the shop told you so, you know the price of lambs at the market and what old so-and-so down the road got from the organic butcher chappie, and I bet when Mrs Green comes in in a moment for her ingrowing toenail you know the names and ages of each of her grandchildren.'

'She doesn't have grandchildren. Tom's not old enough, and Rebecca's still at university—'

'I rest my case,' he said drily, and Anna gave a self-conscious laugh.

'OK, I give up,' she said, a touch of mockery in her voice. 'Blame it on continuity. It might be something to do with the fact that I've been here off and on for the past thirty years. You might like to try it some time. Staying in one place has a lot to recommend it.'

She stripped off her gloves, bundled up all the disposable waste and put it in the yellow clinic waste bin.

Max watched her silently, making her antsy and nervous. 'Don't you have something useful to do, like look up Mrs Green's notes?' she asked acerbically.

One eyebrow arched expressively, but he turned to the paperwork on the desk and scanned it. 'She's on beta blockers,' he said thoughtfully. 'People sometimes get pincer nails with them. I wonder if that's what is wrong with her, or if she's got ordinary ingrowing toenails. The notes aren't very specific.'

Anna changed the paper over the couch, laid another trolley and turned to him. 'Shall I fetch her?'

'If it's not too much trouble,' he said mildly, and she pressed her lips together to hold back the retort and went out to find Mrs Green.

She limped across the waiting room, and Anna frowned

at her. 'You really are in a bad way, aren't you?' she said with sympathy.

'Oh, dear, don't talk about it! It's driving me mad. It's been getting worse and worse, but I've been ignoring it because Rebecca's home for the summer and I've been enjoying her company, but now I can't go anywhere with her and it's just ridiculous!'

'Don't worry, we'll soon have you sorted out. How's she getting on? Enjoying Liverpool?'

Mrs Green rolled her eyes. 'Oh, loves it! She says the social life is brilliant. Tom misses her, though. I didn't think he would because they fight all the time, but he's really enjoyed having her back for a while. I don't know what we'll do without her when she goes back.'

Mrs Green came to a halt just outside the door, and tugged at Anna's sleeve. 'This new man—Dr Carter. What's he like?' she whispered.

A total pain in the neck, she wanted to say, but professionalism prevailed. 'He's good,' she said truthfully. 'I'm sure you're in good hands.'

'Have you seen him do anything?'

She nodded. 'Yes—two ops this morning. He's very careful and thorough.'

Mrs Green relaxed visibly. 'Good,' she said in relief. 'I was so worried when I realised Suzanna had gone on maternity leave. I thought it wasn't for another week or so, but then I saw her in the shop yesterday and I was worried all night!'

Anna smiled and patted her arm. 'No need to worry. He's fine. Come on in, I'll introduce you. I'm sure you'll get on like a house on fire.'

Even if I don't, she added to herself. Except they had once, of course. They'd got on too well, from the moment they'd first clapped eyes on each other in the surgery in Gloucestershire...

'Hi.'

Anna looked up, straight into the most stunning blue eyes she'd ever seen, and felt her heart crash against her ribs.

'Hi,' she replied, and wondered if it was just her imagination or if she really sounded that breathless. 'Can I help you?'

'Tantalising thought,' he murmured, a lazy, sexy smile teasing those sensuous lips. 'Actually, I'm looking for the senior partner. I'm Max Carter, the locum.'

She took his outstretched hand, and felt a jolt of electricity up her arm. 'Anna Young. I'm the practice nurse. Well, I am at the moment. I expect I'll be tealady in a minute. John's out on a call. Shall I put the kettle on and fill you in?'

He followed her into the tiny kitchen, his presence making the air so thick with tension that she could hardly breathe, and watched her as she made coffee for them both.

'So, what's it like here?' he asked as they sipped their drinks a moment later.

'Crazy,' she said with a laugh. 'Everyone's lovely. All you need is a sense of humour and you'll survive.'

He did more than survive. He fitted right in, and every time Anna emerged from her room he seemed to be there. On his third day, he invited her out for a drink. She went, and it was wonderful. They shared the same zany sense of fun, liked the same music, chose the same food from the bar snacks menu.

Later that week he asked her out for dinner, and took her to an intimate, bijou little restaurant in Cheltenham where they ate lobster and crêpes and drank too much wine and laughed until the tears ran down their cheeks.

Then they came out of the restaurant and Max hailed a taxi, and when they fell into it, giggling, he looked at her and said, 'Where to?'

Suddenly the laughter died, replaced by a blazing heat which had been simmering gently under the surface for the whole week. 'You could come back for coffee,' she offered.

He nodded, and she leant forwards and told the taxi driver her address. Five minutes later they were there, letting themselves into the once-elegant Georgian terraced house where she had a flat.

They didn't bother with the coffee. Instead, as the door closed behind them they went into each other's arms, and their mouths met in hungry, devouring kisses that left them both aching for more.

He stayed that night, and the night after, and the night after that. Then it was Monday, and he was on call, and he went—reluctantly—back to his own flat and stayed there for a couple of nights.

He was tired. They both were, hardly having slept for the previous nights, and in order to preserve their sanity and professional competence they agreed to stay in their own homes. In practice this meant one or other of them getting up and getting dressed in the middle of the night, and after a while they gave up again and resigned themselves to exhaustion, unless Max was on call.

Then he stayed alone at his flat, and Anna missed him the entire time. They'd become so close it seemed strange to sleep without him, and Anna couldn't imagine them ever living apart.

Then, during the third week, Max became a little distant. He seemed tired, more so than usual, and she sometimes caught a preoccupied expression on his face.

'Are you all right?' she asked him on one occasion.

He nodded. 'Yes, I'm fine. Just thinking about something.'

'A patient?'

He nodded. 'Yes, a patient,' he agreed.

'You shouldn't bring your work home,' she scolded gently, cuddling up to him. 'Want to talk about it?'

He shook his head. 'No. It's OK, really.' He turned his head and looked down at her, snuggled against his shoulder. 'Want to go to bed?'

She smiled. 'I always want to go to bed with you,' she teased.

His smile was thin and weary. 'I could do with sleeping,' he warned. 'Don't expect a wild night of passion.'

She chuckled and stood up, pulling him to his feet. 'You can sleep. There's always the morning.'

But in the morning he was gone when she woke, and she found him at work, peering at something down the microscope they used for quick checks on bloods and things.

'You sneaked off,' she grumbled gently, standing behind him and hugging him over the back of the chair.

'Sorry. Work to do,' he told her, still peering.

She let him go and went into the kitchen, putting the kettle on. When she came back out he was putting some samples into a path lab envelope. 'I just want to take these up to the lab,' he said, and left her there.

She shrugged, made herself some tea and curled up in

the corner, scanning through her notes for the morning surgery and mentally checking that she had the inoculations she was going to need. It was OK. Everything was fine, and she settled back and finished her tea and wondered what specimens he'd taken to the lab.

Odd, at that time of the day. Oh, well. Perhaps it was some histological sample he'd taken the day before. Maybe he was in a hurry for the result.

They went out for dinner again that night, and afterwards they went back to her flat.

He wasn't tired that night, she thought. Far from it. Their lovemaking reached new heights, and left them both shaken with the intensity of it.

'I love you,' she said softly, and his arms tightened convulsively.

'Anna,' he whispered.

He didn't say the little words, but she knew he meant them.

At least, she thought she did.

Then she woke in the morning to find him gone, a note from him propped up against the kettle. It filled her with foreboding, and she held it with trembling fingers for an age before she could open it.

Dear Anna,

By the time you see this I'll be gone. I'm sorry to leave you like this, but I can't stay. There are all sorts of reasons why I have to go, but I'll miss you, you've been a lot of fun. Don't have regrets. Life's too short for regrets. Just remember the good times.

Max

Not even 'love, Max'. Just 'Max'.

She screwed up the note and threw it in the bin, then, without even stopping to dress, she jumped in her car and drove to his flat. He was gone, a neighbour told her, peering curiously at her nightdress.

She went home, curled up in a chair and howled. Handfuls of soggy tissue later, she had a bath, got dressed and walked miles, ranting at him as she paced up and down the Cotswold hills in a fury of bitter recriminations and desperate longing.

He couldn't have gone—not for ever! How would she cope without him?

She phoned her mother and blurted out the whole sorry mess, and her mother gave her telephone hugs and said, 'Come home for the weekend.' So she did.

And there, lo and behold, was a vacancy for a practice nurse. Too gutted to stay in Cheltenham, she handed in her notice, moved back to Wenham Market and then discovered to her absolute horror that she was expecting a baby.

Anna deliberated for ages, then wrote a letter to Max and waited with bated breath for his reply.

It never came. All that came was her own letter, with RETURN TO SENDER—NOT KNOWN AT THIS ADDRESS stamped all over it.

She tried again, but the same thing happened.

She wrote to the locum agency that he'd come through, asking for a new forwarding address, but was told that he'd stopped working for them and there was no way to contact him.

So that was that. She had a baby on the way, no father on the horizon, a job she was about to have to give up. Without the love and support of her parents and the practice staff, she would have sunk without trace.

Then Harry was born, undoubtedly the best thing that had ever happened to her in the whole of her twenty-six years, and she put thoughts of Max on the side and concentrated on giving her baby the best start in life she could manage.

It was hard—impossibly hard at first—and financially always difficult, but she managed, and it had slowly grown easier. People had accepted her and Harry, and she'd felt very much a part of the community.

And it had been fine until last week, when Max had turned up again out of the blue and thrown her carefully ordered emotions into pandemonium.

He finished Mrs Green's foot, leaving her with just the central section of the nail so that the painful tightly curled edges were gone and wouldn't trouble her again. Anna bandaged the battered and bloody toe and reflected that she hadn't registered anything he had done.

She'd been miles away, reliving those wonderfully romantic moments in his arms, and it seemed almost intrusive of him and Mrs Green to be there. She'd tuned them out so absolutely that she wondered if she'd done anything stupid.

Apparently not, because Max said nothing, and he would have done. He didn't tend to hold back.

The rest of the day was routine and passed without incident, until she reached the end of her day. Then she found a note from Max in Reception.

Would like to come round tonight to see photos etc. Would nine o'clock be all right? That should give you time to put Harry to bed. Leave me a note to confirm.

M

Not even 'Max'. He was getting briefer, she thought drily. Soon he'd be signing things with a cross.

'Nine is fine. See you later. Anna.' Her reply was even more brief.

She went home, looked around and had a guilt-driven tidying fit. Then she shoved the vacuum round, rescued Harry's toys from the dust collector and wormed the cat, which took the hump and stalked off, tail twitching furiously.

'Bedtime,' she said to Harry at seven-thirty.

He whinged, grumbled and squirmed all the way up the stairs, through the bath and into bed, but in the end he fell asleep in seconds.

Then, just when she thought she might grab a moment to change and clean herself up, the doorbell rang.

She opened the door to find Max there, looking disgustingly appealing in a faded blue shirt, which matched the changing blue of his eyes, and a pair of jeans that did wicked and wholly unprintable things to his body.

Help, she thought, I'm going to be alone with him!

She took him into the sitting room, put on the overhead light on maximum and pulled out the baby albums, then headed for a chair. 'Here you go. Baby photos.'

He sat down next to her and took the albums, then lifted the first one. He opened the cover, stared at the pictures for a moment then closed his eyes.

'I'm sorry you had to go through it alone,' he said heavily.

'You could have been there, if you hadn't disappeared so effectively. I tried to write, but there was no getting through to you. Not known at this address and all that. Anyway, Mum was with me.'

He nodded, then looked down at the pictures again. She glanced across, and felt her face colour. He was looking at a picture of her breast-feeding the newborn Harry.

'I'd forgotten that one was in there,' she muttered, embarrassed that he should see something so personal.

'It's beautiful,' he said softly. 'I'm glad you breast-fed him. There's something so primitive—so erotic and right about it. I wish I could have seen it.'

'You could have seen it. All you had to do was stick around,' she reminded him—again.

He shook his head. 'No.' He turned the pages in silence, except for the odd question, and she could feel the tension radiating off him.

After a while he shut the albums and stood up. 'I think I'll call it a night, I'm tired. Mind if we do this again? I'd like to ask you more.'

She realised with a shock that it was after eleven o'clock.

'Sure. Not tomorrow, I've got something on. Maybe Thursday?'

His mouth moved automatically in a polite, social smile. 'That would be lovely,' he agreed, and turned away, but not before she'd seen the pain in his eyes.

He could have been there—he could have had it all, she reminded herself as she watched him walk away. He could have, and he'd chosen not to.

Well, having made the bed, he could lie in it, she thought

crossly, and tried not to remember the pain in his eyes or the weary set of his shoulders.

It was five years too late to appeal to her sense of decency. Frankly, he was lucky she was prepared to do this much.

She closed the door, turned off the sitting-room light and went to bed, evicting the cat from the middle of it. He came back, though, and she let him. He was undemanding company, and conversation with him wasn't complicated by lies and half-truths and mixed emotions.

It took her ages to go to sleep.

CHAPTER THREE

'IS THERE any chance you could get a babysitter for tomorrow?' Max asked Anna the following morning.

She stared at him, puzzled and a little suspicious. 'A babysitter? I thought you were coming to me. That's what we agreed.'

He looked down at his hand, his fingers tracing a pattern on the edge of the desk. 'I thought perhaps you could come to me—I could cook something.'

She laughed. 'You? Cook? No,' she said bluntly. It was too scary—too much like a date, and that made her nervous. She had weak enough defences around him, without him setting up some big seduction scene.

He sighed. 'I'm not trying to proposition you, Annie,' he said, proving for the nth time that he could read her mind. 'I just want to be able to talk openly, and with Harry in the house it's difficult. Anyway, there's something I want to tell you.'

'So tell me,' she said bluntly. 'Whatever it is, just tell me. It can't be that secret or important.'

His face closed, and she thought she'd been a little harsh, but he needed to know that he didn't affect her any longer. She *had* to have some distance, or she was going to go crazy.

'Forget it,' he said, a little shortly. 'You're probably right. It isn't that important.' He scooped up a pile of notes, turned on his heel and headed for the door, leaving her in the office with a terrible suspicion that she had just made a very hurtful mistake.

'So what? He hurt you,' she muttered under her breath.

David Fellows came up behind her and put an arm around her shoulders. 'All right, my dear?' he asked, an expression of concern on his face.

She shrugged and eased out of reach. 'Fine. Busy.' And I'm not going to discuss Max with you, she thought, however kindly you might be.

'Just wondered. You've been looking a bit preoccupied recently. Nothing to do with Max, is it?'

'Of course not. We're just colleagues,' she said firmly, and headed for her room and a bit of peace and privacy.

Her patients provided a little light relief that morning—children for inoculation, an elderly lady for an ulcer dressing, Mr Bryant with his sinus on his finger for a fresh dressing on the incision—she knew them all, and chatted happily to them, pushing Max Carter to the back of her mind.

He didn't stay there, though. She worried about whatever it was he'd wanted to tell her, and her callous dismissal of its importance, and after lunch she sought him out in the little garden behind the practice and apologised.

'You got me too early in the morning—never was a morning person, remember?' she added with a wry smile, and then regretted it, because all sorts of warm and intimate images came flooding back to her and swamped her reason.

'Yes, I remember,' he said softly, and she knew that he was remembering, too. Oh, darn. Why had she brought it up?

'Anyway,' she went on, 'if you still want me to come over—yes, I could get a babysitter. I think you're right, it would be easier to talk about Harry if he wasn't in the house. He comes downstairs sometimes to find me, and I wouldn't want him to overhear something that upset or confused him.'

Max nodded agreement. 'That was what I thought. If it's the idea of my cooking that's putting you off, don't worry,' he said, a slow, teasing smile playing around his lips. 'I've learned to be quite self-sufficient in the past few years.'

'Just something simple,' she warned him. 'No candle-light or rubbish like that, or I go straight back home again.'

He smiled. 'No candlelight. There's a fluorescent strip light in the kitchen-breakfast room of my cottage—will that do you?'

'Perfect,' she said crisply. 'What time? I need to arrange the babysitter.'

'Eight? Eight-thirty? What time does Harry go to bed?'

'Six-thirty. He gets up with the lark, disgustingly cheerful,' she told him flatly. 'It's another fault inherited from his father.'

Max grinned. 'Is that right? It must be hell for you.'

'Trust me, it is. Right, I must ring the sitter and get back to work. I've got another surgery starting in a minute.'

She went back inside, leaving him sitting there on the edge of a low wall in the sunshine, surrounded by all the greenery of the garden. She glanced back, and found his eyes on her, regarding her thoughtfully. For a moment their eyes locked, and then his mouth twitched in a travesty of a smile. She turned away, suddenly hot, and wondered if she'd actually survive the evening with him without sacrificing her principles and falling into bed.

More to the point, did she *want* to survive in this emotional and physical vacuum she'd been in for so many years? She thought again of their lazy mornings, the gentle, teasing, sensual way he'd woken her, and she almost moaned aloud.

He had been so tender, so clever, so incredibly good at making her feel well loved. He'd been so good at it that she'd never had the desire or inclination to try again with anyone else. It hadn't seemed fair to the very few kind, pleasant men with whom she'd had low-key, short-term relationships to expose them to certain failure.

She pushed the thought from her mind and rang her neighbour, Jill Fraser, arranging for her to have Harry for the night. They worked a reciprocal system, and it saved her having to overuse her parents and wear out their goodwill—and just at the moment Jill owed her loads of time. Anna had had her three children more times than she cared to remember just recently, since Jill's husband had walked out yet again.

She'd been able to sympathise. At least Harry's father had only left her with one child, and he'd had the grace to disappear and stay away—until now. No, she thought, she didn't want to rekindle the flames of her old romance. It would be emotional suicide. She'd just deal with the business of Harry's photos and so on, and hear what he had to say.

She wondered yet again what it was Max wanted to tell her. Was he married?

The thought chilled her. 'You're stupid,' she growled at

herself. 'You don't want him anyway—how can it make any difference if he's married? He's probably going to tell you he's only here for a week.'

She resigned herself to waiting for their meeting on Thursday night, and concentrated on her patients. It was a short day for a change, with no evening surgery for her, and she picked up Harry from her mother and took him for a walk, then did some washing, tidied up and threw the cat's bed in the washing machine, to his utter disgust.

He decamped to her best tapestry cushion, and sat there, sulking, for the rest of the night, before joining her on her bed.

'You are a nuisance,' she told him firmly, shoving him out of the way, but he purred and rubbed himself against her face, leaving hairs stuck all over it.

'Oh, cat,' she grumbled, wiping the hairs away and pushing him down the bed again to the bottom. 'You could go outside and hunt mice, if you were a respectable cat instead of a fat and indolent pyjama case.'

'Mreouw,' he squawked, and settled down with a sigh to lick himself thoroughly from end to end.

'You'll get hairballs,' she said self-righteously, tugging the pillow into the side of her neck and wondering what Max had to say.

A chilling thought occurred to her. What if he'd never married or had children because he had an inheritable disorder? Some recessive gene he carried, or some bizarre and insidious disease that only showed itself in later life? Maybe he wanted to warn her that Harry would inherit it?

Panic washed over her, and she got out of bed and made herself a hot drink, pacing round the house as she drank it.

'You're mad,' she told herself at three in the morning,

when she was on her third hot chocolate. 'It's nothing. It will be about something totally inconsequential, and you'll laugh at yourself. He said it wasn't important. Just wait. You'll find out soon enough.'

She went back to bed, evicted the cat from the warm, snuggly bit between the top of the quilt and the pillow, and lay down in a sea of hair.

Darned cat. She turned the pillow over, shifted the quilt and eventually fell asleep. Two hours later Harry climbed into bed with her and woke her by the simple expedient of peeling back her eyelids and saying hello.

She groaned and reached for him, pulling him under the quilt and snuggling him for a moment. Sometimes he'd go back to sleep again but, just her luck, this time he refused. Bouncingly, revoltingly cheerful, he sat up and pulled the quilt off her and grinned.

'Breakfast time,' he announced, and dragged her down the stairs to the kitchen.

'Harry, it's only six-thirty,' she wailed, trailing after him. 'We don't have to get up till seven-thirty.'

'But I'm hungry,' he said reasonably, squirming into the cereal cupboard and coming out with his favourite box. He handed it to her expectantly and, resigned, she switched on the kettle, poured his cereal out into his bowl, sloshed milk onto it and flopped into a chair.

The cat appeared, meowing and trying to look cute, and she sighed and fed him as well.

'Where yours?' Harry asked through a mouthful of cereal.

'I'm not hungry,' she told him, getting up to make her tea. Six or seven cups should do it, she thought with slight hysteria, and pulled down a mug from the cupboard.

It said WORLD'S BEST MUM on the outside, and she loved it. She filled it with steaming tea, splashed a bit of milk in and hoofed the cat off her chair, before slumping into it and listening, eyes closed, to the sound of Harry chomping.

Max was puzzled. He had a patient, a woman of fifty called Valerie Hawkshead, who was complaining of headaches and light-headedness. She had slight arthritis, muscular aches and pains but was otherwise healthy. According to the notes, she took pills for the aches and pains, and they used to work for the headaches, but they didn't seem so effective any longer and she was starting to forget things and wondered if she was getting Alzheimer's.

Suzanna had made a note that she thought the headaches were from analgesic over-use, and she'd eased her off them and put her on an anti-anxiety drug and done a battery of tests, all normal.

Now today she was back with her husband, looking slightly unkempt and withdrawn, and according to her husband she'd lost weight.

Max tried a mini-mental state test, and she scored 12 out of 30—hardly bothering to respond to some of the questions. That didn't seem to him like the reaction of a woman suffering from analgesic over-use, or even marked anxiety. It was something more than that, his intuition told him—something deeper.

More sinister.

Max trusted his intuition.

'I want to refer you to a neurologist,' he said. 'He can examine you and see if he can get to the bottom of the headaches and forgetfulness. OK?'

They were quite happy, and so he sent them off and dictated the letter later. Hopefully the neurologist would pick up on any problem. In the meantime, he had Annie coming round that evening for a meal. The place looked even drabber than usual and he still had to go shopping for some of the ingredients.

Just so long as Mrs Bootle had red and green peppers, courgettes and mushrooms he'd be all right. Knowing his luck, though, they'd come on Friday for the weekend, which wouldn't help him tonight.

He checked his watch, debated whether or not he'd got time and rang the shop. 'I don't suppose you could put a few things together for me, could you?' he asked Mrs Bootle, and she agreed without hesitation.

He dictated his list, gave up on the durum wheat flour and ploughed on with his surgery until he'd finished it. Then he glanced at his watch.

Six-thirty, and he hadn't even picked up the shopping or started the main dish. By seven he was home, by seven-thirty he was on his way to the shower, with the sauce bubbling on the back of the stove and the pasta piled up ready, and before he was finished and organised, the doorbell rang.

'You're being silly,' Anna told herself twelve hours after her revoltingly early breakfast. She had a whole plethora of outfits spread around her bedroom, and not one of them did she deem suitable.

Jeans were too casual, the trouser suit was too formal, the dress was too eveningy, the skirt was boring and she wore it for going to the dentist and things like that.

Which left the long, soft cotton dress that clung and

draped and was both casual and dressy, and which she felt good in. Max had never seen it before, but that wasn't a problem with the majority of her wardrobe. So far he'd only seen her uniform and her jeans.

She turned her attention to her hair. Up or down? She chewed her lip, brushing out the long strands and studying it critically.

Down. No, up.

She threw the brush across the room, went into the bathroom and showered with undue care and scented shower gel, all the while getting more and more irritated with herself because it wasn't supposed to be like this and it shouldn't matter what she wore or how she smelt or if her hair was up, down or dropping out!

His cottage was on the outskirts of town, down a secluded little lane. It was in a lovely setting but it was looking a little tired. For the umpteenth time she wondered why he didn't settle down and buy himself a nice house, even if he didn't want to get married and have children and ties. She rang the doorbell and waited, and heard his footsteps running down stairs.

He opened the door, wearing only a pair of jeans and a T-shirt, bare feet sticking out from the bottom of the jeans. He looked gorgeous, and all the reasons why this was a bad idea came crashing back to her.

He grinned, making it even worse. 'Sorry, I'm on the drag. I was cooking and got carried away and forgot the time. Come on in.' He led her through to the kitchen, giving her a tempting view of firm, hard thighs and a neat bottom snugly encased in worn, soft denim the exact shade of his incredibly lovely eyes.

She sighed quietly. How could he have so much power over her still? He'd walked out on her, leaving just a short, unemotional note that trampled her dreams in the dust, and yet still she only had to look at him and her knees went weak.

Hormones, she told herself. There had been something in the news about falling in love being like a psychiatric illness, altering levels of certain hormones in the body and changing behaviour. At the time she'd recognised the syndrome as something from which she'd thought she'd recovered.

Now, following him through the little cottage, she wasn't so sure.

They went into the kitchen so he could check on the pasta sauce that was bubbling gently on the hob, and he offered her a glass of wine.

Trying to soften her up to seduce her? He didn't need any help. 'I'll have water, please,' she said, and he pulled a bottle of mineral water from the fridge.

'This all right?'

She nodded, surprised that he would have anything so—what? Civilised? He used to poke fun at people who paid huge sums of money for bottled water, and here he was with his own supply!

That wasn't the only change, she realised as they ate. He could cook now, too, probably better than she could.

'This is delicious,' she told him appreciatively, twirling strands of pasta round her fork. 'Where did you learn to make such a lovely sauce—or did you cheat and buy it?'

He chuckled. 'In Italy,' he told her, leaning back in his chair and sipping his wine thoughtfully. 'I spent six months there, doing a little locum job. It was fun. I lived with a real Italian mama, and she took me under her wing. I learned to cook all sorts of things. I made the pasta, too. It's a handy little skill—it's dead easy and it impresses people no end.'

It worked—she was impressed. She was also falling under his spell again, and to keep her emotional distance was getting harder and harder.

She had to keep reminding herself that leopards didn't change their spots, and if he'd walked out on her once, he could do it again, but her warnings fell on deaf ears.

She succumbed to a glass of wine, then another, and they settled down on the sofa with the pictures of Harry, and she told him all about her pregnancy and his birth, and how kind everyone had been.

'I missed you, though,' she told him, not meaning to but finding the words just spilling out. 'Even though you'd walked out like that, I still missed you.'

He bowed his head. 'I'm sorry,' he murmured. 'It was hell for you, and I should have been there.'

Was it genuine remorse in his voice? It sounded like it. 'I tried to tell you about it,' she said, 'but my letters came back. You'd moved, or just returned them. I don't know.'

'I moved.'

She nodded. 'I hadn't—but I suppose you didn't want to know anyway, or you would have kept in touch.'

His hand came up and cupped her cheek. 'I'm sorry,' he said gruffly. Their eyes locked, and after the longest moment, as if in slow motion, his head descended.

She had plenty of time to move, to get away from him, to do what she'd said she'd do and stop anything like this happening. Instead, like a traitor, her arm stole round his neck and drew him down, and their lips met.

It was like coming home.

After all these years, she could still remember the feel of his mouth, the texture of his skin, the firm pressure of his lips. He tasted of coffee and mints and a lingering trace of brandy, and she moaned softly and threaded her fingers through his hair, urging him closer.

He shifted against her, drawing her body up against his and deepening the kiss. She felt the velvet sweep of his tongue, the gentle coaxing pressure of his lips, and she forgot all her warnings to herself.

This was where she belonged—here, with him, in this embrace. His hand left her cheek and trailed softly, tormentingly down, to settle lightly on her breast. She arched against it and he squeezed gently, making her ache with longing.

'Max,' she sighed against his lips, and his breath drifted raggedly over her cheek.

'Let me love you,' he whispered unevenly, and the longing grew until she nearly cried out.

'Yes,' she whimpered, 'oh, yes. Please.'

He stood up and drew her to her feet, leading her upstairs to the bedroom. She didn't notice it—didn't notice anything except the feel of his arm around her shoulders, the hard jut of his hipbone against her side, the heat of his body radiating through his clothes.

He stripped them off, then with shaking hands he took the hem of her dress and peeled it gently over her head.

She felt suddenly naked and vulnerable, standing there in her basic chainstore bra and pants. Would he notice the changes in her body? The thickening of her waist, the little bulge below her tummy button where her muscles hadn't quite gone flat after Harry?

Her breasts weren't as firm, either—would he mind? Would it put him off?

'You're lovely,' he said unsteadily. 'Oh, Annie, I've missed you so much…'

He held his arms out to her, and she flew into them, clinging to him and letting herself absorb the feel of his body. She was right, he was thinner. Leaner, really, perhaps more mature—and hot. So hot. She ran her hands down the firm column of his spine, and he moved against her restlessly.

'I need you,' he whispered, his breath teasing at her hair, and she took his hand and led him to the bed, sinking down onto it and drawing him down beside her.

He was shaking all over, his body trembling under her hands, and he couldn't unfasten her bra. She slipped the catch and threw it aside, and his hands were there to catch her and cradle the soft warmth of her breasts.

His mouth was hot, closing over one aching, straining peak, his palm roughly caressing the other while she cried out with need. 'You're so lovely,' he said, his lips trailing down over her hipbone and laying soft, hot kisses against the curve of her thigh.

'Max, please…!'

He stripped away their last remaining scraps of clothing, then moved over her, his body meshing with hers in one smooth, effortless homecoming that made her cry out with joy.

'Oh, Max,' she sobbed, and he trapped her face between his hands and plundered her mouth. She moved restlessly against him, and with a ragged groan he gave up all pretence of control and drove into her, sending her over the brink into glorious freefall.

She heard his cry, felt the stiffening of his body against hers, and then they were drifting slowly back down to earth, cradled in each other's arms. Tears clogged her lashes and threatened to choke her, and she turned her head into his neck and bit her lip. She wouldn't cry. She wouldn't…

'Oh, Annie, I've missed you,' he said, and his voice cracked. His head dropped against her shoulder, his chest heaved and she gave up her feeble attempt at controlling her own tears and let them fall.

Five years, she thought. I've longed for him for five years. He's my other half, the other part of me, and he's come back. All the anger, all the bitterness—just a defence, because I love him, and I always have, and I always will.

He lifted his head and kissed away her tears, his own eyes deep pools of emotion. 'It's been so long,' he murmured. 'I thought I must have exaggerated what it was like for us—thought my memory must have built it up into something that it wasn't—but I was wrong. It was every bit as beautiful as I remember—maybe even better.'

She thought he was going to say more—perhaps tell her that he loved her—but he turned his head away, dragging in a deep breath and letting it out on a shaky sigh.

He rolled away from her, collapsing onto the bed beside her, and drew her up against his side, his hand idly smoothing the skin of her back with slow, lazy strokes.

So where do we go from here? she wondered as she lay cradled in the crook of his arm, her legs tangled with his and her ear listening to the steady rhythm of his heart. Did she dare to hope this time? He was older now, more mature. Would he stay? Or would he go again, leaving her in tatters once more?

'I don't have ties,' he'd said.

Perhaps Harry would have the power to change him, where she had failed. It was unlikely, and a few days ago she would have said impossible. The other night it had sounded as if he didn't want anything to do with the boy apart from a periodical update. Now he made it sound as if she were the most wonderful woman he'd ever met, and he'd missed her.

Would it be enough, this time?

'I need a drink—shall I bring a bottle of water back to bed?' he murmured, hugging her gently against his side.

'Please.'

He slid out of the bed, padding soundlessly across the room and down the stairs. She heard him pottering about, and sat up, naked, on the bed, her arms hugging her knees. While she waited for him to come back, she looked around her at the little bedroom of his rented home.

It was lit only by the soft glow coming from the bedside lamp he'd turned on when they'd entered the room, and even in the mellow light it was bleak, lacking warmth and character, and she felt sad for him that he seemed to live permanently in these sorts of surroundings. It just seemed so—temporary, really. Rootless. As if it didn't matter.

The night had grown cool, and the slight breeze from the open window dallied over her skin, pebbling her nipples and bringing goose-bumps up all over her. She gave a little shiver, and stood up, pulling the quilt back. It was silly to be cold.

She was about to climb back in under the covers when she spotted a piece of paper on the floor by the bed, sent flying, no doubt, by their hasty disrobing. She picked it up, glancing at it out of idle curiosity, and felt the blood drain from her face.

It was a letter to Max, telling him when his next appointment had been scheduled for.

Nothing odd in that, except that it was from the hospital that housed the country's foremost oncology unit.

And Max had an appointment there, which could only mean one thing…

Anna closed her eyes, then opened them again and re-read the letter in case she'd made a mistake.

No. There it was in black and white, directed to him at a London address, presumably his last temporary post.

And, suddenly, it all fell into place. The constant moving around, the refusal to settle or have ties, the lack of commitment to anywhere or anything—all typical of a man under a death sentence.

How long had it been going on? A year? Two?

Horror trickled over her like cold water.

Now that she'd found him again, was she about to lose him?

'Here—I've brought us some goodies to snack on.'

She turned her head slowly and looked up at him, the letter lying unnoticed in her nerveless fingers.

'What does this mean?' she asked him with deadly calm, fluttering the sheet of paper.

He glanced down, and sighed. 'Oh, hell,' he said softly.

'Hell what? What does it mean? Max, tell me what's wrong with you,' she said, mustering as much firmness as she could.

He put the tray down on the bedside table, took the letter from her and put it down as well, then wrapped her hands in his.

'It's a follow-up appointment,' he said softly.

'I can see that,' she said, dreading his answer but needing to hear it—needing to have her fears confirmed. 'What for? Why?'

He took a long breath, then met her searching eyes.

'That's what I was going to tell you. I've got non-Hodgkin's lymphoma.'

CHAPTER FOUR

SHOCK held Anna motionless for an endless moment, then she snatched her hands free and stood up, crossing to the window and wrapping her arms around her waist.

Lymphoma.

Oh, God, no.

It was dark outside, only the distant lights of the village breaking the velvet blackness. She shivered in the cool stream of air, and then felt a soft towelling robe settle comfortingly around her shoulders. Max's hands cupped her arms, drawing her back against him.

'I told you it wasn't important,' she said in a hollow, incredulous voice. 'I had no idea—'

'Of course you didn't. It doesn't matter.'

'It does!' she cried softly, turning in his arms and looking up into those beautiful blue eyes. They were in shadow and she couldn't read them, but his hand came up and cupped her cheek, and his thumb caressed her jaw with tender, slow strokes.

'I'm glad we made love before you found out. Otherwise I might have thought it was pity. You know—

last privileges for a condemned man and all that.' He smiled, a wry, crooked smile that tore at her heart.

Tears swam in her eyes, but she blinked them away. 'Don't,' she protested. Her arms slid round him, and she buried her face in his chest and bit her lip hard. 'How long?' she mumbled.

'How long have I had it? Five years.'

Her head came up sharply. 'Five years? So you knew? When you were with me, you knew?'

'I began to suspect. I'd found a lump in my groin—just a pea, really, nothing significant. It didn't hurt, I had no other symptoms. I thought it was just a lymphatic reaction to infection, probably—something I didn't know I'd done. A little cut, a splinter or something. I couldn't find anything, and it didn't go away.'

'So what did you do?'

'I took a biopsy and sent it off.'

'Yourself?'

He nodded. 'And it came back positive. I went to an oncologist privately and he confirmed low-grade follicular non-Hodgkin's lymphoma. That was the day before I left.'

She eased away from him, sliding her arms into the sleeves of his dressing-gown and belting it tightly, as if to protect her from what she was hearing.

'Why did you leave?' she asked desperately. 'Why like that, with just that note? Why didn't you tell me?' Her voice was starting to crack, and she wheeled away, going to stand by the window and staring out into the dark, quiet night. In the distance a dog barked. She hardly registered it. All she could think was that he'd gone, run away when he should have stayed and talked it through with her. If he'd loved her at all—

'I wanted to protect you. We hardly knew each other, Annie. It wasn't fair to expect you to go through all that with me.'

'All what?' she stormed, turning on him furiously. 'Sharing the burden? Supporting you in your treatment? Cheering you up and helping you when you were down?'

'Exactly,' he said sadly. 'How could I ask that of you after only three weeks—even if they were the best and most wonderful three weeks of my life? I missed you, Annie. Believe me, it was the hardest thing I've ever done, and so many times I nearly tried to contact you.'

'You should have done.'

He shook his head. 'Why? To tell you I wasn't in remission any more? That it had come back, and was threatening me again? Or the next time? Or when I was lying in hospital, being blasted by drugs before having the stem cell treatment as a last-ditch attempt at knocking it on the head?'

He laughed softly. 'You wouldn't have wanted me, Annie. I was thin to the point of gaunt, I looked like death. I'd lost my hair, I'd lost my faith in myself. I wasn't worth having.'

Tears welled up and scalded her cheeks. 'Oh, Max. Do you really think that would have made any difference to me? I would have been there for you.'

'Sacrificing yourself. I thought if I left you, you might find someone else—someone you could marry and have children with. It was the only thing that comforted me, thinking that you might have found happiness.'

She laughed, a tiny, humourless huff of sound. 'Happiness? Yes, I found happiness, eventually. With your son. *Our* son.' She clenched her fists, hanging onto her temper by a hair. 'You had no *right* to make that decision for me. It was my decision to make, not yours.'

He was silent for a while, then shook his head. 'Maybe I didn't want you there,' he said softly.

She felt the rejection right through to her bones. It held her stunned, unable to move, to breathe, to think.

She dragged in a lungful of air and let it out again in a whoosh. 'I'll go,' she whispered, frantically scrabbling around on the floor for her clothes. 'If you don't want me here…'

'Annie, stop it.'

'I can't stop it,' she wept. 'Just let me go.'

'No.' His hands came out and caught her shoulders, drawing her up against his chest. 'No, Annie, don't run. Stay and talk about it—'

'No!' She drummed her fists against his chest impotently. 'Max, please!'

'Shh.' His hands soothed her, stroking slowly up and down her spine, and she sagged against him, sobbing helplessly.

'It's all right, my love,' he murmured, but she knew he was lying. It wasn't all right, and it hadn't been all right in a long, long time, and it probably never would be again.

What if he'd died? She would never have known! All these years she'd pictured him with another woman, and instead he'd been ill, fighting death alone…

'You should have told me!' she yelled, pummelling his chest again, the hot tears refusing to be held in check.

'I'm sorry. Maybe I should have done. I just wanted to spare you the pain. It was such a brief affair. I thought you'd get over me.'

She dropped her hands and moved away, drawing herself up and hugging her arms around her waist again to distance herself. 'Well, I didn't. I still love you. So what happens now?'

He sighed. 'I don't know. I'm in remission at the moment. It's as near as I'll get to a cure. It may come back, it may not. They may be able to destroy it again if it comes back, they may not. I have no idea. It's just one of those damn things, like dog muck on your shoe. You can wipe it off, you can get rid of it, but that last trace seems to linger.'

He shrugged. 'You just learn to live with it. It's like asthma or high blood pressure or diabetes. You treat it, you deal with it, and you know that it will probably kill you in the end, but it's a vague sort of end. It may be years—many, many years. A lifetime. It may be just a few short months. No one knows. That's the hardest thing to deal with, to learn to live with—the terrible uncertainty. It's like the sword of Damocles hanging over you, held by a bit of frayed thread. I couldn't ask you to share that, and I wouldn't.'

She swallowed, trying to visualise such an uncertain future. No wonder he wouldn't settle down.

'What about Harry?' she asked, choked by tears. 'Is he ever going to know you're his father?'

'No.'

'But he has a right—'

'He has a right to a secure future. He has a right to happiness, and confidence in his own mortality. I won't take that away from him, Anna, and I won't let you do it either.'

Anna. He'd called her Anna.

It made her feel cold inside.

'He has a right to his father, too.'

'To watch me die? To watch me endure another series of treatments? To not know if this time I'm coming home?'

'Yes! Yes, he has that right. He's a human—he's not just a child. You can't shield him from reality. People get ill. That's why I'm a nurse and you're a doctor. And people die.'

But not you. Please, God, not you. She turned away, blinking hard and biting her lip until she could taste the salt of her blood.

'Annie.' His voice was soft, his hands gentle. 'Come to bed. Let me hold you.'

She turned, burrowing into his chest, and he led her to the bed and tucked her under the quilt, their snack forgotten. He held her close, his heartbeat steady under her ear, and he seemed so alive, so well and normal and vital that she could hardly believe what he'd told her.

Maybe she'd wake up soon and find it was all a dream?

Max held her, his hands moving rhythmically over her shoulders and down her back, soothing her. Tears clogged his lashes, and he blinked them away. They could have had so much together.

He tipped her chin, his mouth finding hers and kissing her tenderly, and she clung to him, kissing him back as if she was starving for him.

Maybe she was. He understood that.

He peeled away the dressing-gown and kissed every inch of her, noting the changes—the softer fullness of her breasts, the gentle curve of her abdomen, the slight widening of her hips. She'd lost that youthfulness, become a ripe, fertile woman in her prime, and he found her somehow more beautiful, more intoxicating than the slender girl she'd been.

Her hands were all over him, fluttering feverishly as he

teased and tormented her with hot, suckling kisses and sliding caresses. 'Please,' she begged, and he moved over her, his body trembling with the effort of holding back his own response.

She felt so good. So well. So alive. He sought her mouth frantically, as if he could draw life from her to conquer the demon that stalked him.

He felt her body start to tighten, and she bucked beneath him, crying out. He caught her cries, their kiss muffling his deep groan as his body stiffened against her, shuddering with the force of his release.

'I love you,' she whispered, and he couldn't hold the tears any longer. They fell on her face, running down into her hair, mingling with her own as they welled from her beautiful eyes.

'I'm sorry,' he said raggedly. 'Annie, I'm sorry.' He didn't know what he was sorry for—for dragging her into this sorry mess, for leaving her the first time, or because he was going to leave her again.

And this time, he'd make sure it was for ever…

'You can't go,' she said flatly. 'You have to stop running. You have a son. Even if I don't mean anything to you, he should. At least get to know him, even if you don't tell him who you are. You can at least spend some time with him, with us. I can tell him you're here for a while and you're lonely, and so we're going to be your friends.'

'And then leave, when Suzanna comes back to work? Walk out on you again?'

She shook her head, trying to stay calm. 'I would like you to stay—or take us with you.'

'I can't. I won't.'

'You don't know that. Give yourself time. Max, I'm a health professional. I understand that we can't save everyone. What I do, as a nurse, is improve quality of life. There are many ways of doing that and, if you've only got a limited amount of time, don't you owe it to yourself to make that time happy?'

His jaw clenched, and he turned away. 'I can't, Anna,' he said in a strangled voice. 'Don't push me, please.'

'At least stay until Suzanna comes back,' she pleaded. 'Even if you don't see Harry, at least stay with me. Let me have some memories—please?'

He looked back at her, his eyes tortured. 'You don't know what you're asking,' he said roughly.

'Yes, I do. I know exactly what I'm asking, and I know it takes courage—more courage than running away again.'

She let the words hang, and after a while he bowed his head and gave a heavy sigh. 'I'll think about it.'

Her shoulders dropped with relief. It was only a slight concession, but at least she wasn't going to come out of her morning surgery and find him gone.

'Just promise me something—if you decide you have to go, say goodbye. Don't leave me again—not like that.'

He nodded slowly. 'All right.'

'Thank you.'

She wheeled round and yanked his consulting-room door open, almost running down the corridor to her room. She had five minutes before her first patient—five minutes to get her wildly see-sawing emotions under control and dredge up a professional demeanour.

She managed it, but only just.

Mr Bryant came in to see her for his dressing, and looked at her keenly. He'd known her all her life, and she just hoped he wouldn't say anything kind, or she'd dissolve.

'You look a bit wat'ry, my dear,' he said as she bent over his finger. 'Took the hay fever, have you?'

She nodded, hoping he wouldn't know she'd never suffered so much as a single sneeze from a pollen allergy. 'It must be bad at the moment—there must be something about that gets to me.'

Called Max, she added to herself, and dismissed the thought firmly. She had to work, had to concentrate and deal with her patients. It would give it time to sink in, give her subconscious time to assimilate it.

'It's looking better,' she told Mr Bryant, peering critically at his fingertip. 'I think it's starting to heal properly at last. I should think you're relieved.'

'Tell you the truth, it's never really troubled me,' he confessed. 'It were the wife sent me along. Said it looked unsightly and she weren't going out with me again till I did something about it. Not that we go out much, mind. Just Friday nights down the Rose and Crown, for the darts. I've played for years, but she's just decided to join in, and she's in the women's team,' he said, clearly proud of her. 'I couldn't mess that up because of my finger, now, could I?'

Anna smiled. 'Well, you're safe now, then. You can still go down to the Rose and Crown together on Fridays. It sounds like fun.'

He nodded. 'We enjoy it. Bit of light relief at the end of the week, 'specially in the winter. You ought to come along—you ever played darts?'

She laughed. 'Yes—I missed the board every time. I nearly put someone's eye out with one throw. I haven't tried since,' she admitted ruefully. 'Anyway, I can't get out easily because of Harry.'

Mr Bryant's eyes softened. 'He's a lovely little chap. Saw him the other day out for a walk with your mother, bless her. Dear little fellow. Gave me a great big smile, he did. Shame you haven't got a man to take care of you, my dear. I know it's none of my business, but a boy that age needs his mother, and I reckon you need him, too. Less hay fever that way.'

And he lifted his hand in farewell and stomped out of the surgery, leaving her laughing wryly. And she'd thought she'd fooled him!

Friday afternoon was her afternoon off, and she left the surgery at lunchtime without seeing Max. He was out on call, apparently, and so she went home with a strange, hollow feeling inside, changed out of her uniform and went round to see her mother.

Perceptive woman that she was, she took one look at her only daughter and pushed her into a chair. 'Stay here,' she ordered softly, took little Harry by the hand and led him off to find her husband.

Moments later she was back, walking straight up to Anna and engulfing her in a wordless hug.

All the fears she'd stifled for the past twelve hours or so welled up in a great hideous tide, and she buried her face in her mother's soft and comforting bosom and howled her eyes out. Finally, after what seemed like an age, she hiccuped to a halt, and her mother smoothed her hair one last time and handed her a fistful of tissues.

She blew her nose and wiped her cheeks, stifled another bout of weeping and watched as her mother bustled about with the kettle.

She made two mugs of tea, put them down in the middle of the table and pushed one towards Anna. 'Do you want to talk about it?' she asked gently.

Anna sniffed and tipped her head back, looking up at the ceiling for strength and inspiration. There was none to be found. 'He's dying,' she said flatly. 'Max. He's got lymphoma. That's why he left me.'

'Oh, my love…' Her mother's warm, capable hand closed over hers, squeezing hard. 'Oh, darling, I am so sorry.'

The tears started again, and Anna dashed them away impatiently. 'He's in remission. He might be all right for years and years, but he won't stay. He won't listen to me—he says he'll think about staying till Suzanna comes back, but he won't stay after that, and he doesn't want Harry to know who he is, and I can't persuade him and I don't know what to do! I can't bear to lose him again…'

She dropped her head onto her arms, and sobbed helplessly, while her mother held her hand and murmured the sort of words she said to Harry when he fell and scraped his knees. Universal words, meaningless sounds that soothed and comforted and took away the pain.

Words she should have said to Max when he'd been lying in hospital, all alone.

She pushed herself up and gulped her tea, sniffing hard. 'He's so damn stubborn,' she said on a hiccuping sob. 'He just won't listen to me. It's my decision whether I can cope with it or not.'

'And can you?' her mother asked gently.

Anna sighed. 'I don't know. Better than I can cope with him leaving me, and not knowing if he was alive or dead—'

She broke off, pressing her fingers to her mouth to hold in the fear.

'How does he feel about you?' her mother asked.

She shrugged. 'He said he'd missed me. He said leaving was the hardest thing he'd ever done. He said he thought he must have misremembered how it was with me—'

She broke off, colouring, and wondered what her mother would think if she realised she'd spent the night with him.

'And had he?' she asked softly.

Anna shook her head. 'No. We still…' She floundered to a halt, unsure how to phrase it, but her mother understood.

'Sometimes it's just right, I suppose. Your father and I met and fell headlong in love. There was no doubt, no question of waiting to be sure. We *were* sure, right from the first moment we set eyes on each other.'

She coloured softly and looked away. 'That's why we were married so quickly. Everyone thought it was because I was pregnant, but it was just that we couldn't stay away from each other, and it wasn't like it is these days. People didn't just live together—at least, not in the country.'

She smiled. 'So we were married, just eight weeks after we met, and thirty-four years later we're still here. I suppose we've been incredibly lucky. We've both got our health, we're happy, we've got a lovely daughter and a beautiful grandson—the only thing I would change is your happiness, and that's been something that's troubled me ever since Max came into your life.'

'You're very fortunate,' Anna told her wistfully. 'Treasure him. Not everyone gets the chance.'

Sarah Young swallowed hard and patted her daughter's hand. 'I know. I do.' She stood up, clearing away the cups—bustling to keep her emotions in check, Anna thought. She turned and gave Anna an over-bright smile. 'So how about giving me a hand to get lunch?'

Max drove slowly through the lanes, looking for Culvert Farm. He checked his directions again, and wondered if he'd passed that little turning or not.

He wasn't exactly concentrating. All he could think about was Anna, and how incredibly sweet it had been to lie in her arms last night. She wanted him to stay. He laughed wryly. If she only knew how easy it would be to do that, to give up being noble and let her share the uncertainty of the coming years.

But he couldn't, because of Harry. Oddly enough, if it hadn't been for the boy he might have stayed this time, but he couldn't trash the kid's life like that. What if he came out of remission and went downhill fast? It could happen. If he was on his own, nobody else would be affected and it wouldn't matter.

Still, she'd made a very tempting offer. Stay until Suzanna came back off maternity leave, she'd suggested, and make memories with her. It was unbelievably tempting—so tempting he thought he'd do it. Why not? They were both going to be hurt anyway. It might as well be worthwhile.

A bubble of something rose in his chest, and he realised it was happiness. It was the first time for five years—he almost hadn't recognised it. Yes, he'd stay, and make memories with her, and then he'd go, taking his memories with him to comfort him through the months and years ahead.

But he wouldn't think of that now. He'd concentrate on finding his patient, then going to see Anna and asking her to have dinner with him. Perhaps they'd go somewhere in the village, or in a nearby town. He'd ask if she had any preference.

Humming softly, he turned down the little lane he'd missed the first time, swung into the yard of Culvert Farm and cut the engine.

A man in overalls and boots was crossing the yard, and he smiled. 'Wonderful day,' he called.

The man nodded. 'You looking for David Bliss?'

'Yes—I'm the doctor.'

'I'm his son—he's inside. I'll take you in.'

He followed the man through the open doorway, past the sleeping collies that opened one eye and watched him warily, up the narrow winding cottage staircase to a bedroom.

'Father, Doctor's here,' the man said, and left them to it.

'Mr Bliss? I'm Dr Carter—I've taken over from Dr Korrel. I understand you've been having pain in your chest and you're a bit breathless. Is that right?'

The man heaved himself up the bed a little and nodded, puffing slightly from the effort. He looked congested, Max thought, his fingers a little swollen, his face round. His breathing seemed laboured, and a quick examination revealed all the symptoms of angina and congestive heart failure.

'Where do you feel the pain, and when?' he asked, checking his patient's chest with a stethoscope. It sounded like a soggy sponge.

'Up the middle, really. Sometimes down my arm a little, but not much. More into the armpit.'

Max nodded, sat him up and listened to the back of his chest, then took off the stethoscope and tucked it in his pocket.

'I think your heart's struggling a bit to keep your fluid levels right, and that's making it hurt periodically,' he told the elderly man. 'I'm going to give you some pills to take some of the fluid away from your lungs, and that should make you feel better quite quickly. You will find you need to pass water more often, though.'

He nodded. 'My sister's on them water tablets,' he said. 'Has been for years. Father was as well.'

'Perhaps it's something you all suffer from, then. Well, as you know, if it's kept under control it's nothing to worry about, but I want to put you on some pills for your heart as well, and I want you to try these. You pop one under your tongue if you have a pain, and if the pain goes, we'll know it's nothing to worry about, just a touch of angina. If the pain lingers or gets worse, I want to know straight away, all right?'

He went back out into the sunshine, found Mr Bliss's son and told him what he'd found, and then drove back to Wenham Market. There was no reply from Anna's house, but Jill Fraser stuck her head out of an upstairs window. 'She's at her mother's,' she said cheerfully. 'Did you have a good time last night?'

'Yes—thank you,' he said, a little taken aback. 'Were you babysitting?'

'That's right. Go and find her—you might have to go round the back, they'll probably be in the garden with a paddling pool in this lovely weather. We're just going to the beach.'

Max nodded, thanked her and drove down the lane,

turning onto the gravel sweep in front of the Youngs' farmhouse. He rang the bell twice, and then one of the dogs bounded lazily up to him, barking a greeting, and he ruffled its ears and asked it where the others were.

It bounded back round the side of the house, and he followed a little hesitantly. He didn't like just walking in on them like that, but Jill had seemed to think it would be all right.

'Hello, anybody home?' he called, and the other dog ambled up, too hot to bark or do anything more kinetic than wave its tail.

Anna appeared, looking a little surprised to see him, and he apologised.

'Your neighbour told me to come round the back,' he explained.

'That's fine. Come on in, I just wasn't expecting you. I thought you were out, doing calls. Harry's in the paddling pool.'

There was a splash and a shriek, and Harry came tearing round the side of the shrubs, dripping wet and laughing gleefully. He skidded to a halt and looked up at Max.

'Hello,' he said curiously. 'Have you come for tea? Grannie's just getting some.'

He looked at Anna, and she shrugged. 'It's up to you. We'd like you to join us—you know you're welcome.'

He hesitated. The boy was there, drawing him like a magnet, and yet this wasn't part of his plan.

'We've made lemon drizzle cake,' Harry confided, and that did it.

Max smiled wryly. 'Thank you, that sounds wonderful. I'd be delighted to stay.'

'You need shorts on,' Harry told him, and then ran off

again. There was another splash, and a shriek from Grannie who was presumably soaked. Max chuckled and followed Anna round the shrubbery into the garden, his heart lighter than it had been for years.

Maybe this wouldn't be so hard, after all.

'Will you stay for supper?'

Max smiled at Mrs Young and shook his head. 'I don't think so. I have to go back for evening surgery in a minute. Actually, I was going to ask Anna if she wanted to join me for dinner.'

Anna's eyes met his searchingly. 'Dinner?' she said doubtfully. 'I just ate three slices of cake.'

He smiled. She always had loved cake. 'We could eat lightly—or just have a drink. It doesn't matter.'

'I'll have Harry,' her mother offered. 'He can stay the night with his grandparents. He enjoys that.'

'He was with Jill last night,' Anna said without thinking, and then coloured.

Her mother ignored her embarrassment. 'Well, that's all right,' she said. 'He loves coming here, it's like a second home, and we love having him. You have little enough social life, darling. You go out. You can always put him to bed before you go, if you're worried about not seeing him. It's not as if you've been at work all day today, is it?'

In the face of such common sense, Anna couldn't think of a single valid reason why she shouldn't go out with Max that night, whatever he had in mind. Perhaps he'd decided what he was going to do, and would tell her.

She felt a surge of adrenaline. If he was going to tell her he was leaving, surely he wouldn't have spent the entire afternoon with her and Harry, laughing and playing with his son, kicking balls around on the lawn and spreading sunblock on his nose and cheeks like a practised father.

'That would be lovely,' she said, without giving herself any more time to vacillate. 'Eight o'clock?'

He nodded. 'Maybe by then the cake will have worn off and you'll be able to eat,' he teased.

'On top of that lot?' She laughed. 'Hardly. I'll be like a house if I eat that much.'

He smiled indulgently. 'Don't hold back on my account. I like the new you. You were too skinny before.'

She coloured furiously, and he suddenly seemed to realise her mother was sitting in earshot, valiantly trying to pretend that she couldn't hear every word.

He cleared his throat and got to his feet. 'I'll see you at eight, then. Thank you for a lovely afternoon.'

She smiled up at him. 'You're welcome. See you later.'

She watched him go, then thought of that evening. Was he going to tell her that he'd decided to stay? Or had he stayed that afternoon just making memories, as she'd suggested, and was going to say goodbye that night? Only time would tell.

CHAPTER FIVE

'THIS is bliss,' Max said, stretching out luxuriously on the grass beside the river.

They were lying near a weeping willow, its branches hanging low over the water, and a cool breeze wafted over them, dispelling the heat of the day. Swans drifted in the current, paddling lazily to hold their positions, and there was the occasional splosh from the riverbank as a little vole or something plopped into the water.

It *was* bliss, but Anna was on edge. She wanted to know what he was thinking, and he didn't seem to be about to bring up the subject. Unable to help herself, she challenged him.

'Are you going?'

He opened his eyes and sat up slowly. 'Going?' he echoed. 'I'm not going anywhere—most particularly not until my food arrives.'

She rolled her eyes. 'You know what I mean. Are you going to stay and see out this locum job, or are you running away again?'

'Is that how you see it? Running away again?'

'Don't you?'

'Not really.' He gave a short, hollow laugh. 'I'm probably a fool, but I thought I'd stay for now.'

Relief washed over her like a tidal wave. 'I just wanted to know,' she said, trying to sound unmoved. 'And what about Harry? Will you see him—get to know him at all? You seemed to get on well today.'

He rolled onto his front and propped himself up on his elbows, regarding her steadily. 'I don't know. I could easily fall for him. I think I probably have. I don't want to hurt him when I go—and I am going,' he said firmly. 'It's up to you whether I see him or not in the interim.'

She looked away, stifling her disappointment. One step at a time, she cautioned herself. 'I think you should see him, but maybe just as a friend, at least for now. I don't want him hurt either, and he will be if you tell him you're his father and then leave.'

He nodded. 'That's what I thought. So, in the meantime,' he asked softly, 'what are we going to do to make these memories of yours? Any particular fantasies you have in mind?'

Anything with you in it, she could have said, but she didn't. She didn't think it was a good idea to be too up-front—and, anyway, if she played her cards right, she could use this time together to get so far under his skin that he couldn't bear to leave them.

'Making love under a willow,' she said, her voice whisper-soft.

One eyebrow shot up. 'Not this one at this precise moment, I take it?' he said with a chuckle.

She looked around the crowded pub garden and shook

her head with a smile. 'Not this one, and not now, no. But some time, somewhere.'

His eyes darkened. 'OK,' he agreed slowly. 'Anything else?'

She settled down on the grass, getting into the game. 'Oh—midnight skinny-dipping at the beach?'

His mouth twitched. 'Like prison food, do you?'

She laughed softly, then became wistful again. 'Waking up with you,' she said without a trace of a smile. 'I loved waking up with you.'

He looked away. Too close to home, she thought. 'What about you?' she asked. 'Any memories you want to make?'

'More than I care to think about,' he said gruffly, and rolled over and sat up, staring down into the slowly moving water. He propped his elbows on his knees, fisting one hand and wrapping the fingers of the other over it tightly. 'A picnic,' he said after an age. 'Going for a picnic on a perfect day—with Harry. Maybe going to the zoo? Walking in the countryside, by a river. Lying in on a Sunday and reading the papers. Fighting over the colour supplement. Making love in the shower.'

Five years ago they'd only had two Sundays together, and he'd been on call for one and she'd had a long-standing commitment on the Saturday night before the other, and so neither time had they been able to have a lie-in. Maybe this time, if she could persuade her mother to have Harry—?

'Number forty-two?'

'That's us,' Max said, getting to his feet and going over to the waitress to fetch the plates. 'Do you want to sit at a table, or can we manage here?' he asked her.

'Here,' she said without hesitation. 'Or nearer the river.'

'Those swans might get a bit too interested if you go nearer,' he warned, and so they stayed where they were, in the shelter of the willow, and ate their ham and prawn salad with fresh crusty rolls and creamy butter, washed down with ice-cold mineral water.

It was delicious—cool and light enough to eat even after pigging out on her mother's cake, and yet tasty and interesting.

'Lovely ham,' Max commented.

'It's wild boar ham, from a totally free-range herd. All the food here's organic. That's why I suggested it.'

He raised an enquiring brow. 'Have you gone organic, then?'

She shook her head. 'Not entirely. Wherever possible or reasonable, though. My father's an organic farmer now—has been for over ten years. He's doing much better than he was, because the demand is growing. The sheep are all grass fed without prophylactic medicines, and he raises geese and bronze turkeys for Christmas, again all organic and free range.'

'What about Mr Bryant? What does he do?'

'Oh, arable—all sprayed within an inch of its life. It's a problem, actually, because one of our fields is adjacent to one of his and we can't graze the ewes on it because of the spraying.'

'That's a bit of a pain. Is the field wasted?'

She shook her head. 'No. It's all right for the turkeys because he sows spring wheat, not winter wheat, so there's no spraying when we're growing them on. We keep trying to persuade him to grow something else there, but he's a bit resistant. Knows what he knows, and all that. He's very nice about it, but he's a nice man,' she added, remembering his remark about hay fever.

She picked up a cherry tomato in her fingers and ate it. 'So, what about you?' she asked. 'Do you still eat the most awful rubbish, like you did?'

He laughed. 'No, not really. I decided if I was going to fight this thing I ought to give my body the best possible chance, so I learned to cook and count grams of fat, and I eat tons of fresh fruit and veg, and I've cut down on meat now. I eat a lot of fish and chicken, pulses, that sort of thing, and virtually no packaged convenience foods. I like fresh ingredients.'

'Hence your fresh pasta last night.'

'Hence my fresh pasta every time I cook it.'

He put his plate down and met her eyes. 'Want to go and make some memories?' he asked softly.

She put her plate on his and stood up. 'Where are we going?'

'I don't know. My cottage? We could go for a walk down the lane to the river.'

She smiled. 'Is there a weeping willow?'

'No. There's a willow, but it's quite cheerful. Anyway, it's a bit muddy and there are lots of little bugs and things at night.'

So they went back to his cottage, and wandered down the lane hand in hand and found Max's cheerful willow, and sat on a fallen branch and talked until the light was fading.

Then they strolled back, arms wrapped round each other's waists, and in the kitchen they hesitated.

'Coffee?' Max offered.

She shook her head. 'Maybe later,' she murmured, summoning up her courage. Perhaps he didn't want her. Perhaps she was taking it for granted…

'Maybe,' he said softly, and drew her into his arms. 'I wouldn't have believed it was possible, but I think you're more beautiful now than you were before.'

Her cheeks warmed. 'You're just an old smoothie,' she said, flattered despite herself. 'You're just buttering me up so you can have your evil way with me.'

'Rumbled,' he said with a chuckle. 'Did it work?'

She smiled up at him. 'Oh, yes, it worked.'

They took Harry to the zoo on Sunday afternoon—after a morning spent building memories of squabbling over the colour supplement and making love in the shower. Harry adored his father, and it seemed it was mutual.

Excellent, she thought. If he gets in deep enough, he won't be able to walk away. They fed the llamas, oohed and aahed at the elephants and big cats, and giggled at the giraffe.

Then they went back to Anna's house and she cooked for Max, for a change, while he bathed Harry and got him ready for bed.

They came down more or less dry and looking so like each other it made her breath catch in her throat, and she thought she was going to cry again.

Fortunately the cat made a nuisance of itself and got on the worktop, and under cover of the diversion she got herself back under control. They ate their supper, a chicken casserole with baby new potatoes and tiny carrots, and then it was time for Harry to go to bed.

'Will you stay for coffee?' she asked him as Harry chased the cat into the sitting room.

'Do you want me to?'

She shrugged. 'It's up to you. It'll take me some time

to put him to bed—we always read for a while. And…' She hesitated, not knowing quite how to put into words her reluctance to behave as they had in the privacy of his cottage with Harry in the house, but he read her mind again.

'Don't worry. I'll go. I don't want to make things awkward for you. I've had a wonderful weekend. Thank you.'

And without further ado, he bent forward, kissed her cheek circumspectly and ruffled Harry's hair on the way past.

"Night, sport. Be good. See you soon.'

"Night, Max,' Harry piped. 'See you soon, too.'

She caught a glimpse of his face as he went through the door, and his mouth was set in a bitter-sweet smile. And no wonder, she thought. Harry was the only child he would ever have—at least, she imagined so, unless he'd taken advantage of the sperm bank before his treatment had started. He hadn't talked about it, apart from telling her that there was no danger of pregnancy, and she didn't feel somehow that she could ask. It was rather a personal issue, after all, even with their history.

And what was their history? she wondered sadly. A wild and hot affair five years ago and, judging by the way their current relationship was shaping up, another hot and wild affair now, interspersed with trips to the zoo and the beach. No wonder she didn't feel she could ask him about the sperm bank. She really didn't know him at all.

She sighed and ruffled Harry's hair. 'Shall we go and find a story?' she asked.

'Can we have Peter Rabbit?'

'Again?' she teased.

'Or Tom Kitten.'

The old Beatrix Potter books from her childhood were

his favourites, to her surprise. All the modern, highly coloured books left him cold. He much preferred the simple, beautifully illustrated animal fantasies that she had enjoyed so much as a child.

'We'll go and look, shall we?' she said, and five minutes later he was curled up in the crook of her arm, laughing at the antics of Tom Kitten and his sisters. Ten minutes later, he was asleep.

Max could have stayed. He could have joined in story time, but, in fact, Anna was glad he'd gone home. She needed a breathing space, time to think, time to come to terms with Thursday night's revelation. It was only Sunday, and she'd hardly been out of his sight the entire time.

She needed time alone, and she imagined he did, too.

So much had happened, and yet nothing had changed.

He was still leaving, and Harry still didn't have a father, and she was going to be alone again.

The thought was unbearable.

He was getting in too deep. Spending just about every waking minute since Thursday—and many sleeping ones—with Annie, that had been a mistake. And as for Harry, he thought the child could easily break his heart.

He was a darling, with a highly developed sense of fun and an insatiable curiosity. He'd never stopped asking questions the whole time they'd been at the zoo, and Max began to understand why people found their much-loved children so exhausting. They seemed to run on some kind of rocket fuel, but fortunately, like rockets, after a while they fizzled out and went quiet, at least for a while.

He wondered what story Annie had read him, and found

himself driving past at a quarter to midnight to see if she still had her bedroom light on.

She didn't, but there was a faint glow that probably came from the landing. He wanted to stay there, parked outside, protecting them like some kind of guardian angel.

That was when he realised he was in over his head.

For the next few days, they gave each other space. It wasn't easy for either of them, and yet they both seemed to need it, and by some unspoken mutual agreement they chatted at work, and then went their separate ways.

Max, particularly, wondered if it had all been a big mistake and if he should have gone when he'd had the chance. He'd told her now, though, that he would stay for a while, and stay he would, even though it was killing him.

Instead of beating himself over the head with it, though, he concentrated on his patients. There was plenty to do. It was a busy practice, and as she'd predicted it wasn't long before Jill Fraser, Anna's neighbour, brought one of her children in.

'This is Will,' she said, sitting down with the screaming baby on her lap. 'I think he's got another ear infection.'

'Oh, dear.' Max slid his chair forward and felt the baby's head, and it was hot. That might have been because he was crying, or because he had a fever. 'Could I look in his ear?' he asked, and directed Jill to turn his head to one side and hold it firmly against her front.

She had obviously done it before, probably numerous times with her three children over the years. She had that resigned look of the long-suffering mother, and Max wondered if she was all right herself, or if she was suffering from stress.

'I just want to check the ear with another device,' he explained. 'It tests the mobility of the middle ear—if there's liquid in there, or pus, it will tell me because that will make the whole mechanism less mobile. The eardrum becomes stiff, the little bones inside don't move properly, and that sort of thing.'

'Does it hurt?' she asked.

He shook his head. 'No, it doesn't hurt—it's just a little probe that seals in the ear, attached to this thing like a gun.'

'Oh, good,' Jill said with a laugh. 'Are you going to shoot him?'

Max smiled. 'Been a bit rough, has it, over the last few days?'

'A bit?' Her smile wobbled, and she turned away. 'You could say that. It wouldn't be so bad if I had someone to share it, but I don't, not since Mick walked out yet again.'

Definitely stressed, Max thought. 'Was this recently?' he asked, fitting the right-sized probe in the tympanometer and placing it in the child's ear. Within a second he had his result—the sound returning to the machine was diminished, which meant the child's ear was full of fluid.

'Two months ago,' Jill replied, mechanically stroking the baby's head to soothe him. 'That was the third time he left. I won't have him back again. It's when they come and go it's so hard. You go through all the grieving for the relationship, and then they come back, and then they go, and you do the grieving again but this time there's hope, and then they come back, and go—it's hell. I wish he'd just go and stay gone.'

Max sat back in the chair and studied her body language. She was dealing with the baby all right, but she was tense, her shoulders hunched, her neck stiff, and it was his bet that if she relaxed she'd howl her eyes out—and the baby, not unnaturally, was picking up on it.

'Let me see the little fellow,' he said, reaching out for the child. The baby relaxed against him almost instantly, sensing his calm presence even though he was a total stranger, and Jill sighed as the noise diminished to a dull sniffle.

'Do you want to make an appointment to come and see me on your own for a chat?' he asked. 'I think you're very stressed, and maybe I can do something to help you.'

'Put me on tranks, you mean?' she said sceptically. 'No, thanks.'

'Not tranquillisers, necessarily. I don't like them any more than you do, but there are other things. Have you tried St John's wort? It's a relation of rose of Sharon. It's brilliant for TATT—tired all the time. It happens to so many people we've even given it a name! Unfortunately, I can't prescribe it, because it's not a recognised remedy, being herbal, and it's not regulated in the same way, but if you can afford it, it may well help you.'

'I'll try it. It certainly sounds like me.'

'Now, getting back to the baby for a minute, he's definitely got fluid in his ear, and he might have a condition called glue ear, when they get sticky gunk in the ear all the time. If so, he might need to be referred to a specialist. I'll give him something to take, and you need to give him paracetamol syrup, but I don't want to give him antibiotics because these ear bugs get very resistant and most of the time the body can sort itself out if you give it long enough. OK?'

She nodded.

'Now, about you. Try the St John's wort, and come

back to see me if it's not working or if you can't wait that long—it might take a week or so to kick in. Be patient. And if you want to chat, just come in. OK? I'll fit you in.'

'Thanks.' She smiled, a fragile smile that he sensed would dissolve into tears at the slightest provocation, and took her baby off his lap while he printed out the prescription and handed it to her.

'Take care,' he said, and she nodded and left.

'I wish he'd just go and stay gone.'

Max closed his eyes. Was he doing the same thing to Anna? And to himself?

'Oh, hell's teeth,' he sighed, and pressed his buzzer for the next patient.

He saw Anna later, and found a quiet moment to ask her about Jill. 'Do you think she's depressed and stressed out any more than normal? She brought the baby in with an ear infection and I thought she seemed very flat.'

'I noticed that,' Anna said thoughtfully. 'I was going to keep an eye on her.'

'Would you? I'd be grateful. What's her financial situation like? I've recommended she takes St John's wort, but, of course, I can't prescribe it and it isn't cheap.'

'Oh, Mick's more than generous,' Anna said drily. 'He just won't give them his time. Too busy doing what he wants to do—which most of the time seems to be other women. But, no, she's not that short of money, I don't think.'

Max nodded, and wondered why a man married to an attractive, pleasant woman like Jill Fraser would need to play the field. A flaw in himself, he thought, but the end result was the same, possibly, no matter why he left.

Was he himself behaving as badly as that? He was doing it for their sakes, though.

'Penny for them,' Anna murmured.

He gave a short laugh. 'Not a chance.' He suddenly realised how much he'd missed her in the past few days and nights. 'I don't suppose you could find a babysitter, could you?'

'Tonight?'

He shrugged. 'If possible, but if not then tomorrow?'

She was silent for a moment, then she smiled sadly. 'OK. I'll ask my parents. Do you want him to stay overnight?'

Their eyes met, and heat seared between them. 'It's up to you,' he said, putting the ball back in her court. 'I thought, as it's so hot, we might go swimming in the sea tonight.'

'At midnight?' she asked, and he could see the anticipation in her eyes.

'Uh-huh.'

She swallowed. 'I'll ask. I'm just going round there for lunch. I'll tell you later.'

He watched her go, anticipation tightening his gut, and wondered if he was insane to stay, to make her memories, to indulge both of them in this lunatic folly.

Probably, but it was beyond him to stop. He didn't care how much it hurt later. He'd deal with it then. For now, he wanted to be with her every minute of every day.

Making memories.

It was a gorgeous night. They found a deserted stretch of beach, with sand at the waterline and pebbles at high water, and near the top of the sand Max built a little campfire with driftwood and they sat beside it, staring out over the moonlit sea.

The light gleamed on the lazy swell, and the soft rush of the breaking waves lulled their senses. It was hypnotic, enchanting and utterly romantic, and Anna wanted to stay there with him for ever.

'Fancy a walk?' Max asked, and she nodded.

'Can do. Are we going far?'

'I doubt it.'

She stood up, brushing sand off her bottom, then took off her shoes and rolled up the hems of her jeans. Max did the same, and then, arm in arm, they strolled along the waterline, gasping with laughter every now and then as a more adventurous wave curled coldly around their ankles.

Then one particularly big wave came and soaked them to the knees, and Anna screamed and ran up the beach, Max in hot pursuit.

He chased her back past their little campfire, down towards a breakwater, and when she reached it she was too slow to climb over.

'Got you,' he said victoriously, and turned her, laughing, into his arms.

'That's cheating—I had to stop,' she protested, but it was a token protest and she was happy to be caught—especially when he silenced her by the simple expedient of cutting off her air supply with a kiss.

The resistance and laughter drained out of her, and she leant into his arms, slid her hands round and tucked them in the back pockets of his jeans and groaned softly with pleasure. It seemed like days since he'd kissed her, and with the sighing of the surf in the background, the utter peace and tranquillity of the night, the vast openness of the sea beside them, she couldn't have designed a more perfect setting.

His mouth was gentle, coaxing, sipping and teasing at her lips, trailing hot, open-mouthed kisses over her throat and down the open V of her blouse.

He opened first one button, then the next, his lips following his hands to kiss every inch of skin as it was revealed. She felt the cool salt air on her skin, the hot moisture of his tongue followed by the cooling breeze, and wondered how it was possible for sensation to be so heightened by the romance of the night.

Because it *was* heightened, without question. Unbearably heightened, every sense alert, aware, more receptive than ever before.

There was no sound apart from the soft rush of the sea and their breathy sighs, their bodies caressed by the cool fingers of night air whispering over their skin. They were utterly alone, wrapped in a private world, and they could have been a hundred miles from civilisation, not just a matter of minutes.

He lifted his head and rested it against hers, his breathing ragged. His fingers fumbled to do up her buttons, and, regretfully, she moved to help him. It was common sense. They weren't miles from anywhere, and anyone could have walked along the beach and found them.

'Do you want your swim, or do you want to go home?' he asked softly.

'Swim,' she said instantly. 'Are we going to be daring?'

He chuckled. 'Why not? We can stay in the water if anyone comes along. Anything to help your fantasies along.'

They looked around, then stripped off their clothes and ran headlong into the sea, gasping with shocked laughter as they hit the water. Once they were in it was wonderful, the sea caressing them like liquid velvet, rocking them gently in the slow, languid swell.

They kissed again, just affectionate, loving touches in the silvering moonlight, and then hand in hand they walked out of the sea, water streaming from their skin and leaving silver trails in the sand. They dressed, sandy legs and all, and limped and picked their way over the stones to the car park.

Anna didn't bother with her shoes. Instead, she brushed off the loose sand, swung her feet in and left them to dry while Max, properly shod again, drove them home.

They arrived back at his cottage at after one, showered off the salt and sand and went to bed, their hair still damp, too impatient to dry it properly. It had been days since they'd been alone, and their hunger had been sharpened by anticipation.

Anna took everything he had to offer, and in return she gave him everything she had to give, and later, lying quietly and drowsing in the still of the night, she thought back over the evening.

It was a beautiful memory. She would file it away carefully, smoothed flat and placed with infinite care where she could view it on demand, and she would treasure it.

CHAPTER SIX

AS THE days turned to weeks, almost as many weeks as they'd had before, Anna grew to know and love Max even more. They seemed so in tune with each other that it was uncanny, and without the threat to his future, life would have been perfect.

Oddly it wasn't the threat of his death that troubled her. More that he would go, and that she would lose such time as he did have left. And the frustrating thing was that it could, and probably would, be years and years. It was entirely possible that he would outlive her, and yet she seemed unable to persuade him to stay longer than he had agreed, or to tell Harry who he was.

'What about your parents?' she said one day, as they were sitting in the garden of his cottage, staring out over the countryside and sipping wine. 'Have you told them about Harry?'

He looked at her as if she had lost her mind. 'My parents? No, of course I haven't told them! What would I tell them?'

Anna laughed incredulously. 'That you have a son? Max, Harry's their grandson, a part of you that will live on.

Don't you think they have a right to know about him? And what about Harry? Don't you think he's entitled to their love and friendship as he grows older? And what about uncles and aunts and cousins? It's not just you you're depriving him of, Max. It's your entire family. Do you really think that's fair?'

He looked away, his face drawn into troubled lines. 'I don't know. I don't know what to do, Annie,' he confessed wearily. 'Part of me wants to pretend this isn't happening, and just ignore it. Another part insists on staring it in the face.' He turned to her, his eyes unshuttered for once, open and revealing. 'I love you. Whatever happens, I want you to know that.'

She sighed harshly round the lump in her throat. 'This sounds like another of your "I'm doing for your own good" speeches, Max. Maybe *I* want to be the judge of what's good for me and Harry. Especially Harry. He's always talking about not having a father.'

Max looked shocked. 'What have you told him? I didn't even think, but I suppose he must wonder because his friends have fathers. So what did you say?'

She lifted her shoulders in a quick shrug. 'I told him that I loved his father very much but he had to go away. He wants to know when he's coming back, and I keep telling him never. He asked again the other day.'

He froze, shock written on his face. 'What did you tell him?' he demanded hoarsely.

'The same. What could I tell him?' she asked bitterly. 'That he was here—that he'd already met his father and liked him? That his father loved him but wasn't man enough to deal with it?'

'That's not true!' he protested. 'You know that's not true.'

'Isn't it?'

She stood up and brushed down her skirt. 'I'm going home. Don't bother to come. I'll walk.'

And she turned on her heel and left him.

Max contemplated finishing the bottle of wine but thought better of it. Instead, he sat staring blankly out over the darkening countryside, considering what Anna had said and wrestling with his conscience. Finally coming to a conclusion, he stood up, carried his glass inside and dumped it in the sink, picked up his car keys and headed north, out along the A14 to Cambridge.

He arrived at his parents' house at something after ten, and let himself in through the back door. His parents were in the kitchen, feeding the cat, loading the dishwasher—doing all the usual family chores before bedtime—and they took one look at him and froze.

'I've got something to tell you,' he said, and the glass slid out of his mother's fingers and shattered all over the floor.

He dredged up a smile. 'Not that. I'm still in remission. It's something else—something I should have told you weeks ago.' He looked around restlessly, unsure how to go on, but his parents were quicker.

'Better get this glass cleared up while the kettle boils,' his father said practically. 'Max, hold the cat. Clare, mind your feet, darling. Just stand still.' He whisked the broom around her, then ran a wet cloth over the floor to pick up any tiny bits. Max shut the cat out and made coffee while his mother posted the last of the dishes into the machine.

'Right,' Henry Carter said, dusting off his hands. 'Let's

go and sit down somewhere comfortable while you get whatever this is off your chest.'

Bless him, Max thought. He'd been a tower of strength through his illness. Maybe he could see a way through this.

They sat down, his parents watching him expectantly, and because there was no subtle way to do this, no easy way into the conversation, he said bluntly, 'I've got a son. He's called Harry, he's four years old and he doesn't know I'm his father.'

Shock held them motionless for ages, and then the questions started. When? How? Why hadn't he known? When did he find out?

And then the one he was dreading.

'When can we meet him?' his mother asked, on the edge of her seat, her face expectant and excited.

'You can't,' he said flatly. 'I'm not going to tell him who I am. It's not fair—in case anything happens.'

Of course, they went through all the arguments Anna had been through, and he gave them all the same replies until he began to feel like a programmed robot. Press button A to start, he thought impatiently, and stood up.

'Listen, I only told you because I thought you ought to know. If anything happens to me, I want you to contact Anna. I'll make sure you always have her correct address, and I'll keep you up to date with photos of Harry and so on, but I'm leaving Wenham Market as soon as my contract is up, and I won't be back. All communication with her will be by letter, through solicitors. All right?'

His mother burst into tears, his father stood up and gave her shoulder an agitated pat, before coming over to him and standing in front of him, toe to toe.

'Don't you think Harry has a right to his father?' he asked quietly. 'How would you have felt if I'd had an illness and cut you out of my life? Wouldn't you rather have done the things we did when you were a little boy? Gone fishing, kicked footballs, lain awake all night in the woods, looking for badgers—wouldn't you rather have had that than known nothing about me? Even if it meant you had to lose me, wouldn't it have been better to have had that first?'

Max looked down. The floor swam in front of his eyes, and he blinked. 'It's not the same.'

'How is it not the same? Except that you already have four years to make up for?'

'I want to meet him,' his mother pleaded from the sofa. 'Max, please—can't you bring him over? You don't have to tell him who you are—just invite them both here for lunch on Sunday, and we won't say anything, I promise. Just let us meet him—' She broke off, struggling with her composure again, and Max gave a short sigh.

'Dammit, Mother, don't cry,' he said gruffly. 'This is hard enough.' His voice cracked, and he went out to the kitchen and put the kettle on again to give himself something to do. The cat attacked his shoelaces, and he picked her up and tickled her chin. 'You're just like Anna's cat,' he told her. 'Wicked and into everything.'

She purred and butted his chin, and he hugged her and wished he could settle down in one place and maybe have a cat of his own—something on which to lavish all the love and devotion in him that was going to waste.

His mother came up behind him and slipped her arms round his waist. 'I'm sorry,' she said in a rather damp voice. 'I didn't mean to nag you. I know it has to be your decision, but perhaps you could think about it? Or maybe we could pop in to visit you and they could be there, almost by accident?'

'That might be better,' he conceded gruffly. 'I'm not just trying to be awkward, Mum. I feel the future's so uncertain I can't bear to expose him to it. It seems cruel.'

'And what does Anna think?'

He sighed. 'Anna agrees with you.'

He felt his mother's lips press lightly against his shoulder, and a lump formed in his throat.

'You must do what you think is best. Just let us know. Now, are you going to stay the night and drive back in the morning, or do you want another drink before you go?'

'I'll stay—if I may? I'm feeling pretty tired.' Too many nights with Annie, he thought sadly, filling up her memory banks…

Anna felt guilty. She'd stormed out without giving Max a chance to discuss it, accused him of not being man enough to deal with what was after all an incredibly painful and sensitive issue, and now she felt guilty.

Who was she to judge Max? She'd made mistakes with Harry. Every parent did. Maybe Max was no different. Whatever, she'd been unfair, and she couldn't sleep.

Because she'd planned to spend the evening with Max, Harry was staying with her mother, and so she didn't have to worry about him. She got out of bed and dressed quickly in her jeans and a sweater against the chilly night, and ran out to her car. She'd go round and see him and apologise, and then maybe stay the night.

If he forgave her.

The house was in darkness. It was after midnight, so it

wasn't surprising, but his car wasn't on the drive, and she knew he wasn't on call.

A terrible cold fear crawled over her, seeping into her bones and filling her with a hideous dread.

'No!' she whispered. 'Not again. Max, no!'

She threw the door open and ran round the bonnet, hammering on his front door with her fists. 'Max!' she screamed. 'Max! Wake up. Open the door! Open the door!'

She slid to the step, her face against the cool wood burning with emotion and anxiety. She lifted her fist again and dropped it feebly against the door, a sob rising in her throat. 'Max? Please, Max, no…'

It was her fault. She'd driven him away, pushed him too hard, made an already difficult situation intolerable for him, and so he'd left her, gone away without a word.

'You promised,' she wept brokenly. 'You promised to tell me…'

She pounded the door again. 'Max! Damn you, answer the door!'

A light came on down the lane, in the neighbouring cottage a few hundred yards away. She saw a curtain twitch, and bit her lip. She had to live in this village. She couldn't be found weeping and ranting on his doorstep.

Mustering the last remnants of her common sense, she struggled to her feet and climbed back into the car. She couldn't drive away, though. She couldn't see, and the faster she blinked, the faster she misted up again.

'Oh, hell,' she mumbled, scrubbing her eyes with a tissue. 'Max, you promised…'

She gave up fighting, folded her arms over the steering-wheel and wept until she was too exhausted to move.

Eventually, as the sky lightened in the east and the birds began to stir, she fell into an uneasy and troubled sleep.

She was woken by the car door opening, and Max's voice anxiously rousing her.

'Annie? Are you all right? What's wrong? Dear God, my love, what is it?'

He was here! He hadn't left—or if he had, he'd come back! And he'd called her his love. She sat up stiffly and met his troubled eyes. 'I thought you'd gone,' she said simply.

Max was gutted. He looked at her, so dear, so precious, at the grief in her face and the pain in her eyes, and he dragged her from the car and crushed her to his chest.

'Silly girl, of course I haven't gone!' he said roughly. 'I've been with my parents—I stayed the night. I've just come back to shower and change for work.'

'I couldn't believe it,' she told him, staring incredulously at him, touching his face as if to make sure he was real. 'I thought you'd left again without telling me, and you promised, but I was unfair to you—that's why I came back, to apologise, and you weren't here…' She hiccuped to a halt, and Max hugged her again, guilt stabbing through him.

'I'm sorry,' he whispered into her hair. 'You weren't unfair, you were right. I went to tell my parents about Harry.'

Her head snapped up and her eyes locked with his. 'And?' she said hopefully.

He sighed. 'They want to meet him.'

'That's wonderful,' she said softly. 'Oh, Max, that's wonderful—'

'I still don't want him to know—not yet, at least.' He heard that last qualifying remark, and wondered if Annie had noticed it.

'Not yet?' she echoed. 'But maybe—later?'

Damn. 'Slip of the tongue,' he told her, watching the hope die in her eyes and hating himself. 'Annie, don't. I've had all I can deal with for now, and you have, too. Come inside—I need you. I missed you last night.'

'I missed you, too. I always miss you.'

He hugged her, unable to speak, and once through the door he drew her into his arms and kissed her hungrily. He didn't want to think any more, didn't want to ponder on the right course of action. He just wanted to hold her, to love her, to lose himself in her sweet warmth and let her love wash over him.

'Where's Harry?' he asked softly.

'With my parents. He's been there for the night.'

He remembered now. It seemed so long ago. He'd sat up with his parents, talking to them, until nearly one, and it was only six now. He held out his hand, and she took it, and wordlessly he led her upstairs to his bedroom and took her in his arms again.

'We'll be late,' she protested half-heartedly.

'No, we won't. I promise.'

He lied. She left him in the shower and rushed home, and they arrived almost simultaneously in their separate cars a scant two minutes late.

'Well, we almost made it,' he said with a wry smile, and she laughed softly and disappeared to collect her notes.

He checked his messages, scooped up his notes and went into his consulting room. His parents had been thrilled about Harry, he thought, and he was sure it was because they'd thought he'd never have another chance. He'd taken advantage of the sperm bank facilites—just in case, by a miracle, he should be cured and meet up with Annie again—but he hadn't held out much hope, and nor had his parents.

Funny, until Annie had pointed it out it had never occurred to him that he was cheating them of their grandson.

He'd have to set up an impromptu get-together—a casual drop-in that gave them all a chance to meet without ceremony. Perhaps if they arrived just as he was taking Annie and Harry out for the day. They could join in...

Hmm. Interesting thought. He picked up the first set of patient notes, scanned them briefly and pressed the buzzer. He'd have to see what they were all doing this weekend, perhaps.

He soon forgot about his parents and Harry. It was a busy morning, made more hectic by a number of patients who came to see him with a whole list of things wrong with them.

'While I'm here, Doctor...' It was becoming an oft-repeated remark that was threatening to mess up his schedules beyond redemption.

Then Valerie Hawkshead was brought in by her husband as an emergency. They had been driving through town, and she'd had a seizure in the car. Could he see her?

He could. He was puzzled, and concerned. She'd come in two or three weeks ago and had had an urgent referral to a neurologist, once he'd dismissed any other obvious cause of her forgetfulness and headaches. She'd been sent back to him as suffering from depression with retardation, and needing drug therapy to alleviate this.

Unhappy with the diagnosis, he'd given her something suitable and was following her up regularly. This, though, was totally out of the blue, and threw a whole different light on the situation.

It was also potentially much more serious, he felt, and his unease grew when he saw her.

She was depressed, listless, her eyes seemed unfocussed and she had clearly gone downhill drastically. She was also suffering from a blinding headache, and needed urgent hospital assessment.

'I want her to go back to the hospital for a scan,' he told her husband. 'I'm not happy. This is not what I would have expected, and I think we need to find out what's caused it and why. I think it's perhaps a little bit more complicated than we'd all anticipated.'

He wrote a letter, handed it to them and asked them to go straight to the hospital radiology department. If, as he suspected, they found a brain tumour, and provided they were able to remove it successfully, she might find all her symptoms resolved themselves.

If not—well, if not, it could be terminal.

Assuming he was correct, of course. There was always a chance that he was mistaken, but he feared not. There was still the possibility of Creutzfeldt-Jakob disease—CJD, or mad cow disease as it was commonly and mistakenly called—or syphilis in a late stage. He couldn't tell, and there was no future in speculating.

That the hospital would admit her he was sure. He wondered how her family would cope, and how she would progress, and not for the first time he was frustrated that he would be unlikely to see their story through to the end.

The lack of continuity in patient care distressed him—so many times he picked up things that had a long-term treatment plan, and had to hand the patients over before he'd seen it through. It was frustrating, and it was also professionally undesirable because he was failing to build up a picture of many treatments that might help with future cases.

There was an answer, of course. Annie was pushing him towards it, but he didn't feel it was fair to his patients. What if he came out of remission and had to go for treatment, and was off for some weeks or months? Was it fair to expect patients to have to make do with a locum under those circumstances?

And, anyway, he thought drily, no practice in its right mind would take him on, knowing he had lymphoma. It was too risky, too uncertain a future to gamble on.

Whatever.

He pressed the buzzer for his next patient, suddenly aware that he'd been staring into space and had a queue of patients still to see.

Lack of sleep and too much emotion, he thought tiredly. Perhaps tonight he'd go round and visit Annie and Harry, and just sit and chat for a while, then go home for an early night.

He must remember to ask how Jill Fraser was getting on, on the subject of continuity and follow-up. Perhaps he'd even pop in to see her.

The doorbell rang, and Anna dusted her hands on her apron and followed Harry down the hall.

'Hello, sunshine,' Max said to the child, then looked up at her and smiled.

The sun came out in her heart, and she smiled back, holding the door wide. 'Come on in. We're still not ready—Harry's been helping me.'

He ran a laughing eye over her flour-spattered form, and grinned. 'Is it safe to eat?' he asked under his breath, and she laughed.

'Of course. It's going to be good, isn't it, Harry?'

Harry nodded. 'I put the eyes in,' he informed Max.

His eyebrows shot up, and Anna laughed again. 'In the gingerbread men. Nothing ghastly, don't worry. I'm not doing culinary experiments.'

'I'm relieved to hear it. Listen, I'm just going to pop in and have a chat to Jill for a moment, OK? I won't be long. Put the kettle on, I'm dying of thirst.'

He kissed her floury cheek and went out again, and she closed the door and went back to the kitchen to finish the preparations. They were having a barbecue, with chicken breasts cut into chunks and skewered with peppers, tiny onions and cherry tomatoes, and organic sausages in buns with fried onions, and loads of salad, the gingerbread men to follow.

Assuming they ever got into the oven.

'Harry, darling, that's enough buttons. Let's cook them now.' She slipped the tray into the oven, Harry standing well back as instructed, and then she told him he could sit down opposite the oven door and watch for them to go nicely brown.

'They're brown, Mummy,' he called excitedly almost before she was out of the kitchen.

'Harry, they can't be. Give them five minutes. Look—see the clock? See this long hand? When it gets to here, look again. All right?'

He nodded, and watched the clock unblinkingly. Every time she came back into the kitchen for something else, he was still in the same position, until in the end he called her again.

'They're brown now,' he yelled, and she went back in and opened the oven door.

'Not quite. Watch the hand to here,' she said, and then the doorbell rang again.

Harry pelted down the hall and struggled to reach the lock, and she took the safety catch off the top and opened it to let Max in.

'How is she?' she asked, following Harry slowly down the hall.

'Better, she thinks. I suspect it's as much because someone noticed as it is the St John's wort, but it is supposed to be very good. She certainly seems more cheerful and on top of things, but that might be because the baby's better.'

'Are you here for the evening now?' she asked with a smile.

'Yes. Come here.' He glanced down the hall at Harry, glued to the clock, and propelled her into the sitting room.

'They're ready,' Harry yelled, and Max laughed softly and kissed her anyway, just briefly.

'Later,' she promised, and then there was a scream from the kitchen and Max dropped her and sprinted down the hall.

She ran after him, to find him holding Harry screaming over the sink, cold water already running over his arm. There was a thin white line across his forearm—from the edge of the oven, she imagined—and guilt savaged her.

'What were you doing, darling?' she asked, soothing his brow and hugging him.

'They were ready,' he sobbed. 'I just wanted to take them out before they got burnted.'

'I'll take them out. You stay there with Max and let that cool down.'

She opened the oven, and still the biscuits were hardly cooked. But she'd had enough of his obsessive watching, and they would cook a moment longer on the oven tray. She pulled it out, put it out of Harry's reach and turned the oven off.

'Right. Leave them alone. They're for pudding, understand? Later.'

He nodded miserably, perched on the draining-board with Max holding his arm firmly but gently under the water. 'I just di'n't want them to get burnted,' he said again, and buried his face in her shoulder.

'I think it's all right. Have you got anything to put on it?' Max asked.

'Aloe vera—that's it there,' she said, pointing to a spiky succulent on the window sill. 'Just break a piece off and slice it up the middle, but mind the spikes at the sides.'

'What do you do with it then?' he asked, slicing with her vegetable knife.

'Tape it on for the night. By tomorrow it won't hurt and will almost have cleared up. It's a bit slimy, but it works wonders.'

She dried Harry's arm, and then taped the piece of juicy leaf in place. 'There,' she said with satisfaction. 'Now, let's go and start the barbecue before anything else happens.'

'Want a gingerbread man,' Harry said petulantly.

'No, they're hot, you'll burn your tongue and I can't stick aloe vera on that. Anyway, they're for pudding.'

They went outside, just in time to see the cat legging it down the garden with a string of sausages in tow.

'Oh, Felix, you horrible cat!' she wailed.

It was too much for Max. He leant back against the fence and laughed till his sides ached.

'Just for that you can starve,' Anna said repressively.

'I could nip to the shop for some burgers,' he offered.

'They're shut. Don't worry, I've got more in the freezer. I swear, one day I'm going to skin that cat.'

'A likely story,' Max said mildly, settling down in one of her garden chairs in the shade of the apple tree. 'This is such a pretty garden,' he murmured, looking round.

She glanced at it, and wondered if he could see the years of work that had gone into rescuing it from dereliction. Not that she'd done it alone, or the house. Her father and mother had been wonderful, in between telling her she was mad and ought to live with them instead of buying her own place, but she'd wanted privacy and a little emotional distance, and most of the time she was sure she'd done the right thing.

She found more sausages, and they cooked them and the chicken kebabs when the coals were hot, and then they had Harry's over-buttoned and slightly under-done gingerbread men for pudding with a dollop of organic ice cream which was the wickedest thing she'd ever tasted.

'This can't be healthy,' Max remarked, scraping the last trace from his bowl.

She laughed. 'Who said anything about healthy? It's stuffed with cholesterol and calories. It's just organic—it's not poisoned with sprays and chemicals and hormones and antibiotics. It doesn't mean it can't be wicked.'

'I want more,' Harry announced, but she shook her head.

'You've had more than enough to eat, young man. It's time for your bath and bed—you're late, and you've had too many nights with Grannie recently.'

'Want Max to bath me,' he said.

'Then ask nicely,' Max told him, firmly but gently.

'Please, will you bath me?' he asked him, and Max, only too willing by the look on his face, took his son by the hand and led him into the house, while Anna cleared up the dishes, washed up and indulged herself in a little sentimental cry.

Another memory, she thought.

Max had forgotten how easy it was to get wet, bathing young children. He hadn't spent all that much time with his nephews and nieces recently, but it all came flooding back, as it were.

I blame it on the mother, he thought wryly, getting another soaking from the water-pistol. Giving up, he wrestled it from the child, chucked it into the basin and pushed his sleeves up further.

'Right, hairwash and out,' he said, and laid the child back to wet his hair. He shampooed it carefully, laid him down again to rinse it and once more marvelled at how like his nephew Thomas Harry was.

A great wave of love washed over him, and he lifted the boy out, wrapped him in a towel and sat down on the lid of the loo seat to dry him. He squirmed and giggled and tried to get away, but Max managed to pin him down until he'd tickled him dry all over, and then he chased him along the corridor to his bedroom, bribed him into his pyjamas with the promise of an extra-long story, then settled down at the head of the bed, Harry tucked under his arm and a book in his hand.

That was how Anna found them an hour later, both fast asleep.

She woke Max gently, and he blinked and shifted carefully away from Harry, easing off the bed without disturbing him.

He needn't have worried. Harry rolled over, snuggling down under the quilt with a little sleepy noise, and they went downstairs.

They didn't talk for fear of disturbing him, but Max was glad of the silence. To be honest, he didn't think he could speak. Emotion was welling up in him, and when they reached the sitting room, as if she understood exactly what he felt, Anna opened her arms and hugged him.

'You don't have to go,' she reminded him. 'You could be part of this.'

He swallowed hard. 'Don't, please. Not tonight. Just hold me.'

So she held him, her hands tracing lazy circles on his back, and he dropped his head into the curve of her neck and let the soothing touch wash over him.

She was right. He could stay—but at what cost to them? And could he really ask them to pay the price?

CHAPTER SEVEN

'ABOUT my parents,' Max said the following day.

They were sitting in the tiny bit of garden at the back of the practice, perched on the wall in the sunshine, taking a well-earned rest. 'What about your parents?' Anna asked, blowing the steam off the top of her coffee.

'How about you and Harry coming to my place on Sunday for tea in the garden, and they can just "drop in", as it were, in passing?'

Anna sensed that it was a huge step forwards for Max, one he was taking reluctantly for the sake of his parents. 'Sounds fine,' she told him, concentrating on her coffee so he wouldn't see how pleased she was. 'What time do you want us? And do you want help with the tea?'

He grinned wryly. 'I was going to ask the tearoom for some goodies,' he confessed. 'Supporting local industry and all that.'

'Nothing to do with the fact that you don't want to cook,' she teased.

'I love cooking—I'm good at it,' he reminded her archly. 'I just don't do cakes. King Alfred and I have a lot in common. Talking of which, how's Harry's burn?'

'Fine. I took the aloe vera off this morning, and it looks perfectly all right—there's a little red line, but it's not sore. You ought to have a plant.'

'There are all sorts of things I ought to have,' he said, and she didn't know if she'd imagined it or if there had been a trace of sadness in his voice.

Poor Max. It was all so simple, and he just couldn't see it.

'I'll give you a rooted bit,' she promised. 'Now, getting back to Sunday—do you want me to make a cake, or cut some sandwiches or something? It mustn't look too staged or Harry will smell a rat.'

'He will?'

'He's four, not stupid,' Anna reminded him. 'People he knows don't have big teas unless it's for a birthday party or Grannie and Grandad at Christmas.'

'I concede to your superior knowledge,' he said with a grin. 'I'll buy a cake—unless you can make one of those wicked chocolate ones they sell in there? But we can make sandwiches. Can you get hold of some of that wild boar ham we had in the pub?'

She wrinkled her nose. 'I can, but Harry won't eat it. He only likes egg and cress or banana sandwiches.'

'In which case we'd better have a variety,' Max said, pulling a face. 'I haven't had a banana sandwich for at least twenty-five years.'

'You should,' she said with a laugh. 'They're lovely.'

'Yuck.' He swirled his coffee. 'Do you know Valerie Hawkshead, by the way?'

'Valerie—yes, I do. She and her husband own the fruit shop. Why, has she been in to see you?'

He nodded. He looked concerned, and she wondered what was wrong.

'Problems?' she prompted.

He let out a sigh. 'She came in with headaches and forgetfulness. I sent her to a neurologist, and he said she had depression with retardation. Then she had a fit, and I sent her in again yesterday for a scan. Her husband's just phoned to say they found a brain tumour of some sort, and they've removed it.'

He put his mug down. 'I knew it was more than just depression or premature dementia. That's why I referred her. I can't believe they sent her back on anti-depressants without doing a thorough screen.'

'Will she be all right?' Anna asked, concerned for the woman she knew only slightly but who had always been pleasant and friendly.

Max shrugged. 'I don't know. It's too early to say if there's any permanent damage done, and I probably won't be here long enough to find out. That's the trouble with locum work. No continuity.'

He sounded disheartened by that, but again Anna didn't comment. She didn't want to patronise him with platitudes about the patients missing him, or insult his intelligence by telling him that Suzanna was perfectly well qualified. He knew that. She just left the seed of discontent growing quietly in a corner of his mind, and took heart from another ally in her fight against his stubbornness.

Sunday was gorgeous. It wasn't too hot, but Max had mowed the lawn with the little push-mower he'd found in the garage, and had tidied up the rose bed a little so the bushes actually had a chance to be seen. He didn't get as much done as he'd have liked, but he'd cleaned the kitchen and generally made the place look a little better, and Anna brought some flowers from her garden for the mantelpiece in the sitting room.

Harry was playing in the garden, dressed in soft, stretchy shorts and a matching T-shirt, and he looked taller.

Ridiculous, Max told himself. It's only been four weeks. How can he have grown?

He stood at the kitchen window, poised in the act of rinsing the cress for the egg sandwiches, and Anna turned off the cold tap and stood beside him.

'He's grown,' he said, and his voice sounded rough and unused.

Anna gave him an odd look. 'Has he? I hadn't noticed.'

'I think so.'

She looked out again, her face softening.

'You really love him, don't you?' Max said, and he felt a pang of…not envy, exactly, but something akin to it. It must be wonderful to have such a relationship with your child.

He turned the tap on again, washing the cress with great vigour and very little skill, and Anna turned the tap off again and took it out of his hands.

'You're supposed to be rinsing it, not mashing it under the tap,' she scolded affectionately. 'I'll do this. You go outside and spend some time with him.'

He threw her a grateful glance and went out to the garden. 'How are you doing, sport?' he asked.

'OK,' Harry said, chasing a grasshopper across the rough lawn. 'Look, it can jump ever such a long way!'

Max sat down beside him, watching the grasshopper out of the corner of his eye, most of his attention on his son.

Son.

The very word was a miracle, never mind the child. He wanted to reach out and hug him, just to prove he was real and not a figment of his imagination. Instead, he found excuses to touch him—lifting him into a tree, helping him down again, turning him round to show him something—almost anything, just to assuage the terrible urge to sweep him into his arms and crush him against his chest.

'I'm just going to see how your mother's getting on with the sandwiches,' he said, and stood up, almost running into the house in his haste to get away before he made a fool of himself.

Anna met him in the hall, her arms coming out to hug him, and he hugged her back and gave himself time to settle.

'All right now?' she asked gently, and he nodded.

'Yes. Don't know what came over me.'

'Love, I would imagine,' she said matter-of-factly. 'It can get you like that.'

She dropped her arms and went back to the sandwiches, and he went into the sitting room, doing a last scan round to make sure it was tidy. Out of the front window he saw his father's car pull up on the drive, and he went back to the kitchen.

'They're here,' he said, and she turned towards him and looked at him searchingly.

'Are you all right?'

He nodded. 'I'm fine. A bit worried they'll say something. How about you?'

She gave a tight smile, and he realised she was nervous. 'I'll live,' she said, and he gave her a quick hug.

'They'll love you,' he promised, and went to open the door.

'Where is he?' his mother whispered.

'In the garden. You can see him from the window. It's a bit of a shock, he's just like Thomas. Come on in and meet Anna.'

He led them through to the kitchen, and they found Anna standing nervously by the sink, her eyes alert, her body quiet.

'Anna, I want you to meet my parents, Henry and Clare. Mum, Dad, this is Anna,' he said, and he suddenly found his heart racing. He wanted them to get on, he realised. *Needed* them to get on. He felt suddenly sick with apprehension, but then Anna smiled and held out her hand, and his mother was moving towards her and wrapping her in a motherly embrace, and he knew it was going to be all right.

They were lovely—Max's father just like him but older, with kindly crinkles around eyes that saw right through that outer shell to the things that really mattered, his mother warm and loving and utterly devoted to her stubborn and courageous son.

Her eyes strayed to the window, and Anna moved back, giving them both a better view.

Clare Carter gasped, the hand covering her mouth trembling with reaction. 'Oh, my goodness, he is so like Thomas! I wouldn't have believed it!' Tears filled her eyes, and Anna could see the yearning in her face.

Henry's, too. He stood beside his wife, one hand comfortingly on her shoulder, and together they stared at the grandson they had thought never to have.

'Oh, Max,' his mother said unsteadily, and Anna slipped out, going down the garden to keep an eye on Harry while they stood and watched him from the window and wrestled their emotions into order again.

'Max's mother and father have dropped in—they're going to stay for tea. Isn't that nice?' she told him.

He didn't even look up. 'Yeah. Have we got 'nough?'

'Should have. What are you doing?'

'I found a whole lot of wood lices. They curl up in your hand—look!'

'No, thanks,' she said, suppressing a shudder and looking away. 'Anyway, they're called lice, not lices.'

'This one's really friendly. Hold it!'

'No!'

He chased her with it, down the garden and back again, giggling and squealing with delight, and finally trapped her against the back fence and held out his empty hands.

'Ha-ha!' he said gleefully. 'No wood lices!'

'Lice,' she corrected automatically. 'You are a horrid tease and it's not fair to the wood lice to run around with them. They'll lose their families and be frightened. Where did you drop it?'

'I put him down—I didn't really have him. I just made you run away.'

She hugged him. 'You are a little beast,' she said affectionately.

'Having fun?' Max asked.

Harry broke away from her and ran to his father, talking

a mile a minute. Then he skidded to a halt and looked up. 'Is this your mum and dad?' he asked.

Anna watched Max, detecting tiny signs of strain around his eyes as he squatted down next to Harry. 'Yes. They've dropped in on their way past—they've been out for the day, and they're going to stay for tea.'

'Mummy said. Hello.' He tipped his head on one side and looked up at them thoughtfully. 'You look like Max,' he said to Henry Carter.

'That's because I'm his father. Sons often look like their fathers,' he told the boy. How true, Anna thought, looking from Harry to Max, and then Harry lobbed a bomb into the conversation.

'I don't have a father,' he told them matter-of-factly. 'He had to go away.'

There was an awkward silence when all of them seemed to be holding their breath, then Harry went on, 'I've got a granddad, though. I 'spect that counts. He's called George. What's your name?'

'Henry.'

Harry's eyes widened. 'I'm Henry, too! 'Cept everyone calls me Harry, but my proper name's Henry. It's short for Harry.'

'Actually, I think it's the other way round,' Max said, breaking the silence.

'Oh. Never mind. Do you like wood lices?' he asked Clare hopefully.

'Not especially, but your—Max does.'

'Especially down the neck,' he murmured under his breath, and Anna chuckled softly.

So far, so good, she thought.

'I'm hungry,' Harry said, relieving them all of the burden of enduring any more of his entomological exploits. Anna had visions of his victimised woodlice, like tiny armadillos, scuttling for cover in relief.

'Shall we go in for tea?' Max suggested.

'Good idea. No insects,' his mother said with a smile.

'I wouldn't bank on it. This is the country.'

They retired to the relative safety of the sitting room, and Anna helped Max carry in the food while his parents sat down in the comfy chairs and were entertained by their grandson.

'Banana sandwiches—my favourite,' Henry said, tucking in.

'Mine, too,' Harry mumbled.

'Don't talk with your mouth full,' Anna corrected automatically. 'Anyway, I thought egg and cress were your favourites?'

'Not any more,' he said, siding firmly with his new friend. 'Me 'n Henry like banana best.'

'Dr Carter,' Anna corrected sternly. 'You can't call him Henry, it's not respectful.'

Harry ducked his head. 'Sorry,' he mumbled, and Henry's hand came out and tousled his hair.

'Don't worry about it, son. You call me whatever you want.'

So long as it's Granddad, Anna thought sadly, and met his eyes. They shared a smile of understanding, an understanding shared by his wife.

Anna went out to the kitchen to refill the kettle for more tea, and Clare Carter joined her and gave her a silent hug.

'He's lovely. Such a nice boy. You've done wonders, bringing him up on your own.'

She smiled wryly. 'I've had a lot of help—my parents have been wonderful, and I've got a super neighbour and very good child-care facilities for some of the time.'

Clare hesitated for a moment. 'If you didn't have to work, would you still want to?' she asked cautiously. 'Because, if it's a question of money, we'd be only too happy to help you. I know Max is being obstinate, but I want you to know we're on your side—'

'What are you girls plotting?' Max asked, coming into the kitchen and sliding his arms round his mother's waist.

'We're just talking about how stubborn you are,' she said bluntly. 'And what a tribute Harry is to Anna.'

Anna coloured. 'You're very kind. He's an easy child.'

'His father was,' Clare said, very quietly. 'It's a family thing. Happy genes or something.'

Happy genes, Anna thought. Max's happy genes were a bit overstretched at the moment. If only he'd give in and let himself have everything that was there, waiting for him on a plate—her love, their son's love, the welcome of her family. So much waste.

She shrugged off the sombre thoughts and smiled. 'They'll think they've been abandoned,' she said, topping up the teapot. 'Shall we go back before they finish all the chocolate cake?'

'Thank you.'

Anna smiled sadly. 'My pleasure. It was little enough to do for them,' she told him. 'Fancy a glass of wine?'

'I fancy a hug.'

'You can have both.'

He grinned. 'Sounds good. I left my car at home anyway, so I can walk back.'

They took their wine into her little sitting room and settled down on the sofa, his arm round her shoulders, snuggled up close. 'This is so nice,' he murmured wistfully. 'Harry asleep upstairs, sitting down here with you—all we need now is the cat.'

Right on cue Felix strolled in, leapt onto Max's lap and settled down, kneading his leg with his claws and dribbling furiously.

'You are disgusting,' Anna said affectionately.

'He's just a cat. Ouch! Not that hard.' He peeled the claws out of his skin, tucked the cat's paws under his chest and tickled his ears. It did nothing for the dribbling, but at least that didn't hurt, and his jeans were destined for the wash anyway. He dropped his head back and sighed.

Life was good. This time with Anna and Harry was building him up, filling his memory banks with so much that was infinitely precious. And for a while, at least, he could forget about the future and just pretend…

Anna didn't have the heart to wake him. Anyway, she didn't want to. She sat there, enjoying the cosy moment, until the night grew dark and she thought Max's neck would suffer from being at such a crazy angle.

She eased out from under his arm and lowered it carefully to his side, then propped his head up on a cushion. He sighed and snuggled into it, and she left him there and went and made them coffee.

It was almost midnight, and he needed to go home to

bed. He was looking tired—a hangover from the treatment? Possibly. His check-up appointment was the following week, and she was beginning to feel anxious about it.

Not consciously, but inside her there was a deep coil of tension winding slowly but surely tighter. She wondered if she'd have enough adrenaline to cope with it, or if she'd run out or collapse before the check-up.

And how did Max feel? Scared? Resigned?

'Mreouw!'

She looked down at her feet, to see Felix rubbing against her legs, staring hopefully up at her and pleading prettily.

'Cupboard lover,' she told him. 'No. You've been fed. You're fat. Go outside and catch something if you're hungry—work off some calories.'

He was either deaf or eternally hopeful. Whatever, she nearly fell over him on the way back to the sitting room because he kept trying to block her path, running ahead and sitting down and squawking.

'Oh, cat, shut up,' she said firmly. 'Go away.'

'Who, me?'

Anna laughed. 'No, the cat. I was just going to wake you up—I've made coffee.'

'Wonderful. I love you. I'm as dry as a crisp.'

He levered himself up a bit on the sofa, and she handed him his mug and curled up at the other end, her toes tucked under his thigh. He dropped a hand over her ankles and stroked them absently with his thumb while he sipped his coffee.

'Ah, that's better,' he sighed, dropping his head back against the cushion. 'Your sofa's too comfortable.'

'You're tired.'

He nodded. 'I know. It's the treatment. It takes the stuffing out of you. Anyway, I'm getting older. I'm thirty-four shortly.'

'Poor old man,' she crooned with mock sympathy.

'You don't have to take the mick,' he said archly. 'I know I'm older than you.'

'Not much. I'm thirty now.'

He looked at her strangely. 'I suppose you must be. I still think of you as that young woman of twenty-five that I fell in love with all those years ago. It's as if you've been suspended in time. Whenever I've thought about you, I've tried to imagine you run to seed with lots of grubby, runny-nosed children. Instead, I find you more beautiful than ever, with only one child, and I may be biased but I think he's the most wonderful child in the world.'

She found a wobbly smile. 'Perhaps slightly biased. I think I might be, too, because I agree. About Harry, anyway. Not about me. I've got squashy and unfit.'

'You're hardly squashy,' he protested. 'Just...womanly.' His eyes darkened, and he groaned. 'Can we change the subject? Thinking about your womanly charms is killing me. I don't suppose we could sneak up to bed?'

'Not unless you're prepared to explain yourself to your son,' she said seriously.

He gave a wry, humourless laugh. 'It was just a thought.' He drained his coffee and stood up. 'Time to go. A brisk walk in the dark might settle my libido down a little.'

'Do you want a torch?'

'Might be an idea. There's no moon tonight. I'd hate to get lost and end up in the ditch with the local drunk.'

'Old Fred? He'll be tucked up in bed at his sister's by now.

She keeps him on a fairly tight rein, but not quite tight enough, unfortunately.' She went out to the kitchen, followed by the cat, ever hopeful, and retrieved the torch for Max.

'Here. I think it's all right. It might not be wonderful. Take care.'

He kissed her, a long, slow, lingering kiss that did nothing to settle either his libido or hers, and then opened the door.

The cat, clearly deciding they were too boring for words, hopped out and darted across the road, just as a car shot down the lane.

There was a bump and a howl of pain, and Anna felt her blood run cold.

'Oh, my God,' she whispered, and ran to the edge of the road. 'Felix? Felix, come here. Where are you, boy?'

'Over there,' Max said quietly, shining the torch. 'He's badly hurt. Have you got a board or a stiff mat we can slid him onto?'

'Doormat?' she suggested, picking it up and shaking the loose dirt off it. 'I'll put something on it,' she said shakily, and yanked a pillowcase off the top of the laundry basket at the bottom of the stairs.

She followed Max over the road and found him hunched over Felix, stroking him gently and talking to him in quiet, soothing tones.

'Let's get him inside into the light,' Max suggested. 'We're all a little vulnerable here if there are any more lunatics like that about.'

He took Felix by the scruff and drew him gently onto the covered mat, then lifted him. The cat cried softly in protest, but otherwise lay motionless, panting and gasping.

'Oh, poor baby,' Anna murmured, stroking his head with trembling fingers. 'Oh, Max, what are we going to do?'

'Take him to the vet. Could your parents come and sit with Harry?'

'You could stay. I'll take him.'

Max shook his head. 'No. It's too hard to do that alone. You don't know how badly injured he is. Where is the vet?'

'Ten minutes down the road. I'll ring.'

They'd set the cat down on the sofa, and it was obvious from the strange angle of the limb that one back leg was broken. His face looked battered as well, and Anna bit her lip. Was his jaw broken? The last thing she needed at the moment was a stupendous vet bill.

She rang the vet, filled him in and arranged to meet him, then rang her parents. Her father was out of the door before she'd put the phone down, and arrived as they were loading the cat into her car.

'Don't worry about the boy,' he said, hugging her. 'Hello, Max. Going with her?'

He nodded, and her father said, 'Good man.' He watched them pull away before going inside.

Anna held the cat on her lap on the mat. Her carrier was broken, and she'd kept meaning to get another. Maybe if he came home… 'Turn left—there it is.'

The vet was waiting for them, and met them at the car, lifting Felix gently by the scruff and under the chest and carrying him through to the surgery.

'I'll have to anaesthetise him and X-ray him to make sure his chest isn't compromised,' he said. 'That leg's definitely gone, and possibly his jaw. When did he last eat?'

Anna for once didn't have to feel guilty. 'Hours ago. He was nagging.'

'Good. Right, if you could sign the consent form, I'll do it now, and then you'll know, if you want to hang on.'

She stopped him. 'Is it—? Will the cat recover? Would it be kinder to put him down?'

The vet pulled a face. 'Hard to tell without the X-rays. We need to see what's wrong, but if it's just the leg he should be all right. If it's his pelvis, his bladder and bowel nerves could be affected. We'll have to wait and see.'

'Do whatever's necessary,' Max interrupted. 'If you think it's fair to the cat, do whatever you have to do. I'll pay for it.'

'Max, you can't!' she protested.

'I can. I opened the door.'

'But it's not your fault—'

'Could you please sign the consent form for the X-rays? You can decide who pays for what once we know if he's going to make it, but I'd like to knock him out. He's in a lot of pain.'

Anna signed, her hand trembling, and then looked up. 'Can we come with you and watch?'

'Sure you want to?'

Anna nodded. 'I'm a nurse, he's a doctor. We won't faint or get in the way.'

The vet smiled. 'Come on, then. You can look at the X-rays and see what he's done.'

He clipped a little fur off Felix's foreleg, injected him with anaesthetic and the cat subsided into sleep. 'Right, let's arrange him for these pictures.'

He positioned the body, laid long tubes like sandbags over his limbs to hold them steady and exposed the plates.

Once they were developed and he was sure they showed everything he wanted to see, he put the cat in a cage on soft synthetic bedding, gave him water for when he woke up and showed them the plates.

'Right. Well, for a start he's going to be a compromised cat, but it could have been worse. The head's all right—bottom jaw's a bit mangled, but I gave it a good wiggle and it's not dislocated or broken, just sore. He's shattered an eye-tooth, lost a chunk of skin under his chin but otherwise his head's fine.

'The chest is good, which is a relief. Sometimes they rupture their diaphragms and the abdominal contents push up into the chest cavity and crush the lungs and heart, which isn't good. They usually sit up then and pant, which he wasn't doing, so I didn't think it was a problem.

'Now, this leg, though.' He shook his head. 'He's taken the head right off his femur—snapped it clean off the femoral neck. The problems will arise because the end of the femur may have damaged the bladder nerves, so before I operate I want him to pee. Once he's done that, we'll know it's all right to go ahead. If he doesn't, I'm afraid that's it. He's a dead cat.'

'If he does,' Anna said, feeling sicker and more unhappy by the minute, 'if he pees, then what?'

'Then we have to remove the head of the femur—an excision arthoplasty. It's dead now—it's totally severed and lost all its blood supply, so it will start to become necrotic, so we have to remove it. I'll file off the end of the femoral neck, and that will then float in the muscle, build up a layer of callus in the form of cartilage, and create a new joint—a pseudarthrosis.'

Max nodded. 'My uncle has a pseudarthrosis. He had a hip replacement and it went wrong, and they took it away and left him to heal. It's better now than it's been for years, certainly better than the other one. He just wears a built-up shoe.'

'Which the cat, of course, can't do, so he's going to be walking with a limp, but it's quite a common injury, quite a common procedure for us to carry out, and the prognosis is good.'

'If he pees,' Anna said flatly.

'If he pees,' the vet agreed. 'It may be some time. I've given him a painkiller in there with the anaesthetic, so when he comes round he'll be groggy for a while and then might feel like staggering to the litter tray.'

'Ring me,' she pleaded. 'Ring me when he pees. Any time. At home, in the surgery—whatever. Get a message to me, please.'

The vet nodded. 'I think it's hopeful he will. His pelvis isn't damaged but, of course, the hip joint is part of the pelvis and it's all very close to the nerves. If the swelling spreads, that may cause a problem, but don't worry, I'll ring you the second he's in that litter tray.'

She struggled for a smile. 'Thank you.'

Max thanked the vet as well, then dropped an arm round her shoulders and led her out to the car. Without asking, he put her in the passenger seat and drove her home, and spent the night there in the spare room.

She was glad to have him close. It wasn't close enough, but it was better than in his cottage down the road. She even slept a little, dozing for a few minutes at a time. The night dragged, and only common decency prevented her from ringing the vet and getting him out of bed to check the cat.

At a quarter to seven the phone rang, and she threw herself down the stairs and grabbed the receiver.

'Hello?' she said breathlessly.

'Panic over. He's managed to use his litter tray.'

Relief surged through her. 'Thank you. So what now?'

'Now I go ahead and operate. He'll be here until tomorrow. I want to keep an eye on him and make sure he's all right—make sure all his functions are up to scratch and he's comfortable, and then he'll have to be on cage rest for weeks, I'm afraid.'

'That's fine,' she said weakly. 'I don't mind.'

'I expect he will, though. He'll probably drive you mad, but he can come out for cuddles on your lap. He just mustn't jump up and down on the furniture and, of course, he can't go out until he's properly healed. Anyway, ring up later if you like and see how he got on. I'm sure he'll be fine now.'

'OK. Thank you.'

She put the phone down, shaking with reaction, and found Max's arms round her.

'He peed,' she said. 'He's going to operate this morning.' And promptly howled her eyes out.

CHAPTER EIGHT

FELIX looked incredibly sorry for himself. His leg was shaved at the top, over the hip joint, and there was a line of sutures which Anna hoped he would have the good sense to leave alone, his head was battered and sore, and he was delighted to see them all.

Anna was just delighted that he was alive, and Max insisted on paying the bill. She didn't argue. It came to over a hundred pounds, money she didn't have just lying about, and she vowed to take out pet insurance.

He had to be on cage rest for ages, and for the first few days he was quite good. Because she was out at work all day, she got up early and cuddled him on the bed until she had to get ready, and then again in the evening she had him on her lap in the sitting room, but he was restless and kept trying to jump down, and that was the last thing he was allowed to do until he'd healed.

Harry was wonderfully gentle with him, but she wouldn't let him hold him at first, because she was worried that if Harry prodded a sore bit by accident Felix would scratch or bite him in self-defence. Either that or he'd jump down and hurt himself.

In the end, though, she relented, and he seemed totally content on the little boy's lap and lay there for hours at a time.

It meant she couldn't go out, of course, and so Max did her shopping, Max sat with them in the evenings and, after Harry was in bed and the cat was returned to his borrowed cage, each night Max would systematically drive her up the wall with his goodnight kisses.

Then came the day when Max had to go to London for his check-up.

'When will you know?' she asked him anxiously.

He didn't pretend not to understand. 'A few days,' he said tautly. 'They do the scan, check the blood, run a few tests and let me know. I have to go back for the results.'

She nodded. 'Good luck,' she murmured.

'Thanks.'

She hugged him, unable to help herself, and he hugged her back, his arms tightening so hard he nearly cracked her ribs. 'I love you,' she whispered.

His grip tightened again, just fractionally, and then he let her go. 'I'll be back later. I don't suppose you'd like to get a sitter for the cat and Harry for a few hours and play hooky?'

'I'd love to.' She tried for a smile, but it wouldn't come. She was too tense, too scared, and as the day wore on it grew worse.

It was silly. She kept telling herself it was silly, because he wouldn't get the results today, but it was the fact that the scan would be done and the blood tests taken, and that the whole train would be set in motion.

Without the check-up, without the reminder, they had been able to play at being an ordinary couple and carry on as if nothing had happened.

Was this what it was like for Max always? A long time of forgetting, of putting it out of his mind and ignoring it, and then the harsh reality slamming back?

The sword of Damocles, he'd said, suspended over him on a frayed thread.

She swallowed her fear and tried to concentrate on her patients, but it was difficult. She struggled through her morning surgery, and was just finishing and planning a drive home and a cuddle with her wretched cat when Fred came in.

He'd fallen down, as drunk as a skunk, and been brought in by the local policeman.

'Oh, Fred,' Anna said with a sigh. 'You've cut your head open.'

'Bloody kerb come up and hit me,' he slurred.

'So I see,' she said drily, and smiled at the policeman, another familiar face. 'Stick him there. I'll clean him up and put a stitch in it. Would you like to stay and keep an eye on him? He'll do me for assault, for sure. If you're here, he won't be able to get so exercised.'

The policeman laughed. 'You'll be a good old boy, won't you, Fred?' the young man said, pushing him into a chair in her treatment room and keeping him occupied while she cleaned up the blood down his face and assessed the wound.

'You're going to have a scar, Fred,' she warned, studying the jagged tear. 'Still, we'll soon have you stitched up.'

'Want the doc,' Fred slurred aggressively. 'Not a bloody woman.'

'Fred, shut it, eh?' the policeman said with some affection. 'She's a damn sight prettier than the doctor. Just think yourself lucky. She's younger, too—I expect her eyesight's better. You ought to know when you're well off, mate.'

Anna stifled a smile and swiped Fred's forehead with a spirit wipe. 'Hold still now, this might sting a little.'

'Ow, hell, get her off me!' he yelled, flailing his arms. She whipped the needle out and straightened up.

'Are you going to sit still, or are you going to lie on the bed and I'll tie you down? Which is it to be, Fred? Or you can just go home with your brain hanging out. You never know your luck, some sense might leak in there.'

'Cheeky cow,' he grumbled, but he sat, and she injected him again, putting up with the volley of abuse and invective.

'That's better,' she said comfortingly. 'Now we'll give it a minute to go to sleep, and then I'll sew it together and you'll be good as new.'

Not quite, she thought, standing back some minutes later and studying her handiwork, but better than she'd feared from the state of the cut. At least it had been clean, just a simple split rather than a dirty graze. She didn't fancy her chances of taking a wire brush to his head in this lifetime!

She glanced at her watch as they left, and sighed. She wouldn't get home to Felix, and it seemed unfair to leave him all alone. Now that he wasn't hurting so much, he was bored out of his mind.

She had an idea, and rang her mother. 'Mum, would you mind having Felix in the kitchen in his cage? He could lie there and watch the other cats and the dogs come and go, and Harry could play with him after school, and it would be so much nicer for him.'

'Sounds fine,' her mother agreed. 'I'll get your father to go round with the car and pick him up now, shall I?'

'You're a star,' Anna said, and then hesitated. 'I don't suppose you want Harry for the night as well, do you? Max has been to London for a check-up and tests. I'd just like to spend some time with him tonight.'

'Of course,' her mother said without hesitation. 'He's got plenty of things here. Don't worry about it—and I'll take him to school in the morning if you like. Then you don't have to worry about getting up so early.'

She could feel her colour rising, but fortunately her mother couldn't see it. 'Lovely. Thanks, Mum. I owe you.'

'You owe me nothing,' her mother said gently. 'Just be happy.'

Anna cradled the phone and bit her lip. She'd love to be happy. All she wanted was the chance...

The train journey was interminable, from the hot, overcrowded confusion of the tube to the mercifully air-conditioned but still overcrowded chaos of the mainline service to Ipswich. Max crossed the road, went over the bridge and down to the car park, retrieved his car and headed for Wenham Market. It took half an hour, and without thinking he pulled up outside Anna's house, locked the car and walked up the path.

The door swung open before he had time to touch the bell, and he stepped through the open doorway, kicked the door shut behind him and engulfed her in his arms.

'God, I hate London,' he mumbled into her hair, and kissed her jaw, her cheek, her nose, her eyelids—and then her mouth, settling on those soft, warm, eager lips with a sigh of homecoming.

Reluctantly he drew away, dredging up a lopsided smile. 'We can't,' he groaned. 'Harry.'

'Harry's at Mum's. So's the cat. So, my place or yours?'

He thought of his car, parked outside her house in broad daylight for all to see, and thought of the secluded intimacy of his cottage down its quiet lane.

'Mine? It's more private. I want to be alone with you, without people dropping in or wondering what I'm doing here.'

She nodded. 'Can I stay over?'

He grinned lazily. 'Just try leaving.'

She chuckled. 'Give me a minute to grab some things. I can bring my uniform and then I don't have to come home. Hang on.'

She ran upstairs, her legs flying, and he watched her bottom vanish round the corner with regret. She had a pretty bottom, rounded and soft, without being big—like her breasts. A groan rose in his throat, and he closed his eyes and waited impatiently. He needed two things. A drink was the second. Anna, without doubt, was the first.

He went into the kitchen, drank a glass of water from the tap and was back at the bottom of the stairs as she came down, bag in hand. They all but ran down the path, jumped into his car and didn't quite exceed the speed limit going out to his cottage.

They didn't make it upstairs for a while. Instead, they closed the front door and reached for each other, tearing off their clothes with trembling hands, their eyes fevered, and he lifted her against him and drove into her with a groan of relief. Her legs coiled round him, her mouth sought his and he propped her against the door and plunged into her again and again, until with a shuddering cry she collapsed sobbing in his arms.

His body stiffened, he dropped his head against her shoulder and locked his knees, and when the tremors had passed, he lowered her feet to the floor and kissed her again.

'I love you,' he said raggedly. 'It's been so long.'

'Only a week.'

He gave a strangled laugh. 'Is that all? It feels like months. It's the tension.' He eased away from her and smiled wryly. 'I'm sorry. That wasn't very dignified.'

'I don't care.' Her hand came up and cupped his cheek, her thumb stroking the side of his mouth, dragging the damp skin. 'I love you, too. I've missed you today. It's been such a long day without you.'

Her eyes sparkled, and she blinked and turned away, gathering their clothes in a heap in her arms.

'Let's go to bed,' he suggested softly, and she nodded and went upstairs. He followed her, watching the soft globes of her buttocks tense with every step, and wanted her again. Still. For ever.

He backed away from that thought. Just tonight, he promised himself. Just think about tonight. Don't look ahead. Deal with today. Love her tonight as if it's the last time.

He took the clothes out of her hands and dropped them on a chair, then drew her back into his arms. 'Where were we?' he murmured.

Her arms slid round him and she eased closer, her eyes widening with surprise as she felt his response.

'We were in the hall, up against the front door like alley cats,' she said with a smile. 'Now we're in your bedroom. Shall we take advantage of that nice big bed?'

'What a good idea. I couldn't have had a better one myself.'

He flicked back the quilt, groaned as he watched her slide under the covers, her nipples sassy and pert and asking for attention, and followed her in, drawing her into his arms.

'This time I'm going slow,' he promised.

'Don't change anything on my account,' she said with a laugh, and he groaned and moved over her.

Forget the foreplay, he thought. They didn't need it. They were both wound up so tight they were about to explode, and as he entered her she shuddered and sobbed. He felt her body convulsing round him, her hands raking his back, her mouth hot and eager against his throat, and he abandoned all attempts at finesse and let nature drive him.

It should have been quieter, more gentle, their appetites slaked a little by the first time.

It wasn't. It was, if anything, more devastating, more powerful, more intense than ever before, and as he lay in her arms, unable to move, stunned by the awesome beauty of their loving, he wondered if he would ever find the strength to leave her.

Because he'd promised himself that if by a hideous twist of fate he was no longer in remission then he would go.

It all hung on the results, and the wait was going to be harder than anything he'd had to endure before, because this time there was so much more at stake.

Don't think about it, he told himself. Just enjoy her. Give her what you can. Wait.

Be patient.

And pray…

* * *

'Anna?'

'Yes? Is that Mrs Carter?'

'It is. Anna, I hope you don't mind me phoning—I got your number from directory enquiries. It's about Max.'

Her heart crashed against her ribs. 'What about him?' she asked tensely.

'Nothing bad! Don't worry. It's his birthday on Sunday, but I expect you know that.'

'No, I didn't. He's failed to share it with me,' she said drily.

His mother laughed. 'Oh, well, that sounds like Max. Anyway, he's coming for lunch. I thought I'd ask him to bring you, and he doesn't know it but I've asked the others—Andrew and Frankie and Joel and their other halves, and the children. It'll be a bit chaotic, and I don't know how you feel about it, but I wondered...would you mind bringing Harry?'

Warmth flooded her, the warmth of his family reaching out to her, including her and her son—Max's son, of course, and maybe she was only included as an appendage, but Mrs Carter had seemed genuinely pleased to meet her.

'I'd love to come and bring Harry. The only thing is, you won't say anything, will you? Not to the children. If Max's brothers and sister know, I think that's a good idea, but, please, make sure nobody lets it out. If we decide to tell Harry, I do want it to be a considered decision and not just a blunder.'

Mrs Carter hastened to reassure her. 'Of course. Don't worry, I'll prime them all. Are you going to come with him in the car, or on your own?'

'With him, I think,' she said thoughtfully. 'Otherwise he'll smell a rat. If he doesn't know about the others, he'll just think it's a birthday lunch and we've been invited.' Something else occurred to her. 'Would you like to ask him to invite me, and we'll pretend we've never had this conversation? Then he won't be suspicious.'

Mrs Carter laughed delightedly. 'Oh, Anna, what a good idea. I'll ring him now.'

'Before you go,' Anna said quickly, 'I don't suppose you've got any ideas about what I could give him?'

There was a long silence. 'Nothing lasting—nothing built to endure for generations,' she said finally, her voice tinged with sadness. 'He's got this thing about it. Feels he's not going to be here for long so there's no point. I usually give him clothes or something like that, which he has to have regardless, and make a fuss of him.'

How incredibly sad and defeatist, Anna thought, and wondered what on earth she could give him.

Then it came to her. Flowers. Nobody ever gave men flowers, and yet when her father had been ill once and her mother had given him flowers, he'd been delighted.

Yes. She'd give him flowers, and she'd arrange them herself. A big basket of them to stand on top of the wood-burning stove in his cottage, and look gorgeous. And Harry could draw him a picture.

She went to the florist during her break in the morning and ordered a lined basket, and planned the arrangement. Masses of colour and lots of roses from her mother's garden, with dark green foliage, her favourite combination.

She'd arrange them on Saturday evening—unless Max had plans for the evening, in which case she'd arrange them earlier and hide them in her garden shed. Or, better still, do it at her mother's, where he definitely wouldn't see them. That made sense, as she'd pick the flowers from her mother's wonderful garden on Friday night and condition them in the scullery until she arranged them.

Excellent.

She walked along from the florist to the surgery, and passed Fred lurking near the bus shelter, looking for cigarette ends on the ground. 'Fred?' she said, as she approached, and he jumped guiltily.

'Dear me, Sister, you scared the living daylights out of me—what you trying to do, frighten me to death?'

She suppressed a smile. 'I was expecting you earlier,' she told him. 'You had an appointment to see me this morning to have your stitches out, and you didn't turn up. What happened to you?'

'Oh, the usual,' he said. 'Bad head—it's the arteritis in my neck.'

'You don't have arthritis in your neck,' she told him drily. 'You probably had a hangover.'

'It's my sister's pillows—mean as an old rattlesnake she is, won't buy me a new one.'

'It's a wonder she puts up with you at all, never mind buy you new pillows. Come on, come over to the surgery with me now and I'll take them out for you.'

He mumbled a protest, but she took his arm and guided him across the street, staggering slightly, and propelled him into her room and sat him down. 'Right, this won't take a moment. It's healed quite well, considering.'

'Considering what?' he asked grumpily.

Considering it's bathed in neat alcohol, she nearly said, but then thought better of it. 'Considering it was only a few days ago,' she lied. 'Right, hold still. That's it. Lovely. Off you go, then, and take care.'

'Is that all?' he asked incredulously. 'Could have done that myself with the old cut-throat.'

The idea of him with a cut-throat razor left her cold with horror. 'Go on, Fred, go home.'

'No. Chip shop opens soon. They give me last night's cold fish—I tell them it's for the dog,' he said, wheezing and cackling at his own craftiness.

'Fred, you don't have a dog,' she said patiently.

'I know—clever, ain't it? And they don't know!'

I bet they do, Anna thought with exasperated affection. 'Go on, Fred, hop it. I've got patients to see.'

He grumbled his way out of the door, and she puffed a little air freshener around the room to disguise the smell a bit, then called her next patient.

She recognised the young woman, but she didn't know where from at first. 'Jenny, isn't it? Come on in and sit down.'

'Thanks. First of all, how's the cat?' she asked, and then the penny dropped.

'He's fine—I thought I recognised you. You work at the vet's, don't you?'

'At the moment—I'm pregnant now, so I won't be doing it too much longer. That's why I'm here—for routine blood tests.'

'Oh, lovely. Congratulations. When's it due?'

The girl snorted softly. 'January—and it's not exactly wonderful news. I'm not married, and he's gone off already.'

Anna prepared her syringes and swabbed the inside of the girl's elbow. 'I've got a little boy. He's four, and his father disappeared very early on in my pregnancy without ever knowing. Believe me, it's possible to have a baby on your own and bring it up and do everything a married parent would do. It's just a lot harder sometimes, but at others it's easier, so it sort of balances. Will you have help?'

She nodded. 'My mum. She lives near me. She's going to help me, because I'll have to go back to work. I couldn't get rid of it, though. It's my baby, isn't it?' she said simply. 'I reckon we're stuck with each other.'

Anna smiled at her. 'Just enjoy it. Babies are wonderful, and they grow up so fast. Every stage is different—some are worse than others, but all of them pass. Just remember that when it's teething or has colic or night terrors or temper tantrums. Everything passes!'

'Including pregnancy, thank goodness,' the girl said with a laugh. 'I've been as sick as a parrot for the first few weeks, but now I feel better.'

'Just one thing,' Anna warned her as she dropped the last sample in the bag, 'wear gloves and wash your hands very thoroughly if you handle any cats or dogs or their dirty litter. You can't risk getting toxoplasmosis during your pregnancy.'

'Right. I'll be careful—I had heard about it, but it's so easy to forget. Thanks.'

Anna called her next patient, and Max stuck his head round the door. 'Can we have lunch?' he asked quickly.

'Sure—what time?'

'When you're finished. I haven't got any calls today.'

She nodded. 'OK. I've got two more patients.'

'Fine. I'll wait.'

He blew her a kiss, and she felt a warm glow surround

her that stayed with her after he'd gone. She must have looked different, because both of her patients remarked on how well she looked, and how happy!

She sent the last one off with a new dressing, and went out to find Max. He was in the garden, sitting amongst the roses as usual, and she was suddenly glad she'd decided to give him flowers.

He stood up when she went out and smiled at her. 'Just smell this rose,' he said, and she stuck her nose right into it and sniffed slowly.

'Mmm, gorgeous. It's a Blanc Double de Coubert,' she told him. 'My mother's got some in her garden.'

He looked wistful for a moment, then his mouth tipped in a lopsided smile. 'Lunch?' he suggested.

'Where?'

'I thought we could buy some sandwiches in the shop and walk down to the river. I just wanted some fresh air and space, and I've got something to ask you.'

Sunday? she thought, but said nothing. They went into the shop and bought some sandwiches and a bottle of Max's 'designer' water, and headed down the hill to the river. There was a mill, and they sat on the bank by the mill-stream and munched their sandwiches, and Anna waited.

'Are you busy on Sunday?' he asked finally, taking the last bite of sandwich.

'No—why?'

He shrugged. 'It's my birthday. My mother always does lunch or something for me. She asked me to ask you and Harry. I think they just want to see him again—she hasn't stopped talking about him.'

I know, she nearly said, and stopped herself in the nick

of time. 'That would be lovely,' she said instead. 'What sort of time?'

'Oh, leaving here about eleven, I suppose. We want to be in Cambridge by half past twelve, and I don't want to go like a bat out of hell.'

'OK.'

'And on Saturday night, I thought we'd have our own private celebration,' he said softly, his meaning clear. 'I thought I might take you out for dinner, then lure you back to my den and have my wicked way with you.'

She smiled. 'You won't have to do much luring,' she assured him.

His mouth tipped in a grin. 'Is that right, you hussy?'

'Absolutely. We have to go, we'll be late. You've got an antenatal clinic and I've got to stand in for the midwife.'

'What about tonight?' he asked, getting to his feet and pulling her up. 'Are you doing anything?'

'Visiting my cat,' she said with a laugh. 'Want to join us?'

'Poor old boy. How is he?'

'Less bored than he would be at home,' she replied. 'He'll live. He's driving Mum mad, I think. We could go for a walk through the woods, if you like. I know you won't finish until about six-thirty, but if you come to the farm for supper, we could take a stroll afterwards. Fancy that?'

'Sounds a bit healthy,' he said with a grin. 'Won't your mother mind?'

'Not at all,' she promised, and made a note to ring her mother and warn her so there would be enough to go round. Not that there was any danger that there wouldn't be. She usually did enough for an army.

'Tell me, any news of Valerie?' she asked as they passed the fruit shop.

'Yes—she's progressing well. Her headaches are better, her mind's much clearer and she's feeling more like herself all the time, apparently. Let's just hope it continues.'

They were just turning into the surgery premises when a young lad skidded round the corner on his bike, swerved to miss them and skidded on some loose gravel. The bike flew out from under him, he crashed into the wall and for a second they all froze.

A lorry thundered past, galvanising them all into action. Max ran towards him, with Anna in hot pursuit, and the boy started to get up. Blood poured from his mouth, and he started to shake with reaction.

'It's Paul, isn't it?' Anna said. 'Paul Seager?'

He nodded.

'Are you all right?' Max asked calmly. 'Anywhere particular hurt?'

'Mouth,' he mumbled, and then he closed his eyes and started to cry.

'He's shocked—let's take him in,' Max said, and Anna put her arm round his shoulders and steered him towards the door.

'You picked the right place to fall off, anyway, Paul,' she said, trying to distract him.

The receptionist did a mild double-take. 'Good heavens,' she said, 'I thought we were busy enough, without you two going out touting for business!'

Max shot her a grin. 'Just hold all our patients for a few minutes, could you? We want to make sure there's no harm done.'

'Of course,' she agreed.

Anna pushed the door open, led Paul through the waiting room and said to Max, 'Your place or mine?'

One brow arched eloquently, but he managed to keep a straight face. 'Yours. You've got all the equipment.'

She stifled a laugh. They went into her treatment room and laid the young man down on the couch, and Anna covered him with a blanket while Max washed his hands and snapped on some gloves.

'Right,' he said kindly, 'let's take a look at you, Paul. What have you done to your mouth?'

He opened it carefully, and Max turned back his top lip and found a nasty puncture wound. Two of his teeth were broken, just chipped at the bottom edge, and Max gently but thoroughly checked the wound in his lip to make sure that there were no fragments of teeth left inside.

'Ow,' the boy cried, and Max apologised but carried on. Anna held his hand, and when Max was satisfied she wiped his face, gave him a mouthwash and tidied him up.

'I think your mum's going to have a bit of a fit,' she said, looking at the state of his clothes. His trousers were ripped, his shirt was drenched with blood and he'd dripped on his trainers.

'It's the holidays,' Max said with a grin. 'You'd be safer at school. Right, you need to see the dentist about those teeth, but I don't think you've got an urgent problem. They might be a little bit sensitive to hot and cold for a while, and so will your lip, so be careful to have everything tepid for a bit, OK?'

He nodded.

'Now, anywhere else hurt? Hands, knees, ankles, elbows?'

The boy shook his head. 'My mom'll kill me. These trousers were new.'

'It was an accident,' Anna soothed him. 'Mums only kill when you've been stupid. Trust me, I know.'

'I was being stupid,' Paul said dolefully. 'I was going much too fast. I nearly hit you.'

'Well, if it's any comfort,' Max told him, 'it's a good job you swerved to avoid us, because if you'd gone straight out into the main road like that, that darned great lorry that came along a moment later would have killed you for sure. Tell your mother that. Is she at home at the moment?'

He nodded, his eyes wide.

'Well, perhaps if you give Anna all the details, she can ring your mother and tell her all about your accident, and she can come down and collect you, all right? And I'll make sure your bike's in out of the road so it doesn't get nicked.'

It held them up, of course. They worked their way through the antenatal clinic together, Anna weighing mums and checking blood pressures and urine samples, Max feeling the lie of the babies and listening to their heartbeats and asking about problems.

She finished after the antenatal, but he still had a surgery to do, so she left him to it and went to see her mother—hopefully in time before she cooked the supper, because in all the chaos with young Paul Seager she'd forgotten to ring about Max joining them.

'No problem,' Sarah said with a smile. 'It'll be nice to have him here. Talk to the cat—it's bored to death.'

So Anna sat on the floor beside the cage and tickled the cat through the bars, and her mother handed her a cup of tea and she told her about the flowers she was planning for

Max. 'I hope you've got lots, or shall I go and buy them? I just felt it would be nicer if they came from here.'

'I agree,' her mother said. 'I've got tons, you know that. I always have tons. Just leave me some of the pink stuff for a wedding next week, that's all.'

Anna laughed. 'I won't take that much. I want to be able to carry the darned thing! I thought I'd come and pick them tomorrow morning early and put them in cold water till Saturday. He wants to go out for dinner on Saturday, so I can't do them on Saturday night.'

She had a moment of doubt. 'You don't think he'll feel I'm being a cheapskate, do you?' she asked worriedly. 'Only his mother said he hates anything that lasts, because he thinks it'll outlast him, and I couldn't think of anything else apart from food. Perhaps I should have just ordered him a hamper from somewhere really smart.'

'And spent hundreds of pounds? Don't be silly,' her mother told her. 'Anyway, he'll love them. Men never get flowers, and it's such a shame.'

Thus encouraged, she took Max on a tour of the flower garden later that evening, and made a mental note of the flowers he particularly loved, then the following morning she cut them and put them up to their necks in cold water in the scullery, and on Saturday she made some excuse about the cat and arranged them in her big wicker basket.

'Oh, darling, they're lovely,' her mother said, going all misty-eyed.

'I hope he thinks so. I wonder if I ought to go and get him something else? Chocolates or something? A pen to use for work?'

'No. Stop fussing, and go. You'll be late for dinner.'

'Are you sure you're all right to have Harry again?'

Her mother smiled sadly. 'Of course. It's not for long, after all, is it? Either Max will stay, and you'll all be together, or…' She trailed off.

'Or he'll go, one way or the other,' Anna finished softly. 'I know.'

CHAPTER NINE

ANNA heard her father's pickup truck stop outside Max's cottage at seven the next morning. She slipped out of bed without waking him, crept downstairs in his dressing-gown and opened the door.

'Where do you want them?' her father asked.

'On the wood-burner in the sitting room. I'll open the door.'

She led him silently through, and helped him put the flowers down on the black iron stove. They filled the empty wall above, and looked wonderful.

'Clever girl,' her father said, hugging her. 'Wish him a happy birthday from us. Here's a bottle of wine for you to share later.'

He handed her a bottle of bubbly, and she kissed him and closed the door softly behind him.

'Annie?'

She went to the foot of the stairs, the champagne still in her hand. 'Hi. Did I wake you? Sorry. Someone came to the door.'

'Have they gone?'

'Yes.'

He padded downstairs, dressed only in a pair of hastily tugged-on jeans, and stopped dead in the sitting room doorway.

'What's that?' he asked, his face a picture.

'Happy birthday,' she said softly.

He looked at her, stunned. 'Are they for me?'

She nodded.

'From you?'

Again, she nodded.

'They're beautiful! Oh, Annie…' His voice cracked, and he dragged her into his arms and hugged her till she thought her ribs would break. 'No one's ever given me flowers before,' he mumbled into her hair, and after a moment he lifted his head.

His eyes were sparkling, his lashes clogged, and he went over to the arrangement and breathed deeply. 'It's got those wonderful roses in it—the ones with the French name—and the gladioli, and the—oh, all sorts!' He turned to her, laughing. 'You took me round the garden and pumped me about these,' he accused, pointing a finger at her chest. 'You crafty little minx.'

'Of course. Women are devious,' she said, thinking of his mother and the surprise party waiting for him. Perhaps she'd better change the subject! She held out the bottle. 'This is from my parents. They said happy birthday.'

He took it and looked at her. 'I'll put it in the fridge, and we can have it later. Just now I want to thank you properly.'

They picked Harry up from her parents at eleven o'clock, and Max thanked them for the wine and for donating the flowers. Her mother had a big kiss, which gave her pink-eye, and her father hugged him and patted him awkwardly on the back.

'Have a nice day,' they said warmly, and Anna strapped Harry into his booster seat in her car and they set off. They were taking her car so that Max could drink, as it was his birthday celebration, and Anna had a feeling the family intended him to celebrate it whether he wanted to or not! It took just over an hour, and by the time they arrived Harry was beginning to fidget.

They turned onto the drive and Max heaved a sigh of relief. 'Thank God for that. I did wonder if the whole darned clan would be here—my mother's not beyond that.'

Anna said nothing. She was too busy biting her lip. She parked the car on the drive, beside one other, and wondered where the other cars were hidden. In the garage, perhaps? It looked big enough, and the car on the drive wasn't arousing his suspicions.

'Whose is that?' she asked, indicating it.

'Oh, Mother's. She always leaves it out. Too lazy to put it away. Come on, let's go and find them. Out you get, Harry.'

He was heading for the side of the house when the front door opened and his father appeared. 'Hello, Max. Happy birthday, son. Anna, Harry, hello. Come on in. You've made good time.'

'Anna's driving. You can blame her if we're early,' he said with a smile, and hugged his father. 'Good to see you again. You look well.'

'You look pretty good yourself. Come on in, let's find your mother.'

She followed them through the door, and Max's father

said to him, 'I think she's in the drawing room. Go on in, I just have to do something in the kitchen.'

He held back, and Max opened the door, to find streamers and balloons and all sorts dangling round the room. 'Mother?' he said, bemused, and then people jumped up from behind the furniture. He stood there, totally astonished, a stunned expression on his face.

'Happy birthday!' they all chorused, and he laughed and hugged them all, one by one. 'Mother, I'll get you,' he threatened, but he didn't sound cross at all.

He turned to Anna. 'Did you know about this?' he asked, and all eyes swivelled to her.

'I confess,' she said with a smile.

He shook his head despairingly, and then he caught sight of Harry and froze.

'By the way, everyone, let me introduce you,' Clare was saying. 'Anna, this is Joel, and his wife Patty, and their children Thomas and Daisy, and this is our daughter Frankie, and her husband Rick, and their children Emily and Stephen—oh, I don't know where they are. Under the table, I think. And this is Andrew, and Julia, and little Sophie. Everybody, this is Anna, a colleague of Max's, and her son, Harry.' She peered round. 'Where is Harry, by the way?'

'Here,' he said, coming out from behind Anna and peering at something in his hand. 'I found a spider. It's dead.' Then he looked up and smiled, totally unaware of the impact he was having, and said, 'Hello.'

There was a collective intake of breath, and all eyes were glued to him. All adult eyes, anyway. The children were too busy playing tag. After a stunned second they pulled themselves together and started talking all at once.

Max heaved a sigh of relief and grabbed his mother, dragging her out of the room.

'Do they know?' he asked in an undertone.

'Yes—the adults.'

'I'll kill you if this goes wrong,' he threatened.

'Nothing's going to go wrong,' she promised. 'It's a little party. Just enjoy it.'

Lunch was a splendid affair, a huge sit-down meal for all sixteen of them at a great refectory table which had been somehow carried out to the garden and placed in the shade of a lovely tree. Admittedly they were a bit squashed up, but nobody seemed to mind, and the children were all muddled up amongst them and helped and corrected and encouraged by all the adults regardless.

Harry joined in without hesitation, wedged between Frankie and Joel, and he seemed to be having a wonderful time.

Wine flowed, because nobody was driving for ages. Anna was cautious and restricted herself to one glass of champagne, just in case Max decided they needed to leave suddenly if things got out of hand.

After the meal everyone retired, groaning, to the garden chairs dotted around in the shade, or sat on the grass under the trees on rugs. Some carried on drinking wine, others had tea or coffee. Having made sure Max and Harry were happily engaged, Anna went into the house to see if she could help with the clearing up.

Predictably, the women were in the kitchen, and as she walked in they fell silent. Not surprising, Anna thought. She and Harry were bound to have been the topic of conversation.

'Can I help?' she asked.

Clare handed her a teatowel. 'You could wipe up the crystal—it can't go in the dishwasher. Frankie, darling, put the kettle on. Julia, show Anna where the crystal goes.'

Patty was up to her elbows in suds, and smiled at Anna as she picked up the first glass. 'Nice to meet you, by the way. I didn't get a chance to talk to you at lunch, we were too far apart. You're very brave, agreeing to do this, you know. Clare can be a bit of a bully.'

Clare laughed. 'You exaggerate. I didn't have to bully at all, did I?'

'How can she say yes, Mother?' Frankie said with a smile.

'Actually, she didn't have to bully me,' Anna admitted. 'I wanted to meet you all. I've been telling Max how unfair it is to keep Harry from his family, but he's—'

'Stubborn?' Julia offered. 'Runs in the family, like wooden legs,' she said drily. 'The whole lot of them are tarred with the same brush. Stunning blue eyes and utterly intractable. Talk about mules being difficult.'

'We're wonderful!' Frankie protested, and Patty and Julia laughed.

'In your dreams,' Patty said fondly. 'He's gorgeous, by the way. He's a credit to you.'

Anna followed the direction of her gaze through the kitchen window, and saw Harry playing with the others. It was some kind of organised game, and he was joining in with the others as if he'd always been there. She felt her eyes prickling, and blinked hard.

'Thank you,' she said in a low voice. 'I've always wondered if he had any cousins. I'm an only child, so Max's family were his only hope. I'm so glad he's getting on well with them.'

Clare put her hand on Anna's shoulder. 'Anna, you won't forget where we are, will you? If you and Max should part again, or if anything should happen to him, God forbid, you won't forget we're here, will you? You're part of the family now, you and Harry. With or without Max. I mean that.'

Anna couldn't help the tears. They welled up in her eyes, and she blinked them away and turned into Clare's arms, hugging her hard. 'Thank you,' she said unsteadily. 'Thank you so much.'

'Oh, Lord, you're going to start us all off,' Frankie said, sniffing. 'Come on, they'll be in here in a minute, demanding tea, and the place is still in chaos.'

Clare released her and went back to sorting her salads and leftovers, Patty handed her another glass, Julia started wiping down the worktops and Frankie, redundant at that moment, went outside and started gathering up abandoned wineglasses.

The chatter became more general, and they included Anna whenever possible, telling her stories about the family, asking her about her life and Harry's childhood and her own parents, until she felt she'd known them all for years.

And she knew that no matter what happened to Max, they'd be there for her, like a loving safety net, supporting and sustaining each other through whatever was to come.

She felt the tension ease out of her, the tightened coil of fear inside shift and relax—not much, but just a little. Enough. All they had to do was get through the next few days until Max got his results, and somehow even that seemed less terrifying now than it had.

A problem shared, and all that.

* * *

It was a lovely day.

Clare had said it would be, and she'd been right, of course. It went without a hitch.

Well, almost. There was the spellbinding moment just after the huge birthday cake had been brought out, blazing. Max had blown out the candles quickly before the tree caught fire, and they'd all sung 'Happy Birthday', and then, in a clear, piping voice, one of the children called Harry Thomas, and everyone froze.

Then Daisy started laughing. 'emily called Harry Thomas,' she crowed. 'Isn't that funny?'

'But he looks like Thomas,' Emily said petulantly.

There was another pregnant silence, then Frankie said lightly, 'When I was at school there was a girl who looked just like me. We were always getting into trouble for each other's scrapes. I never worked out if we got into half or twice as much trouble. I suspect twice.'

And the conversation picked up seamlessly, and Max started to breathe again. 'That was close,' he said to Anna under his breath. 'I think we need to get out of here before anything else happens.'

She nodded. 'I agree. The kids are all as sharp as tacks. It won't take them five minutes to work it out if Harry tells them his father went away.'

Frankie appeared at Anna's side and hugged her. 'Incidentally, I think you're just the woman for my brother. He looks happier than he's looked for years. Keep up the good work,' she whispered.

'What are you plotting?' Max asked suspiciously.

'She said I'm wearing you out,' Anna lied with a wink. 'Come on, we need to go. We've got a drive and Harry's tired.'

They made their goodbyes and drove slowly home, and Harry fell asleep in the back of the car. It was nearly nine by the time they got home, and she dropped Max off, pausing to give him a lingering kiss.

'Thank you so much for today,' he said softly. 'I'll see you tomorrow. I'm going to go and enjoy my flowers.' He kissed her again. Turning in the seat, he pressed a kiss to his fingers and laid them gently on Harry's brow. 'Goodnight, little one,' he murmured.

Then he was out of the car, closing the door softly behind him and pushing it till it clicked. Anna drove up to her cottage, took Harry up to bed via the bathroom and slipped him under the covers without really waking him.

She phoned her mother to ask after the cat, curled up in a chair with a cup of tea and reflected on the events of the day. It had been a good day—a wonderful day—and she felt surrounded by the love and acceptance of the entire Carter clan.

That they all adored Max was obvious. What was equally obvious was that they were desperate for an opportunity to love Harry in the same way, and she vowed that, whatever Max decided to do, she would keep in touch with his family.

The flowers made the whole house smell wonderful. Max poured himself a glass of juice, put on a CD of choral music and lay back in his chair, feet up, and relaxed.

He missed Annie, but he felt she was here with him, with the flowers she'd chosen and arranged for him. He breathed deeply, inhaled the delicate, intoxicating fragrance and sighed contentedly.

Harry had had fun, he thought with a smile, remembering how he'd joined in with his cousins. He just seemed to fit right in.

It was a sobering thought. Perhaps Annie was right, he admitted reluctantly. Perhaps it was wrong to deny Harry and the rest of them access to each other.

Still, the results would be revealed in a day or two, and he would have a better idea of what to do. If he was still in remission, then perhaps it was time to tell Harry that he was his father. If not…

If not didn't bear thinking about. He'd have to go through another programme of treatment, another gruelling period of waiting to hear, of further tests, of more treatment, more tests…

He'd worry about it if it happened. For now, he'd listen to the music, enjoy the beauty of the flowers and relax…

'You will come back? No matter what they say, you will come back and tell me, won't you?'

Max hugged Annie gently. 'I will come back,' he said, fear coiling in him. He was lying. If his results were bad, he'd decided not to come back. He'd check into a hotel, then find somewhere else to live. He'd never see her again.

He kissed her hungrily, and she hugged him hard, hanging on till the last moment. 'Annie, I have to go,' he said gruffly, and she released him reluctantly.

He slid behind the wheel and shut the car door, his eyes locked with hers. She knows, he realised. She knows I won't come back if it's bad.

He swallowed, gunned the engine and shot off down the road, blinking hard. Dammit, he wouldn't cry. He wouldn't look back. He wouldn't…

He glanced in the mirror and she was just a blur, standing with one arm upraised, the other wrapped tightly round her waist. She went out of focus, and he blinked again and dragged his eyes back to the road. No point killing himself. Not now, at least.

Not ever. He couldn't do it to his parents, even if there were times when the thought had been more than welcome.

He couldn't do it to Anna, or Harry. There was a picture in his wallet of Harry, laughing, in the garden at the cottage. He was beautiful, mischievous and bright-eyed, and the camera had caught his expression exactly.

At the thought of his son, a huge lump blocked his throat and he swallowed hard. 'Stop thinking about him,' he ordered himself, and turned the radio on to a news programme. Maybe it would take his mind off it.

The train journey was as awful as ever, and he crossed London on the tube and arrived with only five minutes to spare. Nevertheless, he had to wait, and every minute was agony. The hands on the clock seemed to crawl, and he was so tense, so overwound, that when the nurse called his name he felt his heart lurch with fear.

Not for himself, but for all he would lose if this went wrong.

Gathering the last shreds of his self-control, he stood up and walked towards his destiny.

It was the longest day of Anna's life. She'd spent the night with Max, making love tenderly until they were too tired to move, and then sleeping, wrapped in each other's arms. He'd taken the early train, and she'd cleared up the house, taken a couple of dead flowers out of the arrangement and then gone to her parents' house.

Harry was almost a permanent resident now, she thought wearily, and decided that, no matter what today revealed, Harry would know that Max was his father, and she would stay with him and marry him if she had to handcuff him to get him to the altar!

They belonged together, no matter what Max said. 'For better, for worse, for richer, for poorer, in sickness and in health, till…'

She stopped there. No. She'd be positive. He was all right. He was going to be all right.

He had to be all right.

She ran upstairs and found her mother coming out of the bathroom.

'Has he gone?' she asked softly, and Anna nodded.

'Yes. He's getting the early train. Is Harry awake yet?'

'No. Why don't you go and have a cuddle with him?'

She did, sliding under the covers in her clothes and snuggling him up against her. He was small and sleepy and warm, and she tucked her nose into the side of his neck and sniffed. He smelt wonderful, her very own little horror, and she loved him more than she could have believed possible.

'Hello, Mummy,' he mumbled, and turned in her arms, cuddling up against her and jabbing his knees in her stomach. She kissed his nose.

'Time to get up, sleepyhead,' she said affectionately. 'What do you want for breakfast?'

'We've got gooses' eggs, Grannie said,' he told her. 'We're going to have them scrambled on toast.'

'I'd better help you get ready, then, hadn't I, because scrambled eggs don't keep? Up you get!'

She threw back the cover and scooped him out, and he sat on her knee and hugged her and gave her a wet but very welcome kiss.

Dear Lord, he had his father's eyes.

Suppressing another pang of fear, Anna trundled him along to the bathroom, hustled him through the teeth and facewash and loo routine, and then chivvied him into his clothes and downstairs.

'Ah, you're just in time,' Sarah said with a smile. 'Have you had breakfast, darling?'

'Not yet.' She felt warmth creep up her throat. They'd forgone breakfast for another chance to hold each other, and now she was torn between hunger and the sickness of anticipation.

'You need to eat,' her mother tutted. 'Sit. Drink this tea, and I'll do you scrambled eggs on toast with us. Want some bacon?'

'Go on, then,' Anna said, giving in gratefully. She needed to be mothered today, and she was going to let her mother do it. She sensed they all needed it in a way. Closing ranks, she thought, keeping fear at bay.

Thank goodness she had a busy day at work ahead of her.

'Oh, Fred, not again,' she sighed.

He staggered into her room, a blood-soaked rag pressed to his head. "S that kerb—gets me every time,' he muttered. 'I swear they come along and raise it when I'm not lookin'. Turned my ankle and all. Blimmin' nuisance.'

'Let's have you lying down, then,' Anna said patiently,

and helped him onto the couch. She eased his boots off, and a great stench poured off his feet.

'You need some new socks,' she told him, trying not to gag. She covered his feet to trap the smell, and took the soggy rag out of his hand. 'Let's have a look at your face.'

He'd opened up the same cut, of course, barely healed and not yet strong enough for another encounter with the pavement, and she washed it and infiltrated it with anaesthetic.

He was sober this time, but he still protested and complained.

'Right, while that's going numb, let's have a look at your ankle, shall we?' she suggested, and peeled back the blanket. The smell assailed her again, and she eyed his socks with concern. They were soaked, dripping with sweat, probably due in no small part to the rubber boots he always wore.

She peeled them off with her gloved hands, and then blinked in surprise. The heels and soles of both feet were covered in thick, yellowed skin, with cracks and fissures all over the soggy and clearly infected areas.

He had a condition called hyperkeratosis plantaris—roughly translated, too much skin on the soles of the feet—and because they were permanently lying in water in his rubber boots and thin socks, they never dried out and had become infected.

'You need to see a doctor,' she told him. 'Stay here, I'll see if anyone can take a look at you.'

'What 'bout that nice young doc—Carter, innit?' he said.

Her heart lurched. She'd managed to forget, for a moment.

'He's away today,' she said calmly. 'I'll see if Dr Fellows can pop in and have a look at you.'

Dr Fellows did, while she was stitching up the cut on Fred's forehead, and tutted copiously over the mess his feet were in.

'You'll need a prescription for that, something to rub on twice a day, and you'll have to get some better shoes. These rubber boots are all very well in wet weather, but you can't wear them all the time, Fred.'

'Have done for years,' he grumbled.

'Well, you can't now. What size shoe do you take?'

'Eight. Maybe seven. Depends what's in the bins.'

David Fellows rolled his eyes. 'It's illegal to go through people's rubbish, Fred. Anyway, it just so happens we've been turning out the loft and there are lots of my son's old shoes—good leather shoes that he's outgrown. I'm sure there's a pair of size eights in amongst them. I'll look them out and drop them in to your sister for you. There might be some socks and trousers as well.'

'Thank you, Doc,' Fred said, clearly touched. 'Tha's right kind of you.'

'My pleasure. It'll save you going through my dustbin. Anna, I'll do the prescription, if you could make sure he gets it?'

She nodded. 'I'll do my best. Right, Fred, that's your head sewn up again. I think there's a pair of socks in here someone left behind ages ago. Put these on, and go home and take them all off and let your feet dry out a bit. And, now, listen to me, stay away from that pavement!'

'What 'bout my prescription?' he asked.

'I'll get it for you now and drop it by on my way

home for lunch—and I don't want to see you in the pub on the way past!'

She went to the chemist, popped the cream for Fred's feet in at his sister's and went home to the farm. Her mother was just dishing up soup and sandwiches, and she grabbed a bowl and plate and squeezed in.

'Smells good,' she said.

'Harry helped with the sandwiches, didn't you, darling?'

'Egg and cress?'

Her mother smiled. 'Actually, no. Chicken and salad. Harry spread the mayonnaise.'

Which explained why some were dripping with it and others bone dry. Anna didn't care. She loved him. She ate her lunch and dashed back to the surgery, covering another antenatal clinic for David in the absence of the midwife.

There was exciting news as well. 'I've just heard from Suzanna,' one of their very pregnant patients told them. 'She's had her baby—a little girl, three and an half kilos—what's that, about eight pounds?'

'Something like that,' David agreed. 'Oh, that's excellent. Everything OK?'

'Fine, I think. She was born at twelve—two hours ago. She rang just as I was leaving. I'm so jealous, I can't wait for it to all be over.'

Just then the receptionist came out, looking pink and bubbly. 'Dr Korrel's had a little girl—she just rang. Isn't that wonderful?'

'Wonderful,' they all agreed, and then the patient who'd told them dropped a bombshell.

'I don't think she wants to come back,' she said. 'She's

been worrying about it for ages. I wouldn't be at all surprised if she changes her mind.'

And that would leave a vacancy, Anna thought.

A vacancy Max could fill.

Permanently?

The nerves wouldn't be held back any longer. She found it hard to concentrate, impossible to forget.

She left work, went home to her parents' and made herself busy in the kitchen.

She was alone there when Max walked in, and she dropped the knife into the sink with nerveless fingers and turned to him, searching his face for any hint.

He looked exhausted. Lines of strain were etched around his eyes, and he looked very serious.

'Hi,' she said softly. She wanted to ask, but she didn't dare.

'Can we go for a walk?' he asked.

She nodded, scrubbed her hands on the old cotton pinny and took it off, slipping her feet back into her shoes. 'Where do you want to go?'

'Anywhere. The woods?'

They walked in silence for a while, until she thought she'd die of terror. She could feel the tension radiating off him, and she just knew it had been bad news.

'I thought you weren't coming back,' she said at last, her voice shaking with the effort of self-control.

'I didn't know what to do. I've been thinking—about us, about Harry.'

'Max, stay,' she begged, turning to him and taking his hands. 'Please, don't run away again. I don't care if I have to watch you suffer. It can't be worse than not knowing what you're going through and not being there for you. Stay, and be a father to your son, and a husband to me. Marry me, Max. Stay with us, for better, for worse—for ever.'

He stared down into her eyes, his own unfathomable, and then he smiled, a shaky, emotional smile that came from his heart.

'It's all right, Annie,' he said softly. 'I'm still in remission. All the tests were clear. I've come back to ask you to marry me.'

CHAPTER TEN

ANNA stared at Max, dumbstruck.

'But—I thought—you looked so—'

'Unsure? Terrified? I didn't know if you'd say yes. I thought maybe, with this hanging over us, you'd decided you wanted out.'

'I will never want out,' she told him, her voice firm now. 'No matter what happens in the future, I will never want to leave you. Please, believe that. I know remission is only that—that there's no guarantee of a cure. It may be a temporary reprieve, it may be permanent. I realise that. But, whatever happens, however bad it gets, I'll be here. OK?'

He nodded, and his eyes filled. 'Thank you, Annie. I don't think I could leave you anyway. I was going to—if the news was bad, I promised myself I wouldn't come back, but I don't know if I would have been strong enough to stay away. I love you both too much—I need you too much.'

'Thank goodness you didn't need to put it to the test,' she said, reaching out for him. 'Come here. You've just proposed to me and you haven't even kissed me yet.'

'You haven't said yes yet,' he reminded her, a smile flickering around his mouth.

'Yes,' she said firmly. 'Now, kiss me. I've missed you. It's been the most awful day…'

Her voice cracked and she threw herself into his waiting arms. His mouth came down and met hers, hungry and passionate and needy, and she felt her knees go weak.

'I need to sit down,' she told him breathlessly when they came up for air. 'I've been running on adrenaline all day and I can't stand any more.'

He gave a heartfelt chuckle. 'You and me both, darling. How about this log?'

They sat down on the fallen tree, careless of his smart trousers and her uniform dress, and he slung his arm round her shoulder and hugged her to his side.

'I'm sorry I can't give you any guarantees,' he said softly. 'I'd love to be able to say I was definitely cured, but I can't.'

'Max, there are no guarantees. Who's to say I won't die before you of breast cancer or heart disease? Nobody ever knows. It's just the odds that change.'

He nodded. 'I suppose so.' He stroked her hair absently with his fingers, playing with the strands. She could almost hear the cogs turning. 'Where are we going to live?' he asked eventually.

'Ah. A friend of Suzanna's was in today—she's had her baby, and the friend says she doesn't think she'll want to come back.'

His hand stilled, and he turned his head and looked at her searchingly. 'Her job might come up as a permanent one?'

Anna nodded. 'It's possible—but if not, I'm sure there are other permanent jobs around—always assuming you've stopped running now and you're prepared to settle down?'

'I never wanted to run,' he told her. 'And while I was having so much treatment it wouldn't have been fair to take a permanent job, even if I could have persuaded anyone to take me on. But now—I suppose there's no reason why I couldn't.' There was wonder in his voice—wonder and hope and a positive note she'd never thought to hear.

'You could have a garden,' she told him softly.

He nodded. 'The cottage is for sale. Would you fancy living there, or would you want to stay in your house?'

'I'd like the cottage. It's a bit sad—the kitchen and bathroom could do with a bit of attention, and the garden's a wilderness—but it's in a lovely spot. Super for Harry and Felix.'

He chewed his lip thoughtfully, his face serious again. 'Um, I know it's a bit soon to think about it, perhaps, but how would you feel about having another baby?'

She stared at him in astonishment. 'But I thought the treatment—we haven't bothered to use anything. I thought it was because it was safe—that you couldn't?'

'I can't,' he said quietly. 'Well, not like that, anyway. The chemo's knocked out all my sperm-producing cells. But before the treatment, they asked me if I wanted to store any frozen sperm and...I thought...just in case one day I might be cured...I might come and find you, if you weren't married.'

'But you left me.'

'Only because I didn't think it was fair to drag you through that hell. And when they asked about the sperm bank, I didn't think of anybody else, just you. Just in case. To be honest, I thought it was a waste of time, because it wouldn't ever happen, but, yes, it is possible, if you don't mind messing about with all the technical stuff instead of doing it the fun way.'

Her heart bubbled over with happiness. 'I don't care how it happens,' she told him. 'I didn't think we'd ever have another child, and I'd love one.'

'Would you stay at home and look after them?'

'Like a shot,' she said, laughing. 'Absolutely. And you could come home for lunch and sit outside in the garden with us and sniff roses.'

'In January?' he said drily.

'We could have a conservatory.'

He chuckled, then sighed with relief and hugged her. 'So, when are we getting married?'

'Soon,' she said firmly. 'As far as I'm concerned, we're about five years overdue for this. I'm not waiting any longer than I absolutely have to!'

'What do you think your parents will say?' he asked.

'They'll be ecstatic. What about yours? Have you told them the news?'

'Yes—I rang them on the train. I also told them I was going to ask you to marry me. They're waiting to hear, but I don't suppose they'll be surprised. My mother said you'd say yes.'

'Of course I'd say yes. I'd have said yes no matter what they'd come up with.'

'There is one bit of news,' he said, almost as an afterthought. 'They're working on a vaccine—it's designed to seek out and kill any lymphoma cells of that specific type, and once you're vaccinated it's for life. So, if any cells crop up in the future, the antibodies recognise them and blitz them. It's still undergoing trials, but if I can keep well long enough…'

He let the sentence hang, and Anna hugged him. 'That's great,' she said, letting the hope blossom inside her. 'And in the meantime,' she said with a smile, 'we've got a small boy who's desperate for a father. Shall we go and tell him?'

Max nodded. 'Yes, I think so. I think it's time. Let's tell him now.'

They went back to the farmhouse, and found Harry standing on a chair at the sink, washing his hands. George was at the table, reading the paper, a steaming mug of tea on the table beside him, and Sarah was busy at the Aga, stirring something that smelled delicious.

'Max—Anna!' Sarah said, scanning their smiling faces. 'Is it good news?' she asked hopefully, her knuckles white on the Aga rail.

Anna nodded. 'Yes—yes, it's good news. And we've got some more news,' she said, looking at Harry. 'Darling, come here.'

She dried his hands and pulled out a chair, taking him on her lap. 'Do you remember how I told you your father had to go away and leave us?'

He nodded. 'But I don't want him back now. I want Max to be my daddy,' he said, squirming off her lap and heading for his hero.

Max swallowed hard and scooped him up. 'Well, isn't that a good job, Harry?' he said. 'Because I really am your father.'

Harry looked at him thoughtfully. 'Really? My real, proper dad?'

Max nodded, and Harry grinned. Then a shadow crossed his face, and he leant back, looking up at Max. 'Are you going away again?' he asked worriedly.

'No. Never,' Max vowed, and Harry flung his arms round his neck.

'Good,' he said, and snuggled his face into his neck. 'So are you going to get married, like real mums and dads?'

They all laughed, easing the tension.

'Absolutely,' Max said. 'It's going to be the best wedding in the world.'

Nothing was ever simple, Anna thought, scanning through the racks of wedding dresses in the bridal shop on her afternoon off. From the small, quick, quiet wedding she had envisaged, it had escalated into the society wedding of the year—or, at least, that's what it felt like.

There were to be three bridesmaids—Daisy, Emily and Sophie—and three page-boys—Stephen, Thomas and Harry. There were uncles and aunts and colleagues and friends, people from university and old school friends—the list kept growing, and Anna wondered where it would all end.

From a simple meal at the local pub, the reception had grown to a champagne buffet in a marquee on the lawn at her parents' house, in the flower garden, and the church was going to be bursting at the seams.

And Max was loving every second of it.

Anna indulged him. She didn't care, so long as they were married.

She pulled out a dress and looked at it, then put it back. 'They're all so fussy,' she complained to her mother.

'How about mine?'

'Yours?'

'Yes. It's in tissue paper in the trunk in the hall. Let's go home and look.'

It was gorgeous—the softest, finest silk, in a simple style that hugged her curves and fitted as if it had been made for her.

'Oh, Anna, you look lovely,' her mother said, going pink and trying not to cry.

'You're going to be awful, aren't you?' Anna said fondly.

Sarah nodded. 'Probably. You'll just have to ignore me—put a bag over my head or something. What do you think?'

'It might mess up your hat.'

Her mother flapped her hand. 'Not the bag—the dress! What do you think of the dress?'

Anna looked in the long mirror by the front door, and nodded. 'Yes, I think you're right. It's lovely on me. Much better than all those fussy meringues and off-the-shoulder bits of fluff. Not me at all. I'm too short and dumpy.'

'You aren't dumpy!' her mother chastised. 'You're lovely. You're just not a boy.'

'Whatever. We need to get it dry-cleaned, I suppose. And what about the little bridesmaids? Do they need a similar style?'

They'd looked at so many little dresses that they couldn't remember what they'd seen. It needed another trip with the girls.

'There's the veil as well,' her mother said, rooting around in the trunk. 'Here it is.' It was the lightest lace, long enough to form a train, and in the same soft ivory as the dress.

'It's a much better colour on you than white,' her mother said.

'Because I'm a scarlet woman?' Anna offered.

'Because it's more flattering to your skin tone,' Sarah

corrected. 'And you are not a scarlet woman! You're just in love. I can't say I blame you,' she added wistfully. 'He does have the most gorgeous eyes.'

Especially when he's aroused, Anna thought, smiling. They smouldered with promise.

'I can't believe this is all going to happen in just three weeks,' she said, feeling weak just at the thought of all that had to be done.

'Well, it is. The invitations have already gone out—we only have that long.'

'We could have done it quietly,' Anna pointed out.

Her mother laughed. 'No way. This is more than a marriage. It's a celebration of life—of Max's life, of Harry's, of your lives together. It's going to be a party to remember. And that reminds me, I need to ring the photographer.'

Anna went back to work the next day with a sense of relief. Normality at last, she thought. A bit of routine. A few inoculations, taking out the odd set of stitches, taking some blood—wonderful. Sanity.

Then Suzanna brought her baby in for everyone to see, and told David that she wasn't coming back. They were sitting in the garden—Suzanna, David, Anna and Max—and she announced her decision in a calm, quiet voice.

'I'm sorry to dump it on you,' she said to David, 'but I'm so happy at home with the baby, and I never thought I would be. And I hear Max is settled in well and everyone gets on, so I thought—well, as he's staying in the area, maybe he'd like it permanently.'

All eyes swung to Max, and he gave a quiet huff of laughter. 'I'd love it, but don't you have to interview and get it past some regulatory body? Quite apart from which, do you really want to take on someone with lymphoma?'

He stood up and gave them a wry smile. 'Perhaps you need time to think about it—but if the offer's there, the answer's yes.'

And he went out, leaving Suzanna open-mouthed.

'Oh, David, I'm sorry, I didn't realise. But—Anna—I thought you were getting married?'

'We are,' she said gently. 'Anyway, he's in remission, and we're keeping our fingers crossed for this new vaccine. Just in case.'

Suzanna looked back to David, her face distressed. 'I'm sorry. Perhaps I shouldn't have said anything.'

'Don't worry,' he said with a smile. 'I'd already decided to offer him the job. If he has to stop, it won't be his fault, and maybe by then you'd want to come back anyway. There's a hell of a lot of water got to go under a great many bridges before we need to worry about that one, I'm sure. Now, let me have a cuddle with that baby.'

Anna went to find Max to tell him the news. He was in his consulting room, staring blankly across the room.

'He wants you.'

'Now?'

She shook her head. 'For the job. He'd already decided to offer it to you—he was waiting to hear from Suzanna.'

He stared at her for an age, then let his breath out on a gusty sigh. 'Really? He wants me? Annie, that's wonderful!' A smile lit up his face, and he pulled her into his arms and hugged her.

'Pardon me for breaking up the happy party, but could

I have a word?' David said, putting his head round the door, an indulgent smile on his face.

'Come in.'

'I'll go—I've got things to do.'

She closed the door behind her and went back to her room, tidying it in readiness for the afternoon surgery. She restocked her shelves, sorted out the ECG leads and changed the paper on the couch, then went to grab a cup of coffee.

Max and David were in the office, looking at dates and deciding when he would officially take over, while Suzanna and her baby were in the centre of a cluster of practice staff at the other end of the office.

'Excellent,' David said, straightening up and holding out his hand. 'Welcome aboard.'

It was a wonderful start to their marriage, Max thought. A real job, some kind of security, complete remission, the cottage signed and sealed. All they had to do now was get through the wedding!

It was three days away, the forecast was wonderful and ife was good.

Valerie Hawkshead came to see him, her hair slowly re-growing over the incision site on the top of her skull, and she was brighter and happier than he'd ever seen her.

She was to come for regular health checks, in between outine hospital appointments, and it was obvious that she vas doing really well.

'I felt so bad,' she confessed. 'I didn't know what I was oing, who I was—anything. I was so frightened. It was asier to do nothing, to just hide. But I feel so well now, o you suppose I could go back to work?'

Max nodded thoughtfully. 'I would say so. You've got to be sensible. You shouldn't drive because of the convulsion, but that's a legal matter and nothing to do with health really. I wouldn't operate any machinery, though, just to be on the safe side, and don't strain yourself or overdo it. And no carrying heavy bags!'

'I'll let my husband do that. It's just that I'm so bored at home, and it would be lovely to sit in the shop and chat to people. I won't do a lot, I promise.' She leant forward and put her hand on his arm. 'I hear you and Anna are getting married. I think that's wonderful. I hope you'll be very happy.'

He smiled, touched by her good wishes. 'Thank you. I'm sure we will.'

He watched her go, thinking that now he had a chance for continuity, to see cases through, to make a difference. Instead of giving advice that might not be taken, dishing out pills that might have side effects he would never know about, he would be there, to follow up, to provide a better standard of care than he'd been able to in the past.

He had a future.

It might not be as long as other people's, it might not be as smooth, but it was there, and it would be happy. How could it be anything else, shared with Anna and Harry and maybe at some time in the not-too-distant future, another baby?

Peace filled him, warming every corner of his heart, and he found himself impatient for the wedding. Anna was so busy he'd hardly seen her for days, and he'd taken to going to the farm every evening after work and entertaining Harry and the cat while the others plotted and planned.

Felix was out of the cage now, and it was agreed he'

stay with the Youngs until the cottage was sorted out. He was happy there, and there was no point taking him back to Anna's just for a few weeks.

The builders were in, tearing the kitchen and bathroom out and installing central heating and an Aga, a wicked extravagance but a wonderful focal point. The garden could wait until they had more time—perhaps next spring? Whatever.

Life was good.

Anna's mother straightened the veil, and kissed her. 'You look beautiful, darling,' she said emotionally. 'Oh, damn, my mascara's going to run!' She blotted and sniffed, and laughed. Giving Anna one last tweak and kiss, she went out to the waiting car and was swept off to the church.

The bridesmaids and pageboys were to follow in the next car, and then their parents took their own cars, leaving Anna and her father alone.

'You do look beautiful,' her father said gruffly. 'He's a lucky man to have found you. Many women wouldn't have given him a second chance.'

'But it wasn't his fault,' she said fairly. 'He thought he was doing the best thing for me.'

'I take it you've set him straight?'

She smiled. 'Let's put it this way, he won't make any more decisions for me without consulting me. We're going into this together. It's a partnership, and he knows that.'

'Like me and your mother. She looked beautiful in that dress, too. If you do as well as we have, you'll do all right,' he said gruffly. 'She's a good woman, your mother. I hope you're as lucky in Max as I've been in her. She's the salt of the earth, and I love her more now than I ever dreamed of.'

He looked at his watch. 'Where's that car?' he asked, unused to such soul-baring and uncomfortable with it.

Anna stifled a smile. He was a darling, the salt of the earth himself, a straightforward, honest and uncomplicated man, and she loved him dearly. She told him so, and watched the colour climb brick-red up his neck.

'You're a good girl,' he said, and blinked and looked at his watch again.

The wedding car came back, and her father helped her into it and passed her her bouquet, made from the flowers in the garden.

The wedding dress was old, the underwear and shoes were new, the garter was borrowed from Frankie and there were cornflowers in the bouquet.

She perched impatiently in the car, the short journey too long for her to endure. She wanted to be there, to marry Max before he had time to change his mind. There was a tiny, unacknowledged bit of her that was afraid he wouldn't be there, that he would have changed his mind and left without a word.

The little attendants were waiting, and picked up her veil, spaced out boy-girl-boy-girl all round the edge, and slowly, in case any of them tripped and tugged it off, they moved down the step into the church.

The organist was cued into the traditional strains of 'Here Comes the Bride', and as they turned the corner she saw Max standing near the altar rail, his shoulders squared ramrod straight, his brother Joel beside him.

Andrew winked as she passed him, and she smiled, her face relaxing. Max was there, waiting for her, looking like a condemned man at the gallows.

Then one of the bridesmaids tripped, she felt a yank and

stopped dead, and there was a little ripple of laughter through the congregation.

Max turned, and she stifled her laugh and smiled at him, straightening her veil.

His mouth relaxed, widening into a grin, and his eyes were filled with love.

He wasn't going anywhere.

Her father led her to his side, and she looked up at Max and smiled.

His gaze was steady, his eyes clear and unshuttered, and he gave her a tiny wink.

'Hello, gorgeous,' he said under his breath, and her smile lit her eyes.

She handed her bouquet to Emily, the oldest bridesmaid, and smiled at Harry, so self-important in his little page-boy suit, then turned back to the vicar. It was time to marry Max—time to make her vows, the vows she'd mean from the bottom of her heart.

'Dearly beloved,' the vicar began, and she could hear her mother rummaging for a hankie already. The words flowed over her, right up until the point where Max made his vows. His voice was firm, right up to the end, and then on 'till death us do part' he faltered slightly.

'Repeat after me, please,' the vicar said. 'I, Anna Louise…'

She didn't need his help. She knew the vows, had them engraved on her heart. Without hesitation, without faltering, she said clearly, 'I, Anna Louise, take you, Max Henry Stephen, to be my lawful wedded husband, to have and to hold, from this day forward, for better, for worse, for richer, for poorer, in sickness and in health, to love and to cherish, till death us do part, according to God's holy ordinance, and thereto I plight thee my troth.'

His eyes glittered, and his fingers tightened on her hand as he slid the ring onto her finger.

'With this ring, I thee wed,' he said clearly. She didn't hear the rest of the service. She just stood there, staring into Max's incredibly beautiful eyes, and wondered how on earth she could ever love him more than she already did.

'I now pronounce you man and wife,' the vicar said. 'Those whom God hath joined together let no man put asunder. You may kiss the bride.'

And he beamed at them as Max lifted the lopsided veil from her face, laid it carefully back over the flower circlet and kissed her with all the love in his heart.

Her mother broke down and sobbed all over her father's suit, Max's mother and sister and sisters-in-law sniffed and shuffled, and Harry, his fascinated little voice clearly audible, said, 'Does this mean we're going to have a baby?'

EPILOGUE

'DARLING, you are going to have to go to the hospital.'

'Not without Max,' Anna insisted. 'He missed Harry. He's not missing this one.'

Her mother sighed and searched the ceiling for inspiration. 'You are so stubborn. You keep saying Max is stubborn, but he's not a patch on you!'

Anna sighed and paced up and down the sitting room again, pausing at the window to look out. Surely he must be home soon? She could feel the pressure of the baby, the rhythmic tightening of her womb, the steady giving way of the supporting muscles.

It wouldn't be long. Where was he?

She tried sitting, but the baby was too low, and so she stood up again.

'This is ridiculous, Anna,' her mother said firmly. 'I'm going to get your case, and you're going to get in the car and I'm going to take you to the hospital, and Max can meet us there.'

'No. Call the midwife, if you have to do something, but I'm going nowhere without Max.'

She closed her eyes and leant heavily on the back of a

chair, breathing through the contraction. Please, come home, she thought desperately. I need you.

His car swung onto the drive, and he got out slowly and stretched. She sagged against the chair in relief. She was so pleased to see him!

'Max, come now, your stupid, stubborn wife is about to have this baby and wouldn't go to the hospital without you!'

He slammed the car door and strode in, covering the room in two strides.

'What are you doing? Why wouldn't you go, you silly girl?'

'You missed Harry,' she said simply. 'I couldn't let you miss this one.'

He sighed and hugged her, then held her at arm's length and examined her thoughtfully.

'How far on are you? Have we got time to get to the hospital?'

She shook her head. 'No. I don't think so.'

'I'll get my bag. Sarah, call the midwife. Tell her there's no great rush, but it might be an idea if she gets here in time for the champagne.'

Anna perched on the arm of the chair and waited for him to come back with his bag.

'I don't suppose you've got a handy obstetric pack—ah. You have.' She smiled. 'What a good Boy Scout.'

'Cheeky. I must have known you'd pull a stunt like this. Come on, let's get you upstairs. Where's Harry?'

'With his grandfather,' Sarah said. 'Shall I boil kettles and things?'

Max grinned. 'Good idea. I could murder a cup of tea Come on, petal.'

He scooped Anna up into his arms and carried her up the stairs, then paused in the bedroom. 'Stand here a minute. I'll whip the quilt off and put on a clean sheet. Don't move.'

She didn't. She stood there, calm and relaxed, and let him prepare the room. Then he stripped off her clothes, pulled a comfy old T-shirt over her head and helped her lie down.

She made herself comfortable while he went and washed his hands, then he perched on the bed beside her and grinned. 'Did you plan this, or is it just quicker than you'd realised?' he said. 'The head's almost crowning already. This baby's going to be here in a very few minutes.'

She smiled at him, utterly content now that he was home. 'It is a bit quicker, but I had a feeling…'

He shook his head and opened the obstetric pack, spread a waterproof paper sheet under her and laid out the rest of the equipment on another sterile sheet beside the bed.

'Do you want to stand, or walk, or kneel, or just lie there like that?' he asked.

She felt her womb contract again, and felt the pressure building. 'Kneel,' she said, finally losing her cool. 'Max—'

'It's all right,' he said calmly. 'I'm here.'

He locked his arms around under hers and lifted her to her knees, and they knelt on the bed, face to face, and she dropped her head against his chest and moaned softly.

Anna could hear his voice soothing her, and the strong beat of his heart under her ear, and knew she would be all right.

Max held her firmly against his chest, sensing when the baby was about to come from the change in her.

'Hold the headboard,' he instructed, moving just in time to catch the baby as it slithered furiously into the world.

Anna sagged down onto the bed, turning as she did so, and he laid the baby over the soft dome of her abdomen and sighed with relief.

'What is it?' she asked, her hands cradling it against her.

'Alive. Apart from that, I haven't a clue!' he said with a strangled laugh. He lifted the tiny child, slippery and squalling, and inspected it.

'She's a girl,' he said, and sudden, unbidden tears scalded his eyes. 'She's a girl,' he said again, laying her tenderly down and blinking the tears away, before completing the afterbirth and tidying up.

Anna pulled up the T-shirt, lifted the baby to her breast and she suckled immediately. 'Clever girl,' she murmured, and Max swallowed the huge lump in his throat and kissed her.

'You, too. Well done, darling.'

'Can I come in?'

He lifted his head and smiled at Sarah, poking her head round the door.

'I heard the baby cry—is everything all right?'

'Wonderful. Is the tea made?'

'It's brewing.' She smiled. 'Boy or girl?'

'Girl. A daughter.'

Max stood up and found a clean, soft towel, and tucked it round the baby so she didn't get cold. Then he ran downstairs, out to the garden that he loved so dearly, and picked a rose.

Just one, a beautifully scented old-fashioned white rose that was his favourite.

He was a father. Again. Annie, Harry, the baby—no name yet, but no doubt Annie would fight him to the death for her choice—a wonderful job, a cottage in the country and to date, at least, his health.

'Thank you,' he said, to whoever was listening, and, turning, he went inside the cottage, up the stairs and back to his wife and child…

Celebrating Our Authors

MORE ABOUT THE BOOKS

2 Inspiration for writing *Their Miracle Baby* and *Making Memories*

MORE ABOUT THE AUTHOR

4 Author biography

6 Q&A on writing

9 A day in the life

WE RECOMMEND

10 If you enjoyed *Their Miracle Baby* we know you'll love…

INSPIRATION FOR WRITING
Their Miracle Baby and *Making Memories*

I was asked to write *Their Miracle Baby* as part of the Penhally Bay mini-series, and I was delighted to do so because I'd become quite involved with Penhally during the writing of the first book, *Christmas Eve Baby*, and so it was like revisiting old friends. And I love this sort of story. So many couples have difficulties along the way, and to present every story as two normal, healthy, well-adjusted people who meet and fall in love and live happily every after just doesn't seem realistic to me, so I was intrigued to write about a married couple who've tried and failed to have a baby, but who have never really given up hope.

"...I'd become quite involved with Penhally during the writing of the first book... so it was like revisiting old friends..."

And Mike and Fran have a really tough time, because the first thing they need to do is find out if they still love each other – not always something that can be taken for granted! So I had to force them together, in a way, and if any of you know any farmers, you'll know how hard it is to make them take time out. So I had to interfere and play God again. Poor Mike. But it worked, and in the course of falling in love all over again, they realise that a baby isn't necessarily the answer to their happiness. I don't need to tell you, though, if you've glanced at the title, that miracles can and do happen!

And talking of miracles, *Making Memories* is another miracle story in a way, not because of the hero and heroine, but because it was inspired by the quiet courage and determination of a very, very dear friend of mine who has battled lymphoma for the past seventeen years. You will have realised I don't like to make things too easy for my hero and heroine, so I gave Max and Anna a question mark that many of us face in our futures. I'll leave it up to you to write their ending, but this is their journey, and to help them on their way I gave them Harry, a little boy whose father doesn't know he exists until he stumbles on him. Literally!

AUTHOR BIOGRAPHY

My life started in a slightly unconventional way. I was born in Hong Kong, to a mother who was a nurse until she met my father out in Malacca after the Second World War, where he was working for the Hongkong Bank. He was moved around quite a bit, and for the first ten years of my life I lived all over Malaysia. Every weekend we used to go to Penang and swim at the Penang Club, and have cocktails in the bar of the Eastern and Oriental Hotel. I looked it up the other day on the internet – how times have changed! – and, unlike the times, it didn't seem to have changed at all! It brought back so many memories. One day I might go back and take my husband.

Anyway, once we were home in the UK I was sent to boarding school where I spent six years learning how to be self-sufficient and resourceful! And writing all manner of weird stuff for school magazines, English essays, poetry that nobody ever got to see – and the opening salvo of a torrid little novelette I showed to Matron. It's a miracle I wasn't chucked out!

"...Their Miracle Baby is my seventy-fifth book..."

On leaving I started nursing, hurt my back, became a secretary, which gave me skills without which I couldn't do what I now do, and then went to teacher training college where I met my husband and trained to teach Art and Drama. Except I've only ever taught Maths, English and secretarial subjects! Then I had our daughters, and I settled into domestic bliss and read endless Mills & Boon® books in the gaps between feeds and laundry! I started teaching again, had problems with child-care, started my own soft furnishing business – no training, formal or otherwise, please note! – and then after a few years of that when I couldn't cope with the volume of work that seemed to be coming in (I'd ended up doing contract work for hotel refurbs, of all things) I decided to write for Mills & Boon. Why not?

Well, because I wasn't any good, was why not, but I stuck at it, took loads of excellent advice from patient editors on board, and after five rejections I was accepted in 1990 and my first book, *Relative Ethics*, was published in 1991. It seems ages ago, and probably is – *Their Miracle Baby* is my seventy-fifth book! And since then I've written another three, so it can't be all bad.

CAROLINE ANDERSON ON WRITING

What do you love most about being a writer?

Freedom to choose my subject, freedom from routine (although I'm inclined to take that one a little too literally!) and a great bunch of friends in the business.

Where do you go for inspiration?

Nowhere. It comes to me. All the time. Someone will say something, or I'll do something, or there'll be an article in the paper, and I'll think, "Oh…? Well, now, if such and such were to happen…" and off I go again.

Where do your characters come from and do they ever surprise you as you write?

"…I started writing as soon as I learned about story-telling…"

They always surprise me. They (especially the heroes) have a sneaky way of taking over. One of them will say something totally out of left field, and I think, "What! Good grief!" Sometimes I'll go with it, sometimes I put them firmly back in their box. Where do they come from? Dunno. See above!

Do you have a favourite character that you've created and what is it that you like about that character?

My favourite character would have to be one of my heroes, I think. Probably Sam Gregory in *The Baby Bonding* or Patrick Corrigan in *A Wife and Child to Cherish*. But heroine? Probably Maisie Sutherland in *The Baby From Nowhere*, which is definitely one of my all-time favourite books.

When did you start writing?

Oh, as soon as I learned about story-telling! I've always read stories, addicted to Enid Blyton and the Famous Five stories, then Georgette Heyer and Anya Seton, and then after a mild flirtation with serious literature at college, I discovered contemporary romance in the form of Mills & Boon, so I definitely write what I like to read, and I suppose I always have. Even the dire poetry of my schooldays had its footings in the Liverpool Poets and Christina Rossetti – and they couldn't be more different! It was a long time before I learned not to write pretentious rubbish, though. That was probably the most valuable thing I've learned over the years.

What one piece of advice would you give to a writer wanting to start a career?

The same piece of advice that was given to me. It's a job. You get up, get the chores out of the way and GO TO WORK. It's not something I've ever really managed, because there's so much thinking time, but you can take that too literally and then you find you aren't thinking at all, you're just procrastinating. And then you have to get to it and stop fairying about the countryside pretending to plan the plot, or you just lose the plot. Big-time!

What are you currently working on?

A Romance for the Harlequin Diamond Anniversary, about Max and Julia Gallagher, a married couple who have drifted apart and come together again with a life-changing jolt! It's lots of fun, it'll be out in February 2009 and it's going to be called *Two Little Miracles*. Oops. There's that word again! But they are deeply cute…

Could you tell us about your future projects?

No. Not because I'm coy, but because I don't let myself think about them because I'm so easily distracted – see above! But I can tell you that John and I are going to Tuscany in May for a short break, so watch out for an Italian hero coming to a shelf near you in Spring 2009! And in December I'm writing a book set in the Limb Centre of a hospital, because I've recently written a hero who's an amputee, and I was so impressed by the work that they do at the Disablement Services Centre in Norwich that I wanted to give a prosthetist her own story. And there will be another Romance in between those two, and maybe another. It all depends. And that's just this year's schedule!

A DAY IN THE LIFE

Six am. Clock radio bursts into life. If I'm lucky, I'm still asleep. Otherwise I've been fidgeting for hours. Get up, make tea and take it back to bed with dogs and cat, or if John gets to the kettle quick enough, I might get a cup brought to me! Oh, luxury! Then I get up and tackle the day thus: feed dogs, feed ancient pet pony, feed ancient and equally useless chickens, walk dogs, think about book – this is vital planning time and very useful – and then come back to house and make coffee, find two squares – OK, four! – of dark mint chocolate and take to computer, dunk chocolate and suck it while I read yesterday's pearls of wisdom. Edit them. They are mostly plastic beads! Make phone calls. Sneak out for coffee. Come back, fit of guilt, write more, have lunch if I haven't pigged out on cake in a café, write more, walk dogs again, think about dinner, write more because it's easier than cooking, feed horse/collect egg(s)/feed dogs/cat/husband – probably in that order, but not significant in any way except that he makes less noise! – and collapse in chair with glass of wine/coffee/fennel tea, depending on time of night, and veg in front of telly. (Please note no mention of housework. I don't know a single writer who likes it or does it except as an alternative to writing when it hits a brick wall, which it always does in the course of every book. Luckily I have a lovely couple who come and scrape up the dog hair every week and wash an inch of mud off the kitchen floor. One day I'll have a flat and no pets. Hah!) Watch news, if I can stay awake, then go to bed and wake without fail with an amazing idea which, also without fail, I will have forgotten before I drift off again. One day I'll get a notebook…

"… I go to bed and wake without fail with an amazing idea which, also without fail, I will have forgotten before I drift off again…"

If you enjoyed *Their Miracle Baby,* we know you'll love…

A Doctor, A Nurse: A Little Miracle
by Carol Marinelli

Nurse Molly Jones decided that if she was ever to bump into Luke Williams again, she would be super-slim, sleek-haired and dressed to impress… Instead, Molly has just finished a night shift on the children's ward, slightly the worse for wear, when she discovers that paediatrician Luke is back in town – with his four-year-old twins!

Single dad Luke is as dedicated and charming as she remembers. But Molly's heart has been broken before: once when Luke left, and once when she discovered that, for her, motherhood was never meant to be. All Molly has ever dreamt of is a family, and with Luke it looks as if all her dreams might just come true. And then she realises that she and Luke have created a little miracle of their own…

Sheikh Surgeon Claims His Bride
by Josie Metcalfe

Surgeon Zayed Khalil is formidable, yet scarred. The only solace he finds is in his work. He's dedicated, professional and brilliant. And he's come to Penhally Bay to set up a specialist children's unit at St Piran Hospital.

Emily Livingston is in awe of her new boss, but she's noticed the pain behind his dark eyes. Her instinct to reach out to him is as overwhelming as the underlying attraction between them. But Zayed closed his heart long ago.

Could this beautiful young doctor be the woman to show him how to live again, even love again?

Turn the page for a sneak preview from
Sheikh Surgeon Claims His Bride
by Josie Metcalfe –
the tenth book in the
Brides of Penhally Bay series:

BRIDES OF PENHALLY BAY

Bachelor doctors become husbands and fathers – in a place where hearts are made whole.

SHEIKH SURGEON CLAIMS HIS BRIDE

by

Josie Metcalfe

'*That* is one of the good things about coming back to Penhally,' Emily murmured aloud, mesmerised by the changing colours in the streaks of cloud against the horizon while she waited for the sun to sink into the sea at the end of another perfect summer's day.

And *there* was another benefit to coming back to her home town, she added silently as a good-looking man stepped into view on the sand and proceeded to strip his clothing off.

'Oh, yes!' she breathed as the last golden rays outlined each new vista, from broad shoulders and a wide chest decorated with an intriguing swathe of dark silky-looking hair to a tautly muscled belly and slim hips, all covered by darkly tanned skin. 'That is *definitely* a good reason for living near a beach.'

As she watched, he began an obviously well-practised routine of stretches before progressing to a seriously strenuous workout. For just a moment she wondered if he was putting on a show for her benefit, but there was no way that he could know she was there. This little alcove at the base of the rocks was one of the first places to be thrown into shadow as evening began to fall, and had been a favourite spot of hers ever since she'd come to live with her grandmother in her teens.

It wasn't until the man finally turned to walk into the sea that she noticed that he was limping fairly heavily, and her professional interest was raised. Had he injured himself during that punishing drill he'd just put himself through, or could the disability itself be the reason for the routine?

The light level had fallen too much by now for her to see any evidence of an injury, and while he had probably come to the beach at this time so that he could have some solitude, the idea of leaving anyone to swim alone when they might get into difficulties and need assistance wasn't something she could contemplate.

'Well, it's no hardship to sit here a bit longer,' she murmured. The air was still warm and even though a playful breeze had started up as the sun began to go down, she was perfectly sheltered where she was. Then, of course, there was the fact that she would have a second chance to look at that beautiful body when whoever he was finally emerged from the water.

In the meantime, she had some serious thinking to do and a mountain of guilt to come to terms with.

She'd been away for such a long time while she'd gone through her arduous medical training and had only realised that it had been far too long when a visit had revealed the dreadful secret her grandmother had been hiding.

'I didn't want you to come home just to watch me die not when you had all those exams to take,' she'd explained stubbornly when Emily had arrived for a long weekend visit to give her the latest good news in person

She'd been so looking forward to seeing Beabea's fac

when she told her that she'd just been offered the plum job she'd been after at St Piran's Hospital. Admittedly, it was only a six-month placement, but she had high hopes that there might be a permanent position she could apply for at the end of that time.

The taste of triumph had turned to ashes in her mouth when she'd realised just how little time she had left with the only family she possessed in the world.

With her grandmother's permission, she'd spoken to the oncologist at St Piran's the next day, hoping against hope that there was room for some glimmer of optimism—an operation, perhaps, or chemotherapy—but, if anything, the prognosis was worse than she'd thought.

'She could have several months, but I really think it's unlikely,' the kindly man had said, leaving Emily feeling sick to her stomach. 'With this sort of thing, the patient is usually fairly well, despite the devastation going on inside, right up until the last couple of weeks. That's the point when she'll need to come into hospital or transfer into a hospice—somewhere where they'll be able to monitor the pain medication, because she'll need it by then.'

'If she's put on PCA, couldn't I take care of her at home?' Emily had pleaded, knowing just how much her grandmother loved her little cottage. The place was full of years of love and so many happy memories, and if she was put on a morphine pump for patient-controlled pain relief, Emily wouldn't have to worry that she wasn't giving her grandmother the correct dose.

'You could, initially,' he'd agreed. 'But we've found that it's often far too stressful for the patient to stay at home right to the end, knowing that their relatives are having to do so much for them and watching them die by inches. In the end, the two of you will find that you'll know when it's time to make the move, for both your sakes.'

And in the meantime, Emily had started her new job under Mr Breyley and had obtained permission to spend her off-duty hours far further away than the immediate vicinity of St Piran's.

Their little system had worked well, with Emily taking care of her grandmother's needs before she drove the hour to St Piran's, knowing that Beabea still had many friends in the Penhally area, including several in the medical profession in one capacity or another, who would be dropping in throughout the time she herself was away on duty.

And while her grandmother slept for longer stretches each day, Emily took herself off for walks along the harbour, past the Penhally Arms and the Anchor Hotel. Each time she glanced in she saw that holidaymakers and locals alike were enjoying themselves, and it seemed somehow wrong that they were oblivious of the life-and-death battle that was going on just around the corner.

A time or two she'd sat at the café on the end of the row, sipping a long frothy latte while she watched the holidaymakers leaning on the parapet of the bridge, wh were watching the waters of the river Lanson hurrying o the final stretch of their journey to the sea.

She'd stood there a time or two herself, gazing dow at the chuckling, purling waters tumbling over the rock while she'd pondered on the timelessness of the view. S little had changed from the first time she'd balanced o the parapet on her stomach as a teenager, risking a painf dunking if she'd gone head first over the edge. And yet, even though the stones and the water hadn't changed, everything else had.

She was a different person from that teenager, a doctor, now, with the job of her dreams. And her grandmother, who had always seemed so ageless that she might live for ever, was now a shrunken old lady with thin grey hair and papery skin and barely enough energy to breathe.

In fact, apart from working under Mr Breyley, which was everything she'd hoped for and more, the one bright spot in her day was if she managed to make it to the beach to complete her mind-numbing run along the hard-packed sand before her mystery man arrived.

Several times she'd been tempted to speak to him, to let him know that she was there and to get her first good look at his face, but that would have spoilt the fantasies she'd been weaving about him, especially if she found out that he was only someone she'd gone to school with.

Then there was the fact that he might see her as some sort of voyeur, hiding in the rocks while she watched him put himself through his nightly torment, but she could always counter that accusation by pointing out that she was doing nothing more than acting as an unofficial lifeguard. Not that she thought that would cut much ice with a man who seemed so driven and so utterly self-contained. In fact, his focus seemed so intense that she found it difficult to imagine that he was the sort who would ever relax enough to reveal a softer side to his nature.

'But that won't stop me imagining one,' Emily murmured as he set off into the water again lit only by the dying rays of the sun.

MILLS & BOON
100
YEARS
of pure reading pleasure